STORIES FROM HEAVEN

Earll Erving Supnet

En Route Books and Media, LLC
Saint Louis, MO

ENROUTE
Make the time

En Route Books and Media, LLC
5705 Rhodes Avenue
St. Louis, MO 63109

Contact us at
contactus@enroutebooksandmedia.com

Cover Credit: Sebastian Mahfood

ISBN-13: 979-8-88870-522-3
Library of Congress Control Number:
Available online at https://catalog.loc.gov

Table of Contents

FOREWORD

In the enchanting world of storytelling, we often find ourselves drawn to narratives that touch our hearts, inspire our souls, and illuminate the beauty of the human experience. *Stories from Heaven* is a collection of tales woven with threads of empathy, resilience, and the transformative power of love.

Through the diverse stories of individuals navigating life's challenges and triumphs, this anthology invites readers to embark on a journey of self-discovery, compassion, and the realization that the extraordinary can be found within the ordinary, encouraging a sense of appreciation and mindfulness.

The title *Stories from Heaven* serves as a guiding light that unifies the entire collection, illuminating the divine essence present in each narrative. While the word "heaven" may evoke thoughts of ethereal realms beyond our reach, it also symbolizes the moments of grace, beauty, and connection we experience daily. These stories remind us that heaven is not just a distant paradise but a realm of love, understanding, and empathy that we can cultivate and share with others.

As you delve into the pages of *Stories from Heaven*, may you be touched by the profound impact of faith and resilience, and the boundless reach of inspiration. Each story is a testament to the belief that amidst life's challenges, there lies a glimmer of hope, a spark of beauty, and a reminder that we are all connected by the threads of our shared humanity, fostering a sense of connection and empathy.

The Essence of Storytelling

Storytelling is an ancient art form that transcends culture, time, and geography. It has the power to weave together the disparate threads of our lives into a coherent tapestry, enriching our understanding of ourselves and others. Through tales of triumph and adversity, we find reflections of our own experiences, and in these moments of recognition, we cultivate empathy.

The stories in this anthology are not merely entertainment; they serve as mirrors that reflect the myriad emotions we experience as human beings. Each character, each situation, resonates with the complexities of life, allowing readers to confront their own fears, dreams, and desires. This collection stands as a reminder that no matter how isolated we may feel in our struggles, we are never truly alone.

Themes of Resilience and Hope

Resilience is a recurring theme throughout *Stories from Heaven.* Each narrative showcases individuals who face trials that test their spirit and resolve. These stories illuminate the capacity of the human heart to endure, adapt, and ultimately thrive in the face of adversity. Whether it is a single mother juggling work and family, a young man overcoming personal demons, or an elderly couple rekindling their love after decades of marriage, the threads of resilience are woven into every tale.

In moments of darkness, hope shines brightest. The characters in these stories, despite their circumstances, find light in the smallest acts of kindness, moments of clarity, and the unwavering support of loved ones. This collective resilience serves as a beacon of hope for readers, reminding us that it is possible to overcome the obstacles life presents. The stories encourage us to find strength in vulnerability, to seek help when needed, and to recognize the beauty in the journey itself.

The Power of Love and Connection

At the heart of *Stories from Heaven* lies the transformative power of love. Love, in all its forms—romantic, familial, platonic, and self-love—acts as a catalyst for change and growth. Each narrative explores how love can heal wounds, bridge divides, and inspire individuals to become the best versions of themselves.

The anthology also emphasizes the importance of human connection. In a world that often feels fragmented and chaotic, these stories remind us of the profound impact that relationships have on our lives. The characters' journeys illustrate how connection fosters understanding, compassion, and a sense of belonging. Through shared experiences, both joyous and sorrowful, the characters discover that they are part of something larger than themselves.

Finding the Extraordinary in the Ordinary

One of the most poignant aspects of *Stories from Heaven* is its celebration of the extraordinary found within the ordinary. Each tale serves as a gentle reminder that beauty exists in the nuances of daily life. From the laughter shared between friends over coffee to the quiet moments of reflection during a sunset, these stories highlight how the simplest experiences can be deeply meaningful.

This theme encourages readers to cultivate mindfulness and appreciation for the present moment. In a fast-paced world filled with distractions, it is easy to overlook the small joys that surround us. The characters in this anthology inspire us to slow down, observe, and cherish the fleeting moments that make life truly remarkable.

A Journey of Self-Discovery

As readers navigate through the pages of *Stories from Heaven*, they are invited to embark on a journey of self-discovery. Each story serves as a catalyst for introspection, prompting us to reflect on our own lives, values, and aspirations. The characters' struggles and triumphs resonate with our personal experiences, encouraging us to confront our fears, embrace our vulnerabilities, and celebrate our victories.

Through this journey, we may find ourselves inspired to take action, whether it be pursuing a long-held dream, reconnecting with a loved one, or simply choosing to practice gratitude. The stories remind us that life is not merely a series of events but a continuous journey of growth and transformation.

The Role of Faith and Spirituality

Faith, in its many forms, is a vital thread that runs through *Stories from Heaven*. It serves as a source of strength for the characters as they navigate their paths. Whether it is faith in a higher power, faith in themselves, or faith in the goodness of others, this belief system provides the foundation upon which they build their resilience.

The anthology invites readers to explore their own beliefs and the role that faith plays in their lives. It encourages a dialogue about spirituality, connection, and the search for meaning. In doing so, it fosters a deeper understanding of the varied ways in which individuals find solace and strength, ultimately enriching the reader's own perspective on life.

In closing, *Stories from Heaven* is more than just a collection of narratives; it is a celebration of the human spirit, a testament to our shared experiences, and a reminder of the beauty that surrounds us. As you journey through these pages, may you discover not only the stories of others but also pieces of yourself.

Let these tales guide you toward a greater understanding of empathy, resilience, and love. May you find inspiration in the ordinary, hope in the face of adversity, and a renewed sense of connection with the world around you. As you close the final chapter, may you carry the essence of these stories with you, allowing them to illuminate your own path and inspire you to share your narrative with the world.

Stories from Heaven beckons you to experience the magic of storytelling, to embrace the extraordinary within the ordinary, and to recognize that within each heart lies a story waiting to be told. Welcome to a world where love reigns, resilience flourishes, and every moment is an opportunity for connection and growth. Let the journey begin.

FAITH AND REDEMPTION

Beyond the Cracked Window

In the heart of a remote Central Asian province, nestled amidst emerald-green fields and undulating hills, there lived a young dreamer named Aisha. Her days were bathed in the soft glow of faith and the teachings of her deeply religious Christian parents. Aisha's heart danced to the rhythm of beauty and inspiration, seeking solace in the whispers of the wind and the caress of the sun's rays on her skin.

Aisha's life, though filled with her parents' love, resonated with an underlying sense of disconnection and self-doubt. The weight of not belonging tugged at her spirit, driving her to wander through the cobblestone streets of her village, her eyes a mirror to her soul's quest for meaning.

One fateful day, as the sun painted the sky in hues of gold and amber, Aisha's wandering footsteps led her to the edge of her village, where an ancient, weather-beaten cottage stood sentinel against time. The air was heavy with the musky scent of earth, and the gentle murmur of a nearby stream serenaded the surroundings.

Intrigued, Aisha pushed open the creaking wooden door, revealing the forgotten secrets of the dilapidated cottage. Dust danced in the light that filtered through the cracked window, bathing the room in a soft, ethereal glow. At this moment, amidst the decay and abandonment, Aisha's eyes alighted upon a weathered painting hanging on the wall.

The painting depicted a breathtaking landscape—a vast desert, its golden dunes stretching to the horizon like waves frozen in time. In the center stood a majestic tree, its branches outstretched as if embracing the heavens. Aisha felt a tug at her heart, a silent calling that beckoned her to unravel the mysteries hidden within the art.

With each visit to the forgotten cottage, Aisha drew more profoundly into the painting's allure. She would lose herself in the desert expanse, feeling the power of God's creation whispering through the grains of sand and the rustle of the solitary tree's leaves. The cottage became her sanctuary, a temporal refuge from the cacophony of her doubts and fears.

As Aisha's pilgrimage to the cottage became routine, the villagers whispered amongst themselves, casting doubtful glances at the young dreamer. They failed to grasp the depth of her connection to the painting, dismissing her actions as frivolous in a world marred by struggle and toil.

But change was on the horizon.

One evening, as the sun dipped below the horizon, casting the sky in hues of rose and sapphire, Aisha's absence tugged at the strings of her parents' hearts. In search of their daughter, they stumbled upon the forgotten cottage, where Aisha knelt before the painting, tears glistening in her eyes like pearls.

Her father, a man of quiet wisdom and unwavering faith, approached her with a tenderness that bespoke of understanding. "Aisha, my child," he began, his voice a gentle murmur that echoed through the silent room, "what draws you to this painting, to this place?"

Through tear-streaked eyes, Aisha poured her heart out, revealing the depths of her soul to her father. "Father," she whispered, her voice raw with emotion, "I see the beauty of God's creation in this painting. I see His grace, majesty, and love for all of us. This desert, this tree reminds me that God's beauty shines through even in desolation."

Her father's eyes brimmed with unshed tears, his heart a symphony of emotions. At that moment, he understood. A true inspiration, he realized, nestled in the most unexpected of places, waiting to be discovered by hearts willing to listen.

Word of Aisha's revelation spread through the village like wildfire, igniting a spark of curiosity and wonder among the villagers. People from all walks of life flocked to the forgotten cottage, eager to witness the beauty that had kindled a flame in Aisha's heart.

The once-ignored cottage, steeped in shadows and dust, bloomed like a desert rose after a rainfall. Its walls echoed with laughter and prayers, its cracked window framing a tableau of hope and inspiration that touched even the most hardened hearts.

As days turned into weeks and weeks into years, Aisha's legacy grew like a tree taking root in fertile soil. Her unwavering faith and boundless love for God's creation became a beacon of light for those lost in the shadows of doubt and despair.

Once burdened by their struggles, the villagers found solace in the simplest blessings that adorned their lives like jewels. Farmers marveled at the intricacies of the fields and the vibrant hues of the flowers that painted the landscape in riot colors. Inspired by the interplay of light and shadow, artisans crafted works that wove tales of tradition and heritage, celebrating the beauty surrounding them.

Even the weary souls, those who had lost their way in the labyrinth of life, sought refuge within the cottage's weathered walls. They witnessed Aisha's transformation, a metamorphosis of spirit and heart that stirred their longing for redemption and grace. Prayers floated like incense in the still air, seeking forgiveness, seeking renewal.

Now pulsing with life and purpose, the forgotten cottage became a beacon of hope in a world clouded by uncertainty and fear. Stories of healing, reconciliation, and faith reborn whispered through the village like a melody carried on the wings of the wind. Once fractured by doubt and division, the community found unity in their quest for beauty and inspiration.

Through Aisha's eyes, they saw the world anew—a tapestry woven with threads of faith and love, a canvas painted with the hues of redemption and grace. The once-abandoned cottage stood tall, its cracked window now a gateway to a realm where miracles bloomed like desert flowers after a rainstorm.

Years flowed like a river, carrying with them the echoes of Aisha's laughter and the fragrance of her unwavering faith. She grew from a young dreamer into a beacon of wisdom and compassion, her heart a wellspring of grace and understanding that touched all who crossed her path.

Aisha's tale, a symphony of faith and resilience, resonated far beyond the borders of her village. Transcending time and space, it reached hearts yearning to glimpse the divine. Her legacy, etched into the annals of history, served as a reminder to look beyond the surface and seek beauty in the most unexpected of places.

And so, in the heart of that far-flung province in Central Asia, amidst the rustling fields and the whispering hills, Aisha's legacy lived on. Once a forgotten relic of the past, the cottage stood as a testament to the unyielding power of faith, the boundless reach of inspiration, and the enduring love of a God who painted beauty in the most desolate of landscapes.

Aisha's story, shared through the ages in hushed whispers and joyful hymns, beckoned to all who listened, inviting them to cast aside their doubts and fears and embrace the beauty hidden in the cracks of their existence.

And so, the legacy of Aisha, the dreamer who found beauty beyond the cracked window, danced on the wings of eternity, a timeless melody that sang of hope, love, and the transformative power of faith.

From Shadows to Sunlight

In the heart of Uzbekistan's Fergana Valley, a married couple named Alisher and Gulistan struggled to make ends meet for their two children. Life had become a relentless cycle of poverty, overshadowed by self-destructive habits that threatened to engulf them.

Alisher, once a promising student, had succumbed to the grip of addiction. His days were lost in a haze of opium smoke, numbing the pain of his unfulfilled dreams. Buried by the weight of responsibility, Gulistan found solace in her vices, drowning her sorrows in alcohol. The once vibrant and loving couple had become shells of their former selves, trapped in a cycle of despair.

Their children, Aziza and Amir, witnessed their parents' daily struggles. A constant sense of unease replaced the innocent joy that should have filled their lives. Hunger gnawed at their young bellies, and the lack of stability cast a heavy shadow on their hopes and dreams.

One fateful day, a ray of light pierced through the darkness, shrouding Alisher and Gulistan's lives. A local charity organization, "Roshan Hayot" (Radiant Life), had set up a community center in their neighborhood. The center aimed to support struggling families, offering counseling, vocational training, and a glimmer of hope for a better future.

Intrigued by the possibility of change, Gulistan attended a support group meeting at the community center. There, she met individuals who had overcome their battles with addiction and self-destructive habits. Their stories resonated deep within her, igniting a flicker of determination to reclaim her life and provide a better future for her children.

Gulistan returned home that evening with renewed vigor. She confronted Alisher, pleading with him to join her in seeking help, to break free from the chains that held them captive. At first resistant, Alisher's love for his family triumphed over his addiction, and he reluctantly agreed.

Together, they embarked on a journey of self-discovery and healing. The road to recovery was arduous, filled with relapses and setbacks. But the community center's unwavering support and the couple's newfound determination propelled them forward.

Days turned into weeks, and weeks into months. Alisher and Gulistan discovered hidden talents and passions they had long forgotten. Once a talented artist, Alisher embraced his gift again, finding solace and purpose in his paintings. Fueled by her love for cooking, Gulistan honed her culinary skills, dreaming of opening a small restaurant someday.

Their transformation did not go unnoticed. The community witnessed a remarkable change in Alisher and Gulistan's lives. Inspired by their resilience, others struggling with their demons sought solace and guidance from the community center. The ripple effect of hope and transformation spread throughout the neighborhood, breathing life into souls trapped in the shadows for far too long.

With the unwavering support of their community, Alisher and Gulistan rebuilt their lives from the ground up. They opened a small art gallery and restaurant, aptly named "Shams" (Sun), symbolizing the dawn that had finally broken through their darkness.

In time, Aziza and Amir's lives transformed as well. The children flourished under the guidance of their reformed parents. With stability and love, they excelled in their studies and pursued their passions. Aziza, inspired by her father's artistic talent, became a talented painter herself, while Amir discovered a love for storytelling and writing.

The family's newfound success did not shield them from life's challenges, but their resilience and the lessons they had learned carried them through. They faced setbacks and obstacles with unwavering determination, knowing they had overcome far greater hardships.

As the years passed, Alisher and Gulistan became pillars of strength and hope in their community. They shared their stories at local schools and community events, inspiring others to believe in their capacity for change. They supported and guided those still battling their demons, reminding them they were not alone.

The Fergana Valley, once plagued by the shadows of self-destruction, was now basked in the warmth of hope and transformation. Alisher and Gulistan's story spread far and wide, touching people's hearts nationwide. Their journey served as a testament to the power of redemption, reminding others that it was never too late to rewrite their narratives.

"From Shadows to Sunlight" became more than just a catchy title—it symbolized the triumph of the human spirit. Alisher and Gulistan's story taught others that the path to change might be difficult, but with perseverance, support, and a deep belief in one's worth, even the darkest of lives can be illuminated by hope.

And so, in the heart of Uzbekistan's Fergana Valley, Alisher, Gulistan, Aziza, and Amir continued to shine brightly, forever grateful for the opportunity to rewrite their destinies and to inspire others to do the same.

Threads of Compassion

In the bustling city of Munich, Germany, a young college man named Markus found himself entangled in a web of doubt and uncertainty. At the tender age of twenty, he had always considered himself an atheist, staunchly dismissing notions of faith as mere superstitions. Yet, within the depths of his soul, a yearning for something beyond the tangible world stirred, a yearning he had long suppressed.

Markus, seeking solace and connection in the vast digital realm, stumbled upon an online chat forum on a seemingly ordinary day. Little did he know that this virtual encounter would profoundly transform his life.

He initiated a conversation with a fellow chatmate, Sophia, among the virtual sea of strangers. With each exchange of words, Markus discovered a kindred spirit in Sophia—a compassionate soul who saw the world through a lens of empathy and understanding. Her unwavering faith in the power of love and compassion captivated Markus, drawing him closer to a truth he had long denied, a truth that was reshaping his entire worldview.

As their online friendship blossomed, Markus yearned for a deeper connection. With trepidation, he suggested meeting in person, and Sophia agreed. The streets of Munich would witness a pivotal moment in Markus's life as he stood face to face with the embodiment of compassion that had ignited a flame.

Captivating and radiant, Sophia exuded a warmth that seemed to envelop everyone around her. Her eyes held the wisdom of ages, and her smile carried the weight of a thousand sunsets. Markus felt an inexplicable sense of peace in her presence, as if he had finally found the missing piece of his soul.

Over countless conversations, Sophia shared her journey of faith—a path she had walked with unwavering conviction and unyielding compassion. Her stories, woven with tales of healing and lives transformed by acts of kindness and love, resonated deep within Markus, slowly unraveling the threads of skepticism that had bound his heart far too long.

As days turned into weeks, Markus immersed himself in Sophia's world. Together, they volunteered at local shelters, offering warmth and nourishment to those forgotten by society. They listened to the stories of the homeless, the marginalized, and the broken-hearted—each tale a testament to the transformative power of compassion.

Through these experiences, Markus witnessed firsthand the healing that compassion could bring. He saw lives mended, hearts mended, and souls reborn from the ashes of despair. The walls he had built around himself crumbled, revealing a newfound vulnerability and a profound connection to the world around him.

Markus's conversion from atheism to faith was not a sudden epiphany but a gradual unfolding of his heart. Sophia's unwavering compassion and embodiment of love had pierced through his doubts, bridging the gap between skepticism and belief. It was not the dogmas or rituals that convinced Markus but the lived experience of compassion in action, an experience that was reshaping his entire worldview.

With each passing day, Markus embraced his newfound faith, not as a rigid doctrine but as a guiding light to navigate the complexities of life. He discovered that religion was not confined to the walls of a church but manifested in the kindness we extend to strangers and the love we offer unconditionally.

The story of Markus and Sophia spread throughout Munich, touching the lives of others who yearned for a deeper connection and a purpose greater than themselves. Their journey became a testament to the transformative power of compassion, reminding others that within each of us lies.

Transience

A single mother named Emily, a beacon of determination, carried the world's weight in the quaint town of Alexander, nestled within the serene county of Genesee. At twenty-four years old, she bravely navigated the treacherous path of life, her every step dictated by the needs of her four-year-old daughter, Lily, who battled severe heart disease. Emily's days were a perpetual juggling act, balancing two jobs to provide for Lily's medical expenses and ensure stability in their fragile existence.

The weight of her responsibilities wore heavily on Emily's slender shoulders, threatening to suffocate her spirit. Exhaustion seeped into her bones, and despair cast a relentless shadow over her heart. Yet, in the depths of her soul, a flicker of resilience burned fiercely, driving her forward through the darkest of nights.

Word of Emily's plight reached the ears of two nuns, Sisters Maria and Teresa, belonging to the revered Missionaries of Charity. Touched by Emily's unwavering dedication and the love she poured into caring for Lily, they embarked on a journey to Alexander. They traveled for days, braving harsh weather and treacherous terrain, their hearts filled with a determination to offer their support and solace to Emily and Lily.

Their arrival in the town was met with curious whispers and a sense of anticipation. The nuns' presence breathed life into the community, stirring hope in the hearts of those worn down by the burdens of life. Emily, too, felt a flicker of hope ignite within her as she awaited their arrival.

The meeting between Emily and the nuns was a collision of worlds, as the paths of faith and resilience intertwined. Sisters Maria and Teresa listened intently to Emily's story, her struggles, and her unwavering love for her daughter. The depth of her sacrifice moved them to the core, resonating with their calling to serve the impoverished and marginalized. As Emily poured out her heart, tears streaming down her face, the nuns held her hands, their eyes filled with compassion and understanding. 'You are not alone, Emily,' Sister Maria said softly. 'We are here for you and Lily.'

Through their shared conversations, Emily discovered a profound truth within the gentle wisdom of the nuns—a reality that transcended her struggles. They spoke of embracing impermanence and finding solace in life's transient nature. Their words carried the weight of experience, their eyes reflecting the countless lives they had touched.

In the days that followed, Emily's bond with the nuns deepened. Together, they embarked on a journey of self-discovery, exploring the significance of embracing impermanence and change. Sisters Maria and Teresa shared stories of their encounters with loss, reminding Emily that life's beauty lay not in its permanence but in the fleeting moments that slipped through our grasp.

A transformation began to unfold as Emily's heart opened to the whispers of transience. She realized that clinging to the illusion of stability only brought suffering, for life was an ever-flowing river, forever changing its course. She learned to cherish the present moment, savoring the precious minutes with Lily, knowing that each breath was a gift to be treasured. 'Thank you, Sisters,' she whispered, her voice filled with a newfound strength. 'Thank you for showing me the beauty in impermanence.'

With the nuns' support and the newfound wisdom she had acquired, Emily discovered the strength to seek help from the community. People rallied around her, offering assistance in various forms. Meals were prepared, medical bills were paid, and a support network was woven around her and Lily. Neighbors took turns looking after Lily, local businesses donated to her medical fund, and the town organized a fundraising event. The city of Alexander became a testament to the power of compassion and unity, each act of kindness a thread in the fabric of their shared resilience.

Emily's journey was not without its challenges. Lily's health remained fragile, and the road ahead was uncertain. The doctors warned of more surgeries, more hospital stays, and the constant fear of Lily's condition worsening. But armed with the knowledge that life was a tapestry of impermanence, Emily faced each day with renewed strength, her heart filled with the love and support of the community.

The Unyielding Spirit

November 8, 2013, dawned like any other day in Tacloban City, Leyte, Philippines. But as the day unfolded, the skies began to darken, and the ominous whispers of an impending catastrophe echoed through the air. Super Typhoon Yolanda, one of the most potent typhoons ever recorded, was about to unleash its fury.

A fisherman named Diego lived in a humble nipa hut by the coast. A man of simple means, Diego was beloved in his community for his kind heart and infectious laughter. He lived with his elderly mother, Ising, and his young daughter, Rosa, an energetic seven-year-old with dreams as vast as the sea her father sailed.

Diego's heart pounded as the first gusts of wind began to whip through their village. He had weathered many storms before, but the sheer force of Yolanda was a force unknown. He fortified their home best, whispering comforting words to his mother and daughter. Yet, beneath his calming facade, his heart trembled with fear.

The cyclone hit with a ferocity beyond comprehension. The winds howled like enraged beasts, ripping roofs off houses, uprooting trees, and turning debris into deadly projectiles. The sea, once a source of livelihood, raged and roared, swallowing entire homes in its mighty waves.

Diego's nipa hut, once a sanctuary, was swept away by the monstrous waves. He held Rosa tightly, his mother clutching his arm, as they found refuge atop a large mango tree. They watched in silent terror as their world was torn apart, their village decimated by the relentless storm.

When the typhoon finally subsided, their village was unrecognizable - a desolate landscape of destruction and despair. But amidst the wreckage, the spirit of resilience began to stir.

Diego, with his world shattered, could have succumbed to despair. He had lost everything - his home, boat, livelihood - but he held onto the most valuable thing he still had: hope. He held Rosa's hand, looked into her frightened eyes, and made a promise. "We will rebuild, Anak," he said, his voice firm with conviction, "We will rise again."

In the following days, Diego worked tirelessly, salvaging what he could from the ruins, rebuilding their home piece by piece. He scavenged for food, fished with makeshift nets, and did whatever it took to provide for his family. His strength did not wane, nor did his spirit falter.

Rosa, inspired by her father's unyielding resilience, mirrored his determination. She helped in any way she could, her small hands attempting to mend what the storm had broken. Even Ising, frail and weak, contributed in her small ways, mending clothes and cooking meals with their scant resources.

The recovery was slow and fraught with challenges. There were days of hunger, nights of despair, moments when Diego wondered if they would ever see better days. But every time he felt his resolve waver, he would look at Rosa and Ising, their spirits unbroken, their hope undimmed. Their resilience became his strength, their courage his inspiration.

Months turned into years, and slowly, life began to return to their ravaged village. The mango tree, once a symbol of their survival, now bore the sweetest fruits. Diego's new nipa hut stood firm, a testament to his relentless resilience. His boat, carved from the wreckage remnants, sailed the seas again. Rosa's laughter echoed in the air, a melody more beautiful than the lullabies of the sea. Even Ising found joy in the most minor things, her spirit burning brighter than ever.

Their journey was not just one of painful struggles and heart-breaking losses but one of resilience. They had weathered the most formidable storm, not with weapons or wealth but with an indestructible spirit and unwavering hope. Their story was not just a tale of survival but a testament to the power of resilience in the face of adversity.

As the sun set on Tacloban, painting the sky with hues of hope, Diego sat by the shore, Rosa nestled by his side. He looked at the sea, oncc a terrifying beast, now a calming expanse of blue. He felt a sense of peace wash over him, a sense of triumph. They had survived. They had rebuilt. They had risen from the ashes.

"Did we beat the storm, Papa?" Rosa asked, her eyes reflecting the vibrant sunset.

Diego smiled, pulling Rosa closer. "No, Anak. We didn't beat the storm. We learned to dance in the rain. We learned to rise, no matter how hard we fall. We learned the power of resilience."

The tale of Diego, Rosa, and Ising is a tale that resonates with every heart that has faced a storm, literal or metaphorical. It is a tale that reminds us of the strength within us, of the resilience that lies at the core of our being. It is a tale that teaches us that no storm is powerful enough to quell the human spirit and that our resilience becomes our most formidable shield in times of crisis.

As the world remembers Super Typhoon Yolanda, let us not forget the destruction it caused and the stories of resilience it gave birth to. Let us not forget the Diegos, the Rosas, and the Isings, who remind us that we can rise even in the face of the most formidable storms. We can rebuild. We can endure because we are, at our core, resilient.

The tale of their resilience is a whisper in the wind, a ripple in the water, a story carved in the heart of Tacloban City. It is a story that echoes across time and space, reminding us of the unyielding human spirit, the power of resilience, and the hope that shines brightest in the darkest storms.

The Beauty Within

The sun hung high in the sky, casting its golden glow upon the bustling courtyard of the Senior High School in Thailand. Students hurriedly made their way to their classrooms, their chatter filling the air like a symphony of youthful energy. Among them was a young Thai boy named Pichai, whose heart was burdened with a secret he dared not share.

A young Thai boy, Pichai was constantly at odds with his peers. While they seemed to embrace their identities effortlessly, he grappled with a profound confusion about his gender. The weight of societal expectations bore down on him, often driving him to seek solace in solitude and self-reflection. His deepest desire was to break free from societal norms and unearth his true self.

As the days rolled by, Pichai observed the world around him with a keen eye. He noticed the beauty in the simplest moments—the way the sunlight danced upon the leaves of the ancient banyan tree or the laughter from friends sharing stories during lunchtime. These everyday moments have held a profound meaning for him, a reminder that true happiness can be found in the most minor things.

One fateful day, Pichai was drawn to the school's art room. He hesitantly stepped inside, his eyes widening at the sight before him. Canvases adorned the walls, capturing fragments of life's delicate nuances. Pichai's heart swelled with longing as he gazed at the vibrant strokes of color, the artists' emotions palpable in every stroke.

It was in the art room that Pichai's life took a turn. Her hair, adorned with streaks of gray, emerged from the shadows. She introduced herself as Miss Supatra, the art teacher. Her eyes, filled with warmth and understanding, met Pichai's. At that moment, Pichai knew he had found a kindred spirit, someone who could guide him on his journey of self-discovery.

"Art has a way of capturing the essence of life," she said, her voice filled with wisdom. "It allows us to express ourselves freely, without the constraints of judgment or expectation."

Pichai's heart skipped a beat as he absorbed her words. He sensed a kindred spirit in Miss Supatra, someone who understood the struggles of identity and the power of self-expression. A flicker of hope ignited within him.

Under Miss Supatra's guidance, Pichai discovered the magic of art. He poured his emotions onto the canvas with a brush, creating a vibrant tapestry of colors that mirrored his soul. Each stroke carried a tale of self-discovery, battles fought, and victories won.

As the days turned into weeks, Pichai's talent bloomed, attracting the attention of his classmates and teachers alike. The once-confused young boy became a beacon of inspiration, his art a testament to the beauty within each of us, waiting to be uncovered.

Emboldened by his newfound confidence, Pichai shared his truth with his closest friends. With bated breath, he revealed his struggles with gender identity, expecting rejection or ridicule. To his surprise, his friends embraced him warmly, their acceptance a balm to his wounded soul. They saw beyond the external labels, recognizing the beauty of his spirit that shone brightly through his art.

Word of Pichai's journey spread like wildfire throughout the school, touching the hearts of students and teachers alike. The corridors buzzed with whispers of admiration and curiosity as students began flocking to the art room to witness Pichai's creations firsthand. They marveled at the raw emotion that emanated from each stroke, the delicate balance of vulnerability and strength that his artwork portrayed.

Pichai's story resonated deeply with many as they, too, struggled with their insecurities and fears. A newfound sense of acceptance and understanding began to take root in the Senior High School hallowed halls. Students who had once felt isolated found solace in knowing they were not alone in their struggles.

Miss Supatra, the catalyst of Pichai's transformation, saw her guidance's impact on her students. She organized an art exhibition within the school, a celebration of diversity and the power of self-expression. The art room transformed into a gallery, each canvas serving as a window into the artist's soul.

The exhibition drew visitors from far and wide as the story of Pichai and his fellow artists spread beyond the confines of the school. People from different walks of life stood before the artworks, their eyes welling up with tears, their hearts stirred with empathy. They saw their journeys reflected in the vibrant hues and intricate details, finding solace and inspiration in the bare vulnerability.

Pichai's parents, initially hesitant to embrace their son's truth, attended the exhibition. As they perused the gallery, their eyes were opened to the depth of their son's struggle, the strength he had summoned to overcome his fears. Tears streamed down their faces, mingling with regret and pride. At that moment, they understood the importance of unconditional love and support.

The art exhibition was pivotal for Pichai and the school community. Once burdened by the pressure of conformity, students began to embrace their unique identities, finding beauty in the most mundane moments. Friendships deepened, barriers crumbled, and a newfound sense of unity permeated the hallways, all sparked by the transformative power of Pichai's art.

Pichai's journey extended far beyond the confines of the school. News of his art and story reached prominent galleries, leading to invitations for him to showcase his work globally. His art transcended borders and language barriers, resonating with people's souls worldwide. Pichai became a symbol of resilience and self-discovery; his story is a testament to the universal power of authenticity.

As Pichai stood before a packed auditorium years later, he reflected on his journey. The applause and admiration washed over him, but what truly resonated was the knowledge that his art had inspired others to find their meaning and purpose. The beauty he had discovered in everyday moments had become a beacon of hope for countless individuals.

In the audience, students from the Senior High School in Thailand sat, their hearts filled with gratitude. They had witnessed the transformation of their school, the emergence of a haven where everyone was celebrated for who they were. They knew Pichai's story would forever be etched in their hearts, a reminder to embrace their identities and find beauty in the simplest moments.

And as Pichai took his final bow, he knew deep within his being that his journey had only begun. The beauty of finding meaning in everyday moments had become his life's purpose, and he vowed to continue sharing his art, his story, and his unwavering belief in the power of authenticity.

The Phoenix's Flight

In the enchanting land of Thailand, where vibrant colors and rich traditions danced harmoniously, there lived a young teacher named Anurak. At the tender age of twenty-seven, he had already faced more challenges than his young heart could bear. But little did he know that within the depths of his struggles lay the seeds of transformation and the power to overcome self-limiting beliefs.

Anurak's world was turned upside down when his beloved mother was diagnosed with a terminal illness. The weight of this devastating news pressed upon his chest like an iron vice, squeezing out every ounce of hope and joy. As the doctors predicted a limited time left, Anurak's family turned to him, their eyes filled with desperation, knowing that his financial capacity was their only lifeline.

With a heavy heart and a determined spirit, Anurak set out on a path of self-discovery and resilience. He looked within, searching for the strength to navigate the treacherous terrain. During those moments of introspection, he realized the shackles that bound him were external and internal.

Anurak had always carried a burden of self-doubt, feeling unworthy of the dreams that danced within the recesses of his mind. He had convinced himself that he was destined for mediocrity, his aspirations diminished by the weight of self-limiting beliefs. But now, faced with the imminent loss of his mother, he understood that he had to rise above these constraints and become the person he was meant to be.

With newfound determination, Anurak embarked on a journey of personal growth. He devoured books on self-improvement, seeking guidance from the wisdom of others who had faced their battles and emerged victorious. He surrounded himself with positive influences, seeking the company of those who believed in his potential.

As the days turned into weeks and the weeks into months, Anurak transformed. He shed his old skin, emerging as a phoenix rising from the ashes of self-doubt. Once obscured by his insecurities, his passion for teaching burned with an intensity that radiated through his every action. Anurak poured his heart and soul into his vocation, inspiring his students to believe in themselves and reach for their dreams.

Amidst the chaos of his journey, Anurak found solace in the beauty of his homeland. Thailand's lush landscapes and vibrant culture served as a reminder of the resilience ingrained within its people. He would wander through the bustling streets of Bangkok, the intoxicating aroma of street food swirling around him, and marvel at the colorful temples that adorned the city—these moments of serenity fueled his determination, reminding him that even in the face of adversity, beauty persisted.

Anurak's unwavering dedication to his craft began to bear fruit. Once disengaged and uninspired, his students shone with a newfound passion for learning. They saw in Anurak a reflection of their potential, a manifestation of what they could achieve if they dared to overcome their self-imposed limitations.

With each passing day, Anurak's financial burden grew heavier. The cost of his mother's medical care and the looming specter of funeral expenses threatened to crush his spirit. But he refused to let despair consume him. Instead, he utilized his creativity and resourcefulness, contacting friends and colleagues for support. Their generosity, Their generosity, combined with Anurak's unwavering determination, helped alleviate the burden that weighed heavily upon his shoulders. Fundraisers were organized, benefit concerts held, and a compassionate community rallied around him, recognizing his character's strength and love for his mother.

As the days turned into nights, Anurak would sit by his mother's side, holding her frail hand and whispering words of love and gratitude. They shared stories of their lives, memories that wove a tapestry of love and connection. In those moments, Anurak discovered the true essence of his mother's spirit—a warrior who had faced countless battles with grace and resilience.

On February 26, 2011, as the world held its breath, Anurak's mother took her final breath. The room was filled with a bittersweet stillness, a mix of grief and relief that swirled in the air. Anurak's heart shattered into a million pieces, but he knew that his mother's legacy would forever live on within him.

After his mother's passing, Anurak found himself at a crossroads. He could succumb to the weight of grief, allowing it to consume him, or he could honor his mother's memory by stepping into the fullness of his potential. Determined to choose the latter, he embarked on a pilgrimage to Wat Arun, the Temple of Dawn.

As the first rays of sunlight painted the sky in hues of orange and gold, Anurak climbed the steps of the temple. The intricate details of the architecture mirrored the complexities of his journey. Each step brought him closer to the realization that he had the power to rewrite his story and transcend the limitations that had held him back for so long.

At the temple's pinnacle, Anurak stood in awe, his gaze sweeping across the city's panorama. The moment's beauty overwhelmed him, and tears streamed down his face as he released the last vestiges of self-doubt. In that sacred space, he vowed to himself and his mother's spirit to honor her memory by living a life of purpose, resilience, and unwavering belief in his potential.

Anurak returned to his teaching career with a renewed sense of purpose. He poured his heart into every lesson, nurturing a sense of self-belief within his students. He shared his journey of overcoming self-limiting beliefs, inspiring them to recognize their inherent worth and the limitless possibilities that lay before them.

Word of Anurak's transformative journey spread far and wide, capturing the attention of educational organizations and media outlets. He became a beacon of hope for those trapped by their self-doubt, a testament to the power of resilience and the strength within each individual.

In the years that followed, Anurak's influence continued to grow. He established a foundation in his mother's name, providing scholarships and support for students facing financial hardship. His story inspired countless others, reminding them that the power to overcome self-limiting beliefs resides within every one of us.

As Anurak stood before a gathering of educators and students, his voice strong and unwavering, he reflected on the journey that had brought him to this moment. The hardships, the heartaches, and the triumphs had molded him into the person he was today—a symbol of resilience, a testament to the indomitable human spirit.

Anurak's message resonated deeply with the audience, his words weaving a tapestry of hope and possibility. As he concluded his speech, thunderous applause erupted, reverberating. Tears glistened in the eyes of those touched by his story, who had been reminded of their capacity to overcome obstacles and rewrite their narratives.

In the years that followed, Anurak's influence extended beyond the borders of Thailand. He became a sought-after speaker, traveling to different corners of the globe to share his message of resilience and empowerment. Through his workshops and seminars, he inspired individuals from all walks of life to confront their self-limiting beliefs, embrace their true potential, and live a life of purpose and fulfillment.

Anurak's journey also led him to connect with others who had faced similar challenges. He met young individuals confused about their gender and identity, providing them with a safe space to share their stories and find acceptance. He became a mentor, guiding them on their paths of self-discovery and helping them navigate the complexities of societal expectations and self-acceptance.

Back in Thailand, Anurak's impact on the education system was profound. He worked tirelessly to advocate for inclusive and empowering teaching practices to ensure that every student had the opportunity to thrive regardless of their background or circumstances. His efforts sparked a revolution in education, fostering a culture of compassion, resilience, and belief in the potential of every child.

As Anurak reflected on his journey, he couldn't help but feel a deep sense of gratitude. Every hardship, every moment of doubt, had led him to this point—a point of profound fulfillment and purpose. He knew his mother, his guiding light, was watching over him, her love and support propelling him forward.

Anurak's story became legendary, passed down through generations, inspiring countless others to confront their self-limiting beliefs and embrace life's boundless possibilities. His legacy continued to shape lives long after he had taken his final breath, reminding people that within the darkest moments, the seeds of transformation and resilience could bloom.

And so, the young Thai boy who had once been confused about his gender and identity had emerged as a beacon of hope, a symbol of the human capacity for growth and transformation. Anurak's journey reminded everyone that the most significant battles are often fought within oneself and that the power to overcome self-limiting beliefs lies within the depths of one's heart and spirit.

As the sun set over the horizon, casting a warm glow across the land, Anurak stood tall, ready to embrace the next chapter of his life. With a heart filled with gratitude and a spirit fueled by unwavering belief, he stepped forward, knowing that his journey was far from over. The impact of his story would continue to ripple through time, inspiring generations to take flight and soar beyond the confines of their self-imposed limitations.

The Art of Living

I first heard about Marcus through whispers in the art community—a reclusive genius whose works were seldom seen but always revered. I was intrigued as a journalist hungry for a story transcending the ordinary. What kind of man could create such beauty yet remain hidden from the world? I felt a magnetic pull to uncover the mystery of Marcus, not just for my readers but for myself.

I arrived at his secluded cottage on a rainy afternoon, where the world feels washed clean, and every breath is a fresh start. Marcus answered my knock with a wary look, his eyes a stormy grey that mirrored the sky. He was hesitant, but curiosity is a powerful force. He let me in.

As the days turned into weeks, I immersed myself in Marcus's world. His art reflected his soul—raw, emotional, and undeniably beautiful. Yet, he guarded his privacy fiercely. Every conversation was a delicate dance, and I often felt tiptoeing on the edge of a precipice.

As we sat by the fire one evening, Marcus spoke about his disdain for fame. "Fame strips you bare," he said softly, staring into the flames. "It takes your art and makes it a spectacle, something to be consumed rather than experienced."

I understood, but my world thrived on stories and exposure. A paradox hung between us, a silent rift we both acknowledged but never addressed. Despite our differences, I felt an undeniable connection growing between us. His presence was a balm to my restless spirit, and I began to see the world through his eyes—where silence spoke louder than words and solitude was a sanctuary.

Then, I stumbled upon a secret. In the attic, hidden beneath a stack of old canvases, I found a letter from a woman named Elise to Marcus. The words were filled with love and pain, revealing a past that Marcus had buried deep. Elise had been his muse, his lover, and her death had driven him into seclusion.

Confronting Marcus about Elise was the hardest thing I had ever done. His face turned ashen, and the hurt in his eyes was palpable. "She was everything to me," he whispered, his voice breaking. "When she died, a part of me died with her."

At that moment, I saw Marcus not as an enigmatic artist but as a man haunted by loss, struggling to find meaning in a world that had taken so much from him. I realized that my quest for a story had been selfish. I had invaded his sanctuary, prying open wounds that had barely healed.

Yet, amidst the chaos, love blossomed. We confronted our fears and vulnerabilities, learning to navigate the delicate balance between privacy and openness. Marcus taught me the value of shielding one's soul from the greedy eyes of the world while I showed him the beauty of sharing his gift, not for fame, but to touch lives.

Our journey was not easy, but it was transformative. We learned that genuine connection requires vulnerability, that love is a risk worth taking, and that the past, no matter how painful, can lead to new beginnings.

As I write this, I think about the story that brought me to Marcus. It was never about unveiling a reclusive artist but about discovering the art of living. In the end, Marcus's greatest masterpiece was not his paintings but the life we built together—a testament to resilience, love, and the healing power of human connection.

And so, I close this chapter not with a revelation but with a truth: Sometimes, the most profound stories are not the ones we uncover but the ones we live.

LOVE AND CONNECTION

The Canvas of Our Hearts

I always believed that success was a solitary journey. After all, I had climbed the ladder rung by rung, sacrificing countless nights and relationships for the sake of my business empire. With its cold, imposing architecture and bustling streets, Moscow was the perfect backdrop for my relentless pursuit of achievement. Yet, the solitude wrapped around me like the heavy winter fog that often blanketed the city.

On an unremarkable Tuesday, I first saw her as I sipped my usual black coffee at a quaint café near the Arbat. Mia burst into the room with the energy of a summer storm, her vibrant scarf fluttering behind her like a banner of defiance against the dreary Moscow winter. She was the antithesis of everything my life had become: colorful, unpredictable, and unmistakably alive.

She approached the counter, eyes scanning the menu with an artist's curiosity, as if every item had a story waiting to be told. I was captivated by her presence, unable to tear my gaze away.

Our eyes met, and she smiled, a smile that felt like sunshine breaking through a decade-long cloud cover.

"Do you mind if I sit here?" she asked, pointing to the empty chair.

"Not at all," I replied, surprised by my willingness.

We talked about everything and nothing. She was a painter, a free spirit who saw the world not just as it was but as it could be. Her work descriptions were so vivid that I could almost see the brushstrokes on the canvas, the colors blending and dancing in a way that mirrored her personality.

As the weeks turned into months, our conversations grew more profound. We spent hours walking along the Moskva River, her laughter contrasting with the icy wind that nipped at our faces. I opened up to her in ways I never had with anyone else. She had a way of peeling back the layers of my guarded heart, revealing the vulnerable man beneath the businessman's façade.

But Mia had her scars.

One evening, as we stood on a bridge overlooking the river, she confessed her fears. Her past relationships had left her wary and uncertain, and she struggled to believe that something as beautiful as what we had could last.

"I paint because it's the only way I know how to express my emotions," she said, her voice barely a whisper. "But when it comes to love, I'm terrified. What if it all falls apart?"

Her words struck a chord within me. I realized that we were both prisoners of our pasts, held captive by the fear of vulnerability. Yet, here we were, two souls intertwined by destiny, standing on the precipice of something extraordinary.

"Mia," I said, taking her hand in mine, "we can't let our fears dictate our future. We're stronger together than apart. Let's face this, not as individuals, but as partners."

Her eyes shimmered with a mix of hope and apprehension. "Do you believe we can do this?"

"With all my heart," I replied, and for the first time in a long while, I felt a sense of conviction that went beyond business deals and profit margins.

As spring arrived, Moscow transformed. The snow melted, revealing the city's hidden beauty, much like Mia and I had uncovered each other's true selves. We spent our days exploring art galleries, attending concerts, and dreaming of an increasingly possible future.

One evening, as the sun set over the horizon, casting a golden glow across the city, Mia and I found ourselves at the same café where we had first met. She reached into her bag and pulled out a small canvas.

"I painted this for you," she said, handing it to me.

It was a portrait of us, standing on the bridge, our hands intertwined, the city of Moscow sprawling behind us like a silent witness to our journey. The colors were vibrant yet harmonious, capturing the essence of our love.

Tears welled up in my eyes as I looked at the painting. "It's beautiful, Mia. Thank you."

She smiled, her eyes reflecting the warmth of the setting sun. "David, you've taught me that love is worth the risk. Together, we can create something even more beautiful than any painting."

At that moment, I understood that true success was not measured by wealth or accolades but by the connections we forged and the love we shared. Mia and I had found each other in a city known for its harshness, and together, we had discovered the courage to open our hearts.

As we walked hand in hand through the streets of Moscow, I knew our journey was beginning. And for the first time in my life, I felt truly alive.

The canvas of our hearts was no longer blank but filled with the vibrant strokes of a love that had the power to overcome any fear, any obstacle. And that, I realized, was the most tremendous success of all.

Whispers of the Aegean

In a quaint, sun-drenched province of Greece, nestled between olive groves and the cerulean Aegean Sea, lived a woman named Claire. Her red hair, kissed by the Mediterranean sun, cascaded down her shoulders, and her eyes held the depth of the sea's mysteries. She was a foreigner in a land of old myths and new beginnings, teaching English to eager young minds in the cobblestone village of Vassara.

Claire had come to Greece to escape the ghosts of her past relationships, seeking solace in the ancient hills and the simplicity of village life. The villagers welcomed her with open arms, and she quickly found a friend in Nikos, a local olive farmer. Nikos was a man of few words but abundant kindness. His laughter echoed through the olive trees, and his presence was as steady as the mountains surrounding them.

Their friendship blossomed over shared meals, long walks by the sea, and countless cups of strong Greek coffee. With his dark hair and warm, compassionate eyes, Nikos became Claire's anchor in this new world. They shared secrets under the starlit sky, their conversations flowing as naturally as the waves that lapped the shore.

As the months turned into years, Claire's heart began to stir with feelings she could no longer ignore. She found herself yearning for Nikos in ways that frightened her. The scars of past betrayals etched deep within her heart made her wary. Vulnerability felt like a distant dream, one she was too afraid to chase.

One balmy evening, as the sun dipped below the horizon, painting the sky in hues of orange and pink, Claire and Nikos sat on the beach, their feet buried in the cool sand. The sound of the waves was a soothing lullaby, and the air was thick with unspoken words.

"Nikos," Claire began, her voice barely a whisper, "do you ever wonder what it would be like to be truly loved by someone?"

Nikos turned to her, his eyes reflecting the fading light. "Every day, Claire. Every single day."

Her heart pounded in her chest, each beat louder than the last. She wanted to tell him how she felt, but the fear of rejection, of losing the one person who had stood by her side, held her back.

Days turned into weeks, and the weight of her unspoken love grew heavier. One evening, as they walked through the olive grove, the scent of blossoms in the air, Claire could no longer bear the silence. She stopped and looked at him, her eyes brimming with unshed tears, her heart pounding so loudly she was sure he could hear it.

"Nikos, there's something I need to tell you," she said, trembling.

He stepped closer, his brow furrowed with concern. "What is it, Claire?"

She took a deep breath, the words tumbling out before she could stop them. "I think I'm falling in love with you. I've been so scared to say it, but I can't keep it inside anymore."

For a moment, Nikos was silent, his expression unreadable. Claire's heart sank, the fear of rejection tightening its grip on her. But then, a slow smile spread across his face, and he reached out to gently cup her cheek.

"Claire, you have no idea how long I've waited to hear those words," he said softly. "I've loved you from the moment I saw you, but I was afraid you'd never feel the same."

Tears of relief and joy streamed down Claire's face as she realized the depth of his feelings. All this time, they had both been too afraid to leap, too worried about the what-ifs and the maybes. But now, at this moment, all those fears seemed insignificant compared to the overwhelming love that filled her heart.

At that moment, under the ancient olive trees and the watchful gaze of the stars, they shared their first kiss. It was a kiss that spoke of promises, of healing, and of a love that had been waiting to be discovered.

As the seasons changed and the village buzzed with the warmth of summer, Claire and Nikos's love blossomed. They were inseparable, their bond growing stronger with each passing day. The villagers, who had watched their friendship bloom, now celebrated their love with joyous hearts.

Years later, as they stood hand in hand, watching the sunset over the Aegean, Claire realized that true love was not about the absence of fear but finding someone worth facing those fears for. She had found someone in Nikos, and he had found someone in her.

And so, in the heart of Greece, among the olive groves and the whispers of the sea, two souls who had been afraid to love found their courage in each other. Like the ancient myths of the land, their love story was one of timeless beauty and enduring strength.

In the end, love is not about never being hurt; it is about finding the one who makes every risk, every fear, and every moment of vulnerability worth it. And Claire and Nikos had done just that, creating a legacy of love that would be remembered.

Footprints of Empathy

Once upon a time, in the breathtaking high valleys of Mongolia, three brothers embarked on a journey that would forever change their lives and how they understood the world. It was winter, and the snow-capped mountains stood tall against the clear blue sky. This story, born out of an actual scenario, delves into exploring the importance of empathy in relationships and highlights the struggles of a young Thai boy named Aiden, who found himself confused about his gender and identity.

The eldest brother, Kazuki, was known for his wisdom and gentle nature. He possessed an innate ability to understand others, to feel their pain and joy as if they were his own. The middle brother, Takeshi, was a passionate and adventurous soul, always seeking new experiences and unearthing hidden truths. The youngest brother, Hiroshi, was filled with compassion and had an uncanny knack for connecting with people on a deep emotional level.

One cold winter's day, Aiden, a timid and introverted boy from Thailand, arrived in the high valley. His heart was heavy with confusion and a sense of isolation. Aiden struggled to find acceptance in a society that often imposed rigid expectations on gender and identity. The young boy felt lost, yearning for someone who could understand and truly see him for who he was.

As fate would have it, Aiden's path crossed with the three brothers during his stay in Mongolia. Intrigued by his quiet demeanor and the sadness in his eyes, Kazuki, Takeshi, and Hiroshi decided to extend their empathy and offer their friendship to the young boy.

The brothers spent countless hours with Aiden, listening to his fears, dreams, and aspirations. They created a safe space where he could openly express his confusion and explore his true identity. Aiden, still unsure about himself, felt a sense of relief and warmth in their presence. The brothers' unwavering support and understanding began to chip away at the walls he had built around his heart.

Together, they embarked on thrilling adventures, traversing the snowy landscapes and embracing the beauty of nature. Aiden discovered solace in the vastness of the Mongolian wilderness, finding parallels between the natural world and the complexities of his own identity. With their boundless empathy, the brothers guided him through this journey of self-discovery, helping him recognize that his worth was not defined by societal norms but by the love and acceptance he found within himself.

Amid their exploration, Aiden encountered various hardships, moments of self-doubt, and the harsh judgments of others. However, the brothers' unwavering support shielded him from the storm. Their empathy was a beacon of hope, reminding him he was not alone in his struggles.

Through their collective experiences, the brothers discovered that empathy was a virtue and a transformative force capable of healing wounds and bridging divides. They realized that embracing empathy gave them the power to create a ripple effect, inspiring others to be more accepting and compassionate.

As winter slowly faded into spring, Aiden's journey of self-acceptance and empowerment reached a pivotal moment. With the support of his newfound brothers, he embraced his true identity, coming out as non-binary. The weight that burdened his soul for so long lifted, and he felt an overwhelming sense of liberation.

Word of Aiden's transformation spread throughout the high valleys of Mongolia, reaching the ears of others who had felt the weight of societal expectations and the pain of hiding their true selves. Inspired by Aiden's courage, individuals from different walks of life gathered in the high valley, seeking solace and understanding.

Under the guidance of the three brothers, a community formed—a tapestry woven with threads of empathy, acceptance, and love. People shared their stories, fears, and dreams, finding strength in each other's vulnerability. The high valley became a sanctuary where individuals could unapologetically be themselves, free from judgment and prejudice.

Aiden's journey had ignited a spark, setting ablaze the hearts of those who yearned for authentic connections. The community flourished, and with each passing day, the importance of empathy resonated more deeply. It became the cornerstone of their relationships, a guiding principle that allowed them to see beyond surface-level differences and connect on a soulful level.

As the seasons changed, so did the lives of those touched by Aiden's story. The once-confused young boy transformed into a beacon of hope, sharing his experiences and advocating for greater acceptance and understanding. Aiden's voice echoed through the valleys, reaching far and wide, encouraging others to embrace empathy and create spaces of belonging.

The impact of Aiden's journey extended beyond the high valleys of Mongolia, inspiring people in distant lands. His story was shared through various mediums, captivating the hearts of individuals who had never set foot in the high valley. From bustling cities to remote villages, the power of empathy began to permeate relationships, challenging preconceived notions and fostering more profound connections.

Back in the high valley, Aiden continued to thrive, surrounded by the love and support of his chosen family—the three brothers and the community they had built together. With their guidance, he found strength in his vulnerability, embracing his unique identity with pride. Aiden's journey had taught him that his worth was not defined by societal expectations but by the love and acceptance he received from those who indeed saw him.

Years passed, and Aiden's story became woven into the fabric of the High Valley's history. The community flourished, symbolizing empathy and acceptance in a world that often struggled with understanding and tolerance. The high valley stood as a testament to the power of human connection, reminding all who ventured there of the importance of embracing one another's differences.

And so, the exploration of empathy in relationships, sparked by the meeting of three brothers and a young Thai boy in the winter of Mongolia, found its rightful place in people's hearts worldwide. Aiden's journey, as inspiring and emotional as it was, became a timeless tale of resilience, self-discovery, and the transformative power of empathy. This story would continue to touch and inspire generations to come.

Brushstrokes of Fabulousness

Once upon a time, in a small town nestled in the heart of the Midwest, a young boy named Ethan embarked on a journey of self-discovery that would forever change his life and those around him. Born into a devout Catholic family, Ethan grew up surrounded by strong religious beliefs and traditions. But little did he know that truth was waiting to be unveiled within the confines of his own heart.

Ethan's artistic soul yearned to express itself through colors and brushstrokes. His passion for art was fueled by the vibrant stained glass windows that adorned the local Catholic church. As a child, he would gaze at the intricate designs, mesmerized by their beauty and the stories they told. Ethan found solace and a glimpse of his truth in the presence of these windows.

As he grew older, Ethan began to question his own identity. In the quiet moments of introspection, he realized that he was gay. The weight of this realization bore heavy on his young shoulders, for he feared rejection from his family and community, knowing that his truth conflicted with the teachings of his faith. But the desire to live authentically burned within him, a flame that could no longer be extinguished.

Summoning up all his courage, Ethan approached his parents one evening, his heart pounding with anticipation and fear. With trembling words, he confessed his truth, expecting judgment or disappointment. To his surprise, his parents embraced him warmly, their eyes filled with love and acceptance. They assured him that their love for him was unwavering and that his journey of self-discovery was a path they would walk alongside him. Their support was a beacon of light in his darkest moments, giving him the strength to continue on his path of self-discovery and acceptance.

With his parents' acceptance, Ethan experienced a profound sense of liberation. The chains of fear and self-doubt dissolved, allowing his artistic spirit to soar. Inspired by the stained glass windows that had captivated him since childhood, Ethan volunteered to redesign the church's windows, infusing them with a new perspective that mirrored inclusivity and love.

As Ethan devoted countless hours to his creative endeavor, his passion manifested in each stroke of the brush. He experimented with different techniques, blending colors and creating unique patterns. The vibrant colors danced on the glass, breathing life into the stories they depicted. His art became a bridge, connecting the teachings of his faith with the reality of his own identity. With a touch of humor and wit, he painted scenes of Jesus surrounded by diverse individuals, embracing them with open arms. He intended to create a sanctuary where people, regardless of their sexual orientation, could find solace and acceptance.

Word of Ethan's transformative artwork spread throughout the town. Congregants flocked to the church, their eyes widening with awe and their hearts opening to a new understanding. They marveled at the beauty of the stained glass, the stories they told now resonating with a more profound sense of compassion and empathy. The church, once a place of rigid tradition, became a space where people could explore their identities and beliefs, thanks to the transformative power of Ethan's art.

Ethan's art transformed not only the physical space of the church but also the hearts and minds of those who entered. People who had once held prejudices or reservations now questioned their beliefs, their hearts softened by Ethan's art's message of love and inclusivity. The church became a place where individuals felt seen and accepted, a refuge where their journeys of self-discovery were acknowledged and celebrated. The community, too, began to change. Conversations about acceptance and diversity became more common, and people started challenging their biases and preconceptions.

Ethan's artistic talent flourished as the years passed, radiating beyond the church walls. His creations reached galleries, museums, and people's hearts far and wide. Ethan's art's impact went beyond his small town's confines. His paintings, infused with love, acceptance, and a touch of humor, resonated with people from all walks of life. They became symbols of hope and inspiration, reminding individuals to embrace their authentic selves and celebrate the diversity that enriches our world. His art was a testament to the power of self-expression and the universal language of creativity.

Ethan's story spread through various media outlets, capturing the attention of art enthusiasts, activists, and those seeking their paths of self-discovery. His journey became a testament to the power of authenticity and the profound impact that acceptance can have on an individual's life.

Art galleries were filled with Ethan's vibrant masterpieces, each telling a story of resilience, love, and the beauty of embracing one's true identity. His name became synonymous with courage and creativity, a beacon of light for those trapped in the shadows of conformity.

But amidst the recognition and acclaim, Ethan remained grounded and humble. He never forgot the support of his loving parents and the unwavering acceptance they had shown him. Their open-mindedness had allowed him to flourish, and he dedicated his success to them, always expressing gratitude for their love and understanding. Their support was a source of strength for Ethan and a testament to the power of love and acceptance in fostering self-discovery and personal growth.

As the years passed, Ethan's art took on new dimensions. He ventured into other mediums, using his talents to advocate for LGBTQ+ rights and to shed light on the struggles faced by marginalized communities. His work became a fusion of activism and creativity, a powerful force for change. His early pieces, inspired by the stained glass windows of his childhood, were vibrant and full of life. But as he grew and his understanding of his identity deepened, his art became more introspective, exploring themes of self-acceptance and love. His later works, often featuring diverse individuals and symbols of LGBTQ+ pride, were a testament to his journey and a call to action for others.

Ethan's artistic journey became a source of inspiration for countless individuals who, like him, were searching for their true selves. Through his art, he encouraged others to embrace their unique identities, celebrate their strengths, and find the courage to live authentically.

Amid his artistic endeavors, Ethan never lost his sense of humor. He believed that laughter could heal wounds and bridge divides. His paintings often featured whimsical characters and playful scenes, reminding viewers not to take life too seriously and to find joy in the simplest moments. This touch of humor was not just a reflection of Ethan's personality but also a powerful tool in his art, helping to break down barriers and foster a sense of shared humanity.

With each stroke of the brush and every canvas he filled, Ethan's legacy grew. His art touched hearts, sparked conversations, and fostered understanding. He became a symbol of the significance of self-discovery, showing the world that embracing our true selves can lead to a life filled with purpose, love, and creativity. However, the impact of his art was not just external. It also transformed Ethan's own life, giving him a sense of purpose and fulfillment that he had never experienced before. His art was a means of self-expression and a tool for personal growth and understanding.

As Ethan reflected on his journey, he realized that his art was not just about personal expression; it was a gift he could use to make a difference in the lives of others. And so, he continued to paint, create, and inspire, knowing that his journey of self-discovery had become a catalyst for change in the hearts and minds of those who encountered his work.

As the sun set on the canvas of Ethan's life, his artistic legacy would forever illuminate the path for others to embark on their journeys of self-discovery, acceptance, and the pursuit of a life lived authentically.

Willow Creek

The quaint town of Willow Creek is nestled between rolling hills and winding streams. It was here that Sarah, a beloved community member, faced the greatest challenge of her life.

Sarah, a 42-year-old administrative assistant and single mother, was diagnosed with stage III breast cancer after a routine check-up. The news hit hard, leaving Sarah and her 12-year-old daughter, Emily, fearful and uncertain. Sarah had always been the rock in Emily's life, providing love, stability, and strength. Now, it seemed the foundation of their world was crumbling.

The close-knit community of Willow Creek had long been a source of comfort and camaraderie for its residents. When word of Sarah's diagnosis spread, the town's collective heart sank. Yet, rather than succumb to despair, the community rallied around Sarah, offering meals, childcare, and emotional support during her darkest days.

Sarah's determination to fight the disease and maintain a positive outlook inspired those around her despite daunting odds. She approached each day with a resolve to live fully and cherish every moment for herself and Emily. Though sometimes tinged with pain, her laughter became a powerful reminder of the human spirit's resilience.

Sarah and Emily walked through Willow Creek's picturesque park one crisp autumn afternoon. The leaves, with vibrant reds and golds, reflected their tumultuous yet beautiful journey. Clutching her mother's hand, Emily looked up with teary eyes and asked, "Mom, are we going to be okay?"

Sarah knelt, her eyes meeting Emily's with unwavering love and strength. "Yes, sweetie. We will be okay. No matter what happens, we'll face it together. And we have so many people who love us and are here to help. We are never alone."

As the weeks turned into months, Sarah's battle with cancer became a tapestry woven with moments of hope and hardship. She underwent grueling treatments, often finding herself exhausted and in pain. Yet, even on the most challenging days, she found solace in her neighbor's and friends' small acts of kindness.

One particularly challenging evening, Sarah received a surprise visit from Mrs. Thompson, an elderly widow who lived down the street. She brought a homemade casserole and a scrapbook filled with photographs and heartfelt messages from the community. "We wanted you to know how much you mean to all of us," Mrs. Thompson said, tears glistening.

Sarah flipped through the pages, her heart swelling with gratitude. There were pictures of neighborhood barbecues, holiday gatherings, and countless smiling faces. Each message was a testament to the impact Sarah had on their lives. "Thank you," Sarah whispered, feeling a renewed sense of hope. "This means more than you know."

Inspired by her mother's strength and the community's support, Emily organized a charity run to raise funds for breast cancer research. She enlisted the help of her classmates, and soon, the entire town was abuzz with excitement. On the day of the event, hundreds of people gathered, wearing pink ribbons and determined expressions. Sarah, although weak, stood at the starting line, her heart brimming with pride.

As the runners took off, Sarah watched with tears in her eyes. She felt a deep connection to each person there, knowing their support was not just for her but for everyone who had ever faced a similar battle.

In the months that followed, Sarah's health gradually improved. The treatments, combined with her indomitable spirit and the love surrounding her, began to show positive results. Though the road ahead was still uncertain, Sarah held onto hope with both hands.

One evening, as the sun set over Willow Creek, casting a golden glow on the town, Sarah sat with Emily on their porch. They watched fireflies dance in the twilight, their tiny lights flickering like beacons of hope. "Mom," Emily said softly, "I'm so proud of you."

Sarah smiled, her eyes filled with love. "I'm proud of us, Emily. We've been through so much, but we've faced it together. And no matter what the future holds, we have hope. And that makes all the difference."

The story of Sarah and Emily became a cherished narrative in Willow Creek, a reminder that even in the darkest times, hope can light the way. Their journey touched the hearts of all who knew them, proving that anything is possible with love, community, and unwavering determination.

RESILIENCE AND TRANSFORMATION

"Yes, we can."

The villagers united in their cause and redoubled their efforts, working day and night—word of their unwavering perseverance spread, and soon, neighboring villages sent help. The school became a symbol of resistance, a beacon of unity against the darkness threatening to engulf them.

In a moment of quiet reflection, Sara recalled a day many years before when she had been a student herself. The teacher then was a kind older man who profoundly impacted her. One day, he had brought a small potted plant to class.

The teacher said, "This plant is like our community. It needs care, love, and strength to grow. If we neglect it, it withers. But if we nurture it, it will bloom even in the harshest conditions."

Sara had nurtured that lesson in her heart through the years. And now, she was passing it on to the next generation.

Meanwhile, Rafiq watched the village's defiance with growing unease. He remembered his days in the school, the dreams he once had, now buried under layers of cynicism and regret. One night, unable to sleep, he wandered to the school. He stood outside, unseen, watching the villagers work together. A memory surfaced—his younger self, sitting at a desk, filled with dreams of becoming someone who could make a difference. He felt a flicker of warmth, a spark of hope amidst the cold emptiness he now felt.

The next day, Sara found Rafiq waiting for her outside the school. His stern demeanor seemed to have softened, his eyes less cold.

"Sara," he began, his voice hesitant, "I see how much this school means to you and the villagers. I remember what it meant to me once."

Sara looked at him, her heart pounding. "Rafiq, it's not too late to make a difference. You can help us instead of standing in our way."

For a moment, Rafiq's face was a battlefield of conflicting emotions. Finally, he sighed deeply. "What do you need?"

Sara, cautious but hopeful, outlined the school's immediate needs. Rafiq listened, nodding occasionally, and when she finished, he promised to provide the materials and resources necessary for the repairs.

True to his word, Rafiq delivered. He brought in supplies, organized work crews, and even rolled up his sleeves to help with the labor. The villagers watched in astonishment as the man they had once feared, now a symbol of change, worked alongside them. Slowly, suspicion gave way to acceptance and then to gratitude.

One evening, as the sun set in a blaze of orange and pink, Sara and Rafiq sat on the school's steps, watching the children play.

"Why did you change your mind?" Sara asked softly.

Rafiq was silent for a moment. "I remembered what this place once meant to me. I realized I'd lost sight of what was important. Power and wealth blinded me, but seeing the villagers' determination and the children's hope brought back something I thought I'd lost forever."

Sara smiled, a sense of profound relief washing over her. "People can change, Rafiq. You've shown that."

The transformation of the school became a turning point for Valtari. The villagers' efforts and Rafiq's newfound support brought about a remarkable renewal. The school was not just repaired but improved. New books filled the shelves, the walls were painted vibrant colors, and a playground was built for the children.

The official reopening of the school was a day of celebration. The entire village gathered, their faces glowing with pride and joy. Sara stood at the front, her heart swelling as she looked at the transformed school and the hopeful faces of the children.

"Today," Sara began, her voice steady and filled with emotion, "we celebrate more than just the reopening of our school. We celebrate our unity, our resilience, and our hope. This school is a testament to what we can achieve together."

Standing beside her, Rafiq nodded. "I once lost my way, but this community showed me the path back. For that, I am forever grateful."

The villagers erupted in applause, their cheers echoing through the village. That night, as the stars twinkled above, the town of Valtari felt a sense of peace and purpose that had long been missing.

Years passed, and the school continued to thrive. It became a place of learning and community where the values of kindness, resilience, and unity were taught and lived. Sara remained a beloved teacher, her influence extending far beyond the classroom.

Rafiq, now a respected elder, often visited the school, sharing his experiences and lessons with the children. He had found redemption in the very place he once sought to destroy, and his transformation became a powerful story of hope and change.

One day, a young boy raised his hand as Sara taught a new group of students about constellations.

"Miss Sara," he asked, "do the stars ever change?"

Sara smiled, her eyes reflecting the light of the stars in the night sky. "The stars remain the same, but our perspective changes as we grow. And sometimes, if we look closely, we can see patterns and possibilities we never noticed before."

The boy nodded thoughtfully, and Sara looked out at her students, feeling fulfilled. They had found their way to the light together in a world that had once seemed so dark.

Thus, in the village of Valtari, the legacy of hope and unity lived on, a testament to the power of perseverance, the possibility of redemption, and the enduring strength of a community bound by love and purpose.

Echo

Jake Donovan stood before the rusted mirror in his cramped studio apartment, guitar slung over his shoulder. The calloused tips of his fingers caressed the strings, and he took a deep breath. The local talent show was just hours away, and Jake could already hear the whispers of the past creeping in, reminding him of betrayal and broken dreams.

Two years ago, Jake was on the brink of something great. His band, Echoes of Tomorrow, was gaining traction, and the future seemed bright. But then came the betrayal—Lucas's best friend and bandmate had signed a solo deal behind his back, effectively dismantling the band. The betrayal had cut deep, and Jake had slipped into a spiral of bitterness and obscurity.

With the talent show looming, Jake saw a glimmer of hope, a chance for redemption. He knew Lucas would be there, having heard rumors of his participation. This wasn't just about winning; it was about reclaiming his passion and confronting the ghost of his past.

At the venue, the atmosphere buzzed with anticipation. Jake's heart pounded as he scanned the crowd, his eyes landing on Lucas. The years had been kind to him; his confident stance and easy smile were unchanged. A flicker of recognition passed between them as their eyes met, followed by a heavy silence.

"Jake," Lucas said, approaching him. His voice was softer than Jake remembered. "It's been a while."

Jake nodded, his jaw clenched. "Yeah, it has."

Lucas sighed, rubbing the back of his neck. "Look, I know there's a lot to say, but maybe we can talk after the show?"

Jake's eyes narrowed. "We'll see if there's anything left to say."

As the night progressed, the talent show unfolded with a mix of performances, each competitor pouring their heart into their art. When Jake's turn came, he took the stage, the spotlight casting a halo around him. The first strum of his guitar sent a hush through the crowd, and for a moment, he felt the old fire reignite.

His fingers danced across the strings, weaving a melody of pain, loss, and a yearning for redemption. His raw and unfiltered voice carried the weight of his journey, and as the final note resonated, the audience erupted into applause. Jake's heart swelled with bittersweet pride.

Lucas was the last to perform. As he stepped onto the stage, Jake felt a pang of envy. Lucas had always had a magnetic presence, and tonight was no different. His performance was polished, and his voice was smooth and controlled. Yet, beneath the surface, Jake sensed a vulnerability, a hint of the Lucas he once knew.

When the applause died down, the judges deliberated, and the tension in the room was palpable. Jake's mind raced with conflicting emotions — the desire to win, the fear of facing Lucas, and the hope of finding closure.

Finally, the host announced the results. "The winner of this year's talent show is... Jake Donovan!"

The crowd cheered, and Jake's heart skipped a beat. He had done it. But as he looked at Lucas, standing off to the side, a mixture of relief and guilt washed over him. He had won, but at what cost?

After the show, as the crowd dispersed, Lucas approached Jake. "Congratulations," he said, his voice sincere. "You deserved it."

Jake nodded, the bitterness in his heart softening. "Thanks, Lucas. But we need to talk."

They found a quiet corner backstage, the noise of the departing crowd fading into the background. Lucas took a deep breath, his eyes meeting Jake's with regret and determination.

"Jake, I know I messed up," Lucas began. "I was selfish and ambitious, and I didn't think about how my actions would affect you or the band. Signing that solo deal was the biggest mistake of my life."

Jake's eyes searched Lucas's face, looking for any sign of insincerity. But all he saw was genuine remorse. "Why now, Lucas? Why tell me this now?"

Lucas sighed. "Because I've been carrying this guilt with me for too long. And seeing you tonight and hearing your music reminded me of why we started this journey in the first place. We had something special, Jake. Something worth fighting for."

Jake felt a lump form in his throat. The anger and resentment he had harbored for so long began dissipating, replaced by a longing for the bond they once shared. "So, what do we do now?" he asked, his voice barely above a whisper.

Lucas smiled, a glimmer of hope in his eyes. "I was thinking... maybe we could perform together. Just like old times. One last song, for the sake of what we had."

Jake's heart skipped a beat. The idea of playing alongside Lucas again felt both terrifying and exhilarating. But as he looked into his former bandmate's eyes, he realized this could be the bridge to healing old wounds and reigniting a shared passion.

"Alright," Jake said, his voice firm but with a hint of vulnerability. "Let's do it. One last song."

They retrieved their instruments and returned to the stage, which was now empty but for a few lingering staff members cleaning up. The dim lighting gave the room an intimate feel, and as they tuned their guitars, an unspoken understanding passed between them.

Lucas strummed the first chords, and Jake joined in, their melodies intertwining in a nostalgic and new harmony. They chose a song they had written together during their early days—a piece that spoke of dreams, friendship, and the unyielding spirit of youth.

As they played, the years of bitterness and separation melted away. Their music filled the room, echoing the purity of their shared journey. It was as if they had never been apart, their connection through the music more vital than ever.

When the last note faded into silence, Jake looked at Lucas, a smile breaking across his face. "I missed this," he admitted. "I missed us."

Lucas nodded, his eyes glistening with unshed tears. "Me too, Jake. Me too."

The few remaining staff members applauded slowly, and a sense of peace settled over Jake. More than winning the talent show, this impromptu performance felt like a true victory.

In the following days, Jake and Lucas spent hours talking, reminiscing, and planning their future. They decided to revive Echoes of Tomorrow with a renewed sense of purpose and understanding. They reached out to their old bandmates, who, despite initial hesitations, welcomed the idea of a reunion.

Their first official performance as a reunited band was set for a local music festival. Jake felt a mixture of nervousness and excitement as they took the stage. The crowd was a sea of faces, many of whom had followed their journey from the beginning.

Lucas stepped up to the microphone, his voice steady and confident. "Thank you all for being here tonight. This next song is about forgiveness, redemption, and the power of friendship. It's called 'Echoes of Redemption.'"

The crowd cheered, and as Jake played the opening chords, he felt a sense of completeness he hadn't experienced in years. The song flowed effortlessly, their harmonies blending in perfect unison. It was a testament to their journey — the pain, the betrayal, and the ultimate reconciliation.

Jake's eyes scanned the crowd as they played, landing on a group of young musicians watching with rapt attention. He saw the same hope and dreams he and Lucas once had in them, and it filled him with a renewed sense of purpose.

After the performance, a young woman approached them as they packed up their equipment. "You guys were amazing," she said, her eyes shining with admiration. "Your music spoke to me."

Jake smiled, remembering the impact music had on him at her age. "Thank you. What's your name?"

"Emma," she replied. "I'm a musician, too, and you guys are a huge inspiration."

Lucas leaned in, a twinkle in his eye. "Well, Emma, keep following your passion. Music can heal and unite people, even in the toughest times."

As Emma walked away, Jake turned to Lucas. "You know, we should mentor young musicians like her. Share our experiences and help them navigate the industry."

Lucas nodded, his face lighting up with enthusiasm. "I like that idea. Let's do it."

Jake and Lucas revived their band in the following months and started a mentorship program for aspiring musicians. They held workshops, offered guidance, and provided a platform for young talent to shine. Their journey of redemption became a beacon of hope for others, showing that even the deepest wounds could be healed through the power of music and friendship.

Jake's life had come full circle. From the depths of despair and betrayal, he had found his way back to his true passion, rekindling the bond with his best friend. He felt deeply grateful as he stood on the stage, looking at the crowd of hopeful faces. The echoes of the past had led him to a future filled with promise, and he was eternally thankful for that.

The Canvas of Redemption

A woman named Emily lived in the heart of New York City, where dreams and nightmares often share the same bed. She was no stranger to the intoxicating highs and devastating lows that life in this relentless city could bring. A recovering addict, Emily's journey was a testament to the precarious balance between self-destruction and self-discovery. As I sit here in my cozy apartment, with the skyline painting its masterpiece outside my window, I can't help but ponder: Can we ever truly escape our past, or do we learn to paint over it?

Emily's battle with addiction had been a fierce one, a war waged in the shadows of alleyways and the sterile confines of rehab centers. Her struggle was etched into her soul, each scar a reminder of nights spent chasing a fleeting euphoria. But now, she was determined to rebuild her life, brick by fragile brick. She had traded her needles for a journal, her toxic relationships for the solace of solitude, and her despair for a glimmer of hope.

Her days were a mosaic of therapy sessions, support group meetings, and quiet moments in between, during which she grappled with the ghosts of her past. During one of these moments, in the stillness of her small apartment, Emily discovered something extraordinary. She had always been drawn to art, but it was a forgotten passion buried under layers of addiction and regret. One rainy afternoon, she stared at an old, dusty set of paints and brushes tucked away in a corner.

With a hesitant hand, she dipped a brush into a pool of vibrant blue and let it glide across a blank canvas. It was as if the colors whispered secrets to her, urging her to pour her pain and hope onto the canvas. Each stroke was a release, a step towards healing. The more she painted, the more she felt a sense of purpose, a connection to something greater than herself.

Emily's newfound passion for painting became her therapy, a sanctuary where she could confront her demons and celebrate her victories. Her canvases told the story of her journey—a tale of redemption, resilience, and rebirth. The swirls of color and the intricate patterns reflected her inner turmoil and growing sense of self-worth. As she painted, she began to see herself not as a broken woman but as an artist in creating her magnum opus.

However, like any journey worth taking, Emily's path had setbacks. There were days when the weight of her past threatened to crush her spirit when the temptation to escape into old habits loomed large. During these moments, she turned to her support group, a motley crew of individuals bound together by their shared struggles and unwavering belief in second chances.

One evening, after a particularly grueling therapy session, Emily sat on a park bench, her sketchbook in hand. The city around her buzzed with life, but she felt profoundly isolated. Then, a fellow group member, Jack, a wiry man, sat beside her. Jack had battle scars, but his eyes held a wisdom that only came from surviving the darkest nights.

"Emily," he said softly, "you're stronger than you think. Every stroke of that brush is a testament to your courage. You're not just painting your pain but your future."

His words resonated with her, and she realized that her art was more than a coping mechanism—it was a beacon guiding her toward a better tomorrow. She continued to paint, each canvas a chapter in her story, each stroke a declaration of her resilience.

As months passed, Emily's confidence grew. She mustered the courage to showcase her work at a local art gallery. The night of the exhibition was a whirlwind of emotions. She stood amidst strangers who marveled at her creations, their admiration a balm for her battered self-esteem. It was a night of validation, a night where she saw herself through the eyes of others—as an artist, a survivor, a woman worthy of love and respect.

Amid the crowd, she spotted a familiar face—her estranged sister, Lily. Emily's addiction had strained their relationship, but tonight, there was a glimmer of hope. With tears, Lily approached her, pulling her into a tight embrace. "I'm so proud of you, Emily," she whispered. "You've come so far."

That night, under the soft glow of the gallery lights, Emily felt something she hadn't felt in a long time—self-acceptance. She realized that her worth was not defined by her past mistakes but by her ability to rise above them. Her journey was far from over, but she now had a compass to guide her—a paintbrush that transformed her pain into something beautiful.

As I sit here, reflecting on Emily's story, I am reminded of art's power to heal, transform, and connect us to our most authentic selves. Emily's journey is a testament to the fact that within each of us lies an untapped reservoir of strength waiting to be discovered, nurtured, and expressed. It made me wonder: How many of us are silently carrying our hidden talents, our potential masterpieces, just waiting for the right moment to emerge?

Emily's life, once marred by shadows and despair, had become a canvas of vibrant possibility. Her art was a mirror reflecting not only her struggles but also her triumphs, her resilience, and her hope. It reminded us that a spark within us can ignite a path to redemption even in our darkest moments.

As seasons changed, so did Emily. She moved into a larger apartment with ample space for her growing canvases and art supplies collection. Each painting she created was a testament to her evolving journey, a visual diary of her battles and victories. Her work began to attract attention beyond the local art scene. Critics praised her unique style, calling her a "raw, unfiltered voice in the art world."

One evening, as she prepared for another exhibition, she received an unexpected phone call. A prominent art gallery in SoHo wanted to feature her work in a solo exhibition. For a moment, Emily was speechless. The gallery director's voice echoed through the phone, "Your work speaks to the soul, Emily. We believe it deserves a wider audience."

The day of the SoHo exhibition was a milestone in Emily's journey. She felt a profound sense of accomplishment as she stood among her paintings. The gallery was filled with art enthusiasts, critics, and collectors, each captivated by her work's emotion and depth. Reporters asked about her inspiration, and she spoke candidly about her past, struggles, and how painting had become her lifeline.

In the crowd, she noticed Jack, her steadfast supporter and friend from the support group. He gave her a thumbs-up, a simple gesture that conveyed a world of encouragement. Emily reflected on how far she had come as the night drew close. She had transformed her pain into purpose, her despair into hope. She had found her voice, not just as an artist but as a woman reclaiming her life.

Emily's journey taught her that recovery is not a destination but a continuous process that requires patience, self-compassion, and an unwavering belief in the possibility of change. She learned to forgive herself for past mistakes and embrace the person she was becoming. Her art was more than a means of expression; it was a testament to her resilience and a beacon of hope for others who walked a similar path.

As I sit here sipping my coffee and watching the city lights twinkle, I can't help but marvel at the transformative power of creativity. Emily's story reminds us that no matter how lost we may feel, there is always a way to find our way back to ourselves. Sometimes, it's through the love of friends and family; sometimes, it's through discovering a hidden talent that allows us to see the beauty within us.

In a city that never sleeps, where dreams are often elusive, and hope can feel like a distant star, Emily found her salvation in the most unexpected place—a blank canvas. Her journey reminds us that we all have the power to rewrite our stories, to paint over the pain, and to create a masterpiece from the fragments of our lives.

And so, as I close my laptop and prepare to face another day in this bustling metropolis, I carry the lessons of Emily's journey with me. Ultimately, we are all artists of our lives, capable of creating beauty from chaos, strength from vulnerability, and hope from despair. And who knows? We may discover that our masterpieces are not just for the world to see but for us to believe in ourselves.

The Mediterranean Mosaic of Hope

I couldn't help but wonder, can the beauty of a place mend a heart that's been shattered by loss? Is the warmth of a sun-kissed village and the innocence of a child's love possible to weave a tapestry of hope out of threads of despair?

The azure waters of the Mediterranean gently caressed the shores of a Greek village, its whitewashed houses with blue shutters clinging to the cliffs like eternal sentinels. In this idyllic setting, Tom and his young daughter, Sophia, sought solace from a past that still cast its long shadow.

Tom, once a man brimming with life, was now a mere shell. His laughter and dreams drowned in the sea of sorrow that was his wife's untimely death. Each day was a battle against the waves of depression threatening to engulf him. His only anchor was Sophia, a spirited six-year-old with hair the color of chestnuts and eyes that mirrored the Aegean Sea.

Sophia, the heart and soul of their small household, was a beacon of light in their darkest days. Her laughter echoed through the narrow alleys, her joy as infectious as the scent of blooming jasmine. She had an unshakeable belief in her father, a faith that Tom found comforting and overwhelming. But even her boundless energy couldn't entirely dispel the shadows in his heart.

Tom's days were a monotonous blur of routine—preparing simple meals, tending to their small garden, and taking Sophia to the local school, where she quickly made friends and charmed her teachers. He found solace in the predictability, yet he felt like a ghost, merely existing rather than truly living.

One golden afternoon, as they wandered through the vibrant marketplace, Sophia tugged Tom's hand, pulling him towards a small antique shop. The shop was a treasure trove of forgotten memories, filled with trinkets and relics from bygone eras. Sophia's eyes widened with wonder as she explored the dusty shelves.

"Daddy, look!" she exclaimed, holding up a weathered wooden box adorned with intricate carvings.

Tom took the box from her, his fingers tracing the delicate patterns. He opened it to reveal a collection of old letters, photographs, and mementos. Among them was a letter addressed to him in Eleni's elegant handwriting. His heart pounded in his chest as he unfolded the paper, the familiar scent of her perfume wafting up to meet him.

My Dearest Tom,

If you are reading this, I am no longer by your side. I know your heart is heavy, and I wish I could be there to ease your pain. But remember this: you are stronger than you realize, and Sophia needs you more than ever. She is your beacon of light, your reason to smile again.

Find beauty in the small moments, the everyday miracles. Hold onto hope, even when the world is crumbling around you. I believe in you, Tom. I always have and always will.

With all my love,

Eleni

Tears welled up in Tom's eyes as he clutched the letter. It was as if Eleni's words had transcended time and space, wrapping him in a warm embrace. A flicker of hope ignited in his heart for the first time in a long while.

Sophia wrapped her tiny arms around his waist, Sensing her father's emotional turmoil. "It's okay, Daddy. Mommy's watching over us. She wants us to be happy."

At that moment, Tom realized that his daughter was wise. She had an innate ability to see life's beauty and find joy in the simplest things. Her resilience and Eleni's words inspired Tom to reclaim his life.

He began to make small changes, starting with their daily routine. Instead of rushing through their chores, he took the time to savor the moments with Sophia, sharing stories and laughter. They explored the village together, discovering hidden gardens, ancient ruins, and breathtaking vistas. Tom even picked up a paintbrush, rediscovering his passion for art that he had long abandoned.

As the weeks turned into months, Tom's outlook on life profoundly shifted. He still had his dark days, but they were fewer and farther between. Sophia's unwavering belief in him and the small moments of joy they shared became his lifeline, guiding him toward a brighter future.

One sun-drenched afternoon, they climbed to the top of a hill overlooking the village, the sea stretching out endlessly before them. Tom felt a sense of peace over him as they sat on a weathered stone bench, watching the sunset in a blaze of color. He looked at Sophia, her face lit up with pure delight as she chased after a butterfly, and he knew that Eleni was right. Happiness can be found in the smallest of moments.

Tom took out his sketchbook and began to draw, capturing the beauty of the scene before him. The vibrant hues of the sunset, the delicate flutter of the butterfly, and Sophia's joyful expression flowed from his pencil onto the paper. It was a mosaic of hope, a testament to the power of love and resilience.

As the sun dipped below the horizon, painting the sky in shades of pink and gold, Tom felt a newfound sense of purpose. He realized that his life wasn't defined by his loss but by the love that continued to surround him. In Sophia's laughter, the beauty of their village, and the cherished memories of Eleni, he found the strength to move forward.

At their cozy home, Tom and Sophia settled into their evening routine. After dinner, they curled up on the sofa, a warm fire crackling in the hearth. Sophia's eyes were heavy with sleep, but she looked up at her father with a contented smile.

"Daddy, can you read me a story?" she asked, her voice tired.

Tom nodded and reached for a book from the shelf. The familiar words wove a comforting spell as he read aloud, lulling Sophia into a peaceful slumber. He watched her momentarily, marveling at her innocence and the depth of her love. She was his anchor, his guiding light.

Tom carefully tucked Sophia into bed, gently kissing her forehead. He returned to the living room and retrieved Eleni's letter from the wooden box. He read it once more, letting her words seep into his soul. Eleni had believed in him; now, he was also starting to believe in himself.

The following morning, Tom and Sophia walked hand in hand to the village square, where a local festival was in full swing. The air was filled with the lively sounds of music and laughter, the aroma of freshly baked bread and roasted lamb wafting through the streets. Colorful banners fluttered in the breeze, and children danced with abandon.

Tom felt light in his step as he and Sophia joined the festivities. They danced to the rhythm of the bouzouki, their laughter blending with the melodies that echoed through the square. For the first time in a long while, Tom felt truly alive.

As the day turned to night, the villagers gathered for a traditional bonfire. Tom and Sophia sat close to the flames, their faces aglow with the warmth of the fire. The stars sparkled above them, a reminder of the vast beauty of the world and the endless possibilities that lay ahead.

Tom looked at Sophia, her eyes wide with wonder as she watched the dancing flames. He realized that they had come a long way since Eleni's death. They had faced their darkest days together and emerged stronger, their bond unbreakable.

I couldn't help but wonder if happiness isn't about having everything we want but finding beauty in what we have. In a village steeped in tradition and bathed in the golden light of the Mediterranean, Tom and Sophia discovered that love and resilience could heal even the deepest wounds.

Their journey was far from over, but they faced it with hope and a renewed sense of purpose. As they walked home hand in hand, the night air filled with the promise of new beginnings, Tom knew they were not just surviving; they were genuinely living, one precious moment at a time.

And so, in a place where the sun kissed the sea and the past whispered through ancient stones, a widowed father and his young daughter found their way back to joy. It was a mosaic of hope, a testament to the enduring power of love, and a reminder that even in the darkest times, there is always light to be found.

Climbing Beyond Fear

The sun was peeking over the horizon, casting a golden hue over the snow-capped peaks of the Ruby Mountains. A group of ten hikers, each bundled in layers of warm clothing, stood at the base of the trail, their breath visible in the crisp morning air. Among them was Jake, a 28-year-old with a bright smile and an even brighter spirit, who had volunteered to be their guide despite his limited experience. He was known for his boundless enthusiasm and genuine kindness, which earned him the group's trust.

As they began their ascent, the mood was light, filled with laughter and excitement. The trail was challenging but manageable, and the hikers felt confident under Jake's leadership. However, as they climbed higher, the path became steeper and more treacherous. The weather turned, the sky darkening with ominous clouds that promised a storm.

By late afternoon, the group was enveloped in a dense fog, the visibility reduced to mere feet. The once-clear trail was now obscured, and the temperature dropped sharply. The hikers huddled together, their faces etched with worry. Jake, sensing their fear, tried to maintain his composure.

"We'll be okay," he said, his voice steady. "Let's stick together and take it slow. We'll find our way."

As they trudged forward, the fog thickened, and the wind picked up, howling through the mountain pass. The hikers' steps grew more uncertain, their confidence waning. They came to a narrow ledge, a sheer drop on one side and a rocky wall on the other. The sight of it stopped them in their tracks.

"Jake, are you sure about this?" Sarah, a seasoned hiker, asked skeptically. "This doesn't seem safe."

Jake swallowed hard, his heart pounding. What no one knew was that he had a crippling fear of heights, a phobia that had haunted him since childhood. He had hoped to avoid any precarious paths, but now, leading this group to safety meant facing his deepest fear.

"We don't have a choice," Jake replied, trembling slightly. "We need to keep moving before the storm gets worse."

Taking a deep breath, he stepped onto the ledge, his legs shaking. He kept his eyes forward, refusing to look down. The hikers followed individually; their trust in Jake outweighed their fear. The wind whipped around them, and the fog made it impossible to see more than a few feet ahead.

Halfway across the ledge, Jake's foot slipped on a loose rock, sending small stones tumbling into the abyss. He froze, his breath caught in his throat. Panic surged through him, threatening to paralyze him completely. But then he heard a voice behind him.

"Jake, you've got this," said Tom, the group's oldest member. "We believe in you."

Those simple yet powerful words reignited a spark of courage within Jake. He steadied himself, gripping the rocky wall with renewed determination. Slowly, he continued, guiding the others step by step until they were all safely across.

Relief washed over the group as they reached a small plateau, but their ordeal was far from over. The storm was full of heavy snow and biting winds, and they needed to find shelter quickly.

"Look over there," said Maria, pointing to a dark shape in the distance. "Is that a cave?"

Jake squinted through the snow and nodded. "It looks like it. Let's check it out."

They hurried towards the cave, their movements hampered by the deepening snow. As they reached the entrance, they found it was a cave, offering refuge from the storm. They huddled inside, grateful for the temporary respite.

"Jake, you did great out there," said Sarah, her earlier skepticism replaced with admiration. "I don't know how you kept it together."

Jake smiled weakly, the adrenaline still coursing through him. "Honestly, I was terrified. Heights aren't exactly my thing."

The group stared at him in surprise. "You mean you're afraid of heights?" asked Tom.

Jake nodded. "Yeah, I always have been. But I couldn't let that stop me—not when your lives depended on me."

Silence filled the cave as the hikers processed his words. Then, one by one, they began to speak.

"You were brave, Jake," said Maria. "You faced your fear for us. That's something we'll never forget."

"Yeah," added Tom. "You proved that courage isn't the absence of fear but the triumph over it."

As the storm raged outside, the hikers found warmth from the fire they managed to start and the bond forming among them. They shared stories, laughed, and talked about their lives, each moment bringing them closer together.

By morning, the storm had passed, leaving a pristine blanket of snow that sparkled under the clear blue sky. Jake and the others emerged from the cave, their spirits lifted by the sun shining down on the mountains. The air was crisp, and the world seemed transformed as if offering them a fresh start.

“It looks like we survived the worst of it," said Tom, stretching his stiff limbs. Now we just need to find our way back."

Jake nodded, feeling a renewed sense of responsibility. "Let's stick together and take it slow. With the sun out, we should be able to navigate better."

The group set off, and their steps became more confident. The snow was deep, but they took turns breaking the trail, working as a team. Jake led the way, his fear of heights now a distant memory. Now and then, he glanced back, ensuring everyone kept up and encouraging them with a smile or a word of support.

As they descended, the landscape changed from rugged cliffs to gentler slopes, and the trail became more defined. The hikers felt a growing hope, knowing they were getting closer to safety. They shared snacks and water, and their camaraderie was evident in how they looked out for one another.

Around midday, they reached a clearing from which they could see the valley below. The sight of civilization—tiny buildings and winding roads—cheered the group. They quickened their pace, eager to return to warmth and comfort.

Finally, after hours of trekking, they arrived at a small mountain lodge. The staff welcomed them with hot drinks and blankets, and the hikers sank into chairs, grateful for the hospitality. As they sipped their cocoa, they reflected on their journey.

"Jake, you pulled us through," said Sarah, her eyes filled with gratitude. "I don't think we would have made it without you."

Jake shook his head modestly. "I couldn't have done it alone. We all worked together. That's what got us through."

Tom raised his cup in a toast. "To Jake, our fearless leader, and all of us, for sticking together and supporting each other."

"To Jake!" the group echoed, clinking their cups.

As the days passed, the hikers parted ways, each returning to their lives with stories to tell and memories to cherish. Jake, too, returned home, but the experience forever changed him. He had faced his greatest fear and discovered a strength he never knew he had.

Months later, the group reunited for a celebratory hike, this time on a less challenging trail. They laughed and reminisced about their adventure, the bond they had formed as strong as ever.

"Remember the ledge?" Tom teased, winking at Jake.

"Oh, I'll never forget that," Jake replied with a chuckle. "But it taught me something important."

"What's that?" asked Maria.

Jake said thoughtfully, "Sometimes, the greatest challenges reveal our true potential. "And that with hope and unity, we can overcome anything."

The group nodded in agreement, their hearts warmed by the shared sentiment. The once a symbol of treacherous danger, the mountains now stood as a testament to their resilience and solidarity.

So, the hikers continued their journey, not just through the trails they walked but through life itself, carrying with them the lessons learned and the friendships forged in the heart of the Ruby Mountains.

Leo's Miracle Cove

In the village of Solace Bay, nestled between rugged cliffs and the endless expanse of the ocean, lived a fisherman named Leo. With a face tanned and weathered by years of labor under the sun, Leo was a man of few words but boundless determination. His eyes, a deep, oceanic blue, held stories of countless dawns and dusks spent battling the sea. With its quaint cottages and cobblestone streets, Solace Bay was a place where the sound of waves was a constant companion, and the scent of saltwater lingered in the air. But now, the village grappled with a famine that threatened to erase its existence.

The once generous sea had turned stingy, and day after day, the fishermen returned with empty nets and heavier hearts. Whispers of abandoning the village began to float on the wind, but Leo couldn't bear the thought. The sea was his life, and Solace Bay was his home. He promised himself and his fellow villagers that he would venture further into the stormy sea, no matter the risk, to find the fish to save them.

Long before dawn one early morning, Leo prepared his boat. A small yet sturdy wooden vessel creaked softly as he loaded it with his fishing gear. His wife, Maria, handed him a small sack of provisions. Her eyes, a mirror of the sea's depth, were filled with worry, but she knew better than to try and dissuade him. She kissed him softly and whispered, "Come back to me, Leo. Come back to us."

Leo nodded his resolve as firm as the cliffs that surrounded their bay. He pushed off from the shore, the rhythmic sound of the oars slicing through the water mingling with the distant cries of waking seagulls. The sea was calm for now, a deceptive tranquility under a sky that was beginning to bruise with the promise of a storm. Dark clouds loomed on the horizon, and the distant rumble of thunder was a reminder of the peril ahead.

As the hours passed, the sky grew darker, and the waves grew taller, turning the sea into a churning beast. The storm was upon him. The wind howled like a wild creature, whipping the sea into a frenzy, and rain lashed against his face like a thousand tiny needles. But Leo pressed on, his thoughts anchored to the hungry faces of the children in the village, older people who could not fend for themselves, and Maria, waiting for his return.

Just when it seemed that the storm would claim him, Leo saw something strange through the sheets of rain—a faint, almost ethereal glimmer of light. He steered his boat towards it, his heart pounding with fear and hope. As he drew closer, he realized it was a narrow opening in the cliffside, a hidden cove bathed in an otherworldly glow.

With great effort, Leo navigated his boat through the opening and into the calm, sheltered waters of the cove. The sight that greeted him took his breath away. The cove was teeming with fish, more than he had ever seen in one place. The water sparkled with their silvery bodies, a living treasure that seemed almost miraculous.

Leo wasted no time. He cast his nets, and they filled almost instantly, the weight nearly overwhelming him. He worked tirelessly, his muscles burning with effort but his heart soaring with hope and gratitude. By the time the storm began to wane, his boat was laden with fish, enough to feed the entire village for weeks.

The journey back to Solace Bay was arduous, but the storm had spent much of its fury. As Leo neared the familiar shoreline, he let out a shout of triumph. The villagers, anxiously waiting, rushed to the shore to greet him. Their faces, moments ago marked by worry, now shone with joy and relief.

Maria threw her arms around him, tears streaming down her face. "You did it, Leo. You saved us."

Leo held her close, his own eyes wet with tears of gratitude. "No, Maria. We did it. The sea gave us a miracle, and we will never forget it."

In the days that followed, the village of Solace Bay found new strength. The hidden cove, known only to them, became a well-guarded secret, a source of sustenance in their time of need. And Leo, the quiet fisherman with a heart as vast as the ocean, symbolized hope and resilience.

The famine passed, but Leo's journey into the storm became a legend, a reminder that even in the darkest of times, miracles could be found by those brave enough to seek them. With its resilient people and unwavering faith in each other, Solace Bay continued to thrive, forever grateful for the day the sea revealed its hidden treasure.

Fusion Hearts in La Rioja

In the heart of La Rioja, Spain, where the rolling vineyards painted the horizon in lush green, and the scent of saffron and olive oil permeated the air, the annual Culinaria Competition was about to unfold. The cobbled streets of Logroño were alive with the buzz of anticipation as chefs from all corners of the globe prepared to showcase their culinary prowess. Emma and Max, two culinary titans, were about to embark on a journey that would intertwine their lives in ways they could never have imagined.

Emma, a fiery redhead from Ireland, had built a reputation for her innovative take on traditional Spanish cuisine. Her dishes were a fusion of flavors, a testament to her adventurous spirit and willingness to push culinary art's boundaries. Her emerald eyes sparkled passionately as she meticulously prepared ingredients in the bustling market square. Across the plaza, Max, a tall and brooding German chef, was equally engrossed in his preparations. On the other hand, his dishes celebrated tradition, a testament to his respect for the classics and his belief in the power of simplicity. His piercing blue eyes and chiseled features had won him many admirers, but his true love was the art of cooking.

Their rivalry was well-known in culinary circles. Emma's daring fusion dishes often clashed with Max's purist approach, and their heated debates at previous competitions had become legendary. Yet, this year was different. The competition had introduced a new twist: rival chefs had to team up.

Emma and Max's faces contorted with shock and anger when the announcement was made. They approached each other warily, like two predators sizing up their prey, their rivalry palpable in the air.

"This should be... interesting," Emma said, her voice dripping with sarcasm.

"To say the least," Max replied coolly, his accent sharp as a knife.

Forced to collaborate, their initial days were a whirlwind of tension. Every decision, from the selection of ingredients to the presentation of dishes, became a battleground. They found themselves constantly struggling to find a balance between their contrasting styles. Yet, beneath the surface, something else was simmering.

As they spent more time together, Emma began to see beyond Max's stern exterior. She noticed how he tenderly handled fresh produce, his eyes softening as he spoke of his grandmother's recipes. Max, in turn, was captivated by Emma's creativity and infectious enthusiasm. Her bright and unrestrained laughter began to echo in his thoughts even after they parted ways each evening, marking the subtle shift in their relationship.

One night, after a particularly grueling day in the kitchen, they found themselves alone in a vineyard, the moonlight casting a silver glow over the grapevines. Emma, her red hair glinting in the soft light, looked at Max with a newfound respect.

"You know," she said softly, her voice filled with surprise and admiration, "I never imagined I'd say this, but I'm glad we're doing this together."

Max's eyes met hers, and for the first time, his stern expression melted into a smile. "Me too," he admitted. "We make a good team."

Their partnership flourished, and their dishes began to reflect a harmonious blend of their styles. They created masterpieces that celebrated both tradition and innovation, earning the admiration of their peers and judges alike.

Just as their bond solidified, a shadow from Max's past reappeared. Isabella, a stunning Italian chef with raven-black hair and eyes as dark as espresso, entered the competition. She had once been Max's lover, and their breakup had left deep scars.

Isabella's arrival stirred old emotions in Max, and Emma couldn't help but feel jealousy. As the competition intensified, so did the tension between the three chefs. Isabella's presence was a constant reminder of the past Max had never fully reconciled with, and Emma questioned the strength of their budding relationship.

One evening, after a particularly heated exchange with Isabella, Max found Emma in the kitchen, her face a mask of hurt and confusion.

"Emma, I need to explain," Max began, his voice heavy with regret. "Isabella and I... we had a history, but it's over. I never felt for her what I feel for you."

Emma looked at him, her eyes searching his for the truth. "Max, this is all so complicated. I need to know where we stand."

Max took her hands in his, his touch gentle yet firm. "Emma, you are my present and my future. Isabella is my past. I've learned from my mistakes, and I won't let them ruin what we have." His sincere words, filled with the weight of his past and the hope for their future, began to mend the rift between them.

His sincere words began to mend the rift between them. They refocused on the competition, and their determination was more vital than ever. The tension with Isabella, once a source of discord, dissipated as they realized their love was more potent than any past relationship.

In the final round, they presented a dish encapsulating their journey: a fusion of Irish and German flavors with a Spanish twist. The judges were mesmerized, not just by the taste but also by the story of unity and love that the dish represented.

When the winners were announced, Emma and Max stood hand in hand as their names echoed through the grand hall. They had done it. They had won not just the competition but also each other's hearts.

As they celebrated under the starlit sky of La Rioja, surrounded by the warmth of their newfound friends and the beauty of the Spanish landscape, Emma and Max knew that their story was beginning. They learned true love is about overcoming differences, embracing each other's strengths, and facing challenges together. It's about building something beautiful out of the varied ingredients life throws at you.

The following day, as the sun painted the vineyards in hues of gold, Emma and Max sat together, sipping on rich, local wine and planning their future. The air was filled with the intoxicating aroma of blooming lavender and ripening grapes, and the gentle hum of bees provided a soothing soundtrack to their conversation.

"What's next for us?" Emma asked, her voice soft and hopeful.

Max smiled, his eyes reflecting the serene beauty of the landscape.

"I was thinking we could open a restaurant together.

A place where we can blend our styles and create something unique.

What do you think?"

Emma's face lit up with excitement. "I love that idea! We could call it 'Fusion Hearts'—a tribute to how we came together."

Their plans took shape quickly, and soon, they traveled across Europe, gathering inspiration and perfecting their craft. They visited bustling markets in France, sampled street food in Italy, and learned ancient techniques in Greece. Their love grew stronger everywhere they went, nurtured by shared experiences and mutual respect.

Meanwhile, back in Spain, the culinary world buzzed with news of their victory and blossoming romance. Emma and Max had become a symbol of unity and innovation, an example of how love and collaboration could transcend rivalry and competition.

Watching from a distance, Isabella found herself reflecting on her journey. Seeing Max and Emma's happiness, she realized that holding onto the past prevented her from finding her path. She approached them one evening during a celebratory dinner in a quaint Spanish tavern.

"Congratulations," she said, her voice sincere. "You've created something extraordinary, both in the kitchen and your lives. I wish you all the best."

Emma and Max thanked her, appreciating her gesture of goodwill. Isabella's words marked the end of an old chapter and the beginning of a new one for all three chefs.

Months later, Emma and Max stood outside their newly opened restaurant, Fusion Hearts, in a charming village in La Rioja. The building was a rustic yet elegant space adorned with wooden beams, terracotta tiles, and large windows that offered stunning views of the surrounding vineyards. The scent of fresh herbs and spices wafted from the kitchen, blending with the crisp, clean air.

Their first night was a resounding success. Guests from all over the world came to taste their creations, and the atmosphere was filled with laughter, clinking glasses, and contented sighs as people savored each bite. Emma and Max moved through the dining area, greeting guests and sharing their stories, their faces glowing with pride and joy.

As the evening drew close, they stood together on the terrace, watching the stars twinkle above the vineyards. Max wrapped his arm around Emma, pulling her close.

"Can you believe we've come this far?" he asked, his voice filled with wonder.

Emma leaned her head on his shoulder, her heart full. "I can. Because we did it together."

Their journey from rivals to partners, from hate to love, had taught them the true essence of collaboration and respect. They had discovered that love, like a perfect dish, requires the right blend of ingredients: trust, communication, and the willingness to embrace each other's strengths and flaws.

Fusion Hearts became more than just a restaurant. It was a testament to the power of love and teamwork, where people from all walks of life could unite and celebrate diversity's beauty. Emma and Max's story inspired many, reminding them that even the most significant challenges could be overcome with passion, dedication, and a little love.

And so, under the starlit skies of La Rioja, amidst the vineyards and the rich tapestry of cultures, Emma and Max's love story flourished, a beacon of hope and inspiration for all who crossed their path.

Love Among the Canopy

Love found me in the heart of the Amazon rainforest, where the canopy of trees seemed to touch the heavens. It wasn't just a love for the lush green foliage or the symphony of tropical birds; it was a love that took root most unexpectedly with the most unexpected person.

Alex and I met during a mission to save the critically endangered Harpy Eagle. We were both environmentalists, driven by a passion to protect the planet's dwindling wonders. For Alex, the jungle was a second home. Her knowledge of the flora and fauna was comprehensive, and her dedication was unyielding. On the other hand, I was more of an idealist, drawn to the cause by a sense of duty to future generations. I wanted to leave a world worth inheriting.

Our base camp was deep within the jungle, where the air was thick with the scent of earth and life. We spent our days tracking the eagles, documenting their behavior, and setting up cameras to monitor their nests. The work was exhausting, but Alex's presence made it refreshing. She had a way of making even the most mundane tasks feel like an adventure.

One evening, as the sun dipped below the horizon, casting a golden glow over the treetops, Alex and I sat by the campfire. The crackling flames mirrored the sparks between us. She shared stories of her childhood, how her father had taught her to respect nature, to see it not just as a resource but as a living, breathing entity. I found myself captivated, not just by her words, but by her passion. At that moment, I realized my feelings for her went beyond admiration.

Our romance blossomed amid our mission. We became inseparable, our bond growing stronger with each passing day. But the jungle is a place of trials, and our commitment to the cause and each other was soon tested.

One fateful day, a torrential downpour turned into a full-blown storm. The river swelled, and the ground beneath us became a treacherous quagmire. We were out, miles from the safety of our camp, when the storm hit. Lightning cracked the sky, and the roar of the water was deafening. We sought refuge in a small cave, huddled together for warmth and safety.

As the hours passed, the storm showed no signs of abating. The cave began to flood, and panic set in. In the chaos, Alex slipped and hit her head. She lay unconscious, her breathing shallow. I felt a surge of fear unlike anything I had ever known. The thought of losing her was unbearable. I cradled her in my arms, whispering words of comfort, praying she would wake up.

When she finally stirred, the relief was overwhelming. But the storm had left its mark on both of us. Exhausted and weak, we knew we had to find a way back to camp. The journey was difficult, with fallen trees and swollen rivers blocking our path. But we pressed on, driven by the sheer will to survive and the need to protect each other. The storm had tested us, but it had also transformed us.

We finally made it back to camp, battered but alive. The near-death experience had shaken us to our core. In the aftermath of the storm, as we sat by the fire again, we truly confronted our feelings. The fear of losing each other had brought our love into sharp focus. It was no longer something we could ignore or set aside for the sake of the mission.

"Sam," Alex said, trembling, "I don't want to waste another moment. Life is too fragile, too precious. I love you."

Her words pierced through me, filling the void that fear had created. "I love you too, Alex. More than anything. We've faced so much together, and I want to face everything with you."

From that moment on, our commitment to the cause and each other became intertwined. We continued our work but with a newfound sense of purpose. Our love gave us strength, and our mission gave our love meaning. We fought against poachers, risking our lives to protect the eagles and their habitat. Each victory, each life saved, felt like a testament to our bond.

Years later, as I stand on the edge of the jungle, watching the eagles soar above, I am filled with fulfillment. Alex is by my side, her hand in mine. We have built a life rooted in love and dedication to a cause greater than ourselves. The jungle, once a place of trials, has become our sanctuary.

Ultimately, we saved not just the eagles but also each other. Our love, forged in the Amazon's heart, has withstood life's storms. As I look into Alex's eyes, I know that no matter what the future holds, we will face it together with unwavering love and unyielding commitment.

Because sometimes, it's amid adversity that we find our true selves. And in those moments, we discover the depth of our capacity to love and be loved.

As the sun sets, casting long shadows over the jungle, I think back to that fateful day when the storm nearly tore us apart. It wasn't just the near-death experience that changed us; it was the realization that life is fleeting, and love is what gives it meaning. We can spend our days fighting for a cause, but our victories are hollow without love.

Alex and I have since expanded our mission, educating local communities about the importance of conservation and sustainable living. We've built schools and clinics, empowering the people who call this jungle home. Our efforts have created a ripple effect, turning former poachers into protectors of the species they once hunted. It's a testament to the power of change, the kind that starts with two people and spreads like wildfire.

A young girl approached us one day as we set up a new educational center. She had the same spark in her eyes that I saw in Alex when we first met. She told us her name was Maria, and she wanted to become an environmentalist to save the animals and the trees. Alex knelt and handed her a small, carved figurine of a Harpy Eagle, a symbol of hope and resilience.

"Never forget," Alex said, "that you have the power to make a difference. No matter how small the action, it can change the world."

Maria's eyes lit up, and at that moment, I saw the future we had been fighting for. It wasn't just about saving the eagles or the trees but inspiring the next generation to carry the torch. Our love had not only changed our lives but had also created a legacy of hope and determination.

As we walked back to our camp, hand in hand, I felt a profound sense of peace. With all its beauty and danger, the jungle had given us a gift. It taught us the true meaning of love and the importance of living with purpose. We had faced the storms and come out stronger, our love unbreakable.

Ultimately, not the grand gestures or the epic battles define us. It's the quiet moments, shared dreams, and unwavering belief that we can overcome anything together. Alex and I have learned that life is not a solitary journey but a shared adventure where love makes all the difference.

As the stars twinkle in the night sky, I pull Alex close. "Thank you," I whisper, my voice filled with emotion.

"For what?" she asks, her eyes soft and full of love.

"Thank you for being my partner, my rock, my everything. Thank you for reminding me that even in the darkest times, there's always a light to guide us home."

She smiles, and I see our past, present, and future in her eyes. "And thank you, Sam, for never giving up on us, on our mission, on love."

We stand there, wrapped in each other's arms, listening to the symphony of the jungle. The journey that began with a shared passion for saving a species led us to a love transcending time and space. It's a love that has weathered storms and faced dangers yet remains as strong as ever.

Because, in the end, it's love that saves us. Love gives us the courage to fight, the strength to endure, and the hope to believe in a better tomorrow. And as long as we have that, we have everything we need.

As the night deepens, I know we will face challenges together no matter what lies ahead. Our love is our most excellent adventure, and the jungle is our eternal witness. With Alex by my side, I am ready for whatever comes next, knowing our love will always light the way.

Beneath the Waves

In the small coastal town of Seabrook, the ocean was more than a body of water; it was a way of life. For Kate, a dedicated marine biologist, and Ryan, a seasoned deep-sea diver, it was their life's calling. Kate spent her days in the lab and on boats, studying marine life, while Ryan explored the depths of the sea, documenting its mysterious beauty. Their paths had crossed many times, but always briefly, like ships passing at night.

A palpable sense of urgency gripped the town one summer morning as news of a potential environmental catastrophe spread like wildfire. An offshore drilling rig had suffered a massive leak, threatening to unleash millions of barrels of oil into the ocean. The town's lifeblood was at stake, and it was up to Kate and Ryan to avert this looming disaster.

Kate's heart pounded as she reviewed the data. "We have to act fast," she said, her voice trembling with fear and determination. "If we don't seal that leak, the entire ecosystem will be destroyed."

Ever the calm and collected diver, Ryan placed a reassuring hand on her shoulder. "We'll figure it out together, Kate. We always do." Their shared responsibility and trust in each other formed an unbreakable bond.

They quickly assembled a team and set sail towards the rig. As they reached the site, the air smelled of oil, and the once-clear waters were now stained with a dark, ominous sheen. Kate's eyes filled with tears at the sight of dying marine life, but she steeled herself. There was no time for despair.

Ryan suited up for a dive, his face set in a mask of determination. "I'll go down and assess the damage. You stay up here and coordinate with the team."

Kate nodded, her heart aching as she watched him disappear beneath the waves. She trusted Ryan with her life, but the dangers of deep-sea diving were always present in her mind. She focused on her work, relying on her intellect and expertise to guide the team.

Hours passed like minutes, and tension hung in the air. Ryan resurfaced, his expression grave. "It's worse than we thought," he said, his voice heavy with exhaustion. "The leak is deep, and the pressure is immense. We need to go down together to fix it."

Kate's heart skipped a beat. She had never gone on such a dangerous dive before, but she knew Ryan was right. They suited up and descended into the depths, the weight of their mission pressing down on them.

As they reached the leak site, they worked in perfect sync, their movements a dance of precision and urgency. Despite the danger, they had an unspoken bond, a connection that had grown through years of shared passion for the sea.

Suddenly, a pressure burst sent debris flying, and Kate was thrown off balance. Panic surged through her, but Ryan was there, his strong arms steadying her. "I've got you," he said, his voice calm and reassuring through the comm link. "We can do this."

With renewed determination, they worked tirelessly, sealing the leak and stopping the oil flow. The moment the last patch was in place, Kate felt relief. They had done it. They had saved the ocean.

As they began their ascent, a strange light caught their eye. Intrigued, they followed it, and what they discovered was beyond their wildest dreams. Hidden deep beneath the surface was an underwater paradise, a pristine world untouched by human hands. Coral reefs bloomed in vibrant colors, schools of fish danced harmoniously, and the water was crystal clear, a sight that filled them with wonder and awe.

Kate's eyes widened in wonder. "It's beautiful," she whispered, her voice filled with awe.

Ryan nodded, his gaze softening as he looked at her. "It's like a hidden treasure waiting to be discovered."

As they floated in that magical place, something shifted between them. The bond they had shared through their work blossomed into something more profound. They realized that, like the hidden paradise, their love had been there all along, waiting to be discovered.\

When they finally resurfaced, the team greeted them with cheers and applause. The leak was sealed, the ocean was safe, and their hearts were full.

In the following days, Kate and Ryan worked tirelessly to clean up the remaining oil and restore the affected areas. Their love grew stronger with each passing day, a beacon of hope amidst the challenges they faced.

One evening, as the sun set over the horizon, painting the sky in hues of orange and pink, Kate and Ryan stood hand in hand on the shore. The ocean, their lifelong passion, had brought them together in ways they had never imagined.

Ryan turned to Kate, his eyes filled with love and gratitude. "We saved the ocean, but it also saved us," he said softly.

Kate smiled, tears of joy glistening in her eyes. "Yes, it did."

At that moment, they knew their love, like the ocean, was vast and deep, capable of withstanding any storm. They had found their hidden paradise beneath the waves and within each other's hearts.

As the months passed, Kate and Ryan's bond only deepened. They worked together on various conservation projects, driven by their shared passion and newfound love. Their success with the oil spill had brought attention to their small town and, with it, funding and resources to further protect the ocean they cherished.

One day, while cataloging marine life, Kate noticed something peculiar. A species of coral, thought to be extinct, was thriving in the underwater paradise they had discovered. "Ryan, look at this!" she exclaimed, her eyes sparkling excitedly. "This coral shouldn't exist anymore. It's a living testament to the resilience of nature."

Ryan grinned, his heart swelling with pride and admiration for Kate. "Just like us, right? Against all odds, we found something beautiful."

Their discovery attracted marine biologists and environmentalists from around the world. Seabrook became a hub for oceanic research and conservation, transforming the small town into a beacon of hope for the planet. Kate and Ryan were at the forefront, synonymous with dedication and love for the sea.

One evening, as they walked along the beach, hand in hand, Ryan stopped and pulled Kate close. "I never thought I'd find someone who understands the ocean the way I do," he said, his voice filled with emotion. "But you, Kate, you see its beauty and its pain. You fight for it, just like I do."

Kate leaned her head against his shoulder, her heart full. "And I never thought I'd find someone who makes me feel so alive, so connected to something greater than myself. The ocean brought us together, Ryan. It's our home, our life, our love."

As they stood there, the waves gently lapping at their feet, Ryan reached into his pocket and pulled out a small, delicate seashell. "Kate, this shell is a symbol of the ocean's endless possibilities, its mysteries, and its beauty. Just like our love. Will you marry me?"

Tears streamed down Kate's face as she looked into Ryan's eyes, filled with love and hope. "Yes, Ryan, a thousand times yes."

Their wedding was a celebration of the sea, held on the shores of Seabrook with friends, family, and colleagues. They exchanged vows under a canopy of stars, the sound of the waves their eternal witness.

Years passed, and Kate and Ryan continued their work with unwavering dedication. They founded a marine conservation institute, educating future generations about protecting the ocean. Their love story inspired many, a testament to the power of passion and connection.

While diving together in their underwater paradise, they found a vibrant and graceful new fish species one day. As they marveled at the discovery, Ryan took Kate's hand and held it close. "Every time we dive, we find something new, something beautiful. Just like our love. It never stops growing, never stops surprising me."

Kate smiled, her heart full of love and contentment. "And it never will, Ryan. As long as we have each other and the ocean, we'll always find our way."

Ultimately, their story was not just about saving the ocean but about finding love in the most unexpected places, resilience, and hope. Kate and Ryan's journey was a reminder that even in the face of adversity, love and passion can create miracles.

As they floated in their hidden paradise, surrounded by the wonders of the deep, they knew that they had found their forever home—not just in the sea but in each other. The vast and untamed ocean had brought them together, and in its depths, they had discovered a love as infinite and enduring as the waves themselves.

Shadows of Trust

I first met Ben in the shadowy confines of a dimly lit interrogation room. His reputation preceded him—Ben, the former thief who had danced through the cracks of the law with an almost poetic grace. I was Rachel, the detective who had spent years trying to bring men like him to justice. We were supposed to be enemies, yet fate had other plans.

Our partnership was born from necessity, not choice. A series of baffling crimes had our precinct in knots, and Ben's unique insight into the criminal world was our last resort. My pragmatic captain had thrown us together, hoping Ben's former life might shed light on the shadows we were chasing.

From the beginning, our relationship was strained. Distrust hung in the air like fog. I saw him as a reminder of all the failures in my career, every criminal that had slipped through my fingers. He saw me as the embodiment of a system that had tried to cage him. But beneath this mutual disdain was a flicker of something neither of us could name—curiosity, perhaps, or the faintest glimmer of respect.

Ben was a puzzle, one that I couldn't ignore. He had a mind as sharp as any blade, eyes that missed nothing, and an intuition that often outpaced my own. As we pored over case files and walked through crime scenes, I realized how invaluable his perspective was. He saw patterns where I saw chaos, connections where I saw dead ends.

Our breakthrough came on a rainy Tuesday afternoon. We were knee-deep in reports when Ben's eyes lit up. "Rachel," he said quietly, "these aren't random. They're all connected to someone I once knew."

His revelation was both a gift and a curse. The crimes were the work of his former accomplice, Marcus, who had resurfaced like a ghost from Ben's past. The news tested our fragile alliance. I questioned Ben's loyalty, unable to shake the fear that he might still be tethered to his old life.

Sensing my doubt, Ben grew distant; the walls we had begun tearing down suddenly rebuilt.

The climax came one night as we closed in on Marcus's hideout. The tension was palpable, each step forward heavy with uncertainty. I watched Ben closely, my hand hovering near my weapon, ready for betrayal. We found Marcus in a rundown warehouse, smug and confident, as if he had been expecting us.

"You've returned to the fold, Ben," Marcus sneered. "I knew you would."

For a heartbeat, I saw hesitation in Ben's eyes, a flicker of the past tugging at him. My heart sank. But then, with a resolve I hadn't seen before, Ben stepped forward.

"No, Marcus," he said firmly. "I've come to end this."

The ensuing struggle was a blur of movement and noise. When the dust settled, Marcus was in cuffs, and the look of betrayal in his eyes contrasted with the relief in Ben's. It was over, and at that moment, something shifted between us.

Our partnership became a bond forged by trust and respect in the following days. I no longer saw Ben as a thief but as a man who had chosen a different path, faced his demons, and emerged stronger. And Ben, in turn, saw me not just as a detective but as someone who believed in second chances.

On a warm summer evening, as we sat on the precinct steps, Ben turned to me and said, "You know, Rachel, I never thought I'd trust a cop."

I smiled, feeling the weight of the past lift. "And I never thought I'd trust a thief."

Ultimately, it wasn't the crimes we solved that defined us but the trust we built. Our journey was a testament to the power of change and the belief that even the most unlikely partnerships can lead to redemption. And as the sun set, casting a golden hue over the city, I knew this was just the beginning of something remarkable.

Redemption

I, Lily, felt a whirlwind of emotion as I navigated the bustling city streets. My brother, Daniel, had been kidnapped, and my world had crumbled around me. Grief and desperation clouded my judgment as I searched desperately for any sign of him. The city seemed to pulse with a life of its own, a mix of hope and despair that reflected my internal struggle perfectly. And then, just as I was about to give up, I met Christopher. A mysterious figure, Christopher, appeared out of nowhere, offering a helping hand. His presence brought a glimmer of hope, but I was wary. Something about him stirred fear and doubt in my heart. Was he really here to help, or did he have ulterior motives? Despite my reservations, I decided to take a leap of faith. I had to find Daniel, and if Christopher could help me, I was willing to trust him. Little did I know that this decision would change my life forever. As we embarked on our journey, Christopher and I encountered many challenges and obstacles. His knowledge of the city's underbelly and his mysterious connections both fascinated and scared me. I soon discovered that Christopher had a hidden past that was somehow connected to my brother's disappearance. But despite my initial distrust, I found myself drawn to him. Christopher's redemption arc was one of the most intriguing aspects of our journey, and I couldn't help but be captivated by his complex character.

As we ventured deeper into the heart of the bustling city, my wariness of Christopher remained, his enigmatic past casting a long shadow over our quest to find Daniel. Yet, I found myself slowly lowering my guard, thanks to Christopher's unwavering faith in our newfound companion. Christopher had a way of lightening the mood with his quick wit and boundless optimism, offering a much-needed respite from the weight of our fears. Christopher, with his brooding gaze and reticence, seemed an unlikely ally. Still, as the days turned into weeks, his quiet strength and unwavering dedication to our cause began to chip away at my doubts. We shared a common goal, and his knowledge of the city's underbelly proved invaluable. I couldn't shake the feeling that he was holding something back, but I trusted that his intentions were honorable for now. The city itself felt like a character in our unfolding story. It pulsed with life, a chaotic blend of hope and despair. Amidst the concrete jungle, we navigated through vibrant markets and shadowy alleyways, encountering a cast of characters that ranged from the eccentric to the downright dangerous. It was a world where nothing was quite as it seemed, and our journey was filled with twists and turns that kept us constantly on our toes. Between our strengths as we navigate perilous nights and treacherous paths, forging a connection built on shared adversity.

On a moonlit night, beneath the starry sky, Christopher revealed his connection to my brother's kidnappers. My heart sank as I realized the truth, but a tiny spark of hope remained. I saw it in his eyes – a chance for redemption. Christopher wanted to make amends for his mistakes; I could sense his sincerity. As Christopher acknowledged his misdeeds, I felt a mix of emotions. I was shocked and heartbroken but also felt a strange sense of peace. Here was a man who wanted to help and right his wrongs. I felt a connection to him that I couldn't ignore. "I know it's a lot to take in, Lily," Christopher said, his voice soft and full of remorse. "But I swear, I'm here to help. I want to make things right, and I'll do everything I can to bring your brother, Daniel, home safe." I searched his eyes, looking for any sign of deceit, but found none. With a nod, I accepted his help, knowing that we might see my brother and bring him back home where he belonged.

Christopher stood at the precipice of a decision, his heart warring between fear and courage. The weight of his past hung heavy on his shoulders, a constant reminder of his failures and the potential consequences of his actions. But my unwavering trust in him shone like a beacon, cutting through the darkness of his doubts. I saw the good in him, a glimmer of hope that he could be redeemed. Empowered by my belief, Christopher found the strength to confront his demons. He knew that saving my brother, Daniel, could be his chance at redemption, a way to make amends for his past mistakes. With me by his side, he took the first step towards facing his fears, determined to rescue Daniel and find solace in a future free from the shadows of his history. As we embarked on this mission, Christopher's mysterious past unraveled. I discovered his hidden connection to the kidnappers, a revelation that shook my faith in him. But Christopher, driven by his desire for atonement, remained steadfast in his resolve. He shared with me the truth of his past, revealing his mistakes and the path that led him to this moment. With each confession, Christopher felt the burden of his secrets lift, and my trust in him deepened, understanding the power of second chances. Together, we navigated the twists and turns of our journey, facing obstacles and dangers that tested our courage and resolve. Christopher's knowledge of the kidnappers' tactics proved invaluable, and with each challenge, we grew stronger, our bond forged in the fire of adversity. In the end, it was our unwavering determination and trust in each other that led us to success. Daniel was rescued, and Christopher, having faced his past, stood tall, a man transformed by the power of redemption. I, her brother by my side, knew that their journey would forever change our lives, and I was grateful for the mysterious stranger who had become our savior.

Christopher's decision to confront his past was not made lightly. He knew that putting himself in harm's way might be the only way to save Daniel, but it also meant facing the demons he had tried so hard to leave behind. Still, the thought of my trusting eyes and hopeful smile gave him the strength to take this daring step. He had to prove to her and himself that he was worthy of my trust. As he ventured into the heart of the kidnappers' lair, his heart raced with a mix of fear and determination. Every step brought him closer to the possibility of redemption, and he clung to the hope that his actions would set Daniel free and grant him the chance to forge a new path. Unaware of the full extent of Christopher's past, I waited anxiously for news. I felt mixed emotions, torn between her growing trust in Christopher and the lingering fear that my brother might never be found. As the hours ticked by, my mind raced with worries and what-if scenarios. Yet, deep down, I felt a newfound sense of hope, a feeling that Christopher's bravery had kindled within me. Unbeknownst to me, Ethan's daring gamble was about to pay off. His knowledge of the kidnappers' operations, combined with his own unique set of skills, enabled him to navigate the treacherous path he had chosen. With each challenge he overcame, he inched closer to David, his resolve strengthening with every step. The prospect of redemption was no longer a distant dream but a tangible possibility that fueled his every action.

As the sun rose higher, bathing the landscape in warm light, I felt like I was awakening from a dark dream. Standing beside me, Christopher shared a smile, his presence a reminder of the trials we had endured together. It had been a perilous journey, filled with uncertainty and danger, but their unwavering determination had led us to this moment. Daniel's familiar and beloved laughter signaled that our quest had ended. Our journey had been one of hope and trust, a testament to the power of the human spirit. Even in the face of adversity, we have never lost faith, and now, our perseverance has been rewarded. The reunion was an explosion of emotion, a whirlwind of tears and laughter. Daniel's return brought a sense of wholeness as if a missing piece of our hearts had been restored. The darkness that had once shrouded them was now a distant memory, replaced by the radiant light of joy and relief. In that instant, I understood the true meaning of redemption. Our story reminded us that even in the face of unimaginable odds, love and compassion could move mountains and heal wounded souls. The sun, now high in the sky, shone brightly, mirroring the radiance in their hearts. As we embraced, a new chapter began, one filled with promise and the knowledge that no matter the challenges, love would always prevail.

My journey had been fraught with uncertainty and fear, but as I reflected, I realized that it had also been a path of growth and transformation. The once-distrustful young woman had learned the power of trust and the freedom of forgiveness. Christopher, a mysterious figure with a shadowy past, had become an unlikely ally and a symbol of redemption. Our unusual partnership taught me that true friendship could transcend secrets and mistakes. Christopher's desire for redemption was genuine, and his help finding my kidnapped brother, Daniel, became a beacon of hope in my life. As we worked together, I witnessed Christopher's transformation. He became a source of strength and comfort, always ready to offer a listening ear or a word of encouragement. His past mistakes seemed to fade away as he dedicated himself to helping me and righting the wrongs of his previous life. Our connection deepened as we supported each other through their challenges, and I realized that Christopher's presence in my life was a reminder that hope could be found even in the darkest times. The power of grace and the potential for healing through human connection were the key lessons I took from my experience. Christopher's redemption showed me that people could change and that second chances were possible. As I moved forward, I knew that the trust and forgiveness I had learned to embrace would continue to guide me, and I felt a sense of peace knowing that even in adversity, there was always the possibility of solace and redemption.

Echoes of Valor

I am Sam, a soldier haunted by the echoes of war, where the line between courage and fear blurs into a dizzy haze. The battles I once fought now rage within me, a relentless storm threatening to swallow me whole. PTSD has become my uninvited companion, a shadow that clings to my every step, whispering of past traumas and unhealed wounds.

Amid this turmoil, I sought solace in therapy, where I met Dr. Emily, a beacon of empathy in a world of darkness. Her presence was a gentle reminder that moments of tranquility existed amidst the chaos of my mind. She introduced me to Max, a therapy dog whose eyes held a wisdom beyond words, a silent companion who understood the depths of my pain.

With each therapy session, Dr. Emily guided me through the labyrinth of my memories, helping me navigate the treacherous terrain of my trauma. With his comforting presence and unwavering loyalty, Max became a source of strength in moments of weakness. Together, they formed a safety net beneath me, gently urging me to confront the demons lurking in my mind's shadows.

As the weeks turned into months, Dr. Emily shared a revelation that shifted the ground beneath my feet. She, too, bore the scars of war, a silent testament to the battles she had fought and the wounds she had endured. Her confession forged a bond between us, a connection born of shared suffering and silent understanding. In her, I found a kindred spirit, a guide who navigated the tumultuous waters I now found myself in.

With Dr. Emily's guidance and Max's unwavering presence, I embarked on self-discovery and healing. Each therapy session was a step towards reclaiming the shattered fragments of my soul, a process as painful as it was liberating. Through tears and laughter, anger and acceptance, I learned to confront the demons that had long held me captive, to face the shadows of my past with a newfound courage.

One fateful day, as I sat across from Dr. Emily, the weight of my burdens felt lighter, as if the shackles that bound me were slowly loosening their grip. In that moment of vulnerability, she spoke words that resonated deeply within me and echoed the truth I had long sought. The final step towards healing, she said, lay not in erasing the scars of the past but in embracing them as a testament to my resilience and strength.

As I walked out of Dr. Emily's office that day, I felt a sense of peace, a feeling of liberation I had long yearned for. The road ahead remained uncertain, but with her guidance and Max's unwavering support, I had the strength to face whatever challenges lay in my path. The wounds of war will always be a part of me, but they no longer define me.

In the quiet moments that followed, I realized that true healing was not about forgetting the past but about learning to live with it, to carry its weight with grace and acceptance. As the sun dipped below the horizon, casting a golden glow over the world, I knew that I was not alone. In the company of kindred spirits, even the darkest night could give way to the brightest dawn.

The Symphony of Second Chances

I have always believed that life is just like a symphony. Sometimes, it plays melodious tunes that uplift the spirit, while at other times, it tests our resilience with dissonant notes that challenge our very essence. My name is Lisa, and this is how I learned to dance to the rhythm of life's unpredictable melodies.

The world of entrepreneurship has always beckoned me with its promise of freedom and creativity. I embarked on this journey with dreams as vast as the sky, eager to make my mark on the world. However, my path was fraught with obstacles that tested my resolve at every turn. Failure after failure chipped away at my confidence, leaving me drowning in a sea of self-doubt.

During one of my lowest moments, I met him - a man whose presence exuded wisdom and kindness in equal measure. David was a seasoned entrepreneur who had weathered his fair share of storms. He saw something I had long forgotten in me - the spark of passion that once fueled my dreams.

David became my mentor, guiding me through the darkest alleys of my doubts and fears. With each setback, he would remind me that failure was not the end but a stepping stone towards success. His words were a beacon of light in my darkest hours, leading me towards a newfound sense of purpose and determination.

As I slowly began rebuilding my shattered confidence, David shared his story of resilience with me. He spoke of a venture he had undertaken years ago, a dream that had crumbled before his eyes due to circumstances beyond his control. It was a tale of loss and redemption, of picking oneself up after a devastating fall.

One fateful afternoon, as we sat in his cozy office surrounded by the relics of his past endeavors, David revealed a shocking truth that sent shivers down my spine. My current venture was intricately linked to the project that led to his greatest failure. It was as if fate had woven our destinies together in a tapestry of second chances and redemption.

In that moment of revelation, I felt a surge of emotions overwhelming my senses - disbelief, awe, and a profound sense of connection with David. Our shared experiences bound us in a bond that transcended mere mentorship, evolving into a symbiotic relationship of trust and understanding.

With newfound clarity, I realized that my failures were not a reflection of my inadequacies but stepping stones towards growth and enlightenment. The symphony of my life was playing a new tune that resonated with hope and resilience.

As I stood at the crossroads of my journey, I made a vow to myself - to embrace every challenge as an opportunity for growth, to dance fearlessly to the melody of life's unpredictable rhythms. With David by my side, I embarked on a new chapter of my entrepreneurial journey, armed with the wisdom of the past and the courage to shape my destiny.

And so, dear reader, remember this: In the symphony of life, every note, whether sweet or sour, contributes to the beauty of the whole. Embrace your failures as lessons, your setbacks as stepping stones, and never forget that the darkest moments often lead to the brightest revelations.

Ultimately, it is not the destination that defines us but the journey we undertake with unwavering faith and indomitable spirit.

The Last Harvest

Standing in the middle of the old family farm, a place in our clan for generations, I couldn't help but feel the weight of the years that had passed. The worn wooden fence posts, the creaking windmill, and the sprawling fields of golden wheat all felt familiar yet distant. This was where my brother Ibrahim and I grew up, but it had been years since I'd stepped foot on this land, years since we had been close.

When the bank called to say they were foreclosing on the property, a flood of memories came rushing back. I remembered the laughter we shared as children, chasing each other through the tall grass. I remembered the quiet moments sitting on the porch with our mother, watching the sunset over the horizon. These were the moments that bound us, the moments that made us brothers. And I remembered the bitter arguments, the slammed doors, and the harsh words that drove a wedge between Ibrahim and me.

After I left home to pursue my calling in the Catholic priesthood, Ibrahim and I drifted apart. He had chosen a different path, converting to Islam and moving away to start a new life. I won't lie - I was hurt and confused by his decision. How could he abandon the faith of our ancestors? But in my heart, I knew I had also played a role in our estrangement.

Standing on the soil that had nourished our family for decades, I realized I couldn't let it all slip away. This farm represented something more profound than just a piece of land - our legacy, history, and connection to something greater than ourselves. I had to at least try to save it.

With a heavy heart, I reached out to Ibrahim, pleading with him to return home. It took some convincing, but eventually, he agreed. When he arrived, the tension in the air was palpable. We avoided each other's gaze, the old wounds still raw and painful.

But as we walked the fields together, something began to shift. Ibrahim pointed out the spots where he used to hide as a child, and I reminisced about the time we built a tree house in the old oak. Slowly, the walls between us started crumbling, and we opened up about the past - the hurt, anger, and regret.

Then, one day, as we were sorting through the old barn, Ibrahim stumbled upon a worn leather-bound book. It was our mother's diary, a relic from long ago. As we flipped through the pages, we discovered secrets we never knew - Their mother's writings revealed her internal conflicts as she wrestled with questions of faith and identity. Though she remained a steadfast Catholic, she admired Ibrahim's courage in finding his own path. "Faith is not a static thing, my sons," she had written. "It is a constant journey of discovery, questioning, and growing. The path that is right for one may not be right for another. What matters is that you walk it with an open heart." -Stories of her struggles with faith, her dreams for our family, and her deep, abiding love for us, even in our darkest moments.

Tears streamed down our faces as we read her words, words that seemed to bridge the gap between us. The diary was a treasure trove of our mother's innermost thoughts and feelings, and it brought us closer than we had been in years. At that moment, I realized that the true legacy of this farm wasn't just the land itself but the bond of family that had sustained us through it all. Ibrahim and I may have taken different paths, but we were still brothers, forever connected by the memories and love of our mother.

With a newfound determination, we set out to save the farm. We called in favors, negotiated with the bank, and worked tirelessly to keep the land in our family's hands. It wasn't easy, and there were times when we wanted to give up. But each time we felt like quitting, we would remember our mother's words and unwavering faith in us and find the strength to keep going. Our determination was unwavering, our resilience unbreakable.

In the end, we did it. We saved the farm, but more importantly, we saved our relationship. As we stood on the porch, watching the sunset over the fields, I couldn't help but notice how the farm seemed to have come alive again. The fields were greener, the windmill creaked with a new energy, and the air was filled with the sounds of life. Ibrahim put his hand on my shoulder and said, "Thank you, brother. For never giving up on me or on this place."

I smiled and pulled him into a tight embrace. "Thank you, Ibrahim. For coming back home."

At that moment, I realized that the actual harvest we had reaped was not the wheat that filled our silos but the redemption of our bond as brothers. The farm would continue to sustain us physically and spiritually, but the natural nourishment came from the love and forgiveness that had blossomed between us. This was the legacy we would pass on to the next generation, far more valuable than any piece of land.

As the last rays of the sun dipped below the horizon, I knew that no matter what the future held, Ibrahim and I would face it together as brothers once more.

The Space Between

Jennifer had always known that raising Joseph alone would be a challenge. From the moment she held his tiny, red-faced newborn form in her arms, she felt the weight of the responsibility – to nurture, protect, and guide him through the treacherous waters of life without a father figure.

But nothing could have prepared her for just how turbulent those waters would become.

As Joseph grew into a lanky, sullen teenager, the once-sweet boy she had loved with every fiber of her being seemed to vanish. In his place was a stranger - a simmering cauldron of hormones and angst, lashing out with vicious words and slamming doors. Jennifer was constantly on edge, walking on eggshells, terrified of setting off another explosion.

"Why do you always have to be such a bitch?" Joseph would snarl, his eyes blazing with a fury she couldn't understand. "You're ruining my life!"

The words cut deep, carving gaping wounds in Jennifer's heart. All she wanted was to reach out, to wrap him in her arms and make everything better. But Joseph had built an impenetrable wall, pushing her away with each cruel outburst.

Try as she might, Jennifer couldn't get through to him. She poured her soul into their relationship, schemed, pleaded, and punished, but nothing worked. The more she fought, the more he retreated until she felt like she was losing him entirely.

Then, one fateful night, everything changed.

Jennifer had been called to the police station, her stomach in knots, as the officer explained the situation. Joseph, in a moment of reckless anger, had vandalized a neighbor's property, causing thousands of dollars in damage. She faced the prospect of a lengthy legal battle, possible jail time for her son, and the genuine chance of losing him forever.

As she sat across from the judge, watching Joseph's defiant gaze, Jennifer felt a swell of emotions threaten to spill over. She had fought so hard and sacrificed so much to keep her family together, and now, it was slipping through her fingers.

In a moment of sheer desperation, she made a decision that would alter the course of their lives.

"Your Honor," Jennifer said, her voice quaking, "I would like to propose. I will take full responsibility for the damages, and in exchange, I ask that you allow Joseph to come home with me. I understand he needs help, not punishment. Please, give me one more chance to reach him."

The judge eyed her skeptically, then turned to Joseph. "Do you promise to abide by your mother's rules and guidance, young man?"

For a long, agonizing moment, Joseph remained silent. Then, to Jennifer's shock, he nodded slowly, his expression softening ever so slightly.

As they sat in the living room that night, an uneasy silence hung between them. Jennifer ached to reach out, to bridge the chasm that had grown so wide. But she knew she had to tread carefully, to let Joseph come to her in his own time.

And then, in a moment of surprising vulnerability, he spoke.

"Mom, I'm... I'm sorry." His voice was barely above a whisper, laced with shame and regret. "I've been such a jerk to you, and you don't deserve that. I guess... I guess I've just been so scared of losing you that I've been pushing you away."

Jennifer felt her heart swell with a mix of relief and heartbreak. In that instant, she saw her little boy, the one she had cherished and nurtured, still beneath the layers of anger and rebellion.

"Oh, Joseph," she murmured, scooting closer and pulling him into her embrace. "You could never lose me. I will always be here, no matter what."

As she held him, feeling the tension slowly melt from his body, Jennifer knew that this was a turning point. The wall had been breached, and now they could rebuild their more robust and deeper relationship.

In the following days, they worked tirelessly, uncovering the root of Joseph's pain and fear and learning to communicate in a way they had never done before. It wasn't easy, but with each conversation, each shared laugh, each moment of vulnerability, the space between them began to close.

When the final court date arrived and the judge announced that the charges had been dropped, Jennifer and Joseph stood side by side, both with tears in their eyes. They had fought through the darkness and emerged stronger for it.

As they walked out of the courthouse, hand in hand, Jennifer knew that the true victory was not in the legal outcome but in the bond they had forged. In that moment, she saw the future stretched before them—a future filled with understanding, healing, and an unbreakable love that would carry them through whatever challenges lay ahead.

The Unfinished Letters

It was a gray Tuesday morning when Mark's life changed forever. The rain poured down the windows of his sleek sedan as he hurried from his car to the office, his mind already racing with the day's agenda. Mark was a successful businessman with a corner office and a reputation for being a ruthless negotiator. He prided himself on closing deals and growing his company's bottom line.

But on this particular morning, Mark's focus was shattered by a single phone call. As he sat at his desk, the color drained from his face. His wife, Sarah, had passed away unexpectedly during the night. The heartbreaking news left him reeling, unable to process the magnitude of his loss.

In the following weeks, Mark retreated further into his work, using long hours and relentless travel as a shield against the crushing grief. His teenage daughter, Ella, was left alone to navigate her sorrow. The once-vibrant girl withdrew into herself, her once-bright eyes dulled by the weight of her pain.

Mark's absence was not just physical, but it was also a void that echoed through their home. Ella would sit at the kitchen table, staring at the untouched dinner plates, waiting for a father who never came. She would lie awake at night, listening to the eerie silence where her mother's gentle breathing had once been. The weight of her father's absence was a heavy burden on her young shoulders, a constant reminder of the void left by her mother's passing.

One evening, as Ella was cleaning out her mother's dresser, she stumbled upon a stack of unfinished letters. They were addressed to

Mark and written in Sarah's elegant script. Ella's heart raced as she read the words, each a window into her mother's soul.

"My dearest Mark

I know your work is essential to you, but I worry you are letting it consume you. Ella needs you now more than ever. She is struggling, and I fear she is losing herself in the process. Please, my love, find a way to be present for her. She needs her father."

Ella's eyes filled with tears as she read on, her mother's words painting a vivid picture of a family in crisis. Sarah had poured her heart into these letters, pleading with Mark to reconnect with their daughter, to find a way to heal their broken family.

Clutching the letters, Ella made her way to her father's office, her resolve strengthening with every step. When she finally stood before him, Mark was taken aback by the fierce determination in her eyes.

"Dad, we need to talk," Ella said, her voice unwavering. She then presented the unfinished letters, watching her father's expression shift from surprise to anguish.

Mark read each one, his hands trembling, his heart shattering with every word. He had been so consumed by his grief and his work that he had neglected the very thing that mattered most – his family. The realization hit him like a punch to the gut, and he knew then that he had to change. Sarah's words, written in her elegant script, were a stark reminder of his responsibilities as a father and a husband. They were a call to action, a plea for him to step out of the shadow of his grief and be there for his daughter.

Mark consciously tried to be present in Ella's life in the following days. He took her on weekend hikes, shared meals with her, and listened intently as she poured out her heart. Slowly but surely, the rift between them began to heal, and they found solace in each other's company.

As they walked through the park one afternoon, Ella turned to her father, her eyes shining with a newfound hope.

"Dad, I'm so glad we're talking again. I've missed you so much."

Mark felt a lump in his throat as he embraced his daughter tightly.

"I'm sorry, Ella," he whispered, the weight of his regret heavy in his voice. "I've been a terrible father and promise to make it up to you daily."

From that moment on, Mark made a conscious effort to strike a balance between his work and his family life. He still poured his heart into his business, but he also made time for Ella. He set aside specific times for her, ensuring that she never felt forgotten or alone. They went on weekend hikes, shared meals, and had heart-to-heart conversations. Together, they navigated the path of grief, finding solace in each other's company and healing the wounds that had threatened to tear them apart.

As the years passed, Ella blossomed into a confident, compassionate young woman, and Mark knew that he had his wife's unfinished letters to thank for the renewed connection with his daughter. Sarah's words had been the catalyst for change, a reminder that the most essential things in life are not found in the boardroom but in the moments shared with those we love.

In the end, the unfinished letters had the power to heal, a testament to the enduring strength of a mother's love and a father's redemption.

The Daughter's Promise

Ainur gazed out the window of her small apartment in Tashkent, watching the bustling city come alive in the early morning light. As she sipped her strong black tea, her mind drifted to the child sleeping peacefully in the next room - her daughter, Zhana. At just 3 years old, Zhana was the light of Ainur's life, a constant source of joy and wonder. But behind that innocent face, Ainur saw the specter of her troubled past, a legacy she was terrified of passing on.

Ainur had grown up with a mother who was distant, cold, and burdened by her demons. As a child, she had yearned for the warmth and affection that other families seemed to exude so effortlessly. Instead, she was met with indifference, criticism, and occasional bursts of irrational anger. The scars of that upbringing ran deep, shaping Ainur's view of herself and her ability to be a loving, present parent.

As she watched Zhana sleep, Ainur felt a familiar knot of fear tightening in her chest. "What if I end up like her?" she whispered. "What if I can't give Zhana the childhood I never had?" The thought was almost too much to bear.

In the following weeks and months, Ainur poured her heart and soul into being the best mother she could be. She showered Zhana with affection, read to her every night, and made sure she never wanted for anything. But despite her efforts, the nagging self-doubt persisted. Ainur found herself second-guessing every decision, terrified of making a mistake that could scar her daughter for life.

One day, as Ainur was grocery shopping, her phone rang. The number was unfamiliar, but something compelled her to answer. On the other end of the line was a trembling voice - her mother's.

"Ainur," the voice said, "it's me. I... I need to talk to you."

Ainur stood there, frozen, as her mother began to speak. She apologized, with a raw honesty that Ainur had never heard before, for the neglect and emotional distance of the past. "I was so caught up in my pain," she said, "that I couldn't see the hurt I was causing you. I know I can't undo the past, but I'm asking for a chance to make amends."

Ainur felt a whirlwind of emotions - anger, resentment, and a glimmer of hope. She listened as her mother poured out her heart, explaining how the death of Ainur's father had sent her into a downward spiral of depression and withdrawal. "I was afraid to love you, afraid to open myself up, because I was terrified of losing you too. But in the end, I lost you anyway." Her mother's apology was like a balm to Ainur's wounded soul, soothing the pain she had carried for so long.

The words hit Ainur like a punch to the gut. She had spent so many years blaming her mother, so much time and energy trying to be the opposite of her. And yet, here was a woman willing to own her mistakes and beg for forgiveness. Ainur felt the walls she had built up slowly crumbling, and at that moment, she knew what she had to do. She realized that forgiveness was not about excusing her mother's actions, but about freeing herself from the burden of resentment.

In the days and weeks that followed, Ainur and her mother began rebuilding their relationship. It wasn't easy—there were tears, frustrations, and moments of doubt. But with each conversation, shared laugh, and hug, Ainur felt the weight of the past lifting. She saw her mother's genuine efforts to change and be the kind of grandmother Zhana deserved.

As Ainur watched Zhana and her grandmother play together, her heart swelled with a newfound sense of peace and purpose. She realized the cycle of hurt and distance didn't have to continue. She could break it and create a different legacy for her daughter. She made a conscious effort to communicate openly, show affection, and be present in Zhana's life, breaking the pattern of emotional distance she had experienced.

In that moment, Ainur made a silent promise to Zhana—a promise to love her unconditionally and be the kind of mother she had always longed for. As she held her daughter close, she knew that no matter what challenges lay ahead, she was ready to face them head-on, with a heart filled with the courage and resilience she had learned from her own mother's journey.

Letters of the Heart

I never imagined my life would take the turn it did when I received that call. I was Emily, the young woman known for my selfishness, independence, and unwavering focus on myself. My friends often joked that I was the center of my universe, and I wore it as a badge of honor. But life has a way of peeling back the layers of our existence, revealing truths we never thought we'd face.

It was a quiet evening in early autumn when the phone rang. The voice on the other end was soft yet urgent. My grandmother, the one person who had always been a constant in my life, was gravely ill. The hospital needed someone to care for her; as fate would have it, that was me.

I packed my bags reluctantly, a sense of dread hanging over me. I hadn't seen Grandma in years; our relationship was distant and strained. I had always found excuses to stay away, wrapped up in my world. But now, there was no escaping it.

When I arrived at her quaint, old house, I was struck by the memories it held. The smell of fresh-baked cookies, her laughter, and the warmth of her embrace. But those memories were overshadowed by the reality of her frail body lying in bed, her eyes closed, her breathing shallow.

The first few days were a struggle. I fumbled through the tasks of caring for her, feeling awkward and out of place. I was used to taking care of myself, not someone else. But as the days turned into weeks, something shifted within me. I started to see beyond my needs and desires, focusing instead on her well-being.

While cleaning the attic one evening, I stumbled upon a dusty box filled with letters. Intrigued, I opened it and found a treasure trove of correspondence my grandmother wrote. The letters, some yellowed with age, were addressed to me but have yet to be sent. As I began to read, the words transported me to a different time, revealing a hidden chapter of our family's history.

My grandmother wrote about her struggles, her dreams, and her sacrifices. She spoke of a love lost during the war, a child she had to give up for adoption, and the pain of never knowing what happened to him. Each letter was filled with a deep emotion I had never seen in her.

As I read, tears streamed down my face. I realized how little I knew about her, her life, and the strength it took for her to carry on. Her letters were a testament to her resilience and unwavering love for her family, even amid immense hardship.

One letter, in particular, struck a chord with me. It was written on the day I was born. She described the joy she felt holding me for the first time, vowing to always be there for me, to protect me, and to guide me. I felt a pang of guilt for how distant I had been, for all the times I had taken her for granted.

That night, I sat by her bedside, holding her hand, and whispered, "I'm sorry, Grandma. I never realized how much you went through and sacrificed for us. Thank you for everything."

Her eyes fluttered open, and she gave me a weak smile. "It's never too late to change, Emily. Love and compassion are the greatest gifts we can give."

From that moment on, my heart began to transform. Caring for her became less of a chore and more of a privilege. I started to see the world through her eyes, understanding the true meaning of compassion and selflessness. Every small act of kindness, every gentle touch, became a way for me to honor her legacy. Whether it was preparing her meals, helping her with her daily routines, or simply sitting by her side, each action was a step towards a more compassionate and selfless version of myself.

As the days turned into months, I watched her health deteriorate, but our bond grew more assertive. We shared stories, laughter, and even tears. She taught me how to find joy in the simplest of things, how to give without expecting anything in return and live a life filled with love.

When she passed away, it felt like a part of me had gone with her. But her letters, wisdom, and love remained. They became my guiding light, inspiring me to be a better person and to live a life of purpose and compassion. This enduring impact of her legacy is a shared experience, connecting us all in the power of love and selflessness.

Standing by her grave, I whispered my final goodbye, knowing that she had given me the greatest gift of all – the gift of a changed heart. Her legacy of love and selflessness lived on in me, and I vowed to carry it forward to make her proud. I promised myself that I would continue to live a life guided by her values, always striving to be a better person and to spread love and compassion wherever I go.

As I walked away, I felt a sense of peace, knowing that my grandmother's spirit would always be with me, guiding me and reminding me of the lessons she had imparted. The letters I had found, the stories she had shared, and the moments we had spent together were now etched in my heart, forever shaping the person I was becoming.

Life after Grandma's passing was different. I returned to my city life, but I was no longer the same Emily who had left. I carried with me a newfound appreciation for the simple, yet profound, acts of kindness and the beauty of selflessness. I began to reach out to family and friends more often, building bridges I had once burned with my selfishness. This personal growth and transformation is a testament to the power of love and compassion, inspiring us all to strive for a better version of ourselves.

While sorting through my belongings one afternoon, I found the box of letters again. I decided to compile them into a scrapbook, each letter accompanied by a photo or a memento that connected to the story it told. I spent hours carefully arranging the letters and the accompanying items, making sure each page was a tribute to the love and wisdom my grandmother had shared. This project became a labor of love, a way to keep Grandma's memory alive and to remind myself of the values she had instilled in me.

Months later, on what would have been Grandma's birthday, I organized a small gathering at her house. I invited family members, old friends, and neighbors who had known her. We shared stories, laughed, and cried, celebrating her life and impact. I read a few of the letters aloud, and as I did, I saw how deeply they touched everyone present.

One letter, written shortly after my birth, stood out. In it, Grandma had written, "Emily, my dear, life is a journey filled with unexpected turns. But remember, it's not the destination that matters most, but the love and compassion we show along the way. Always strive to be kind, to give selflessly, and to cherish the moments with those you love."

Those words resonated deeply within me, echoing the transformation I had undergone. They reminded me that despite my past mistakes, I had the power to choose a different path, one marked by empathy and generosity.

As the evening drew to a close, I looked around the room, seeing the faces of people who had come together because of the love and wisdom of one remarkable woman. I realized that Grandma's legacy was not just in the letters she had written but in the lives she had touched and the hearts she had changed.

In the quiet moments that followed, I walked through her garden, where we had spent countless hours together. The flowers were in full bloom, a riot of colors and fragrances that seemed to celebrate life. I found a small bench and sat down, reflecting on my journey.

I had started as a selfish, self-absorbed young woman, but I discovered the true meaning of compassion and selflessness through caring for my grandmother. Her letters unveiled a hidden chapter of our family history, giving me a deeper understanding of my roots and inspiring my transformation.

As the sun began to set, casting a golden glow over the garden, I whispered a silent thank you to Grandma. Her love had been a guiding light, leading me to a place of humility and grace. I knew her spirit would always be with me, a constant reminder of the power of love and the beauty of a selfless heart.

At that moment, I promised myself to live a life that honored her memory, to be the kind of person she had always believed I could be—a life filled with love, compassion, and selflessness. As I walked back to the house, I felt a sense of fulfillment, knowing that I was on the right path, guided by the letters of the heart.

In the end, it wasn't just about caring for my ailing grandmother. It was about discovering the true meaning of love, compassion, and family. It was about realizing that the most profound changes come from within and that the power of love can transform even the most selfish of hearts. This realization is a beacon of hope, showing that love and compassion can transform us into better versions of ourselves no matter how self-centered we may be.

The Last Drive

I arrived at my father's house early that fateful morning; the suburban town I grew up in greeted me with its familiar sights and sounds. As I walked up the porch steps, childhood memories flashed before my eyes. The creak of the wooden boards underfoot, the smell of freshly mown grass, and the sight of my father, James, waiting by the door all wrapped me in a nostalgic embrace. James had been living alone since Mom passed away, and every visit was a stark reminder of his loneliness and our growing distance.

"Michael, it's good to see you," he said, his voice full of joy and exhaustion. He looked older than I remembered, his once vibrant eyes now clouded with the weight of his health issues and depression.

"Good to see you too, Dad," I replied, smiling. "How about we go out for breakfast?"

He nodded, and soon, we were driving to the fast-food restaurant he loved. The drive was quiet, and our conversations were limited to small talk. James stared out the window, lost in thought, while I focused on the road, my mind swirling with concern about his well-being.

"Dad, you know you shouldn't be driving much," I said gently. "Your hearing isn't what it used to be, especially with those medications."

He remained silent, his gaze fixed on the passing scenery. I sighed, feeling the weight of our unspoken words.

The day grew warmer as we returned home, and by noon, the house was filled with the lively chatter of my family. My brother

David and his kids had joined us, and the atmosphere was one of joy and reminiscence. Laughter echoed through the rooms, and it felt like everything was as it should be for a moment.

But amidst the joy, I couldn't shake my concern for Dad. I took him aside, away from the laughter and stories. "Dad, you need to take your medications on time, watch your diet, and please, no more driving," I pleaded, my voice tinged with desperation.

His eyes flashed with anger. "I'm not a child, Michael," he snapped. "I can take care of myself."

"Dad, I'm just worried about you," I said, my frustration boiling. "I don't want to lose you too."

The argument escalated, our voices rising above the merriment in the other room. I could feel the tension building, the years of unspoken fears and frustrations finally breaking through.

"I'm not ready to give up my independence," he shouted, his face red with emotion.

"And I'm not ready to lose my father," I shot back, my eyes stinging with unshed tears.

Unable to contain my emotions, I stormed out, packing my things in a flurry of anger and sorrow. As I walked to the driveway, I heard Dad's voice behind me, broken and desperate.

"Michael, please, don't go," he cried, tears streaming down his face. "I love you, son. I'm sorry."

But my own emotions clouded my judgment, and I drove away, the sound of his pleas echoing in my mind. As I reached the airport, my phone rang. It was David, his voice frantic.

"Michael, it's Dad. He...he tried to end his life. He's in the hospital."

The news hit me like a freight train, the weight of my anger and guilt crashing down on me. I rushed to the hospital, my heart pounding with fear and regret. When I arrived, I found Dad surrounded by medical staff; his condition was critical.

I sat beside him, holding his hand, my tears falling freely. "Dad, I'm so sorry," I whispered, my voice choked with emotion. "I love you. Please, don't leave me."

His eyes fluttered open, and the faintest smile crossed his lips. "I love you too, Michael," he murmured, his voice weak. Forgive me."

We spent those final moments together, our hearts laid bare, the weight of our unspoken emotions finally finding release. As he took his last breath, I felt a profound sense of loss and a deep resolve to honor his memory.

In the days and months that followed, I reflected on that fateful day and the lessons it had taught me. I vowed to be more present, more loving, and more attentive to my own family, ensuring they never felt the same loneliness and despair that Dad did.

His last drive, our final journey, became a turning point in my life. It reminded me of the fragility of time and the importance of love and understanding. As I moved forward, I carried his memory with me, striving to live a life filled with the compassion and connection he desperately needed.

Ultimately, it wasn't just about our drive but the journey of hearts finding their way back to each other, even in the face of loss and regret.

Brothers of Bali

When I returned to Bali after graduation, the island's familiar fragrance of frangipani and incense welcomed me. A sense of hope and excitement bubbled inside me. I was finally home, ready to share my vision for our family's resort with my brothers, Adi and Wayan.

Adi, the eldest, was already at the resort, managing it with the same meticulous care our parents had. He believed in preserving the resort's traditional charm, a testament to our cultural heritage. Wayan, the middle brother, was a free spirit, an artist who saw the resort as a potential canvas for his creative expressions. I, Made, the youngest, had grand ideas of bringing technology and modernity to the resort, envisioning it as a global destination.

Our reunion was joyous but quickly turned into a heated discussion about the future. Each of us had a different dream, and our disagreements grew more intense as the days passed. Adi wanted to maintain the resort's authenticity, Wayan dreamed of an artistic haven, and I saw the potential for a tech-savvy, modern resort.

Our arguments became daily occurrences. Adi's conservative approach clashed with Wayan's artistic ventures and my tech-driven ideas. The resort, once a harmonious blend of our parents' dreams, became a battleground for our conflicting visions.

Our guests began to notice the tension, and the resort's atmosphere shifted from serene to strained. Amidst our internal struggles, a new rival resort opened nearby, threatening our business. To make matters worse, whispers of a potential volcanic eruption loomed over us, adding to the growing sense of unease.

One evening, the tension peaked as we sat in the resort's courtyard. Our voices rose, each of us stubbornly defending our ideas, unwilling to compromise. The volcanic mountain in the distance mirrors our brewing storm.

The eruption came without warning. Ash and smoke filled the sky, and the ground trembled beneath our feet. Panic spread through the resort as guests and staff scrambled for safety. In that moment of crisis, our differences no longer mattered.

Adi took charge, his calm demeanor guiding us through the chaos. Wayan used his creativity to organize makeshift shelters and comfort the terrified guests with his soothing music. I leveraged my tech skills to coordinate communication and ensure everyone's safety.

Working together, we managed to evacuate the resort and lead everyone to a safer location. The volcanic eruption, a force beyond our control, forced us to put aside our differences and unite for a common cause. In the face of danger, we rediscovered our bond as brothers.

In the aftermath of the eruption, as the ash settled and the skies cleared, we gathered to assess the damage. The resort we had known was altered, but we saw an opportunity for rebirth amidst the ruins.

Adi, Wayan, and I sat together, our hearts open and our minds clear. We realized that our individual strengths could complement each other. Adi's respect for tradition, Wayan's artistic vision, and my technological innovations were not conflicting, but rather, they could come together to create something unique and inspiring.

We devised a plan that incorporated all our dreams. The resort would maintain its traditional charm, enhanced by Wayan's artistic touches, and modernized with the latest technology to attract a global audience. It would be a harmonious blend of our visions, a place where culture, art, and innovation coexisted.

Months of hard work followed. We rebuilt the resort, each of us contributing our skills and passion. The process was not without challenges, but with every hurdle, we grew closer, learning the value of compromise and collaboration.

Finally, the day of the grand reopening arrived. The resort, now a testament to our unity and shared dreams, stood proudly against Bali's stunning landscape. Guests worldwide came, drawn by the unique blend of tradition and modernity.

I felt a profound sense of accomplishment and gratitude as I stood with Adi and Wayan, watching the sunset over the horizon. We had faced our conflicts, weathered a crisis, and emerged stronger as individuals and as a family.

As the celebrations began, I took a moment to reflect on that evening. The volcanic eruption had been a turning point, not just for our resort but for us as brothers. It forced us to confront our differences, find strength in our unity, and believe in the power of hope and resilience. We realized that together, we could overcome any challenge.

Ultimately, it wasn't about whose vision was right or wrong. It was about realizing that we could create something more significant than alone. The resort was more than a business; it symbolized our journey, growth, and love for each other.

And as the first fireworks lit up the night sky, I knew our story was beginning. Our resort was more than a business; it symbolized our journey, growth, and love for each other. The challenges we faced tested our resolve and our relationship, but they also brought us closer together, showing us the true meaning of family and brotherhood. Our shared journey was a testament to our bond.

As the fireworks lit up the night sky, casting a kaleidoscope of colors over the resort, I felt a deep sense of peace and fulfillment. The guests cheered and clapped, their faces reflecting the joy and wonder we hoped to inspire. It was a moment of pure magic, celebrating our hard work and shared vision.

I looked at Adi and Wayan, standing beside me. Adi's eyes shone with pride; his shoulders relaxed for the first time in months. Wayan's face was illuminated with pure artistic satisfaction, and his dreams finally took shape in the real world. And I felt a surge of gratitude and hope, knowing that our combined efforts had created something special.

"To our parents," Adi said, raising his glass. "And to us—may we continue to honor their legacy and build our own."

"To the future," Wayan added, his emotion-filled voice. "May it be as bright and bold as the colors in the sky tonight."

"And to us," I concluded, feeling the moment's weight. "Brothers, friends, and partners in this journey. Together, we are unstoppable."

As we clinked our glasses and took in the sights and sounds of the celebration, I realized that the resort was more than just a place. It reflected our combined strengths and dreams, a testament to our ability to overcome adversity and work together.

The volcanic eruption had been a catalyst for change, forcing us to confront our differences and find common ground. It taught us the importance of unity, resilience, and the power of hope. We learned that true success comes from collaboration and that our dreams can only be realized through our collective effort.

The journey ahead undoubtedly brought new challenges, but we were ready to face them together. The lessons we had learned, the bond we had strengthened, and the vision we had created would guide us forward.

As the night drew close and the guests began to return to their rooms, I took one last look at the resort. It stood as a beacon of hope and a symbol of our journey. The path we had taken was not an easy one, but it had led us to this moment of triumph and unity.

In the silence of the night, I whispered a silent prayer of gratitude—for my brothers, our shared vision, and the future that awaited us. The stars above seemed to twinkle in agreement, and I knew we were on the right path.

"Together," I thought, feeling the warmth of my brothers' presence beside me. "We can achieve anything."

And with that, I turned to join Adi and Wayan, ready to embrace the next chapter of our story—with hope, resilience, and the unbreakable bond of brotherhood guiding our way.

Grapple Heart

I've always believed that the whispers of our hearts shape our lives, those quiet murmurings that guide us when the world's noise becomes too loud. My name is Sarah, and I've been the steadfast rock in our small mountain town for as long as I can remember. People looked to me for strength, for faith, for answers. But beneath my composed exterior lay a storm of doubts and fears I rarely allowed myself to acknowledge. This is the story of how my son, Alex, and I embarked on a journey of self-discovery, resilience, and faith.

My son, Alex, was a different story altogether. At sixteen, his spirit was as wild and untamed as the mountain winds. He was caught in the throes of adolescence, torn between the desire to forge his path and the weight of the expectations I and the community had placed upon him. His rebellion was his way of screaming to the world that he was his own person, but to me, it felt like a rejection of everything I stood for.

Our relationship was strained, to say the least. Every conversation felt like a battlefield, each word a potential landmine. One evening, after another heated argument about his reckless behavior, Alex stormed out of the house. I watched him disappear into the twilight, my heart heavy with worry and frustration.

Days turned into weeks, and our interactions became even more strained. Then, one fateful afternoon, Alex stumbled upon a letter hidden deep in the attic. It was from his father—my late husband—addressed to him. The letter revealed a secret that shattered Alex's understanding of our family and his own identity. His father had led a double life that contradicted everything I had ever told Alex about him.

Alex confronted me, his eyes blazing with anger and hurt. "Why didn't you tell me?" he demanded. "Why did you let me believe a lie?"

My heart ached as I looked at my son, realizing that my attempts to protect him had only caused more harm. "I thought I was shielding you from pain," I whispered, tears streaming down my face. "I never wanted you to feel betrayed."

Amid our turmoil, a stranger arrived in town. He was an enigmatic figure with a calm and almost otherworldly wisdom. People said he had answers to questions they hadn't even known they were asking. Alex and I, desperate for clarity, sought him out. Little did we know, his arrival would mark the beginning of a transformative journey.

We found him by the river, his eyes reflecting the serenity of the water. "I hear you're looking for answers," he said, his voice gentle yet powerful.

Alex was the first to speak. "I don't know who I am anymore," he confessed. "Everything I thought I knew is a lie."

The stranger nodded. "Sometimes, the truth is hidden beneath layers of fear and doubt. To find it, you must be willing to face those fears and embrace the uncertainty."

I took a deep breath, feeling a sense of vulnerability I hadn't allowed myself in years. "I've always had faith," I said, my voice trembling with emotion, "but now I'm not sure if it's truly mine or just inherited beliefs." It was a confession that would change everything.

The stranger smiled. "Faith isn't about having all the answers. It's about trusting yourself enough to seek them. It's about finding your path, even if it leads you away from what you've always known."

Over the next few weeks, Alex and I embarked on a journey of self-discovery. We talked, really talked, for the first time in years. We shared our fears, our hopes, our dreams. I opened up about my own struggles with faith, and Alex began to understand that his rebellion was a cry for independence, not a rejection of me.

One evening, as we sat by the river, Alex turned to me, his eyes filled with a newfound determination. "I want to know who I am," he said. "Not who others think I should be."

"And I want to support you," I replied, my voice steady with conviction. "Not as the rock of the community, but as your mother who loves you unconditionally."

The stranger's words echoed in my mind: "Faith isn't about having all the answers." At that moment, I realized that faith was about trusting the journey, no matter how uncertain.

Our town continued to whisper about the stranger, but to us, he was more than a mystery. He was a catalyst for change, a reminder that sometimes, we need to lose ourselves to find our true selves.

As Alex and I faced our inner struggles, we discovered that our bond was stronger than any secret or doubt. We learned that the heart's whisper is a powerful guide, leading us to our true selves if only we had the courage to listen.

In the end, it wasn't the answers that defined us but the journey we took to find them. As we stood together, mother and son, we knew that our faith—in each other and in ourselves—was the greatest strength of all.

True Faith

A strict religious regime ruled every aspect of life in a land shadowed by the towering spires of ancient cathedrals. The High Clerics' words were law, and faith was wielded more as a weapon of control than a beacon of hope. A rebellion began to stir within this dystopian society, led by a group of individuals yearning for freedom and truth.

The resistance had humble beginnings. They met secretly in the basements of forgotten buildings and the dark corners of abandoned alleys. This motley crew—teachers, laborers, and former soldiers—was bound by a common yearning for freedom. Their leader, Miriam, was a woman of unshakable resolve and deep faith. She believed that their struggle was not just for liberty but for the soul of their society.

"We fight not to destroy but to rebuild," Miriam often reminded them, her eyes alight with fervor. "Our faith must be our shield and sword, but it must be pure, untainted by the greed and corruption of those who claim to lead us."

They operated in the shadows for months, spreading their message of true faith and hope. They disrupted the regime's propaganda, provided sanctuary to those persecuted for their beliefs, and sowed the seeds of rebellion. Among them was Samuel, a former soldier, now grappling with doubts. He questioned whether using faith as a weapon was right, even against those who had twisted it for their own ends.

The climax of their struggle came on a night shrouded in mist and uncertainty. The rebels had planned a major operation to expose the corruption of the High Clerics. They had obtained documents proving the Clerics' embezzlement of church funds and their secret indulgences in the vices they preached against. As they prepared to broadcast this evidence, a twist of fate revealed a darker truth.

A young recruit, Daniel, stumbled upon a hidden chamber beneath the central cathedral. There, in the flickering light of countless candles, he found the regime's leaders not in prayer but in a clandestine meeting with foreign agents. It was a revelation that shook the rebellion to its core. The High Clerics were not just corrupt; they were actively betraying their land for personal gain.

The news spread like wildfire through the ranks, igniting a conscience crisis. Some, like Miriam, saw this as the ultimate proof of their righteous cause. "We must strike now, with all the power of our faith," she urged, her voice trembling with emotion. But others hesitated Samuel among them. What were they genuinely fighting for if their faith had been so thoroughly corrupted?

In the days that followed, the group fractured. Arguments erupted, and trust eroded. Samuel found himself grappling with profound inner turmoil. He had dedicated his life to this rebellion, but now he questioned the very foundation of their struggle. Was it possible to cleanse their faith, or were they merely perpetuating a cycle of power and control?

In this darkest hour, Samuel had a revelation. One night, as he wandered the empty streets, he encountered an older man, a former priest who had long been cast out by the regime. The older man sat by a crumbling fountain, his eyes reflecting the flickering torchlight.

"You look lost, my son," the old man said softly, his voice carrying the weight of years.

"I am," Samuel admitted, sinking beside him. "I thought our faith could save us, but now I see it's been used to destroy us."

The older man nodded, his gaze distant. "Faith is a powerful force, but it's not about the rituals or the leaders. True faith lives in the hearts of those who believe in compassion, justice, and love. It's not something to be wielded like a weapon, but a light to guide us."

His words struck a chord deep within Samuel. He realized then that their rebellion had been misguided, not in its aim for freedom but in its method. They had sought to overthrow one form of tyranny with another instead of building a new path based on genuine belief and mutual respect.

The following day, Samuel called for a meeting of the remaining rebels. With Miriam by his side, he shared his newfound understanding. "We must abandon the fight against the corrupted faith," he declared. "Instead, let us build a new community based on our beliefs' true principles—compassion, justice, and love. Let us be the change we seek."

It was not an easy transition, but it was the right one. Slowly, they began to gather others who shared their vision. They created safe havens, schools, and places of worship free from the regime's influence. Their message spread and a new hope began to bloom with it. The regime's power waned as more people embraced the rebels' vision of a society based on true faith and mutual respect.

As the new community began to take shape, the transformation was palpable. The rebellion's initial fire, born from intense desperation and righteous anger, evolved into a steady flame of hope and resilience. Miriam, Samuel, and the others worked tirelessly, turning their dreams into reality. They built schools where children could learn free from indoctrination and places of worship where faith was a matter of personal conviction rather than enforced doctrine.

Once a symbol of oppression and corruption, the central cathedral was repurposed into a community center. Its grand halls, which had echoed with the hollow sermons of the High Clerics, now resonated with children's laughter, scholars' discussions, and the heartfelt prayers of those who sought genuine spiritual connection.

Always a beacon of strength, Miriam became a guiding force in this new era. Her deep faith remained unshaken but was now rooted in love and service rather than power and control. She often spoke passionately about the importance of living one's beliefs through actions, not just words, instilling in her community the profound wisdom she had gained from her journey.

Samuel, too, found his place in this new world. His journey from soldier to rebel to community leader had forged him into a man of profound wisdom and compassion. He became a mentor to the younger members of their growing society, teaching them the lessons he had learned about the true nature of faith and the importance of integrity and justice.

Despite their successes, the remnants of the old regime did not disappear overnight. Pockets of resistance and occasional sabotage reminded them that their struggle was far from over. Yet, the new community stood firm, united by a shared vision and an unyielding commitment to their principles.

One day, as Samuel walked through the bustling market square, he saw Daniel, the young recruit who had uncovered the High

Clerics' betrayal, speaking passionately to a group of townspeople. Daniel's eyes shone with the same enthusiasm that had once driven Samuel and Miriam. He spoke of a future where faith was a source of strength and unity, not division and fear.

Samuel felt a surge of pride and hope. The flame of their rebellion had not only survived but had sparked a more significant movement. It was a movement that transcended the old boundaries of religion and politics, uniting people to pursue a better, more just world.

As the sun set that evening, casting a golden glow over the transformed cathedral, Samuel and Miriam stood side by side, reflecting on their journey. They had faced immense challenges but emerged more robust, their faith purified by their trials.

Miriam turned to Samuel, her eyes filled with determination and serenity. "We've come a long way, but much must be done."

Samuel nodded, a smile playing on his lips. "Yes, but we've shown that it's possible to build something beautiful from the ashes of corruption. We've proven that true faith can be a force for good, a light in the darkness."

And so, the community continued to grow, guided by compassion, justice, and love principles. Their story became a beacon of hope for others living under oppressive regimes, inspiring similar movements worldwide. The legacy of their faithful rebellion lived on, a testament to the power of unwavering belief in the face of adversity.

Ultimately, it was not just their actions that made a difference, but the spirit in which they were undertaken. They had chosen to fight not with weapons of hate but with the enduring power of true faith and the unwavering conviction that a better world was possible. The echoes of their journey resonated far and wide, a reminder that even in the darkest times, light can prevail.

As the years passed, the story of Miriam, Samuel, and their band of rebels became a legend—a legend that taught future generations that the most profound revolutions begin not with the overthrow of regimes but with the transformation of hearts and minds.

The Trust Experiment

The sun was setting as I approached the nondescript building where the "Trust Experiment" was set to take place. Nervous anticipation coursed through my veins as I walked through the door, greeted by a room filled with strangers, each with a curious glint in their eyes. We were a motley crew of individuals brought together by a shared desire to explore the depths of trust and human connection.

Our facilitator, a charismatic figure named Dr. Harper, explained the premise of the experiment: a series of challenges designed to push us out of our comfort zones and into a realm where trust and faith in one another were paramount. As the rules were laid out, a sense of skepticism, a natural response to the unknown, crept in. How could we trust people we barely knew with our vulnerabilities and fears?

The first challenge was simple yet profound: We were tasked with sharing a personal story with the group, a story that defined who we were and what we stood for. As each person took their turn, I felt a wave of emotions wash over me—empathy, compassion, and a growing sense of connection with these strangers who were now becoming allies in this uncharted journey.

As the days passed, the challenges became more intricate, testing our trust in one another and our resilience in the face of uncertainty. We were asked to blindfold ourselves and navigate a maze guided only by the voice of our teammates, to trust that they would lead us to safety. In those moments of darkness and doubt, I relied not on sight but on the unwavering belief that my fellow participants had my back.

However, as trust blossomed, so did the seeds of discord. A rift formed within the group, fueled by suspicions and hidden agendas that threatened to unravel the fragile bonds we had worked so hard to build. This conflict mirrored the internal struggle within each of us: the battle between skepticism and the need for cooperation. It was a test of our commitment to trust and our ability to navigate through the complexities of human relationships.

When tensions reached a boiling point, Dr. Harper dropped a bombshell that sent shockwaves through the room. The challenges we faced were random tests of trust and a carefully orchestrated experiment designed to manipulate our emotions and allegiances. We were pawns in a psychological game of trust, where alliances shifted like sand and betrayals cut deep.

As the group grappled with this revelation, I was at a crossroads. Would I succumb to the fear and doubt that threatened to tear us apart, or would I rise above the chaos and embrace trust wholeheartedly, knowing it was the key to our collective survival?

In a moment of clarity, I made my choice. I chose to trust not just in others but in myself, to believe that vulnerability was not a weakness but a source of strength. As I let go of my doubts and insecurities, a profound transformation began to take place within me, a shift from skepticism to faith, from isolation to connection.

In the final challenge, we were asked to navigate a treacherous obstacle course, relying solely on the trust and cooperation of our teammates. As we worked together to overcome each obstacle, I felt a sense of unity and purpose that transcended words. This challenge, more than any other, symbolized our collective journey of transformation. We were no longer strangers but a tribe bound by a shared transformation journey.

As we emerged from the obstacle course, battered but unbroken, I looked around at the faces of my fellow participants, each radiating a newfound sense of confidence and resilience. We had faced our fears, confronted our doubts, and emerged more robust than ever. The once-strangers had become friends, comrades in arms who had weathered the storm of the Trust Experiment together, forming a bond that transcended the experiment itself.

Dr. Harper stood before us, a smile playing on his lips as he gazed at the transformed group before him. "You have all shown remarkable courage, resilience, and trust throughout this experiment," he said, his voice filled with pride. "You have proven that trust is not just a concept but a way of life, a force that can unite even the most unlikely of allies."

As the sun dipped below the horizon, casting a warm glow over our faces, I felt a sense of peace. I knew that the Trust Experiment had forever changed me and had opened my eyes to the power of trust and human connection. I had learned that trust was not just about relying on others but about being willing to be vulnerable, to open my heart to the possibility of connection and growth.

In that moment of reflection, a profound realization washed over me like a wave: the actual test of trust was not in the challenges we faced or the obstacles we overcame but in the willingness to believe in the goodness of others, to see beyond the masks we wear and connect on a deeper, more authentic level.

As we bid farewell to the Trust Experiment and each other, I carried with me a newfound sense of purpose and a deep belief in the transformative power of trust. I knew that no matter what challenges life threw my way, as long as I had confidence in myself and others, I could conquer anything.

The punchline of this story is not just about the experiment itself but the profound lesson it taught me: that trust is the foundation of all meaningful relationships, the catalyst for personal growth, and the key to unlocking our full potential. Trust leads us to unexpected places, connects us with unlikely allies, and transforms us into the best versions of ourselves.

As I walked into the twilight, surrounded by the echoes of laughter and camaraderie, I knew that the Trust Experiment had been more than just an experiment—it had been a journey of self-discovery, a testament to the enduring power of trust, and a reminder that in the end, it is trust that changes not only the world around us but also the world within.

Fe's Last Wish

In a small town nestled amidst rolling hills and golden fields lived Fe, a kind-hearted grandmother known for her warm smile and gentle demeanor. Fe, with her unwavering love and comforting presence, had always been the pillar of strength for her family, especially her favorite grandson, Alex.

Fe had been eagerly looking forward to Alex's university graduation for months, a momentous occasion she wanted to celebrate with all her heart. She spent hours picking out the perfect outfit, imagining the pride and joy filling her heart when she saw Alex walk across the stage to receive his diploma.

Three months before the big day, Fe mentioned to Alex that her sister-in-law, Carrie, had sent her some money and that she wanted to treat him to something special as a token of her love and pride in his achievements. She hoped to create lasting memories with her grandson, to share a moment of joy amidst the everyday hustle and bustle of life.

However, as the days passed, Alex found himself caught up in the whirlwind of assignments, exams, and extracurricular activities at school. He kept postponing his visit to Fe, intending to make time for her once he had a moment to spare. Little did he know that time was slipping away faster than he realized. This imbalance between his academic pursuits and personal life would soon teach him a valuable lesson.

As graduation day drew nearer, Fe's excitement grew, and she longed to see Alex and share his happiness. She called him one evening, her voice filled with love and anticipation, asking him to come over to spend time together. But Alex engrossed in a choir prayer meeting at the church, promised to visit her the next day, unaware of the ticking clock that measured Fe's remaining moments.

The following day, January 25, 2003, brought a sorrowful dawn as the news of Fe's passing spread through the town like a whisper in the wind. Alex's heart shattered into a million pieces as he realized he would never get the chance to fulfill Fe's last wish, see the sparkle of pride in her eyes, and hear her voice filled with love and admiration. This profound loss would soon change his perspective on life and love.

Regret washed over Alex like a tidal wave, drowning him in sorrow and grief. He wept for the missed opportunities, for the moments that slipped through his fingers like grains of sand. He wished he had made time for Fe and had shown her how much she meant to him before it was too late.

As Alex sat alone in Fe's empty house, surrounded by memories of her love and warmth, he silently vowed to cherish every moment with his loved ones and never let an opportunity to show appreciation and love pass him by. Fe's passing had taught him a valuable lesson: that time is a precious gift, and the moments spent with those we love are treasures to be held close to our hearts.

In the quiet of the house, a photo of Fe and Alex stood on the mantelpiece, a testament to their bond and a reminder of the love that transcended time and space. As Alex wiped away his tears, a faint smile touched his lips, for he knew that Fe's spirit would always be with him, guiding him towards a life filled with love, gratitude, and the wisdom to seize every moment as if it were his last.

In the end, Fe's last wish was not just a fleeting desire for a special treat but a timeless lesson in love, forgiveness, and the power of cherishing the moments that truly matter. As Alex stood up, his heart heavy with emotions yet light with newfound resolve, he promised to live each day with purpose and intention, to honor Fe's memory by spreading love and kindness wherever he went.

In the following weeks, Alex devoted himself to spending quality time with his family, cherishing every meal shared, every laugh exchanged, and every quiet moment of togetherness. He learned to slow down, appreciate the beauty in life's simple moments, and express his love openly and freely to those who mattered most. This open expression of love would soon become a cornerstone of his life.

Alex felt a sense of peace over him as he walked across the stage on his graduation day, diploma in hand and Fe's spirit in his heart. He knew Fe was watching over him from above, her love shining like a beacon of light, guiding him on his journey forward.

As he looked out into the crowd, his eyes landed on an empty seat where Fe would have sat, a bittersweet reminder of her absence yet a poignant symbol of her enduring presence in his life. In that moment, Alex understood that Fe's love would always be with him, a source of strength and inspiration to carry him through life's challenges and triumphs.

With Fe's last wish etched into his heart, Alex embarked on a new chapter of his life, guided by the moral values of love, compassion, and gratitude. He learned that in the tapestry of life, it was the threads of love and connection that held everything together, weaving a story of resilience, forgiveness, and the enduring power of love.

And so, as the sun set on that memorable day, casting a golden glow over the horizon, Alex whispered a silent thank you to Fe for the lessons she had taught him, for the love she had bestowed upon him, and for the enduring legacy of kindness and compassion that would forever shape his life.

In the end, Fe's last wish was not a mere request for a special treat but a profound invitation to live a life filled with love, cherish every moment with those we hold dear, and embrace the beauty of connection and family.

And as Alex walked into the embrace of his loved ones, his heart brimming with gratitude and love, he knew that Fe's spirit would always be by his side, a guardian angel guiding him towards a future filled with purpose, passion, and the boundless power of love.

In the quiet of the evening, a gentle breeze rustled through the trees, carrying with it the whispers of Fe's love and the promise of a new beginning. As Alex closed his eyes, a sense of peace settled over him, for he knew that Fe's legacy would live on in his heart, a beacon of light shining brightly through the darkest of nights.

In the end, Fe's last wish had not been a goodbye; it had been a timeless reminder to cherish the moments that truly matter, love deeply and thoroughly, and never take for granted the precious gift of life and the beauty of connection.

And with a heart full of love and gratitude, Alex whispered into the night, "Thank you, Fe, for showing me the way. I will always carry your love with me, and I will live each day in honor of your memory and the enduring power of love."

And so, as the stars twinkled overhead, a new chapter began in Alex's life, illuminated by the light of Fe's love and the promise of a future filled with hope, possibility, and the unwavering belief in the transformative power of love.

In the days and years that followed, Alex carried Fe's legacy wherever he went. He became a beacon of kindness and compassion in his community, reaching out to those in need, offering a listening ear, and helping those struggling. He knew that every act of kindness, no matter how small, could make a difference in someone's life, just as Fe's love had made a difference in his own.

As he embarked on his career and navigated life's ups and downs, Alex never forgot his lessons from Fe. He understood that life was fleeting, that moments were precious, and that love was the greatest gift of all. He made a conscious effort to prioritize his relationships, to nurture connections with his family and friends, and to never let a day go by without expressing his love and gratitude.

Through the highs and lows, triumphs and challenges, Alex held onto the moral values that Fe had instilled in him: the importance of forgiveness, the power of resilience, and the beauty of unconditional love. He knew that in a world filled with uncertainty and turmoil, love would always prevail, which would always light the way through the darkness.

As the years passed and Alex's hair turned silver with age, he looked back on his life with gratitude and love. He knew that Fe's spirit had been with him every step of the way, guiding him, inspiring him, and filling his life with purpose and meaning.

And as he sat on the porch of his home, watching the sunset over the horizon, a sense of peace washed over him. He knew that Fe was smiling down on him from heaven, her love surrounding him like a warm embrace, her laughter echoing in the gentle breeze that rustled through the trees.

And in that moment of quiet reflection, Alex whispered a silent thank you to Fe for the gift of her love, the wisdom she had imparted, and the enduring legacy of kindness and compassion that would forever shape his life and the lives of those he touched.

In the end, Fe's last wish was not a farewell but a timeless invitation to live a life filled with love, embrace the beauty of connection, and cherish the moments that truly matter. As Alex closed his eyes, a smile touched his lips, for he knew that Fe's love would always be with him, lighting the way through the darkness and guiding him toward a future filled with hope, possibility, and the boundless power of love.

And so, as the stars twinkled overhead and the world fell into a peaceful slumber, Alex closed his eyes, his heart full of gratitude and love, knowing that Fe's legacy would live on in his heart, a testament to the enduring power of love and the beauty of a life well-lived.

Beyond the Ashes

In the heart of the Philippines, nestled among the lush landscapes of Pampanga, there lived a man named Emilio. At 42 years old, he carried the weight of a lifetime's worth of memories, some etched in gold, some buried beneath the ashes of a devastating past.

It was a day like any other when the earth trembled beneath his feet, and the skies darkened with the wrath of Mt. Pinatubo. Emilio, a mere 9-year-old boy at the time, sat in his classroom, his innocent eyes filled with wonder as the world outside descended into chaos. The eruption unleashed fury upon the land, swallowing whole villages in a fiery embrace, including Emilio's humble home and his entire family. He was left orphaned, with no one to turn to in the deafening silence that followed the storm.

Emilio was orphaned in the deafening silence that followed the storm, a lone soul adrift in a sea of devastation. His heart was heavy with grief, his spirit shattered by loss; he turned to the heavens above, seeking solace in the embrace of faith. In the darkest hour of his life, Emilio discovered a flicker of light, a glimmer of hope to guide him through the shadows of despair. It was his unwavering faith that became his beacon of hope, guiding him through the darkest times and inspiring him to keep moving forward.

With unwavering faith as his compass, Emilio embarked on a journey of self-discovery and redemption. He clung to the memories of his family, their love and laughter echoing in the chambers of his heart, urging him to rise from the ashes of tragedy and forge a new path illuminated by the light of his faith.

Through the years that followed, Emilio's faith became his anchor, his rock in the turbulent seas of life. Guided by a higher power and fueled by a relentless determination to honor the legacy of his loved ones, he poured his heart and soul into his studies, work, and dreams. Despite the challenges and obstacles that stood in his way, Emilio pressed on, his spirit unbroken, his resolve unwavering.

As the years turned into decades, Emilio emerged from the shadows of his past, a testament to the power of faith, resilience, and the boundless strength of the human spirit. He found success in the face of adversity, love amid loss, and purpose in the depths of despair. His journey was a symphony of triumph and tribulation, a tapestry woven with threads of faith, hope, and unwavering belief in a brighter tomorrow.

And so, as Emilio stands at the precipice of his dreams, gazing out at the horizon painted with the hues of a new dawn, he knows that his journey is far from over. The scars of the past may still linger, and the wounds of yesteryears may still ache, but they serve as a reminder of the resilience of the human spirit, the power of faith, and the enduring legacy of love.

Emilio's story is a testament to the transformative power of faith and resilience. It is a journey from despair to the heights of success, fueled by unwavering faith. His journey is a beacon of hope, a reminder that even in the darkest times, there is always a light to guide us home and lead us to a place of peace, purpose, and fulfillment.

As Emilio looks back on his journey, he realizes that his faith was not just a crutch to lean on in times of trouble but a mighty force that propelled him forward, guiding his steps and shaping his destiny. Through faith, he saw the world with renewed clarity, finding beauty in the broken, strength in the struggle, and purpose in the pain.

Through his trials and tribulations, Emilio learned valuable lessons that transcended the boundaries of time and space. He knew the true meaning of resilience, the art of perseverance, and the beauty of forgiveness. His heart, once heavy with sorrow, now overflowed with compassion, empathy, and a deep-seated appreciation for the fragility and resilience of the human spirit. His story is a testament to the transformative power of resilience, inspiring us all to face our trials with courage and determination, and reminding us of the strength that lies within each of us.

As the sun sets on the horizon, casting a golden glow over the landscape, Emilio closes his eyes and whispers a prayer of gratitude to the heavens above. He thanks God for the trials that shaped him, the losses that humbled him, and the victories that crowned his journey with grace. And in that moment of quiet reflection, he feels a sense of peace wash over him, a peace that transcends understanding and fills his soul with a profound sense of purpose.

Emilio's story is a testament to the enduring power of faith, the transformative nature of resilience, and the redemptive force of love. It speaks to the hearts of all who have faced hardship, loss, and despair, offering hope in the darkest nights and a promise of brighter days. It's a reminder that love, in all its forms, can heal and redeem, turning even the most tragic of stories into tales of triumph, and offering a comforting light in the midst of darkness.

And so, as the stars twinkle in the night sky, casting their gentle light upon the earth below, Emilio stands tall, his spirit unbroken, his faith unwavering. For he knows that beyond the ashes of yesterday lie the seeds of tomorrow, waiting to bloom in the light of a new day. And with a heart full of hope and a soul ablaze with faith, he steps forward into the unknown, ready to embrace whatever the future may hold, knowing that all things are possible with God by his side.

Ultimately, Emilio's story is not just his alone—it is a story of triumph over tragedy, light in the darkness, and faith that moves mountains. It is a story that echoes through the ages, inspiring all who hear it to never lose hope, to never give up, and to always believe that with faith as their guide, they too can rise from the ashes and soar to heights beyond their wildest dreams.

Waves of Hope

In the small coastal village of Everblue, where the sky kissed the ocean with hues of sapphire and the air was imbued with the scent of salt and adventure, lived a fisherman named Jonas. His skin was tanned and weathered, a testament to years spent battling the relentless sea. Jonas was a man of tradition, his heart tethered to the tides' rhythms and the waves' ancient whispers.

Every morning, before the sun had fully risen, Jonas would set sail in his weather-beaten boat, "The Tempest," casting his nets into waters that had sustained his family for generations. He believed that the ocean was a boundless source of bounty, a gift from the gods that would never cease to give.

But as the years passed, the once-teeming reefs near Everblue began to fade, their vibrant colors dulled, and their inhabitants dwindling. The villagers noticed the change but were unsure of its cause. Some blamed it on fate, others on the whims of the sea. Jonas, however, refused to see it as anything more than a natural cycle.

Then came Dr. Clara Hart, a marine biologist with eyes as deep and inquisitive as the ocean she studied. Clara had arrived in Everblue to research the declining reef and propose measures to protect it. Her presence stirred the village, her ideas provoking both curiosity and resistance. Jonas, in particular, saw her as an outsider meddling in affairs she couldn't possibly understand.

Clara approached him one crisp morning as Jonas prepared to set out. "Jonas, we need to talk about the reef," she began, her voice steady but urgent.

Jonas narrowed his eyes. "The reef's been here longer than you or me. It'll outlast us both."

"But not if we continue like this," Clara insisted. "Overfishing, pollution—they're killing it. We need to change our ways."

Jonas shook his head. "Change? Change means losing everything we know."

Their arguments became a daily ritual, each trying to convince the other. Jonas saw Clara as naive, her scientific theories threatening his livelihood. Clara saw Jonas as stubborn, clinging to the past at the expense of the future. The village watched, torn between tradition and progress.

Then, one fateful afternoon, disaster struck. An oil tanker off the coast ruptured, spilling its black venom into the ocean. The slick spread quickly, suffocating the life out of the once-glorious reef. Panic gripped Everblue as fishermen found their nets empty and the water poisoned.

Jonas stood on the shore, his heart breaking at the sight of the dying reef. Clara approached him, her face etched with determination. "We can't fight each other anymore, Jonas. We have to fight this together."

Jonas saw the pain in Clara's eyes for the first time, mirroring his own. He realized she wasn't his enemy; the true enemy was the destruction threatening their shared home. With a heavy sigh, he nodded. "What do we do?"

Clara outlined a plan: they would use every resource to contain the spill and heal the reef. Jonas rallied the fishermen while Clara coordinated with environmental experts. Their joint efforts, a testament to the power of unity, became a beacon of hope in the darkness.

Days turned into weeks, and slowly, the tide began to turn. Though gravely injured, the oil was contained, and the reef showed signs of recovery. Jonas and Clara's collaboration symbolized unity, teaching the villagers that tradition and progress could coexist.

Through their struggle, Jonas found himself changing. He began to see the ocean as a provider and a fragile, interconnected ecosystem. He learned new sustainable fishing practices, ensuring the sea's bounty for future generations. Clara, too, grew, understanding the deep-rooted traditions that shaped the lives of Everblue's people. Their personal growth was a powerful lesson in the importance of understanding and adapting to change.

One evening, as the sun dipped below the horizon, painting the sky with strokes of gold and crimson, Jonas and Clara stood on the shore, side by side. The waters of Everblue shimmered with renewed vibrancy, and the reef's colors slowly returned.

"We did it," Clara said softly, a smile touching her lips.

Jonas nodded, his heart swelling with a sense of accomplishment and newfound respect. "We did it together."

Ultimately, the village of Everblue learned that hope, like the ocean, was vast and enduring. It taught them that change, though daunting, could bring about a brighter future. In Jonas's heart, where resistance once resided, a deep appreciation for the delicate balance of life now flowed.

As they watched the waves gently caress the shore, Jonas realized that true strength lay not in clinging to the past but in embracing the future with open arms. And so, with the reef's revival, Everblue's spirit soared and carried on the waves of hope.

The Garden of Forgiveness

The sun rose on Bellwood Street, casting a golden hue on the quaint homes that lined the road, each with carefully tended lawns and flower beds. At the heart of this picturesque neighborhood lay a shared garden plot, a verdant oasis that once symbolized unity and cooperation, its beauty a testament to the care and dedication of its creators. However, it stood as a battleground between two neighbors, Thomas Reed and Eleanor Clark.

Thomas, a retired schoolteacher, had always found solace in the garden. His meticulous rows of tomatoes, beans, and herbs were a testament to his dedication. Eleanor, an artist with a penchant for wild, colorful blooms, believed in cultivating nature's beauty in its most untamed form. Their differing visions for the garden had sparked a conflict that simmered for years, gradually evolving into a deep-seated resentment.

The feud began innocuously enough. A misplaced rose bush here, a trampled vegetable patch there. But harsh words soon exchanged, and the garden that once brought joy became a source of bitterness. Thomas couldn't let go of the past slights, and Eleanor's frustration grew with each encounter. They both knew their actions were petty, but pride held them captive, preventing any form of reconciliation.

One summer evening, the sky darkened ominously. The weather reports warned of an impending storm, but nothing could have prepared Bellwood Street for the fury that descended upon it. Fierce winds howled, rain pelted the earth, and lightning split the sky. The shared garden lay vulnerable, its delicate plants at the mercy of nature's wrath.

When the storm finally passed, the neighborhood emerged to assess the damage. Thomas and Eleanor stood at the garden's edge, their hearts sinking as they surveyed the devastation. The once-lush plot was a chaotic mess of uprooted plants and broken stems.

Despite their animosity, a sense of shared loss hung in the air. Thomas looked at Eleanor, and for the first time in years, he saw not an adversary but a fellow gardener mourning the same loss. Eleanor met his gaze, her eyes reflecting the same pain and regret, creating a moment of shared understanding and empathy.

Without a word, Thomas walked over to a fallen trellis and began to lift it. Eleanor hesitated, then joined him, her hands working alongside his. As they toiled together, an unspoken understanding passed between them. The garden had been a battleground, but it could also be a place of healing.

Days turned into weeks as Thomas and Eleanor worked side by side to restore the garden. Their conversations, once sharp and cutting, became softer, more compassionate. Thomas shared his horticultural wisdom, teaching Eleanor about soil health and pest control. In return, Eleanor introduced Thomas to the beauty of wildflowers and the importance of biodiversity.

As they rebuilt the garden, they also began to mend the wounds in their hearts. Thomas realized that holding onto past hurts had only brought him misery. Eleanor learned that her passion for beauty did not diminish the value of others' perspectives. Together, they created a space that blended their visions, a harmonious fusion of order and wildness.

One sunny afternoon, as they planted the last of the new seedlings, Thomas paused and looked at Eleanor. "I never told you this, but when my wife passed away, this garden was what kept me going. I suppose that's why I was so protective of it."

Eleanor nodded, her eyes moist with unshed tears. "I understand, Thomas. After my divorce, I needed something to remind me of life's beauty, something to nurture. I'm sorry for all the hurtful things I said."

Thomas smiled, a weight lifting from his shoulders. "I'm sorry too, Eleanor. We both lost sight of what really matters."

The garden flourished under their joint care, becoming more vibrant. It stood as a testament to the power of forgiveness and the strength found in unity, its transformation a living proof of the healing power of reconciliation. The neighbors who once avoided each other now shared laughter and stories, their bond growing stronger with each passing day.

Years later, when a new family moved into the neighborhood, they marveled at the beautiful garden and the friendship between Thomas and Eleanor. The story of their feud and subsequent reconciliation became a lesson for all, a reminder that even the deepest wounds can heal with time, effort, and a willingness to forgive.

The Garden of Forgiveness taught Bellwood Street that while nature can be unpredictable and destructive, it can bring people together, heal, and renew. It showed that the most significant battles are often fought within ourselves and that victory lies not in defeating others but in overcoming our own pride and bitterness.

And so, the garden thrived, a living symbol of hope and redemption, proving that even amidst the fiercest storms, the seeds of forgiveness can bloom into the most beautiful of gardens.

The Tree of Trust

The city of Bayhaven has always been known for its resilience and charm. It is a coastal gem where the salty breeze and the hum of commerce blend seamlessly. At the heart of Bayhaven's bustling business district stands a modest yet thriving tech startup called Innovatech, co-founded by two men as different as night and day: Robert Grayson and Ethan Cole.

Robert, a seasoned entrepreneur, believed in steady growth and sustainable practices. His vision for Innovatech was to create innovative solutions that pushed technological boundaries and upheld ethical standards such as transparency, honesty, and respect for all stakeholders. Ethan, younger and more aggressive, was driven by ambition and the lure of rapid expansion. He saw potential in risky ventures and believed bold moves were necessary to stay ahead in the competitive tech industry.

Their contrasting philosophies had always been a source of tension, but mutual respect, a shared passion for innovation, and their commitment to ethical values kept their partnership intact. However, as Innovatech began to grow, so did their disagreements. Ethan pushed for a lucrative deal with a major corporation known for questionable practices, while Robert advocated for a more cautious approach, fearing the ethical compromises it entailed.

One evening, as the sun dipped below the horizon, casting long shadows over Bayhaven, Robert sat alone in his office, the weight of his decision pressing heavily on his shoulders. He knew rejecting Ethan's proposal could jeopardize their business and strain their partnership. Yet, he couldn't shake off the nagging feeling that compromising their values would ultimately lead to their downfall.

As Robert grappled with his inner turmoil, the weather outside worsened. The news channels buzzed with warnings of an impending hurricane, which Bayhaven hadn't seen in decades. The city braced itself for the onslaught, boarding windows and securing valuables.

When the hurricane hit, Bayhaven reeled with ferocity. Fierce winds howled through the streets, uprooting trees and tearing off roofs. Torrential rain battered the city, flooding roads and homes. Innovatech's office, though built to withstand severe weather, was not immune to the storm's wrath.

Amid the chaos, Robert and Ethan found themselves trapped in the office, their escape routes blocked by fallen debris. The power flickered and went out, plunging them into a palpable darkness. The howling wind and lashing rain created an eerie symphony, accentuating the tension between the two men, which was so thick it could be cut with a knife.

With nothing to do but wait out the storm, they were forced to confront their differences. Ethan broke the silence, his voice tinged with frustration. "Robert, we can't keep playing it safe. If we don't take risks, we'll be left behind."

Robert sighed, his own frustration bubbling to the surface. "Ethan, I understand the need for growth, but not at the cost of our integrity. We built this company on trust and ethical values. If we compromise those, what do we have left?"

As the storm raged on, their argument intensified, each man defending his stance fervently. But beneath the heated words lay a more profound struggle—Robert's internal battle with his conscience and Ethan's desperation to prove himself.

Hours passed, and the storm began to weaken. In the quiet that followed, a sense of clarity emerged. Ethan looked at Robert, his expression softening. "Maybe you're right, Robert. I've been so focused on success that I lost sight of why we started this in the first place."

Robert nodded, a glimmer of understanding in his eyes. "I haven't been completely fair either, Ethan. I've been so afraid of losing our values that I resisted every change. We need to find a balance."

With the dawn came a renewed sense of purpose. The hurricane had left a trail of destruction, but it also brought an opportunity for rebuilding—not just their office but their partnership. Together, they cleared the debris and assessed the damage, working side by side with a newfound respect for each other's perspectives, bringing a sense of relief and closure to the conflict.

In the following days, Innovatech symbolized resilience in Bayhaven's recovery. Robert and Ethan presented a united front, blending their visions to steer the company toward a future that honored innovation and integrity. They made tough decisions together, each learning to trust the other's judgment, instilling a sense of pride and accomplishment in their audience.

Their bond, once strained, grew stronger as they navigated the challenges ahead. Innovatech flourished not just because of its technological advancements but also because of the unwavering trust that now formed its foundation.

Years later, when asked about the secret to their success, Robert would smile and point to a tree that stood proudly outside their office—a tree that had survived the hurricane, its roots deep and unshaken. "That's the tree of trust," he would say. "It reminds us that no matter the storm, with trust and integrity, we can weather anything."

And so, the tree of trust became a living testament to the power of friendship, the strength of shared values, and the triumph of ethical perseverance over adversity. It stood as a beacon of hope and inspiration, proving that true success is built.

Mirror

In the heart of Sydney, my name, Emma Lawson, was synonymous with excellence. As a teacher at an elite international school, I had carved a niche for myself, revered by colleagues and adored by students. My classroom was a sanctuary of knowledge, my methods innovative, and my success stories numerous. But beneath the veneer of accolades and achievements, I harbored a growing arrogance, a silent belief that I was infallible. Little did I know, this belief was about to be shattered by an unexpected journey.

One summer, the school announced an exchange program with a remote village in the hills of Cambodia. The idea was to foster cultural exchange and broaden students' horizons. Confident in my abilities and eager for adventure, I volunteered to lead the group, expecting to impart wisdom to the less fortunate and return home even more celebrated.

The village of Kampong Cham starkly contrasted with the urban jungle I was accustomed to. Nestled amidst lush fields and surrounded by ancient temples, it was a place where time seemed to stand still. The school was a modest building, with children whose eyes sparkled with curiosity despite the lack of resources. I arrived with a sense of superiority, confident that I would revolutionize their education. Little did I know I was about to be revolutionized.

On the first day, I began with a lecture on modern teaching techniques, expecting to captivate my audience. Instead, I was met with blank stares and polite nods. The village teacher, Mr. Chann, a man of few words but deep wisdom, observed quietly. When I finished, Mr. Chann said, "Here, we teach with our hearts."

I was taken aback. I prided myself on my intellectual prowess and ability to inspire through knowledge. However, as days turned into weeks, I noticed the subtle ways Mr. Chann connected with his students. He knew their families, their dreams, their struggles. He taught them not just to read and write but to believe in themselves and value kindness and community.

While exploring the village one afternoon, I stumbled upon a clearing where children played a traditional game. I watched as they laughed and cheered, their joy infectious. At this moment, I realized that I had forgotten life's simple pleasures in my quest for perfection. I was so focused on success that I lost sight of what mattered. This realization was a turning point in my journey of transformation.

That evening, a storm swept through the village, causing a landslide that blocked the only road to the nearest town. The villagers rallied together, working tirelessly to clear the debris. Initially hesitant, I found myself drawn into the camaraderie. I felt a sense of belonging I had never experienced before. I realized that my achievements and accolades meant little in the face of such genuine human connection.

As the days passed, I found myself changing. I spent more time listening than speaking, learning from the villagers' resilience and humility. I helped repair the school, taught the children songs from my homeland, and shared stories of my childhood. In return, they taught me the beauty of living in harmony with nature and community.

One morning, while looking in the mirror, I saw not the confident, accomplished woman I once was but a person humbled by the simplicity and sincerity of village life. I had come to Kampong Cham to teach but had been taught the most profound lessons.

The day before my departure, the villagers organized a farewell ceremony. The children performed a dance they had learned from me, and Mr. Chann presented me with a handcrafted mirror adorned with intricate designs. "This mirror," Mr. Chann said, "is a reflection not just of your face but your soul. May it always remind you of what you have learned here."

As I prepared to leave, I felt a pang of sorrow. But it was accompanied by a newfound clarity and purpose. I realized that true success was not measured by accolades or material wealth but by the impact one had on others and the love and respect one earned.

Back in Sydney, I resumed my duties with a changed heart. My colleagues noticed the difference, and my students felt the shift. I was no longer the distant, revered teacher but a mentor who listened and cared deeply about their lives and dreams. I introduced community projects, such as volunteering at local shelters and organizing charity events, to encourage empathy and kindness and foster a sense of unity among my students.

Years later, when I retired, my farewell was a testament to the lives I had touched. Students and teachers from across the globe gathered to honor me. As I looked into the mirror from Kampong Cham, now hanging in my study, I saw a reflection of a life well-lived, a journey from arrogance to humility, from selfishness to selflessness. I felt deeply grateful and fulfilled, knowing I had lived a meaningful life.

Ultimately, my legacy was not the awards on my shelf but the hearts I had touched and the lives I had changed. The mirror's reflection was a constant reminder of the accurate measure of success.

Moral: True success is not in accolades or material wealth, but in the love, respect, and positive impact one has on others. Humility and empathy are the foundations of a meaningful life.

Mask of Deception

A new face seldom went unnoticed in the small, bustling town of Everwood, where everyone knew everyone. Sarah, a diligent journalist with a penchant for uncovering the truth, was no exception to this rule. So, when a charming new colleague named Daniel joined the Everwood Gazette, she couldn't help but be intrigued. Daniel was charismatic, with an infectious smile and an aura that pulled everyone into his orbit. But for Sarah, there was something more—a spark she hadn't felt in years.

Their friendship blossomed quickly. Daniel's wit and warmth made him a favorite at the office, and his intelligence shone brightly in his investigative pieces. Sarah was drawn to his stories, laughter, and, eventually, his heart. They became inseparable, sharing late-night conversations, dreams, and secrets under the starry Everwood sky.

As their bond deepened, so did Sarah's feelings. She had always guarded her heart, but with Daniel, those walls seemed to crumble effortlessly. They worked side by side, uncovering stories that shook the town and brought about change. During one such investigation, Sarah stumbled upon something that would change everything.

One rainy evening, as Sarah sifted through old archives for a story on a decade-old financial scandal, she found a name she recognized—Daniel's. Her heart pounded as she read through the documents. Daniel was implicated in the scandal, not as a whistleblower, but as a central figure. The documents painted a picture of deceit and betrayal, of someone who had manipulated others for personal gain.

Sarah's world shattered. She felt a cold wave of disbelief, anger, and heartache. How could the man she trusted implicitly, the man she loved, be capable of such treachery? She confronted Daniel that night, her voice trembling as she held out the documents.

"Is this true? Did you do this?" she demanded, tears welling in her eyes.

Daniel's face fell, and the mask of deception slipped. He admitted his past, confessing that he had been young and ambitious and had made terrible choices. He had come to Everwood to start over, to escape the shadows of his past. He swore that he had changed and was no longer the man those documents described.

Sarah was torn. She wanted to believe him, but the betrayal cut deep. She needed time to think and process the swirling emotions within her. For days, she avoided Daniel, throwing herself into her work, trying to make sense of everything.

During this time, she stumbled upon an old journal of her father's, a man she had always admired for his integrity and wisdom. In it, he wrote about the importance of forgiveness and second chances, how people are not defined by their worst mistakes but by their ability to learn and grow from them.

Sarah found herself at a crossroads. She could let the pain and betrayal consume her, or she could choose to forgive and see the man Daniel had become rather than the man he once was. She realized that holding onto anger would only poison her soul and that forgiveness was not about absolving Daniel of his mistakes but freeing herself from the bitterness that threatened to engulf her.

With a renewed sense of clarity, Sarah sought out Daniel. She found him sitting alone in their favorite spot by the river, his expression of remorse and sorrow. She sat beside him, taking his hand in hers.

"I've read my father's journal," she began softly. "He believed in second chances, and I think I do too. But trust needs to be rebuilt, and it will take time."

Daniel looked at her, hope flickering in his eyes. "I understand, and I'm willing to do whatever it takes to earn your trust back," he replied earnestly.

Their journey took work. It was marked by moments of doubt, pain, and healing. But through it all, Sarah and Daniel found a deeper understanding of each other and themselves. They continued their work at the Gazette, uncovering truths and making a difference in their community, but now with a bond forged in honesty and redemption.

In the end, Sarah realized that life's true beauty lies not in perfection but in the ability to grow and forgive. She learned that love is not about finding someone without flaws but about finding someone whose flaws you can forgive and whose heart you can trust.

As the sun set over Everwood, casting a golden glow over the town, Sarah knew that she and Daniel had traversed a difficult path but had emerged stronger. They had unmasked the deceptions of the past and found a future built on trust and love.

At that moment, under the same starry sky where their friendship had begun, Sarah whispered, "We are not defined by our mistakes but by our ability to rise above them."

Daniel squeezed her hand, his heart full of gratitude and love. Ultimately, it was not the mask of deception that defined them but the strength of their forgiveness and the depth of their love.

1999

The halls of St. Dominic's High School were alive with the energy and excitement unique to youth. It was the year 1999, and as I strolled through those corridors, a palpable sense of curiosity and intrigue enveloped me. We were all teenagers, navigating the complexities of adolescence, but there was something about Alex that stood out. He exuded a mysterious aura that seemed to both attract and repel people. I found myself drawn to him, eager to unravel the enigma he presented. Alex moved through the school with a peculiar air. He was popular, yet he kept everyone at arm's length, as if he wore an invisible cloak, shielding himself from true connection. I often pondered about the secrets he kept hidden and the mysteries that lay beneath his quiet exterior. Despite his standoffish demeanor, there was something about him that made me want to get closer, to understand the person beneath the mask he presented to the world. As time passed, I observed Alex from a distance, trying to piece together the puzzle that he was. I noticed how he would sometimes gaze out of the classroom window, his eyes distant and full of unspoken dreams. I saw the way he would linger in the hallways, as if he didn't quite belong anywhere but also wanted to be a part of everything. Little by little, I gathered snippets of information about him, but the more I learned, the more I realized how little I knew. Alex was a closed book, and I was determined to find a way to open it. Then, one fateful day, something unexpected happened. I still remember it clearly, even after all these years.

It was a typical school day, the hallways bustling with the usual chatter and laughter. I turned a corner and there, unexpectedly, was Alex. In that brief moment, our eyes met, and I saw a flash of something—pain, perhaps, or a deep-seated loneliness. Before I could say anything, he quickly averted his gaze and walked away, leaving me standing there, my heart unexpectedly heavy. That moment stayed with me, and I thought about Alex even more than before. I wanted to understand why he kept everyone at a distance. Was he hiding something? Or was he, perhaps, protecting himself from potential hurt and disappointment? I couldn't shake the feeling that there was a deeper reason for his aloof behavior, and I became determined to get through to him. I started seeking opportunities to talk to Alex and engage him in conversation. It wasn't easy, as he often gave monosyllabic responses, but I persisted. Little by little, I began to earn his trust. We would talk about school and our classmates, and eventually, our conversations delved into more personal territories. I shared my struggles and insecurities with him, and slowly, he began to open up in return. As we spent more time together, I learned about Alex's challenges at home and the pressures he felt to conform to expectations that didn't truly reflect his identity. He confided in me that he felt like an outsider at school and in his own life. I listened, supported him, and assured him he wasn't alone. Gradually, a deep bond formed between us, and I felt privileged to be one of the few people who truly knew the real Alex.

High school ended, and life took us in different directions. We promised to stay in touch, but we lost contact as the years went by. I often wondered where life had taken him and if he had found the happiness and sense of belonging he deserved. Then, one day, I received an invitation that would change everything. It was 2024, and I was invited to a reunion at St. Dominic's High School. As I walked into the familiar hallways, now adorned with decorations and filled with the voices of adults reminiscing, I felt a surge of nostalgia. I scanned the room, hoping to glimpse Alex, wondering if he would be there. And then, as if fate had orchestrated it, I saw him. He was standing across the room, and our eyes met. In that instant, I saw recognition, warmth, and a hint of the same mystery that had drawn me to him all those years ago. A smile spread across his face, and I felt my heart lift. We made our way towards each other, and as we embraced, I felt a sense of closure, as if the missing piece of a puzzle had finally been found. The reunion allowed us to reconnect and catch up on the years that had passed. I learned that Alex had faced his fair share of struggles but had also found his path and was now living a life true to himself. He told me that my friendship during those formative years had been a lifeline, giving him the strength to persevere and eventually embrace his true self. As we talked, I felt a deep sense of gratitude and fulfillment. Our high school years had been a time of self-discovery for both of us; now, as adults, we could look back and appreciate our impact on each other's lives. The divide that had once existed between Alex and the rest of the class had long since disappeared, replaced by a sense of unity and acceptance that filled the room with warmth and understanding.

The reunion became a testament to the enduring power of friendship and the ability to forgive, forget, and move forward. It was a reminder that no matter how mysterious or elusive someone may seem, we all share the same fundamental desire to be understood and accepted for who we truly are. As the night drew closer, I felt a sense of peace and resolution. The story of Alex and my journey together had come full circle, and I knew that no matter what life threw our way, the bond we shared would always be a source of strength and comfort.

The Rivalry Renewed

In the rugged landscapes of southern Utah, where red rock formations towered against a backdrop of azure skies, the small town of Redstone lay nestled in a valley. The sun glowed warmly on the sandstone cliffs, creating an otherworldly beauty that enchanted everyone. It was a place where the very earth seemed to sing with the colors of sunset, and friendships were forged in the shadows of towering mesas. Among these friendships, two boys stood out: Ethan and Marcus.

As children, they were inseparable. Their laughter echoed through the canyons as they explored hidden caves and chased after lizards in the warm afternoon sun. They shared dreams of adventure, believing they could conquer the world together. But as they grew older, their innocent bond twisted into a bitter rivalry—a rivalry fueled by misunderstandings, envy, and unspoken words.

Ethan became the town's golden boy, a star athlete whose prowess on the basketball court was unmatched. The community celebrated his victories, and he basked in the glow of admiration. Marcus, however, found solace in his art, pouring his emotions onto canvas and creating breathtaking landscapes that captured the essence of their beloved Utah. But while Ethan's name was chanted in victory, Marcus felt invisible, overshadowed by his friend's success, leading to a fracture that widened with each passing year.

The rivalry reached its peak during their senior year of high school. Ethan won the basketball tournament at the annual Spring Festival, his triumphant shot echoing in the crowd's hearts. Meanwhile, Marcus's art exhibition, filled with stunning portrayals of their hometown, garnered little attention. The applause for Ethan felt like a dagger to Marcus's heart, and at that moment, their friendship crumbled. Words were not exchanged; their silence was deafening, filled with resentment and disappointment.

Years passed, and the vivid memories of their childhood faded into the background. Ethan became the town's beloved coach, inspiring the next generation of athletes, while Marcus retreated into his art, finding solace in the brush strokes that brought him peace. Their lives continued in parallel, each avoiding the other, their rivalry becoming a ghost that haunted their past.

One blistering summer afternoon, the tranquility of Redstone was shattered. Dark clouds rolled in, casting an ominous shadow over the town. The weather forecast had warned of a severe storm, but no one anticipated the fury that was about to unfold. As the first raindrops fell, the townspeople hurried to secure their homes. The once-glistening desert landscape transformed, and panic spread as the storm intensified, turning the dry riverbeds into raging torrents.

Ever the leader, Ethan quickly rallied a group of volunteers to set up emergency shelters and rescue operations. Meanwhile, Marcus, who had always preferred to stay in the background, felt a sense of urgency he could not ignore. He grabbed his supplies, determined to help his community, even if it meant facing the man he had avoided for so long.

They found themselves at the town hall, where the community had gathered to coordinate their efforts. The air was tense as Ethan and Marcus exchanged glances, their past grievances like a heavy fog lingering between them. Ethan was barking orders, directing volunteers to fill sandbags and create barriers against the rising waters.

Marcus, unsure of his role, hesitated in the doorway, watching the chaos unfold.

"Marcus! We need help over here!" Ethan called, his voice cutting through the noise.

Taking a deep breath, Marcus stepped forward. "What do you need me to do?"

"Grab that shovel and start filling those sandbags," Ethan instructed, his tone commanding yet urgent.

As they worked side by side, the atmosphere crackled with unspoken tension. Each glance exchanged was filled with memories of past hurt, but the situation's urgency forced them to set aside their differences. They filled sandbags in silence, the rhythmic sound of shovels hitting dirt punctuating the tense air.

With every bag they filled, they witnessed the strength of their community. Neighbors came together, helping one another, sharing water and food, their laughter mingling with the sound of the storm. Ethan and Marcus watched as young volunteers assisted elderly residents, their resilience shining through the chaos. For the first time, they saw each other not as rivals but as two men bound by a shared purpose.

As night fell, the rain showed no signs of letting up. The storm raged outside, and the floodwaters surged, inching closer to the town hall. Ethan and Marcus took a moment to catch their breath, leaning against the wall, drenched and exhausted.

"I never wanted it to be like this," Marcus finally broke the silence, his voice low. "I wanted to be happy for you but felt like I was always in your shadow."

Ethan looked at him, surprise flickering in his eyes. "I thought you resented me. I didn't know you felt that way."

Marcus's shoulders slumped, the weight of years of burden pouring out. "It was never just about your success. I lost my way, and I blamed you for it."

Ethan nodded, the realization hitting him like a wave. "I'm sorry. I should have reached out to you and seen you for who you are, not just as a rival."

At that moment, amid the chaos, they began to peel back the layers of their resentment. The storm outside mirrored the tumult within them, but the clouds started to part as they spoke. The vulnerability of their shared experience allowed them to confront their pain, and as they did, the walls they had built around their hearts began to crumble.

As dawn broke, the rain finally began to relent, revealing the devastation left in its wake. The streets of Redstone were flooded, homes were damaged, and the community faced an uphill battle to recover. But amidst the chaos, the spirit of the town shone brighter than ever. The storm, once a destructive force, had become a catalyst for change, inspiring the community to come together and rebuild.

The townsfolk emerged, ready to help one another, and Ethan and Marcus joined them. They organized cleanup efforts, worked to provide shelter for those who had lost their homes, and set up fundraisers to aid in recovery. The once-bitter rivals found themselves side by side, their shared purpose driving them forward, uniting them in a common cause.

As they cleared debris and salvaged belongings, they discovered a new respect for one another. They shared stories of their childhood, reminiscing about the adventures they had embarked on and the dreams they once had. Each laugh, each shared memory, was a brick in the foundation of a renewed friendship.

One day, as they stood together on a makeshift platform overlooking the community, Marcus turned to Ethan. "You know, maybe we should create something together—an art piece to honor this town and the strength of its people."

Ethan's eyes sparkled with enthusiasm. "I'd love that! Let's do something that captures the spirit of Redstone."

And so, they began to plan their mural—a vibrant depiction of the storm, the community coming together, and the beauty of forgiveness. They sketched ideas, combining their talents to create a piece that would symbolize their journey and the resilience of their hometown.

Weeks passed, and the mural took shape. The colors danced across the canvas, telling a story of challenge and triumph, of rivalry turned to brotherhood. As they painted, they found themselves laughing and reminiscing, the weight of their past grievances dissipating with each brush stroke.

The day of the mural unveiling arrived, and the townspeople gathered to witness the masterpiece. Ethan and Marcus stood side by side, proud of what they had created and even prouder of the bond they had forged through their shared experiences. The mural was unveiled, revealing a stunning portrayal of the storm, the strength of the community, and the beauty of reconciliation.

As the crowd erupted in applause, Ethan and Marcus exchanged a glance filled with understanding and gratitude. At that moment, they knew they had transformed not only their rivalry but also their lives.

Standing before the mural; the town's mayor spoke. "This piece is not just a celebration of our resilience but a reminder that even in our darkest moments, we can find strength in each other. Ethan and Marcus have shown us that forgiveness and collaboration can heal even the deepest wounds."

The crowd cheered, but the real celebration was the bond that had been rekindled. Ethan and Marcus felt a warmth spread through them, a realization that their journey had come full circle. They had learned that true strength lies not in individual victories but in the connections we forge with others.

As the sun set over Redstone, casting a golden glow on the mural, Ethan and Marcus stood together, their hearts full. They understood that the rivalry that once defined them had transformed into something far more valuable—a friendship built on trust, respect, and the shared experience of overcoming adversity.

In the following days, the mural symbolized hope for the entire community. It adorned the town square, a reminder of their strength and unity. Ethan and Marcus continued to work together on art projects and community initiatives, using their talents to uplift those around them.

One evening, Ethan turned to Marcus as they sat on a bench overlooking the vibrant sunset. "I never thought we could come back from where we were. I'm grateful for this storm—it brought us back together."

Marcus nodded, a smile playing on his lips. "Sometimes it takes a tempest to reveal the beauty of a rainbow. We've grown, and I wouldn't trade this journey for anything."

As the sky shifted from orange to purple, they savored the moment, knowing they had emerged stronger and more connected from the storm than ever. Their rivalry had been renewed, but this time, it was rooted in friendship and mutual respect—a powerful reminder that even in the darkest times, the light of compassion can guide us home.

And in that warm Utah evening, with the echoes of their laughter mingling with the whispers of the wind, they understood that true victory lies not in competition but in the bonds we create with those we love.

Heartbeat of Connection

I remember the day my father, with his warm smile and gentle hands, leaned back in his armchair, his voice a soothing melody amidst our chaotic lives. "Son," he said, "you'll find love when you least expect it." Little did I know that those words would echo in my heart long after he left this world. The day my father shared those words with me, I didn't realize the weight they would carry in my life. His warm smile and gentle manner were comforting in our often-hectic home. We were a family of chaos and noise, but my father always found a way to create moments of calm. That afternoon, as he sat in his armchair, a sanctuary amidst the whirlwind of our lives, his voice was a soft melody. It was as if he had all the time in the world to share his wisdom, even as the world rushed by outside our window. "Son," he began, and I knew this would be one of those moments etched forever in my memory. "Love is a mysterious thing. It cannot be forced or predicted. It often comes when we are not looking for it when we are busy living our lives and pursuing our passions." His eyes, kind and knowing, held a lifetime of experience. I could tell these words were not just a platitude but a truth he had discovered in his journey. Little did I know then that this moment would be a beacon of guidance in my life long after my father's passing. My father's prediction proved true in a way I never expected. Years later, when I had forgotten his words, love found me. It happened on an ordinary day, as I was going about my routine, changing my life forever. In an instant, I understood the depth of my father's wisdom. His memory lived on, his voice echoing in my heart, reminding me that love has its own timing and that the heartbeat of connection is a powerful force that cannot be denied. It was a testament to resilience, to the power of love to triumph above all else.

Life can pull the rug out from under you, doesn't it? When my father passed away, the air felt heavier, each breath a reminder of his absence. The house became a mausoleum of memories once filled with laughter and love. My aunt, a fierce woman with an indomitable spirit, tried to fill the void. "You should meet Dr. Eliza," she insisted, her eyes sparkling with mischief. "She's a brilliant doctor and quite lovely if I say so myself."

I rolled my eyes, dismissing her matchmaking attempts. My father had always believed in love that blossomed organically, not through the orchestrations of well-meaning relatives. But as the weeks turned into months, my aunt kept nudging me toward Eliza. "Just add her on Facebook," she urged, tapping her fingers against her phone. "What's the harm?"

Ignoring her suggestions became a habit. I found solace in the silence, the solitude of grief wrapping around me like a protective cloak. But my father's voice lingered in my mind, urging me to embrace life, to connect. Yet, reaching out felt daunting, a reminder of the loss I was trying to outrun.

As if sensing my turmoil, Eliza began sending messages. "Hi, I hope you're doing okay," she would write, words like gentle breezes brushing against my heart. I read them and admired her kindness, but I never responded. Grief can be a stubborn companion, and I was too entrenched in my sorrow to let anyone in.

Then, one afternoon, I received a message that shook me. "If you don't respond soon," Eliza typed, "I'm going to stop reaching out." The ultimatum was unexpected, a jolt that pulled me from my fog. I stared at the screen, my heart racing. Was I really prepared to let this connection slip away?

That evening, I found myself pacing my tiny apartment, the walls closing in with every step. My father's favorite chair sat empty, and suddenly, I felt the weight of his loss more acutely than ever. I imagined his laughter and advice, and I realized he would want me to embrace life—to live, love, and connect.

With trembling fingers, I finally typed back. "Hi, Eliza. I'm sorry for not responding. I've been going through a lot. Can we talk?"

Our first conversation felt like stepping into sunlight after a long winter. Eliza's voice was warm and inviting, and as we spoke, I found pieces of myself I thought I had lost forever. She shared stories of her patients, her dreams, and her passion for life. I listened, mesmerized, as laughter danced between us, fragile yet robust.

Weeks turned into months, and our connection deepened, threading itself through the fabric of my life. Eliza was unlike anyone I had ever met—compassionate, driven, and fiercely independent. We navigated our differences gracefully, respecting each other's cultural backgrounds and beliefs and discovering the beauty in our diversity.

One evening, under a canopy of stars, I found the courage to ask her the question tugging at my heart. "Eliza," I said, my voice barely above a whisper, "would you marry me?"

Her eyes sparkled like the cosmos above us, and for a moment, time stood still. "Yes," she replied, her voice trembling with emotion. "A thousand times, yes."

At that moment, I understood the essence of love—it wasn't about perfection or compatibility but about understanding, respect, and a shared willingness to grow together. Love, I realized, has the power to transform, heal, and bring out the best in us.

Yet, as our wedding day approached, shadows of doubt crept in. I worried about our families, our traditions, our differences. Would they accept us? Would we be strong enough to weather any storm that came our way?

On the eve of our wedding, my aunt held my hand tightly, her eyes shimmering with tears. "Your father would be proud," she whispered, her voice thick with emotion. "Love knows no boundaries, dear. It's the greatest force in the universe."

Her words resonated deeply, and suddenly, I felt the weight of my father's absence transform into a comforting presence. I could almost hear his laughter and his encouragement, and I knew then that love was indeed a bridge that could connect even the most disparate of souls.

The wedding blended our cultures beautifully, celebrating love that transcended differences. As Eliza walked down the aisle, her smile radiant and her spirit unyielding, I felt a surge of hope. In that moment, I realized that the heart has its own language, which speaks of love, resilience, and the courage to be vulnerable.

In the chaos of joy and laughter, I saw my father's favorite chair in the corner of the room. It was empty yet filled with his spirit, a reminder that once-ignited love never truly dies.

As we exchanged vows, I felt a profound sense of belonging. With each promise, each word spoken, I could feel the presence of love wrapping around us, binding us in a tapestry woven from our shared journey.

And then it hit me — love isn't just about finding someone to share your life with; it's about embracing the connections that come with it. It's about showing up, being vulnerable, and allowing others in, even when life is hard.

As the ceremony concluded and we entered the world as husband and wife, I realized that my father had always been right. Love had found me when I least expected it and in unexpected ways.

With Eliza by my side, I felt ready to face anything. The road ahead was uncertain, but with love as our compass, we would navigate through life's complexities together, hand in hand, heart to heart.

And as I looked into her eyes, I knew that every moment of heartache had led me to this one — the heartbeat of connection, where love triumphs above all else.

Love has no boundaries; it flourishes when we embrace our differences and allow our hearts to connect, showing us that true fulfillment lies in the courage to love and be loved.

The Wilderness Within

In the heart of the Cascade Mountains, where the trees whispered secrets to the wind and the rivers sang songs of ancient times, a group of high school seniors set out on what was meant to be a simple hiking trip. The sun shone brightly that Friday morning, casting a golden light over the rugged terrain and filling the air with the scent of pine and wildflowers. Excitement, like a bubbling spring, surged in the veins of each student as they gathered by the old wooden bus, their backpacks slung over their shoulders.

Among them was Mia, a quiet girl passionate about poetry, whose heartbeat silently followed her dreams' rhythm. She often felt like a shadow, blending into the background, but today was different. Next to her was Jason, the class president, whose confident demeanor masked a deep-seated fear of failure. He had always felt the weight of expectations from his peers and himself. Then there was Hannah, a spirited athlete whose laughter could lift anyone's spirits, yet inside, she battled the pressure of perfection. Finally, Amir, a newcomer from a different town, struggled to find his footing in this group, feeling like an outsider.

Their teacher, Mr. Thompson, clad in a well-worn flannel shirt and a wide-brimmed hat, stood at the front, exuding warmth and enthusiasm. He had a knack for making even the most mundane lessons come alive, and his excitement about this trip was palpable. "Today, we'll not only explore nature but also discover a little more about ourselves," he said, his bright eyes sparkling under the morning sun.

As they entered the forest, sunlight danced through the leaves, casting playful shadows on the ground. Laughter echoed, and the sound of crunching leaves underfoot filled the air. They felt invincible, like explorers in a vast, undiscovered world. With every step, they left behind the mundane worries of high school—grades, popularity, and the looming college decisions that clouded their futures.

However, as they ventured deeper into the wilderness, the atmosphere shifted. The trees grew taller, their trunks thick and ancient, the shadows darker and more foreboding. The path became less clear, winding unpredictably through the underbrush. The laughter faded into nervous chatter as they navigated steep inclines and rocky terrain.

After hours of hiking, they finally reached a stunning vista overlooking a valley painted with the warm hues of autumn. The beauty was breathtaking, but as they took in the view, a sudden gust of wind swept through the trees, rattling the branches like a warning. Mr. Thompson checked his watch, realizing they had lost track of time. "We should head back," he said, his voice steady yet tinged with urgency.

As they turned to retrace their steps, a thick fog rolled in, obscuring their path. Within moments, they were lost.

Panic set in. Jason's bravado faded as he realized they had no idea where they were. "What do we do now?" he asked, his voice trembling, the weight of uncertainty pressing down on him. Mia's heart pounded as she fought against the overwhelming tide of fear. Amir remained quiet, his eyes darting from one friend to another, while Hannah tried to maintain a semblance of calm, though her hands shook with anxiety. The once invincible explorers now felt the chill of uncertainty creeping in.

"Let's not panic," Mr. Thompson said, trying to instill hope. "We'll stay together, retrace our steps, and find a landmark." But as they wandered through the thickening fog, the familiar trees twisted into strangers. The shadows deepened, and doubt crept into their hearts with every wrong turn.

Hours turned into a long, desperate night. They huddled together for warmth, the cold biting at their skin while the sounds of the wilderness surrounded them—the hooting of owls, the rustling of leaves, and the distant howl of the wind. Mia pulled out her notebook, hoping to find solace in words, but the lines blurred as tears filled her eyes. "What if we never find our way back?" she whispered, her voice cracking, the weight of despair heavy.

"Don't say that," Jason replied, his voice barely above a whisper. "We will get out of here." But even he could feel the frost of fear settling in his bones.

As the night deepened, they began sharing their fears, hopes, and dreams. Amir spoke of his family and how he longed to connect with his new friends but felt like an outsider. "I thought I'd fit in, but I just feel lost," he admitted, his voice trembling with vulnerability. He revealed the struggles of moving to a new town and the challenge of leaving behind everything familiar.

Mia shared her dreams of becoming a writer and how she often felt silenced in a world that valued noise over silence. "I write to escape," she confessed, "but what do I do when I can't find my way out?" Her words flowed like a river, revealing her longing to be heard and understood.

Hannah, usually the group's light, revealed her fear of not living up to expectations, her laughter a mask for inner turmoil. "I push myself to be perfect, but I'm scared of failing," she admitted, biting her lip. Her fear was palpable, a shadow lurking behind her cheerful facade.

Jason finally opened up about his fear of not being good enough, a suffocating pressure to lead. "I thought I had to be strong for everyone, but I'm just as scared as you all are," he admitted, tears glistening in his eyes. The facade he had maintained began to crack, revealing the vulnerability beneath.

As they bared their souls to one another, a bond formed stronger than they had ever experienced. They realized they were not just classmates but a family forged in the wilderness. In that dark night, they found solace in shared experiences, their fears intertwining like the roots of the trees surrounding them. In this shared vulnerability, they found strength, a realization that would forever change their perspective on life and relationships.

As dawn broke, the fog lifted, revealing a new clarity. The sun poured over the mountains, illuminating the path ahead. But with the light came a realization—the wilderness wasn't just outside; it was within them. Each had faced their own personal wilderness, a battle of fears and doubts that could either bind or tear them apart. The 'wilderness within' was the untamed, unexplored territory of their own emotions and fears, a landscape they had to navigate to find their true selves and form meaningful connections.

With newfound resolve, they stood together, united in their vulnerability. "We can't do this alone," Mia said, her voice steady now, a spark igniting within her. "We have to support each other." The realization washed over them like the morning sunlight filtering through the trees, brightening their spirits.

Mr. Thompson smiled, pride swelling in his chest. "That's right. The wilderness tests our strength but can also show us the way. If we face our fears together, we can find a path." He looked at each of them, his eyes filled with compassion and understanding. Their journey was not merely about finding their way back but about discovering the strength they held within.

They began to move forward, one step at a time, hand in hand. The trees seemed to part, and the trail became clearer. As they walked, they shared encouragement, each word a thread weaving them closer together. The forest, once intimidating, started to feel like a sanctuary, a place where they could shed their fears and embrace their true selves.

After an eternity, they finally stumbled upon a familiar stream, its gentle flow a beacon of hope. "We're close!" Hannah shouted, joy spilling from her heart. The sound of rushing water filled them with a renewed sense of purpose. They followed the water, laughter mingling with tears of relief. The wilderness, once daunting, transformed into a backdrop of unity and strength, each step bringing them closer to safety.

As they emerged from the forest, the sun hung low in the sky, casting a warm glow. They had faced their fears, discovered their strengths, and found their way back—not just to the trailhead but to one another. Each of them carried a piece of the wilderness, a testament to their shared journey.

As they approached the bus, their hearts swelled with a sense of accomplishment. They were no longer just classmates but a family forged in the wilderness. Mr. Thompson gathered them for a moment of reflection. "What did we learn?" he asked, his eyes glistening with pride.

Jason stepped forward, his voice steady. "We learned that it's okay to be scared but not to be alone in that fear. We need each other." His words resonated with the group, a reminder of the bond they had formed in the face of adversity.

Mia added, "Our dreams don't have to be silenced. They can guide us, even in the darkest times." She felt lighter as if the weight she had carried for so long had been lifted.

Hannah smiled, wiping a tear from her cheek. "Perfection isn't the goal. It's about being real and supporting one another." The relief in her voice was palpable, a testament to the growth she had experienced during their ordeal.

Feeling like he finally belonged, Amir said, "We are stronger together. This experience showed me I'm not alone in my struggles." His words were filled with gratitude, a realization that had blossomed amidst the chaos.

As they boarded the bus, the sun dipped below the horizon, painting the sky in hues of orange and purple. The wilderness had tested them, but it also revealed the profound strength of their hearts. At that moment, they understood that the true wilderness was not the forest surrounding them but the fears and doubts that often lurked within. And just as they had found their way through the physical wilderness, they had also begun to navigate the wilderness within, armed with compassion, friendship, and the knowledge that together, they could face anything.

As the bus rolled away, the mountains stood tall behind them, but their journey would remain forever etched in their hearts—a reminder that the path to finding oneself sometimes begins in the most unexpected places. They looked out at the fading landscape, each lost in their thoughts, yet connected by a shared experience that transcended words.

The wilderness within them had been awakened, a call to embrace their fears, dreams, and vulnerabilities. They knew that life would continue to present challenges, moments that might feel insurmountable, but they also understood that they had each other. In the days that followed, whenever they faced difficulties, they would remember the lessons learned in the Cascade Mountains.

As the bus pulled into the school parking lot, the students filed out, their hearts light and their spirits high. The air was crisp, the scent of autumn leaves lingering as they walked toward the entrance. Each of them felt a sense of purpose, a newfound strength from recognizing their vulnerabilities and understanding the power of unity.

In the following weeks, they carried the lessons of the wilderness into their daily lives. Mia began sharing her poetry at school, resonating with her peers. She discovered that her voice mattered and that her dreams were worth pursuing. Jason took on leadership roles with renewed humility, learning that true strength came from collaboration, not just individual achievement.

Embracing her imperfections, Hannah became a mentor to younger students, helping them navigate their fears and insecurities. She learned that vulnerability was not a weakness but a bridge to connection. Amir found a group of friends who accepted him for who he was, and he blossomed, his laughter now a constant presence among them.

As the seasons changed, the group continued to meet, sharing their experiences, fears, and dreams. They formed a club dedicated to exploring the outdoors, using their love for nature to connect, support, and inspire one another. They organized hikes, camping trips, and community service projects, each adventure further solidifying their bond.

One crisp winter evening, they gathered around a fire pit in someone's backyard, the crackling flames illuminating their faces. Wrapped in blankets, they reflected on their journey, laughter mingling with the warmth of the fire. The stars twinkled above them, a reminder of the vast universe that awaited them.

"Mia, share one of your poems," Jason encouraged, a smile spreading across his face. The group turned their attention to her, eager to hear the words that had once felt so heavy on her heart.

Mia opened her notebook with a deep breath, her fingers trembling slightly. "This one is about our journey through the wilderness," she began, her voice steadying as she read:

"In the heart of the trees, I found my voice,
Amidst the shadows, I made my choice.
To face the fears that danced in the night,
To turn my doubts into wings that take flight".

As she read, her confidence grew, and the words flowed like a river, capturing the essence of their shared experience. The group listened intently, their hearts swelling with pride for her courage.

When she finished, a silence enveloped them, filled with the weight of her words. Then, one by one, they applauded, their hearts echoing with appreciation. Mia's eyes glistened with tears, but this time, they were tears of joy, of belonging.

"Thank you for sharing that," Amir said, his voice genuine. "It's a reminder of how far we've come."

As the night deepened, they shared more stories, each one a testament to their growth. They spoke of dreams, aspirations, and the challenges they faced. It was a celebration of resilience, a recognition of the strength found in vulnerability.

As the fire crackled, Jason stood up, raising his cup in a toast. "To us, our journey, and the wilderness within!" The group echoed his sentiment, their voices lifting into the night sky. They understood that life would continue to present challenges but were no longer afraid. They had each other, a family forged in the wilderness.

In that moment, they realized that the true wilderness was the physical challenges they faced and the emotional landscapes they navigated together. They had emerged stronger, more compassionate, and more connected than ever before.

As the stars twinkled overhead, they made a pact to always support one another, to face the wilderness together, no matter what life threw their way. They had learned that in the depths of fear and uncertainty, they could find strength in their connections and the courage to embrace their true selves.

The wilderness within them had become a source of inspiration, a reminder that even in the darkest times, they could find their way back to the light. This journey would continue long after the hiking trip, one that would shape their futures and guide them through the storms of life.

As they extinguished the fire and headed home, they carried the warmth of their friendship in their hearts, a beacon of hope illuminating the path ahead. They were no longer just high school seniors but adventurers, dreamers, and a family bound by the wilderness they had faced together.

As they looked toward the horizon, they knew that the wilderness within would always guide them, leading them to new adventures, deeper connections, and the courage to embrace the unknown. They were no longer lost in the vast landscape of life; they had found their way together.

Lighthouse

The town of Eldermere lay nestled between rugged cliffs and the restless sea, a place where stories were whispered like prayers and secrets clung to the salty air. The lighthouse stood tall at the edge of the precipice, its beam cutting through the mist like a guardian watching over the small community. To the outside world, Eldermere appeared quaint and idyllic, but beneath its surface simmered a myriad of untold tales.

Evelyn Graves, a journalist known for her relentless pursuit of the truth, arrived on a cold autumn evening, her breath visible in the sharp air. Her heart was heavy with the burden of her past; she had lost her mother to a tragic accident that had spiraled into a scandal, ripping apart her family and leaving her with a reputation tarnished by whispers of incompetence. Determined to reclaim her life, she sought solace in stories, believing that every truth uncovered could heal a wound.

As she drove down the narrow, winding roads, the lighthouse came into view, its light sweeping across the darkening sky. "Keep your eyes on the light," her mother used to say, a guiding principle that had always resonated with Evelyn. Now, it felt like a call to action, a beacon of hope in the darkness, a symbol of the truth she sought to uncover.

Evelyn quickly immersed herself in the town's rhythms, meeting the locals at the café where the scent of baked bread mingled with rich coffee. She listened intently to their conversations, her notepad always at hand, jotting down fragments of life—an elderly man's lament over the sea's changing tides, a mother's pride in her daughter's accomplishments. Yet, as she delved deeper, a pattern emerged: the smiles often masked a deeper sorrow.

"People here are good at hiding their truths," a waitress named Sarah confided one afternoon, her eyes darting to the window as if expecting someone to overhear. "But the lighthouse? It knows. It shines on everyone's secrets."

Intrigued, Evelyn pressed for more, and Sarah hesitated before revealing a whisper of a scandal involving the town's mayor and a missing girl from years past. The story had been buried, but the pain lingered like a ghost haunting the shoreline. Evelyn felt a familiar fire igniting within her—a need to uncover the truth, not just for herself but for the sake of those who had suffered.

As the days turned into weeks, Evelyn found herself entangled in the lives of Eldermere's residents. She interviewed the mayor, a charismatic man who spoke eloquently about progress, yet his eyes betrayed a flicker of something darker when the subject of the missing girl arose. She spoke with the girl's mother, a woman whose heart had withered under the weight of grief, and learned of the lies that had shielded the town from its past. The girl's disappearance had left a void in the community, a wound that refused to heal.

Every conversation peeled back layers of deceit, revealing a tapestry woven with betrayal, guilt, and fear. Evelyn felt the weight of her own unresolved grief pressing against her chest, echoing the pain of those she sought to help. The truth was a heavy burden she carried, a burden that could either heal or destroy.

One stormy evening, as rain lashed against the windows of her rented cabin, Evelyn received an anonymous note slipped under her door. "Leave it alone," it read. "Some truths are better left buried."

Her heart raced, a mix of fear and determination surging within her. The lighthouse's beam flickered through the storm, a reminder that the light of truth, no matter how dimmed, could still guide her home.

The next morning, Evelyn, her hands trembling but her voice steady, confronted the mayor at a town meeting. "What happened to the girl?" she demanded, her words cutting through the air like a knife. Gasps filled the room, and the mayor's face paled as the townsfolk shifted uncomfortably in their seats. Her courage was a beacon of hope in the storm of deceit.

"Enough!" he shouted, his voice cracking. "You don't understand what you're doing. This town has suffered enough."

Evelyn felt the heat of the moment, the eyes of the townspeople boring into her. "But at what cost? The truth is like a lighthouse; it shows us the way, even in the darkest of times."

As she spoke, she caught sight of Sarah in the back of the room, tears streaming down her face. The truth was not just about the girl; it was about the collective pain of Eldermere, the guilt that had festered beneath the surface. Evelyn realized that to uncover the truth was to illuminate the darkness within them all.

That night, as a fierce storm raged, Evelyn stood at the base of the lighthouse, its beam slicing through the tempest. She felt an overwhelming urge to climb to the top, to stand where the light shone brightest. As she ascended the narrow spiral staircase, her heart raced not just with fear, but with hope.

Reaching the top, she looked out over the churning sea, the waves crashing violently against the rocks below. In that stark moment, she understood that the truth was not merely a destination; it was a journey filled with pain and redemption. As she gazed into the abyss, her mother's voice echoed in her mind. "Keep your eyes on the light, Evelyn."

Suddenly, her phone buzzed with a text from Sarah: "Meet me by the lighthouse. I have something to show you." Fear gripped her, but she knew she had to go.

Outside, the wind howled like a banshee as Evelyn met Sarah, who was drenched but resolute. "I found something," she said breathlessly, handing over a weathered journal. "It belonged to the girl. She wrote about the mayor… about the night she disappeared."

Evelyn's heart raced as she flipped through the pages, each word a testament to the girl's vibrant spirit. The final entry sent chills down her spine: "I'm scared. I know something I shouldn't. I just want to be safe." The revelation was a shock, but it was also a key to unlocking the truth.

With the journal in hand, Evelyn knew what she had to do. The truth had to be shared, not just for the girl, but for every soul in Eldermere who had been silenced by fear.

In the following days, Evelyn published her story, detailing the mayor's lies and the community's complicity. The truth shattered the facade of Eldermere, but as the scandal unfolded, something remarkable happened. The townsfolk began to gather, sharing their own stories of pain and loss, finding solace in their shared truths.

As the dust settled, Evelyn stood at the lighthouse once more, watching the townspeople come together, embracing their pasts and healing their wounds. She felt the warmth of the light surrounding her, a beacon of hope in a world that often seemed dark.

Months later, as spring breathed new life into Eldermere, Evelyn prepared to leave. Her heart was lighter; she had not only uncovered the truth but had also helped a community rediscover its strength. As she packed her belongings, she found herself drawn once more to the lighthouse, the light shining brightly against the azure sky.

Standing at the edge of the cliff, she whispered a silent prayer, thanking her mother for the guiding words that had led her to this moment. In the distance, she could see children playing, laughter echoing against the backdrop of crashing waves—a sound that spoke of hope and renewal.

Evelyn turned to leave but paused, feeling the weight of her journey settle around her shoulders. The lighthouse had taught her that while the truth could be painful, it was also a powerful force for good. It illuminated the darkness, allowing love, forgiveness, and healing to flourish.

With a final glance back, she smiled, knowing that the light would continue to shine, guiding the people of Eldermere toward a brighter tomorrow.

In a world often cloaked in shadows, the lighthouse of truth would remain a steadfast reminder that courage, compassion, and honesty could conquer even the most turbulent seas.

The Storm

The sun hung low in the sky, casting a golden hue over the small beach town of Seaview. Soft waves lapped at the shore, whispering secrets to the warm sand. The air was rich with the scent of salt and adventure, the kind of place where worries seemed to dissolve into the horizon. This vacation was a long-awaited escape from the daily lives of the Thompson family—a chance to reconnect, breathe, and laugh. The Thompsons, filled with joy and anticipation, were ready to embrace this much-needed break.

Mark Thompson, a middle-aged man with salt-and-pepper hair, stood by the shore, his feet buried in the warm sand. He watched his two children, Emma and Jacob, splash in the water while his wife, Sarah, unpacked their beach towels and snacks. Mark felt a sense of peace wash over him, a rare feeling these days. The demands of his job as an architect had taken a toll, leaving him exhausted and disconnected from his family.

"Dad! Look!" Emma called, her laughter ringing like music. She was twelve, with bright blue eyes that sparkled with mischief. She waved a conch shell in her hand, her face excitedly lit.

Mark smiled, his heart swelling with affection. "That's beautiful, Em! Bring it here!"

Jacob, the younger brother at eight, joined in the excitement, his energy boundless. He dashed through the shallow waters, his tiny legs pumping with determination. The family was together, and for a moment, everything felt right.

The sky transformed into a canvas of pinks and oranges as the sun dipped lower. Sarah joined them, her lengthy hair blowing in the gentle breeze. "Let's take a family photo!" she suggested, pulling out her phone. They gathered close, arms around each other, hearts full of hope. But shadows lingered beneath the laughter—unspoken words and unresolved tensions lurking like dark clouds on the horizon.

The next day dawned bright and clear, but the forecast held an ominous warning. A storm was brewing far out at sea, but the Thompsons were blissfully unaware for now. They spent the day exploring tide pools and chasing seagulls, their bond momentarily restored.

As evening approached, the sky began to darken. Mark felt an uneasy shift in the air; a tension mirrored their unspoken issues. He had been working late, missing family dinners, and the weight of his absence hung heavily in the air. Emma had grown distant, her laughter replaced with silence. Jacob, too young to fully grasp the tension, sensed the change but couldn't articulate it.

"Let's head back early," Mark suggested, glancing at the gathering clouds. "I think we should pack up for the night."

"Aw, Dad! Just a little longer?" Jacob pleaded, his eyes wide with hope.

"Please, Mark," Sarah added gently. "Can't we just enjoy this moment?"

Mark hesitated, torn between his fatherly instincts and the growing concern in his chest. The clouds darkened, swirling ominously, mirroring the storm brewing within him. He decided to leave, but his heart was heavy with the weight of his decisions and their consequences.

The wind picked up as they returned to their rental house, howling like a restless spirit. Inside, they huddled together, trying to distract themselves with board games and laughter. But as the storm began to rage outside, so did the tension inside.

The wind howled, rattling the windows, and rain pelted the roof like a thousand tiny drummers. Emma retreated to her room, the sound of her door slamming echoing through the hallway. Mark felt a pang of regret but pushed it aside, focusing instead on the storm outside.

"Mark, can you go talk to her?" Sarah asked softly; concern etched on her face. "She needs you."

He nodded, but doubt crept in as he made his way to Emma's room. What could he say? What if she didn't want to talk? He knocked gently, and when no answer came, he opened the door.

Emma sat on her bed, the glow of her phone illuminating her face. "Go away, Dad," she muttered, her voice barely a whisper.

"Can we talk?" Mark ventured, stepping inside. He felt the weight of his unspoken words pressing down on him.

"About what? How you never have time for me?" She looked up, her eyes brimming with unshed tears. "Or how you decided we should leave the beach when I was having fun?"

"Emma..." Mark began, but the words faltered as he saw the hurt in her eyes. "I'm sorry. I thought..."

"You thought what? That I wouldn't care? That you could ignore me, and everything would be okay?" Her voice rose, filled with the pain of neglect. Her emotional outburst was a stark reminder of the depth of her hurt. "I needed you, Dad."

Mark felt a wave of guilt wash over him. "I'm here now. I want to be here. I'm sorry for missing things. I thought this vacation would help us reconnect."

"Maybe it's too late," Emma whispered, turning away.

The storm outside intensified, thunder rumbling like a warning. Mark felt a storm brewing within him, a mix of frustration and sorrow. "Please, Em. I love you. I'm trying..."

But Emma was already lost in her thoughts, and the gap between them widened. He left the room, feeling helpless, and returned to the living room, where Sarah waited. Her expression was a mixture of concern and disappointment.

As the night wore on, the storm outside raged in tandem with the turmoil inside. Rain lashed against the windows, and the wind howled like a beast. The family huddled together, but the distance between them felt insurmountable.

Sensing the tension, Jacob clutched his toy dinosaur tightly. "Are we going to be okay?" he asked, his voice trembling. His innocent question cut through the tension, a stark reminder of the impact of their conflicts on the children. It was a wake-up call for Mark and Sarah, a realization that their issues were not just theirs to bear, but also their children's.

"We're fine, buddy," Mark replied, but he wasn't convinced. The truth was, they were far from fine. The storm had become a mirror, reflecting their inner struggles and unresolved conflicts.

Suddenly, a loud crack of thunder shook the house, followed by a power outage that plunged them into darkness. For a moment, panic surged through Mark. He fumbled for his phone, the glow illuminating their faces.

"Stay close, everyone," he said, sounding brave. But deep down, he felt the weight of their unresolved issues pressing down like the storm outside.

In the darkness, Sarah reached for Mark's hand, her touch grounding him. "We need to talk," she whispered, her voice steady despite the chaos around them.

"I know," he said, the fear in his heart palpable. "But can we do it later? Right now, I need to be here for the kids."

"Mark, they need to see us working through this, too. They're hurting, and we can't ignore it," she urged her voice a soothing balm against the storm's fury.

Mark took a deep breath, feeling the walls of his heart begin to crack. "You're right. I've been so focused on work that I forgot what matters."

Just then, a loud crash echoed outside, and Jacob let out a small whimper. Mark rushed to him, kneeling to meet his son's frightened gaze. "It's okay, buddy. We're together, and we'll get through this."

"But what if the storm gets worse?" Jacob's voice trembled, his innocence piercing through the chaos.

Mark's heart ached. "We'll be safe, I promise. And we'll see how beautiful the beach is again when it's over."

But Emma's words echoed in his mind, a reminder of the rift between them. He looked up at Sarah, who nodded, urging him silently to take this moment to heal.

"Emma," he called gently, moving toward her room. "Can we talk now?"

Silence answered him, but he wasn't willing to give up. He opened the door, stepping into the darkness. "I know you're upset and have every right to be. I've let you down, and I'm so sorry."

The shadows shifted, and he could make out Emma's silhouette. "It doesn't matter," she replied, her tone softer now. "You're always busy, and I feel like I'm not important."

"You are important, more than you know," he whispered, his voice thick with emotion. "I've been so caught up in work that I lost sight of what matters. I've missed so much of your life and want to change that. Can you forgive me?"

Emma turned to face him, her expression conflicted. "I want to, but it's hard, Dad."

"I know," he replied, stepping closer. "But I promise to do better. I want to be there for you—truly there. Can we start over?"

The storm outside peaked at that moment, a crescendo of wind and rain. But inside, a different kind of storm was settling, one of reconciliation and love. Emma looked up, her eyes glistening with tears. "Okay, Dad. I'll try."

Mark pulled her into a hug, the warmth of their embrace melting away the cold distance that had grown between them. "I love you, Emma. More than I can say."

Sarah and Jacob joined them as they stood there, creating a circle of love and support. The storm outside continued to rage, but within the walls of their home, a new storm was brewing—one of hope, healing, and the promise of a better future.

As dawn broke, the storm finally began to subside. The sky transformed from angry gray to a soft, hopeful blue. Mark awoke to the sound of laughter echoing through the house. The power had returned, illuminating their world once more.

He stepped outside, where the beach lay glistening and renewed, washed clean by the storm. The air was fresh, filled with the scent of possibility. Emma and Jacob raced toward the water, their laughter ringing like bells.

Mark turned to Sarah, who stood beside him, her eyes reflecting the morning light. "We made it," he said, a smile breaking across his face.

"Together," she replied, her voice filled with warmth. "We faced the storm and came out stronger."

Mark felt a profound gratitude as they watched their children play. The storm forced them to confront their fears, pain, and love. It had shown them the power of vulnerability and the importance of connection.

At that moment, a wave of realization washed over him. Life was not just about sunny days but about weathering the storms together. Love was not just a word; it was an action, a commitment to show up even when the skies were dark.

As the sun rose higher, illuminating the beach, Mark took a deep breath, feeling lighter than he had in years. "Let's make a promise," he said to Sarah, his voice steady. "Always face the storms together, no matter how fierce they may be."

She nodded, her eyes shining with love. "Always."

And as the waves crashed against the shore, they knew that no matter what storms lay ahead, they would face them together, united in love and faith. The storm had passed, but the lessons learned would last a lifetime.

In the distance, the horizon beckoned, full of new adventures and the promise of brighter days. The Thompson family stood together, ready to embrace whatever came next, hand in hand, heart to heart, forever changed by the storm that had brought them back to each other.

Unspoken Words

In the heart of Manhattan, where the skyline pierces the sky like a promise yet unfulfilled, I found myself standing before the weathered brownstone of my childhood—a monument to cherished and profoundly painful memories. The air was thick with nostalgia, sweet like cotton candy but heavy like a leaden weight on my chest. I had come here to confront a past that felt like a ghost haunting me, lingering long after my mother had left this world in a sudden, heart-wrenching departure. Estranged for years, we had been two ships passing in the night, each lost in our own storms.

As I pushed open the creaky attic door, the musty scent of dust and forgotten dreams enveloped me. It was a place I had avoided for so long, a room filled with shadows and echoes of a childhood that had felt incomplete. My heart raced as I stepped inside, the dim light illuminating boxes piled high, each a treasure trove of memories I had long buried. I felt a mix of dread and curiosity—would I find remnants of happiness or merely the debris of a broken relationship? The emotional turmoil I was experiencing was palpable, making the audience empathize with my journey.

It was there, buried under a tattered quilt and an old baseball glove, that I discovered a weathered box. My fingers trembled as I brushed off the dust, revealing a simple latch. Something about it felt heavy, like it contained not just letters but the weight of my mother's silence, the unspoken words that had lingered between us like a chasm. With a deep breath, I opened the box, the creak of the lid sounding almost like a sigh of relief.

Inside, I found a stack of letters, each carefully sealed and addressed to me. My mother's elegant handwriting sent a jolt through me—how could the same hand that had once scolded me for every misstep now hold the key to our fractured past? I felt a swell of emotions: excitement, anger, and an overwhelming sense of loss. I hesitated, caught between the urge to close the box and the desperate need to understand.

The first letter was dated years ago before our relationship had turned cold. As I unfolded it, the familiar scent of her perfume wafted up, and I was transported back to a time when love felt unconditional. "My dearest," it began, and with those words, I was drawn into her world. She spoke of her dreams, her fears, and the moments that had strained our bond. "I'm sorry," she wrote, "for the choices I made that pushed you away." Anger flared within me, a wildfire ignited by the pain of abandonment. How could she have left me in the dark?

With every letter I opened, I felt the walls of my heart begin to crack. My mother's words painted a vivid picture of a woman struggling against the tide of her own disappointments. In one letter, she recounted the night she had missed my high school graduation, her voice trembling as she admitted, 'I was scared of failing you.' I could feel the echoes of that night, the resentment boiling within me, but as I read on, I was confronted with something unexpected: her vulnerability. She had been just as lost as I felt, grappling with her own identity and choices that had spiraled beyond her control. This vulnerability in her words evoked a sense of compassion in the audience, making them feel for both the protagonist and the mother.

I could see her—my mother, a young woman full of ambition, a dreamer who had sacrificed so much. With each revelation, the anger I clung to began to shift, transforming into an understanding that felt liberating and terrifying. "I wanted to be the mother you deserved," she wrote in another letter, "but I was too busy trying to be perfect." My heart ached as I realized how deeply intertwined our pain had become, bound by the threads of unmet expectations and unhealed wounds.

But the emotions were a double-edged sword. Just when I thought I could forgive my mother, the following letter would unleash a torrent of frustration. "There were nights I lay awake, wishing I could turn back time," she confessed, and I found myself screaming silently, wishing she could have just been there for me. How could she have let fear dictate her choices? How could she have walked away when I needed her most?

Then came the final letter. It lay at the bottom of the box, a simple sheet of paper that felt heavier than the rest. As I unfolded it, my hands shook. 'Please forgive me,' it read. A single line, but it struck me like a lightning bolt. The weight of this final plea for forgiveness was immense, making the audience feel the gravity of the situation. Forgiveness. It felt impossible, a word laden with expectations I wasn't sure I could meet. Anger surged within me, clashing with the understanding I had begun to cultivate. How could I forgive her when I felt so profoundly wronged?

But in that moment of turmoil, a realization flickered within me. Forgiveness didn't mean absolving her mistakes; it meant freeing myself from the shackles of resentment that had bound me for far too long. I had spent years feeling like a victim of her choices, but what if I could rewrite that narrative? What if I could embrace love over pain, understanding over anger? This was the moment I truly understood the transformative power of forgiveness and the possibility of healing from past pain.

As I stood in that dim attic, surrounded by shadows and echoes, the weight on my chest began to lift. I imagined my mother, a young woman filled with dreams, wrestling with her own insecurities. I envisioned her fears and the nights she spent drowning in regret. At that moment, I understood that she had loved me fiercely, even if her love had been imperfect.

With each tear that fell, I felt my heart begin to mend. I folded the letters back into the box, feeling like closure and a new beginning. I wasn't just sealing away the past; I was choosing to let go of the hurt and embrace the possibility of healing. As I stepped out of the attic, sunlight poured in, illuminating the darkness that had clung to me for so long. This was the beginning of my journey towards forgiveness and healing.

I walked away from that brownstone, the weight of unresolved anger lifting. I had faced the ghosts of my past and found the courage to forgive—not just my mother but myself. Life was a beautiful, messy journey, and perhaps it was time to write my own story, filled with love, understanding, and the promise of new beginnings. In the end, forgiveness was not about forgetting but choosing to love, even when the past was painful. And with that, I stepped into the light, ready to embrace the future.

A Place to Call Home

The late afternoon sun filtered through dusty lace curtains, casting soft patterns on the worn wooden floor of the tiny house at the end of San Isidro. The air held a faint scent of Sampaguita (Arabian Jasmin) and something more profound, a hint of memories long buried. Maria stood at the threshold, her heart pounding as she stared at the doorway that led into the life she had once known but had almost forgotten. The house, with its creaking floors and faded walls, seemed to echo the untold stories of the family that had once thrived within its walls.

"Home," she whispered, the word tasting foreign on her tongue. It had been years since she had last stepped inside this house, filled with echoes of childhood laughter and the bittersweet remnants of her grandmother's love. But now, it felt like a ghost of its former self, worn down by time and neglect, much like the relationship between Maria and the woman she had once adored. The once vibrant walls now bore the marks of neglect, mirroring the distance that had grown between them.

Maria was twenty-eight, with dreams that had crumbled like the leaves outside in the crisp autumn air. She had lost her job at a local marketing firm due to sudden downsizing, leaving her adrift and confused. The small apartment Maria had rented, once a sanctuary, became a prison without the means to pay for it. Now, with nowhere else to turn, she found herself back at her grandmother Lola Rosa's doorstep, a place she had vowed never to return to after their last heated argument.

Taking a deep breath, she stepped inside, the floor creaking underfoot as if protesting the weight of her return. Lola Rosa sat in a faded armchair, wrapped in a hand-knit blanket, her frail form contrasting with the vibrant woman Maria had once known. The room was filled with photographs—smiling faces frozen in time, each telling stories of family gatherings and the festive celebrations that defined their lives. But they also held the shadows of unspoken words and unresolved pain.

"Maria," Lola Rosa said, her voice a soft, cracked whisper. The surprise in her eyes quickly morphed into a veil of vulnerability.

"Hi, Lola," Maria replied, forcing a smile that felt more like a mask than a greeting. She crossed the room, the weight of unvoiced accusations heavy between them. "I didn't know where else to go."

Lola Rosa nodded slowly as if contemplating the implications of those words. "You're welcome to stay as long as you need," she replied, her tone devoid of the warmth that once enveloped Maria like a comforting embrace.

As the days turned into weeks, Maria settled into a strange routine. The house was quiet, a solemn witness to the struggles of two women who had once shared a bond stronger than blood. Maria took on the role of caregiver, preparing meals and managing the household, while Lola Rosa battled her illness, each day a reminder of the time slipping away. During the day, the silence was unbearable, filled only by the ticking clock and the rustling of leaves outside. At night, the memories flooded back, tainted with regret.

One evening, while washing the dishes, Maria glanced out the window. The sunset's brilliant oranges and pinks painted the sky, but all she could feel was the heaviness in her chest. She felt the weight of her past—the arguments, the missed family gatherings, and the final estrangement that had driven them apart.

"Lola," she called, her voice breaking the stillness, filled with a longing that echoed through the house. "Can we talk?"

Lola Rosa appeared at the doorway, her eyes reflecting years of wisdom and pain. "About what, anak?" she asked, using the affectionate term for "child."

"About us. About everything that happened." Maria leaned against the sink, the water running over her hands as if it could wash away the regrets she couldn't articulate.

Lola Rosa hesitated, the silence stretching between them like an untraversable chasm. "I've been waiting for you to ask," she finally said, her voice steady.

Maria turned to face her grandmother fully, the weight of the moment pressing down on her. "I was angry, Lola. I thought you didn't care about me. When Papa left, I felt like you abandoned me too."

Lola Rosa's face softened, her eyes glistening with unshed tears. "I was grieving too, Maria. I thought I was protecting you from my pain. But in doing so, I pushed you away when I only wanted to keep you close."

The honesty of those words washed over Maria like a balm. "I didn't realize how much I needed you," she confessed, her voice filled with relief as years of hurt poured out. "I was so caught up in my hurt that I couldn't see yours. I'm so sorry for everything."

A silence enveloped them, filled with the weight of unspoken truths. Lola Rosa moved closer, her frail hand reaching to touch Maria's. "We both made mistakes, but we can still find our way back to each other. It's never too late for forgiveness." These words, heavy with the weight of their shared history, held the promise of a new beginning, a chance for healing and reconciliation.

Over the next few weeks, they shared stories of happier times and the dreams that once filled their hearts. Maria learned of her grandmother's struggles, the loneliness that accompanied her husband's death, and the guilt she felt over her inability to mend their fractured family. Each story was a stitch in the fabric of their relationship, slowly weaving them back together.

One evening, as they sat on the porch watching the twilight settle over the world, Lola Rosa turned to Maria with a severe expression. "There's something I need to tell you," she began, her voice trembling slightly. "The doctors say I don't have much time left."

Maria's heart dropped, panic rising within her. "No, Lola! We can fight this! There must be something…"

Lola Rosa shook her head gently, a sad smile gracing her lips. "Sometimes, fighting isn't what we need. Sometimes, it's about acceptance and making peace with the time we have left."

At that moment, the gravity of their situation settled heavily around them. They were on borrowed time, and every moment counted. Maria felt a wave of desperation wash over her. "I don't want to lose you again," she cried, tears streaming down her face. "You're all I have left!"

Lola Rosa wrapped her arms around Maria, pulling her close. "You're stronger than you know, my dear. You have a life ahead of you. Promise me you'll live it fully, without fear of the past."

Days turned into a blur of laughter and tears as they grew closer. Maria found herself sharing her dreams—of starting her own business, of traveling, of finding love. Lola Rosa listened intently, offering advice wrapped in stories of her youth.

Then, one rainy evening, Lola Rosa suddenly grew quiet as they sat by the fireplace with cups of chocolate. Maria looked over, concerned. "What is it, Lola?"

"I want to show you something," Lola Rosa said, her voice firm yet gentle. She pulled out an old, worn box from the shelf, dust motes dancing in the air as she opened it. Inside were letters, photographs, and a small quilt, meticulously stitched with care.

"This," Lola Rosa said, holding up the quilt, "was made for you. It's a piece of my heart, woven into every thread. I want you to have it."

Maria's breath caught in her throat as she took the quilt, feeling the love and warmth in the fabric. "I can't take this, Lola. It's too precious."

Lola Rosa smiled, the light in her eyes flickering like the dying embers of a fire. "You need it more than I do. It's a reminder that home is not a place but a feeling. You will carry it with you, no matter where life takes you."

With tears streaming down her face, Maria clutched the quilt to her chest. "Thank you, Lola. I promise I will cherish it."

As Lola Rosa's strength waned in the following weeks, Maria became her anchor. They shared quiet moments filled with laughter, stories, and deep conversations about faith and hope. Lola Rosa spoke of her belief in God's plan, and Maria found solace in those words, even as she faced the reality of loss.

One morning, as the first light of dawn crept through the curtains, Maria found Lola Rosa sitting by the window, gazing out at the world with a serene acceptance. "Good morning, Lola," she whispered, joining her by the window.

Lola Rosa turned to her, her smile radiant. "This world is a beautiful place. Full of love and memories. I am so proud of you, Maria."

They shared a moment of silence, the weight of unspoken words lingering in the air. Then, Lola Rosa took Maria's hand in hers. "Promise me that you will live fully. Don't let fear hold you back. Trust in God and yourself."

"I promise, Lola," Maria replied, her heart breaking with the realization of what would come.

That night, as storm clouds gathered and rain began to fall, Lola Rosa slipped away peacefully, her hand still clasped in Maria's. The room was filled with an overwhelming sense of love, a bittersweet farewell that echoed with the promise of new beginnings.

In the days that followed, Maria found herself wandering through the quiet house, now filled with memories of both joy and sorrow. She felt the weight of her grandmother's love surrounding her, urging her to take the following steps. The quilt draped over her bed was a constant reminder of the bond they had shared.

One afternoon, as she stepped outside into the crisp air, Maria felt a surge of determination. She could hear Lola Rosa's voice in her heart, encouraging her to embrace life and chase her dreams fearlessly. The world was vast, waiting for her to explore it.

With each passing day, Maria began to rebuild her life. She started her own business, pouring her heart into something that felt like home. She traveled to places she had only dreamed of, finding joy in life's little things. She volunteered at a local shelter, helping lost others, just as she once had been.

And through it all, the quilt remained with her, a tangible reminder of love, forgiveness, and the unbreakable bond between grandmother and granddaughter.

As the seasons changed, Maria stood on a hill overlooking the town, the sun setting in a blaze of colors. She breathed in deeply, feeling a sense of peace wash over her.

"Thank you, Lola," she whispered to the wind, knowing that love transcended time and space. "I promise to live bravely."

At that moment, she understood that home was not just a place but a feeling carried within her. And no matter where life took her, she always had a piece of her grandmother's heart.

Fading Footsteps

The rain fell against the cobblestones of St. Petersburg, a gentle symphony that matched the melancholy of my heart. I stood outside the old theater, its once-grand façade now a whisper of faded glory, reflecting my struggles. I was Katya, a ballerina whose dreams had crumbled with a single misstep—a twist of my ankle during rehearsal that had left me physically and emotionally shattered.

The theater's empty halls echoed memories of my past, where every pirouette and arabesque had once felt like a gust of wind beneath my wings. Now, I was a ghost in that same space, lingering in the shadows of what could have been. I watched my friends glide across the stage, their bodies moving fluidly, while I sat alone in the back, nursing a cup of bitter tea.

"Katya, are you coming to join us?" Anya's voice called out, laced with concern. I shook my head, unable to muster the energy to pretend.

Days turned into weeks, and I sank deeper into solitude. The laughter of others felt like a distant melody I could no longer hear. I became a spectator in my own life, retreating into a silence that felt safer than confronting my shattered dreams.

Then, one rainy afternoon, he entered my world.

He was tall, with a commanding presence, his eyes a deep shade of blue that seemed to hold a universe of sorrows. I noticed him immediately as he walked into the café, his military jacket slightly worn, suggesting a life on the edge. He chose a corner table alone, and I felt an inexplicable pull toward him.

"Mind if I join you?" he asked, his voice deep and steady, breaking through the fog of my isolation.

"Not at all," I replied, surprised by my willingness to engage.

"I'm Alex," he introduced himself, a hint of a smile playing on his lips, though it didn't quite reach his eyes. "I used to dance with the St. Petersburg Ballet before..." His voice trailed off, a shadow passing over his features.

"Before what?" I pressed gently.

"Before I joined the Marines," he said, a note of bitterness creeping into his tone. "And before I lost my family."

His words struck me like a sharp note in a quiet symphony. "What happened?" I asked, my heart aching for the pain I saw etched on his face.

He took a deep breath, his eyes glistening with unshed tears. "My wife and son... they were taken from me during a robbery. I was deployed at the time. I didn't get to say goodbye."

I felt the familiar pang of grief in my chest, a reflection of my own losses, though they were different in nature. "I'm so sorry," I whispered, wanting to comfort him despite my heartache.

"I thought I could find solace in the military," he continued, his voice raw. "But all I found was more pain. I returned to Russia to escape, to find something of myself again."

"Did you find it?" I asked, curious yet wary.

He looked at me, a flicker of vulnerability breaking through his hardened exterior. "I thought I could dance again, but it feels like a lifetime ago. I'm just... lost."

At that moment, we connected in a way I had not anticipated. Here was a man who understood the weight of loss, who had once danced like I had, only to have life pull him in a different direction. My own burdens felt lighter as I shared my story—the injury that had sidelined me, the dreams that felt like they were slipping away.

"I used to think ballet was my everything," I confessed, my voice trembling. "I don't even know who I am without it."

He nodded, his gaze steady as if he understood my depths of despair. "We're both searching for something we've lost," he said softly. "But maybe we can find it together."

As the days rolled on, we met often, each encountering peeling back layers of our pain. We shared stories over cups of steaming tea, finding comfort in the warmth of each other's company. Alex told me about his time in the Marines, the camaraderie he had experienced, and the guilt that haunted him since the loss of his family.

"I was supposed to protect them," he said one evening, his voice breaking. "I was trained to be a hero but couldn't save them."

I reached across the table, resting my hand on his. "You can't carry that burden forever, Alex. It's not your fault."

He looked down at our hands, vulnerability etched in his features. "And you, Katya? You're not just a dancer. You're so much more than that."

His words hung in the air, a lifeline thrown into the turbulent sea of my grief. I had been so consumed by the loss of my dream that I had forgotten to see the beauty still surrounding me—the laughter of children in the streets, the artistry of life unfolding in every moment.

But as I began to embrace this new perspective, fate intervened again.

One evening, as we walked along the banks of the Neva, the atmosphere turned somber. The air felt thick with unspoken words. Alex suddenly stopped, turning to face me, his expression serious.

"Katya, I need to visit my son's grave," he said, his voice trembling. "I haven't been in months. Would you come with me?"

My heart ached for him, the weight of his request pressing down on me. "Of course," I replied, my voice steady despite the lump in my throat.

The cemetery was quiet, the air heavy with damp earth and fresh flowers. As we approached the tiny grave, I felt a mixture of sorrow and reverence. Alex knelt down, his fingers brushing over the inscription, and I stood beside him, overwhelmed by the moment's gravity.

"I'm so sorry, my love," he whispered, tears spilling down his cheeks. "I thought I could find a way to make it right, but I've failed you."

I knelt beside him, placing my hand on his shoulder. "You haven't failed him. You've carried his memory with you. That's what matters."

He looked up at me, his eyes reflecting pain and gratitude. "I've been so focused on my own grief that I've forgotten how to honor him."

At that moment, I realized that forgiveness was not just about letting go but about embracing love amidst the sorrow. I took a deep breath, letting the cool breeze wash over us. "We can honor our loved ones by living fully, by finding joy in what remains."

He nodded, his expression softening as he took in my words. Together, we sat in silence, allowing our emotions to intertwine, forming a bond that transcended our individual losses.

As the sun dipped below the horizon, casting a golden hue over the cemetery, I felt a clarity wash over me. I had spent so long grieving the loss of my dreams that I had forgotten to embrace the beauty of life itself.

In the weeks that followed, I returned to the theater with newfound determination. The audience was a sea of faces, a canvas of dreams and aspirations. As I stepped onto the stage, I felt the familiar flutter of anxiety but also a renewed sense of purpose. I was not just a dancer; I was a survivor, a woman who had learned to navigate the complexities of loss and love.

Alex watched from the front row, his presence a grounding force as I poured my heart into every movement. With each pirouette, I felt the weight of my past lift, allowing the music to guide my body in ways I had thought impossible. I danced not just for myself but for the memories of those we had lost, the love that remained, and the future we could still embrace.

As the final notes faded into silence, I stood breathless, my heart pounding. The applause echoed around me, a symphony of support and understanding. I could see Alex's face illuminated with pride, his smile a beacon of hope.

At that moment, I finally understood the power of resilience. Life always presents challenges, but it also offers the chance for rebirth and new beginnings.

As I stepped off the stage, Alex met me with open arms. "You were incredible," he said, his voice filled with admiration. "You danced not just with your body but with your soul."

I smiled through my tears, feeling a sense of liberation I had never known before. "Thank you for guiding me back," I replied. "I couldn't have done it without you."

As we walked out into the night, the rain had stopped, leaving the world washed clean and shimmering. I looked up at the stars, a vast expanse of possibilities stretching overhead, and realized that while life may take us on unexpected journeys, the connections we forge along the way truly define us.

As we moved forward together, I knew that our fading footsteps would leave behind a legacy of hope, forgiveness, and the courage to dance through life's storms hand in hand.

The Bridge Between Us

The sky hung like a heavy gray blanket over Manhattan, casting a muted hue over Central Park. The air was crisp, filled with the scent of damp earth and falling leaves, as autumn tiptoed into the city. On a bench beneath a sprawling oak, Tom sat, his hands trembling slightly, not from the chill but from the weight of the news he had just received. Across the park, children's laughter echoed, starkly contrasting the turmoil brewing inside him.

Tom's father, Jack, had always been a man of few words, a stoic figure cast in the mold of a bygone era. Growing up, Tom often felt the coldness of Jack's expectations, the pressure to be perfect, to succeed at all costs. Their relationship had always been a series of unspoken grievances, simmering beneath the surface and erupting occasionally in bitter arguments. Now, as Tom faced the uncertainty of his diagnosis—a chronic illness that threatened to change everything—he found himself questioning the very foundation of their bond, a bond burdened with unresolved issues.

Days turned into weeks, and the city continued its relentless pace, indifferent to Tom's internal struggle. He found himself seated across from Jack in a sterile hospital room, the fluorescent lights buzzing above them like angry bees. The doctor had just delivered the news, the words hanging like a thick fog: "Chronic illness."

Jack's expression was inscrutable, a mask of emotions held tightly at bay. "What does this mean for you?" he finally asked, his voice low, almost a whisper.

"It means... everything changes," Tom replied, his heart racing. "I don't know how to deal with this, Dad."

For a moment, silence enveloped them. The walls felt closer, and the beeping of machines punctuated the quiet like a countdown to an inevitable confrontation. Jack shifted in his chair, the weight of unspoken words pressing down on him. "We need to talk about... us," he said hesitantly.

Tom's eyes narrowed. "Us? You mean the years of you pushing me away? The times I needed you, and you were never there?"

Jack flinched, the truth striking him like a physical blow. "I was trying to prepare you for the world, Tom. I thought... I thought I was helping."

"And what do you think this is doing? I'm sick, Dad! I need you now more than ever!" Tom's voice cracked, the anger and fear swirling into a tempest of emotion.

Jack's face softened, a flicker of understanding breaking through his stoicism. "I don't know how to be what you need," he admitted, his eyes glistening with unshed tears. "I was never taught to express... feelings."

They sat in silence, the air thick with unspoken apologies and regrets. As the days turned into routine treatments and hospital visits, they found themselves sharing small moments—Jack bringing Tom his favorite coffee and laughing at the absurdity of hospital food, which was often bland and unappetizing. The ice between them began to thaw, and each shared a smile, a tentative step toward healing.

One afternoon, as the sun streamed through the hospital window, bathing the room in golden light, Tom turned to Jack. "You know, I've been thinking... maybe we can start over. Not as father and son, but just... two people trying to understand each other."

Jack nodded, a lump forming in his throat. "I'd like that," he said, his voice barely above a whisper. "But I need to know... how do you feel about everything?"

Tom hesitated. "I'm scared, Dad. I'm scared of what this means for my life and for my future. But more than that, I'm scared of losing you, of never really knowing you."

In that moment, Jack reached for Tom's hand, a gesture both foreign and profound. "You're not going to lose me. I want to be here. I want to understand you, and I want you to understand me."

As the weeks passed, they forged a fragile bond built on shared vulnerability and a newfound willingness to communicate. They talked about Tom's fears and dreams, and Jack shared stories of his own struggles, tales from his youth that had been buried beneath layers of pride and expectation. They laughed and cried, slowly beginning to bridge the chasm that had long divided them. Their relationship was transforming, offering a glimmer of hope and progress.

Then came the day when Tom's treatment hit a snag. The unexpected news sent him spiraling back into a pit of despair. Jack rushed to the hospital, his heart racing with worry. When he arrived, he found Tom sitting alone in his room, tears streaming down his face. The doctor had just informed him that his condition had worsened and the treatment plan needed to be revised.

"Why is this happening?" Tom cried, the words spilling out in a torrent of frustration and anguish. "I thought I was getting better!"

Jack approached cautiously, sitting beside him on the bed. "I don't have the answers, Tom. But I do know one thing: we'll face this together."

At that moment, as Tom leaned against Jack's shoulder, he felt a warmth he had longed for his entire life. In that embrace, the physical manifestation of their renewed connection, he realized they were not just father and son anymore. They were allies, fighters in the same battle, united by love and a shared desire for understanding. This moment of shared vulnerability deepened their connection, making it more profound and meaningful.

As they sat there, the weight of unspoken words transformed into a bridge that spanned the distance between their hearts. Tom closed his eyes, feeling the rhythm of Jack's heartbeat against him, a steady reminder that they would navigate the storm together no matter the uncertainties ahead.

And perhaps, just perhaps, that was enough.

The Empty Nest

Standing at the threshold of our home, I could hardly recognize the silence that enveloped us. The laughter of our children, once a constant backdrop, had faded into distant echoes. Our house, once a vibrant tapestry woven with the threads of family life, now felt like a museum adorned with memories that seemed to hang in the air like dust settling on unworn furniture.

It was a crisp autumn afternoon, and the golden leaves danced down from the oak trees lining our driveway. The air was thick with change; somehow, it felt like the world was pressing pause on our lives. I turned to Emily, my wife of twenty-five years, and saw the same bewilderment reflected in her eyes. We stood there, two souls adrift in a sea of unfamiliarity, grappling with the void left by our children's departure.

"Do you remember the first time we brought Lily home?" I asked, hoping to ignite a spark of nostalgia amidst the shadows that loomed over us.

Emily's lips curled into a soft smile, one mixed with sadness. "How could I forget? You were so terrified, you nearly dropped her."

We laughed, but the moment quickly dissipated, replaced by an uncomfortable silence. The memories of sleepless nights and frantic school mornings had kept us connected, but now, with those days behind us, it seemed we were more strangers than partners.

As the days turned into weeks, I found myself wandering through the house, searching for remnants of the lives we once led. I would catch Emily gazing out the window, her eyes distant, as if she could still see our children playing in the backyard. I wanted to reach out, to bridge the growing chasm between us, but each time I opened my mouth, the words caught in my throat.

One evening, as the sun dipped below the horizon, painting the sky in hues of orange and purple, I found Emily sitting on the porch swing. The creaking of the wood echoed the unease that had taken residence in our marriage. I joined her, hesitantly taking her hand in mine. Her skin was warm, yet her expression was cold, and I could feel the tension radiating between us like a thick fog.

"Do you think we've lost ourselves?" she asked, her voice barely above a whisper.

The question hung in the air, heavy and unyielding. I had sensed it too—the way our conversations had shifted, how our laughter had grown sparse. We had poured ourselves into raising our children, prioritizing their needs over our own. But what had we sacrificed in the process?

"Maybe we forgot how to be us," I replied, my heart aching with the truth of it. "We built our lives around them and… now what?"

Emily looked away, tears glistening in her eyes. "I thought I'd be happy when they left, finally having time for myself. But I just feel… empty."

Her vulnerability struck a chord deep within me, and I realized that we were both mourning—not just the absence of our children but the loss of the dreams we had shared as a couple.

"Let's not let this be the end," I urged, squeezing her hand tighter. "We can find our way back to each other. We just need to talk, really talk, about the things we've kept inside."

That night, we stayed up late, peeling back the layers of unspoken resentments. I shared my frustrations about feeling like an outsider in my own family. At the same time, she laid bare her struggles with identity as a mother who had dedicated herself to nurturing our children. We cried, we laughed, and in the quiet moments, we rediscovered the love that had brought us together in the first place.

Over the following weeks, we began to mend the rift between us. We took long walks in the crisp autumn air, holding hands as we reminisced about our early years. We cooked together, transforming our kitchen into a sanctuary of shared laughter and culinary experiments. We even ventured out on spontaneous dates, rediscovering the thrill of each other's company.

One evening, as we sat by the fireplace, Emily turned to me, her eyes sparkling with a newfound light. "I think we're going to be okay," she said, her voice steady and confident.

I smiled, feeling the warmth of hope radiate between us. The emptiness that had once consumed our home was slowly being filled with the rekindling of our love.

As winter approached, I realized that our empty nest was not a symbol of loss but rather an opportunity for rebirth. We were building a new life together, one that honored our past while embracing the future.

Then came the day when our children returned for the holidays. As they burst through the door, laughter and warmth flooded the house, filling every corner with life. I glanced at Emily, and we exchanged a knowing smile.

We had faced our fears and emerged stronger and more united than ever. In the midst of the chaos, I understood that love was not merely a feeling but a choice—a commitment to weather the storms together.

In that moment, I realized that our empty nest was not a void to be feared but a canvas waiting for the brushstrokes of new memories. As I watched our children embrace the home we had built, I knew that the most beautiful chapters of our story were still being written.

Unseen

The faded scent of lavender and old books filled the air in Sarah's childhood bedroom, a comforting balm against the tears threatening to spill. It had been years since I'd last stepped foot in this sanctuary, where dreams were whispered, and secrets were shared, especially the ones we kept from each other. The whispers were tinged with sorrow, the secrets weighing heavy on our hearts. Liam, our best friend, our confidante, the boy who held a piece of my heart for so long, was fading, his laughter silenced by the merciless grip of cancer.

Our reunion felt like a final act of defiance against the inevitable. It was a desperate attempt to capture the fleeting moments of shared laughter and unspoken longing before they slipped away forever. Liam's face, pale and gaunt, held a familiar warmth, a silent plea for us to reconcile, to bridge the chasm that had divided us for years.

The air crackled with unspoken truths, the weight of the past clinging to us like a second skin. The memory of that fateful summer, the betrayal that had shattered our friendship, lingered like a phantom pain. I'd slept with his boyfriend, a moment of weakness that had cost us dearly, a wound that had festered in the silence of unspoken words.

I stood in the doorway, my gaze drawn to the faded lavender wallpaper, its floral pattern a faded echo of the vibrant blooms that once adorned the room. The shelves were laden with dusty books, whispered tales of shared dreams, and secrets. The air hung heavy with the scent of lavender, a potent reminder of our shared history, now marked by the shadow of Liam's illness.

The room was a time capsule, a tangible testament to the bond we had forged, the unspoken promises, the unspoken longing. It was where we had shed our inhibitions, shared vulnerabilities, and whispered our hopes and fears into the darkness. The silence now felt suffocating, a stark reminder of the chasm that had separated us, a chasm that felt impossible to bridge.

The scent of lavender, once a symbol of comfort and shared intimacy, now carried the weight of unspoken grief, a reminder of the fleeting nature of life and the enduring power of regret. It was a fragrance that both comforted and haunted me, a reminder of the fragile threads of our connection, which were now unraveling at an alarming rate.

Liam sat on his bed, propped up by pillows, his eyes a mirror to his pain. He wore a faded blue T-shirt, contrasting the vibrant colors that once adorned his life. Once a thick, unruly mane, his hair was now thin and patchy, a tangible testament to the battle he was waging.

His gaze met mine, and a gentle smile touched his lips, a familiar gesture that sent a wave of bittersweet memories crashing over me. There was a vulnerability in his eyes, a raw honesty that stripped away the years of silence and resentment. He looked so fragile, so vulnerable, and yet, there was a strength in his gaze, a resilience that defied the relentless grip of his illness.

He reached out, his hand trembling slightly, and motioned for me to join him. I sat on the edge of the bed, my gaze drawn to the worn fabric, the countless nights we had spent sharing stories, whispering secrets, and forging a bond that had felt unbreakable.

The weight of the past hung heavy in the silence, the unspoken words, the unaddressed emotions, a tangled web of hurt and anger, betrayal and longing.

The silence in the room felt like a physical presence, a tangible force that threatened to suffocate me. I could feel Liam's gaze on me, searching, questioning. He knew, as I did that the chasm that separated us was more than just a physical distance; it was a chasm carved by the weight of our unspoken truths.

The lavender scent, once a symbol of shared dreams and intimate moments, now felt suffocating. It was a poignant reminder of the years we had spent apart, of the silence that had become a language of its own.

"It's good to see you, Sarah," he finally whispered, his voice raspy and weak.

The words hung in the air, a fragile bridge between two worlds that had once been so close. The pain in his eyes, the unspoken plea for understanding and forgiveness, tugged at my heart.

I took a deep breath, my throat tight with emotion. The scent of lavender was a poignant reminder of our shared past and pain. I wanted to tell him I was sorry, to erase the betrayal that had shattered our friendship, to make amends for the choices that had driven us apart.

But the words stuck in my throat, tangled in a web of guilt, shame, fear, and regret. Liam's illness and his fading presence served as a stark reminder of life's fragility and the urgency of mending the broken threads of our past.

The scent of lavender lingered in the air, a silent plea for reconciliation, a reminder of the love we once shared, the dreams we once held, and the unspoken longing that still lingered between us. We were at a crossroads, faced with the monumental task of confronting our ghosts and forging a path towards forgiveness.

Liam's gentle smile and unwavering belief in our connection spurred us forward, pushing us to navigate the labyrinth of our shared history.

We were forever changed, our lives touched by Liam's grace and our own journey of self-discovery. In the quiet aftermath of our reunion, I felt a profound sense of peace, a newfound understanding of the complexities of life, and the bittersweet beauty of letting go. Liam may be gone, but the unseen threads of our connection, woven through years of shared laughter, tears, and unspoken truths, will forever bind us.

The sun dipped below the horizon, painting the sky with fiery hues of orange and purple as I walked back to my room. I could still feel the warmth of Liam's hand in mine, a silent reminder of the past we had confronted and the forgiveness we had offered each other. But as I closed the door behind me, the familiar scent of lavender and old books couldn't mask the hollowness that settled deep within me.

It was like the betrayal had returned, its ghostly presence weaving through the memories of our shared past. I saw Liam's face again, the laughter lines around his eyes suddenly replaced by a stark, painful emptiness. The warmth that had radiated from him just hours ago seemed to have vanished, replaced by a fragile shell that held the weight of shattered trust.

The summer of our betrayal replayed a relentless slideshow of mistakes and misjudgments in my mind. It started with the sun-drenched days spent lounging by the pool, Liam's infectious laughter ringing in the air as we splashed in the water. He'd told me stories of his budding romance with Mark, how their love felt like a whirlwind, something he hadn't experienced before. He was so full of life and so happy, and I felt like I was witnessing a love story unfold before my very eyes.

But then came the night, a blur of alcohol and misplaced affections. The details were hazy, the memories tinged with shame and regret. Mark was there, his eyes full of longing, and for a moment, I felt a flicker of attraction, a moment of weakness that I would later regret for the rest of my life.

The guilt had gnawed at me for years, a constant reminder of the friend I had betrayed, the love I had stolen. But even worse than the guilt was the pain I had inflicted on Liam. I could see him now, his face etched with hurt, his voice cracking as he tried to understand what had happened.

"I never thought you'd do that to me, Sarah," he had whispered, his words laced with disbelief and a pain that cut deeper than any physical wound.

The betrayal became a chasm dividing us, an invisible wall between our once-unbreakable bond. We couldn't look at each other without seeing the ghost of that summer, the silent accusations that hung heavy in the air. I tried to apologize, to make things right, but my words felt hollow and inadequate.

It was like a part of Liam had died that summer; the trust and innocence that had defined our friendship irrevocably shattered. I had become a shadow of the friend he had loved, a constant reminder of the pain I had inflicted.

The silence that followed the betrayal was even more painful than the words. The unspoken accusations, the unaddressed emotions, festered like a wound left to rot. I avoided Liam, afraid to face the pain in his eyes, the silent plea for an explanation I couldn't provide.

He, in turn, retreated into himself, his laughter subdued, his spirit dimmed. The vibrant young man I had known had become a ghost of his former self, haunted by the betrayal and the loss of our friendship.

The weight of regret pressed down on me, a constant reminder of my terrible mistake. Every time I saw Liam, the guilt would rise, a choking tide threatening to drown me in self-loathing.

In the quiet of my childhood bedroom, surrounded by the scent of lavender and old books, I realized that the pain I had caused Liam was far greater than anything I had ever experienced. He was facing his mortality, his life hanging in the balance, and I had given him one more reason to feel heartbroken.

I had hurt him deeply, a wound that had festered for years, its scars still visible in the pain that clouded his eyes. I had betrayed his trust, shattered our friendship, and left him with a gaping hole in his heart.

The memory of that summer, the summer of our betrayal, felt like a curse I could never escape. Liam's ghost, his pain, and heartbreak, would forever be etched in my memory, a constant reminder of the price I had paid for a moment of weakness.

But as I sat there, surrounded by the echoes of our shared past, a glimmer of hope emerged. Liam had offered me forgiveness, a gift I had never dared hope for. In that forgiveness, I saw a chance to heal, to mend the shattered pieces of our friendship, and to finally make amends for the pain I had inflicted.

The journey ahead would be long and arduous, a path paved with regret, forgiveness, and the hope of rediscovering the love and connection that had once defined us. It would be a journey of confronting my demons, acknowledging the hurt I had caused, and learning to forgive myself for the choices I had made.

As I drifted off to sleep that night, I held onto that glimmer of hope, praying that we could find a way to bridge the chasm that had divided us, rebuild the broken pieces of our friendship, and find a semblance of peace before it was too late.

The air crackled with unspoken truths, the weight of the past pressing down on them like a physical force. Sarah's breath caught in her throat, the lavender scent of her childhood bedroom doing little to ease the tension. Liam's face, pale and gaunt, held a mix of apprehension and a quiet plea for understanding. She knew he needed to hear it to understand the depth of her regret and the years of guilt that had gnawed at her soul. It had been years since they'd last spoken, years since she'd faced the consequences of her actions.

"Liam, I... I never stopped thinking about what I did," Sarah finally confessed, her voice cracking with sorrow and desperation. Her words, long held captive by fear and shame, finally found their way out, a floodgate of emotion bursting open.

"I know," Liam whispered, his voice raspy and fragile. He looked at her, his eyes filled with a sorrowful understanding that mirrored her own pain. He was right; she had never stopped thinking about it. That summer, a whirlwind of youthful recklessness and misplaced desires, had left an indelible mark on their friendship, a scar that had festered in the silence of unspoken words.

"It was wrong, I know," she continued, the tears welling up in her eyes, "I hurt you, and I hurt myself. I didn't understand what I was doing, the depth of my actions, the impact they would have on you, on us."

Liam's gaze remained locked on hers, holding her captive in a silent communion of shared pain. He understood the weight of her confession, the vulnerability she was exposing. The years of unspoken words, the chasm that had grown between them, felt like an insurmountable barrier.

"The truth is, I was afraid," Sarah continued, her voice trembling. I was afraid of you, fearful of what we had, scared of the future I thought we couldn't have. I let my fear control me and push me away."

Liam reached out, his hand fragile and skeletal, and gently took hers. "Sarah, you were young. We were all lost in our own ways. We were figuring things out."

His words, spoken with quiet compassion, pierced through the haze of her self-recrimination. For the first time in years, she felt seen and understood. He wasn't judging her; he was offering her a lifeline of forgiveness, a chance to mend the broken threads of their past.

"We're both hurting," Liam continued, his voice soft but unwavering, "But we don't have to continue to hurt each other. We can choose to heal, to forgive, to move forward."

His words resonated deep within Sarah, a powerful echo of her unspoken yearning for reconciliation. She had always known that forgiveness was thé only path to healing, not just for him but for her as well. But the burden of her actions, the weight of her guilt, had kept her trapped in a prison of self-punishment.

Liam's hand, frail and warm, held onto hers with a tenacity that surprised her. His eyes, though faded by illness, shone with a quiet determination. "Sarah, I'm not asking you to forget," he said, his voice catching slightly. But I am asking you to forgive yourself. To understand that we all make mistakes and can choose to learn from them."

Sarah's tears flowed freely now, a release of pent-up emotion and a wash of gratitude for his unwavering belief in her and their connection. She had always cherished the memories they shared, the laughter, the dreams, and the bond they'd forged. The betrayal had shattered that, leaving them both with fragments of a once-unbreakable friendship.

But in the quiet intimacy of her childhood bedroom, surrounded by the familiar scent of lavender and old books, Sarah felt the beginning of a shift. She felt the weight of the past lift slightly, a glimmer of hope flickering in the depths of her heart. She looked at Liam, his face etched with the ravages of illness but his eyes radiating a warmth that seemed to defy the darkness.

She knew forgiveness wasn't a simple act; it was a journey and a process that wouldn't erase the pain of the past. But it was a path worth taking, a chance to release the shackles of guilt and finally find peace. She squeezed his hand, her own tears mingling with his.

"I want to try, Liam," she whispered, her voice thick with emotion, "I want to try to forgive myself, and I want to try to forgive you. I want to try to heal."

Liam's smile, a flicker of light in the dim room, was as fragile as the butterfly wings of a fading summer. It held a depth of love, a glimmer of hope resonating in Sarah's heart.

As the sun dipped below the horizon, painting the sky in fading orange and purple shades, a sense of quiet acceptance settled over them. The past would always remain, a shadow lingering in the corners of their memories. But the fragile and delicate threads of forgiveness they had begun to weave offered the promise of a new beginning, a second chance to find healing and peace.

As Liam squeezed her hand, a silent message of love and gratitude passed between them, a testament to the enduring power of forgiveness and the strength of their bond. It was a bittersweet moment, a last flicker of hope before the inevitable darkness.

They may have lost years to the weight of their past, but in the face of Liam's illness, they had found a path back to each other, a shared journey of healing and acceptance that would forever bind them together. The lavender scent of Sarah's childhood bedroom, once a reminder of a shattered friendship, now carried the promise of a future woven with forgiveness, compassion, and the quiet beauty of second chances.

Sarah sat on the edge of Liam's bed, the sterile white sheets crisp against her skin. The room, usually a haven of laughter and shared secrets, now felt like a mausoleum, filled with the hushed whispers of grief. Liam, gaunt and pale, lay there, his chest rising and falling with the labored breath of a man fighting a losing battle. He looked at her, his eyes, usually sparkling with mischief, now clouded with a weariness that went beyond the physical.

"I'm sorry, Sarah," he rasped, his voice barely a whisper.

Simple yet profound words pierced through Sarah's carefully constructed walls of guilt and resentment. She hadn't expected an apology, but she was hoping for it. For years, the weight of her betrayal had burdened her, a constant reminder of the chasm she had created between them.

Liam's forgiveness, offered freely and unconditionally, was a gift, a precious offering that shook her to her core. It wasn't just forgiveness for her actions that summer, but a forgiveness that transcended the specifics of her betrayal and embraced the entirety of her being.

"Don't be," Sarah whispered, her voice thick with unshed tears. "I should have been there for you. I should have been a better friend."

Liam squeezed her hand, a gesture of understanding and acceptance. "It's okay, Sarah. It's all okay. We all make mistakes."

His words, imbued with a wisdom beyond his years, struck a chord within her. She saw in his eyes a love that was not diminished by her actions but transcended the pain and the anger. He offered her a chance to move forward, heal the wounds of the past, and embrace a new chapter.

"But, Liam, I hurt you so much," she said, her voice breaking with emotion. "I can't just pretend it didn't happen. I have to live with the consequences."

He smiled weakly, the light in his eyes dimming for a moment. "We all live with the consequences, Sarah. But that doesn't mean we have to live with the burden of the past. Forgiveness isn't about forgetting. It's about letting go."

His words resonated deeply within her. For years, she had been carrying the weight of her guilt, the burden of her actions. It had become a part of her, a heavy anchor that kept her tethered to the past, preventing her from moving forward.

Liam's forgiveness offered her a lifeline, a chance to break free from the chains of self-recrimination. But it wasn't just about him forgiving her. It was about her forgiving herself.

The thought of forgiving herself felt daunting, insurmountable. She had hurt Liam, shattered their bond, and betrayed the trust he had placed in her. How could she ever forgive herself for that?

Liam's gentle hand on her arm pulled her back to the present. "It's okay, Sarah," he said, his voice raspy but firm. "It's time to let go."

His words were a balm to her soul, a soothing whisper that eased the relentless ache of guilt. He wasn't just forgiving her for his sake. He was doing it for her, urging her to find peace within herself.

Sarah's heart ached with a mix of gratitude and sorrow. She knew that Liam's illness was taking its toll, both physically and emotionally. Yet, he was still focused on her well-being, offering her a gift of desperately needed acceptance.

"I can't promise I'll ever be able to forgive myself," she whispered, her voice choked with emotion.

Liam smiled, a flicker of his usual warmth illuminating his pale face. "You don't have to promise anything. Just try. Just take a step. Let go of the pain. You deserve to be happy, Sarah."

His words, simple and profound, resonated deeply with her. She knew he was right. She deserved to be happy and to find peace within herself.

She took a deep breath, the air catching her throat as she battled the rising emotions. She looked at Liam, his gaze steady and unwavering.

"Okay," she whispered, the word a promise to herself as much as to him. "I'll try."

Liam squeezed her hand, a silent message of gratitude and love. He was leaving her, his presence a fading memory, but the invisible threads of their connection remained, a testament to the enduring power of forgiveness. They were forever changed, their lives touched by Liam's grace and journey of self-discovery.

In the quiet aftermath of their reunion, Sarah felt a profound sense of peace. She had taken a step, a small but crucial step, towards healing. Liam's forgiveness had unlocked a door within her that led to the possibility of self-forgiveness, of letting go of the pain, and of embracing a future filled with hope.

She knew that the journey wouldn't be challenging. The scars of the past would always remain, but Liam's gift of acceptance had given her the strength to face them. She would never forget the pain, but she would no longer be defined by it.

As she walked out of the hospital room, the fading light of the setting sun casting long shadows across the parking lot, Sarah felt a weight lift from her shoulders. It was a weight that had been there for years, a constant reminder of her mistakes.

Now, it was gone, replaced by a sense of purpose, hope, and profound gratitude for Liam's unconditional love and forgiveness. He might be gone, but the lessons he had taught her, the invisible threads of their connection, would remain with her forever.

Sarah walked towards her car, her steps lighter than they had been in years. She had a long road ahead, but she was no longer alone. Liam had given her the gift of forgiveness and, with it, the gift of a second chance—a chance to find peace within herself, embrace the beauty of life, and live a life worthy of his love.

Sarah and Liam sat on the edge of her childhood bed, the faded lavender scent mingling with the dust motes dancing in the afternoon sun. Their laughter, once a familiar symphony, was now a fragile melody punctuated by moments of silence, a bittersweet reminder of the years lost and the precious time they had left.

"Remember the time we snuck out to the beach after curfew?" Liam asked, a ghost of a smile gracing his pale lips.

Sarah's throat tightened. "How could I forget? We were caught red-handed, scrambling back to your house with sand in our hair and a heart full of mischief."

Their shared memories, woven with threads of youthful exuberance and the unspoken intimacy of their bond, were a poignant tapestry, each image a testament to the unbreakable connection that had bound them for so long. They talked about their first kiss and shared dreams, anxieties, and fears, peeling back layers of their past and revealing the vulnerabilities that had once shielded them.

"I was such a fool that summer," Sarah confessed, her voice thick with regret. "I let my insecurities cloud my judgment and hurt you in a way I never meant to."

Though dimmed by illness, Liam's eyes held a depth of understanding. "We were both young, Sarah. We made mistakes, and we both paid the price."

With all its pain and regret, the past hung heavy between them, a reminder of their shared mistakes and the long road to forgiveness. Yet, they acknowledged the imperfection of their past, recognizing the beauty of their flawed human connection. The betrayal hurt, and years of silence were part of their story, a testament to the complexity of their bond.

"We weren't perfect, Liam," Sarah said softly. "We stumbled, we fell, and we hurt each other. But through it all, there was something... something powerful that held us together. We were friends, we were confidants, and we were, in our own way, always there for each other."

Liam nodded, his gaze fixed on the fading sunlight streaming through the window. "You were my rock, Sarah. Even when I couldn't see it or pushed you away, you were always there, waiting for me to come back."

As they spoke, the weight of their past gradually lifted, replaced by a newfound understanding. They recognized that their connection, flawed and imperfect as it was, was a testament to the power of human resilience. They had endured, learned, and found their way back to each other, albeit under the shadow of a looming goodbye.

"We're not perfect, Sarah," Liam whispered, his voice raspy. "We're just... us. And that's okay. That's enough."

Sarah reached for his hand, her own trembling slightly. "It's enough, Liam. It's more than enough."

At that moment, as the sun dipped below the horizon, painting the sky in hues of orange and purple, they found solace in their shared imperfections. The tears that fell freely were not tears of sadness but tears of acceptance, love, and forgiveness. They had found their way back to each other, which was a testament to the enduring power of human connection, a connection that transcended time, betrayal, and even the fragility of life itself.

Their laughter, now tinged with a bittersweet melancholy, echoed in the quiet room, a testament to the memories they had made, the lessons they had learned, and the strength they had found in their shared vulnerability. The beauty of their imperfect love, a love that had weathered storms and endured the passage of time, was a beacon of hope, a reminder that even in the face of loss, even in the face of inevitable endings, the human spirit could find solace in the embrace of forgiveness, in the shared laughter and tears that bind us together.

The fading light of dusk cast long shadows across Sarah's face as she sat by the window, the lavender scent of her childhood room a comforting presence. Liam was gone, his laughter silenced by the cruel hand of fate, but the echoes of his voice lingered in the corners of her memory, a bittersweet symphony of shared laughter and unspoken truths. He had left, but he had left a legacy that would forever shape her perspective, a testament to the enduring power of human connection, forgiveness, and the courage to face the unknown.

Although Liam's illness was a catalyst for their reunion, it became a crucible, forging a new understanding between them. The weight of the past, the betrayal that had shattered their friendship, was confronted with a raw honesty that stripped away layers of resentment and fear. In the face of mortality, their past transgressions had shrunk, overshadowed by the immensity of their shared history, a tapestry woven with threads of laughter, tears, and unspoken promises.

Liam's gentle smile, a beacon of forgiveness and acceptance, offered Sarah a profound gift, a release from guilt and regret. His unwavering belief in the power of their connection had spurred her to confront her demons, shed the armor of self-protection, and embrace the vulnerability beneath. In his final days, she had seen a reflection of her heart, a fragile yet resilient soul yearning for connection, love, and forgiveness.

Liam's passing had left a gaping void in Sarah's life, a silent reminder of the ephemeral nature of existence. But within that void, something had blossomed – a newfound appreciation for the fragility of life, a deep understanding of the importance of connection, and a profound gratitude for the moments shared with those she loved.

In the aftermath of Liam's departure, Sarah navigated the treacherous waters of grief, her world a kaleidoscope of sorrow and bittersweet memories. Yet, amidst the darkness, a beacon of hope flickered – the legacy of Liam's unwavering love, his unwavering belief in the power of forgiveness, and his steadfast commitment to human connection.

She carried those lessons within her, a guiding light in the uncertainty ahead. Liam had taught her the importance of vulnerability, of acknowledging her own imperfections and embracing the imperfections of others. He had taught her the transformative power of forgiveness, not only for others but for herself. And he had taught her that even in the face of loss, the threads of human connection remained, an invisible tapestry that bound us together, a testament to the enduring power of love.

As the seasons turned and the world moved on, Sarah was drawn back to the lavender-scented room of her childhood. It was a sanctuary where she could revisit the echoes of Liam's laughter, the whisper of his voice, and the enduring legacy of their shared journey.

She could almost hear him say, "Sarah, don't let the fear consume you. Forgive yourself, forgive others, and never stop believing in the power of human connection. Life is a fleeting gift; cherish every moment, and embrace the beauty of letting go."

And so, Sarah carried on, her heart a vessel of both sorrow and hope. She moved forward, her steps guided by Liam's legacy, a testament to the enduring power of forgiveness, the resilience of the human spirit, and the beauty of love that transcends time and circumstance.

The city's quiet hum outside my window starkly contrasted with the peaceful stillness that enveloped me. It was a stillness born of both sorrow and a newfound understanding. Liam was gone, his laughter silenced by the cruel hand of fate. The memories of him, vibrant and alive just a few days ago, now shimmered like fragile, iridescent bubbles, threatening to burst at the slightest touch. Yet, I felt a sense of peace, a quiet understanding transcending the grief. Liam's illness had been a catalyst, a harsh reminder of life's fleeting nature, forcing me to confront the ghosts that had haunted my past.

My journey back to my childhood bedroom, the scent of lavender and old books a familiar balm to my soul, had been a pilgrimage. I'd returned to face my demons, to mend the fractured threads of our friendship, and to seek the forgiveness I so desperately craved. The weight of the past had clung to us, a suffocating blanket of unspoken words and bottled-up emotions. The betrayal that had shattered our bond, the summer I'd slept with his boyfriend, a moment of weakness that echoed through the years, had left an indelible mark.

But in the face of his illness, Liam had offered a glimmer of hope, a gentle nudge towards reconciliation. His unwavering belief in our connection and his unspoken plea for us to mend the broken pieces of our past gave me the courage to confront the truth. Through tearful confessions and heartfelt apologies, we shed the armor of resentment, revealing the fragile vulnerability beneath. We acknowledged the hurt, the anger, and the fear, but most importantly, we learned to forgive each other and, most importantly, ourselves.

Liam's passing had left a gaping hole in my life but also awakened a sense of purpose within me. The echoes of his voice, the warmth of his smile, and the lessons he'd taught me about love, forgiveness, and the fragility of life resonated deep within my soul. The memory of his hand squeezing mine, a silent message of gratitude, love, and acceptance, played like a comforting melody in my mind.

Liam's illness had not only shattered my heart, it had broken my worldview. It had shown me the importance of living life to the fullest, cherishing every moment, and letting go of anger and resentment. The lessons he'd taught me weren't just about forgiving him; they were about forgiving myself.

The past few weeks have been a blur of memories, emotions, and a profound sense of healing. The weight of the past has lifted, replaced by a sense of lightness and a newfound appreciation for life's precious moments. Liam's passing has been a painful reminder of the impermanence of life, but it has also been a catalyst for growth and self-discovery.

I was no longer the same person who had hurt Liam. The woman staring back at me in the mirror was more robust, more resilient, and more open to life's possibilities. I still carried the scars of my past, but they no longer defined me. Instead, they served as reminders of the transformative power of forgiveness, the importance of human connection, and the bittersweet beauty of second chances.

As I stood in my childhood bedroom, the scent of lavender and old books comforting me, I realized that Liam's legacy lived on within me. The lessons I'd learned, the empathy I'd discovered, and the strength I'd gained through the experience would shape the woman I was becoming. The echoes of his voice, the warmth of his smile, and the love we had shared would forever remain a part of me, guiding me on my journey through life.

The echoes of the past were no longer a source of pain but a source of strength. They reminded me of the importance of forgiveness, the power of human connection, and the bittersweet beauty of second chances. Liam was gone, but his memory, love, and the lessons I'd learned from him would forever remain a part of me. I knew that the road ahead would not be easy, but I was no longer afraid. I had faced my ghosts, learned to forgive, and was ready to embrace the future with a renewed sense of hope and gratitude.

Life was a tapestry woven with threads of joy, sorrow, and everything in between. Liam had taught me that the most beautiful threads were often the ones that were interwoven with love, forgiveness, and the courage to face our past. His absence left a hole in my heart, but his memory, like the faded scent of lavender in my childhood bedroom, would always remain, a comforting balm against the uncertainties of life.

The rain hammered against the cafe windows, blurring the cityscape into a hazy watercolor. Inside, the air was warm and comforting, the aroma of coffee and cinnamon mingling with the soft chatter of patrons. Sarah sat by the window, her latte untouched, her eyes fixed on the rain-streaked glass. Liam's words echoed in her mind, his gentle encouragement to open herself to new possibilities and trust again.

She'd spent months consumed by grief and self-recrimination, Liam's absence a gaping hole in her life. Now, she felt a flicker of hope, a spark of curiosity that hinted at a path beyond the shadow of the past.

It started with a chance encounter at the bookstore where she'd volunteered since Liam's passing. He was tall and lean, with a shock of unruly brown hair and eyes that held a kind warmth. They'd locked eyes across the aisle, a silent connection forming in the hushed ambiance of the bookshop.

His name was Ethan, and he introduced himself with a hesitant smile. He was a writer, a poet, actually, drawn to the bookstore for its tranquil atmosphere and the scent of aged paper. He'd shared his work with her, his words weaving a tapestry of emotions, capturing the essence of love, loss, and hope.

Their conversations flowed effortlessly, the initial awkwardness quickly fading into shared laughter and intellectual sparring. He challenged her perceptions; his views on love and life refreshingly contrasted with hers. He wasn't afraid of vulnerability; his words were imbued with honesty and a deep appreciation for the complexities of human emotions.

He didn't shy away from the darkness she carried, the shadow of betrayal that lingered over her heart. He listened intently, his empathy radiating from his warm gaze. He made her feel understood and accepted, not just for the woman she was now but for the woman she was becoming.

Ethan didn't ask her about Liam directly. He knew, sensing the unspoken sorrow that clung to her like a phantom limb. He didn't intrude, but he was always present, reassuring in her life. He made her laugh again, reminding her of the simple joys she'd forgotten in the throes of her grief.

Their walks through the park were a symphony of shared laughter and stolen glances. He showed her a different side of the city, hidden alleyways filled with vibrant street art and quiet cafes tucked away from the bustling crowds. They explored art galleries, their conversations sparked by the brushstrokes of artists who captured the essence of the human experience.

Ethan challenged her assumptions, his perspective on love starkly contrasting her own. She'd always believed that true love meant forever, a concept shattered by Liam's betrayal. Ethan, however, spoke of love as a journey, a tapestry woven with threads of joy, sorrow, and the bittersweet beauty of change.

He spoke of second chances, of finding love in unexpected places. He made her believe that her heart, battered and bruised by the past, could heal and open itself again to the possibility of happiness.

Their connection felt different, more profound than anything she'd experienced before. It wasn't just physical attraction but a deep understanding, a shared wavelength transcending words. He saw her beyond her past, recognizing the resilience she carried within.

There were moments when fear crept in, the ghosts of Liam's betrayal whispering doubt in her ear. But Ethan's unwavering presence, his gentle reassurance, chased away the darkness, reminding her of the strength she'd discovered within.

As weeks turned into months, she began to see her life through a new lens. The pain of loss still lingered, a constant reminder of Liam's absence, but it was overshadowed by the newfound joy that Ethan brought into her life.

She wasn't sure where this journey would lead, but she was no longer afraid to embrace the unknown. She was finally ready to let go of the past to open her heart to the possibilities ahead. The lavender scent of her childhood bedroom, once a symbol of her shared dreams with Liam, now carried a hint of a new, unexpected fragrance.

Looking out at the rain-soaked cityscape, she realized that forgiveness wasn't just about letting go of the past and allowing yourself to be loved again. The possibility of an unexpected and beautiful future shimmered in the misty rain, beckoning her forward. The path ahead was uncertain, but for the first time in a long time, she wasn't afraid to take the first step.

Sarah stood on the porch of her childhood home, the familiar scent of lavender and old books washing over her. The air was tinged with a melancholy that clung to her like a shroud, yet a strange sense of peace lay beneath it. It was the kind of peace that comes after a storm when the wind has died down, and the wreckage is still evident, but the clouds have parted, and a ray of sunshine breaks through. The past few days had been a whirlwind of emotions, a journey through the labyrinth of her past, a reckoning with the ghosts of her past and the remnants of a love that had once burned so fiercely.

Liam's death, while expected, was a brutal reality, a stark reminder of life's fragility. But in the wake of his passing, Sarah felt a lightness, a sense of release she hadn't expected. The weight of their unspoken truths had finally been lifted, replaced by a quiet understanding, a deep well of forgiveness that had been years in the making.

The journey had been arduous, fraught with tears and confessions, a painful excavation of buried emotions. Yet, in their willingness to confront the truth in that shared vulnerability, they had rediscovered a strength they never knew they had. Liam's unconditional and unwavering forgiveness had been the catalyst for her own. It was a gift she carried, a precious weight that had broken the chains of her self-imposed guilt.

She walked through the threshold of her childhood home, the memory of Liam's presence lingering in the air. The house, once filled with laughter and dreams, now resonated with the echoes of their shared past. Each room, each creaking floorboard, whispered tales of their friendship, the joy they had shared, and the pain they had endured.

As she wandered through the rooms, Sarah realized that she was no longer the girl who had stood on the porch of this house, burdened by the weight of her past. The girl who had been consumed by guilt, fear, and the ache of lost friendship. She was stronger now, more resilient, her heart lighter, bearing the scars of her journey, and she also had the newfound wisdom that came from facing her demons and emerging victorious.

She was drawn to her childhood bedroom, the sanctuary where she had spent countless hours dreaming, writing, and escaping the world's complexities. The room remained much the same, the scent of lavender and old books still filling the air, a comforting reminder of the girl she once was.

Sitting on her bed, she picked up a dusty diary, its pages filled with her teenage musings, hopes and dreams, fears and anxieties. Each entry was a window into her past, a testament to the girl she had been and the woman she was becoming. As she read through the faded entries, she was struck by the depth of her emotions, her words' raw honesty, and her heart's undeniable strength.

She closed the diary, a bittersweet smile playing on her lips. It was a reminder of how far she had come, of the journey she had endured, and the lessons she had learned. Liam was gone, but his presence was woven into the fabric of her being. He had taught her the power of forgiveness, the importance of embracing vulnerability, and the enduring strength of the human spirit.

Sarah drifted into a reverie, a tapestry of memories and emotions weaving together. She saw Liam's smile, heard his laughter, and felt the warmth of his presence. She remembered the pain of their betrayal, the ache of their separation, the joy of their reconciliation, and the fragile beauty of their forgiveness.

And as she sat there, surrounded by the remnants of her past, Sarah felt a sense of profound peace. She had come full circle, a journey that had begun with sorrow and ended with a quiet acceptance of life's complexities. She was no longer burdened by the weight of her past but empowered by its lessons, the invisible threads of forgiveness and love woven into the fabric of her being. She was more robust, more resilient, and more grateful than she had ever been. She was ready to embrace the new chapter in her life, carrying Liam's legacy with her, a reminder of the enduring power of human connection, the beauty of second chances, and the transformative power of forgiveness.

The lavender still bloomed, a gentle reminder of Liam's presence in Sarah's life, a fragrance that carried his spirit, love, and wisdom. His memory lingered like a comforting presence, a quiet reassurance that he was still with her, even though his physical form was gone. Sarah's childhood bedroom, once a haven of shared secrets and laughter, had transformed into a sanctuary of remembrance where she could connect with Liam's essence.

The scent of lavender, a symbol of peace and tranquility, was a constant reminder of the profound lessons Liam had taught her about forgiveness, love, and the importance of human connection. The lavender blooms outside her window seemed to mirror Liam's fading strength, a stark reminder of life's fragility and the preciousness of each passing moment. Yet, amidst the sorrow, a gentle light of hope flickered. Liam had shown her that even in the face of adversity, love could bloom, and forgiveness could heal the deepest wounds.

Liam's legacy transcended the boundaries of time and physical presence. He had taught her to confront her past, to own her mistakes, and to extend grace to herself and others. His unwavering belief in her, even when she doubted herself, had instilled a newfound confidence within her. The memories of their shared laughter, their heartfelt conversations, and their journey toward reconciliation filled her heart with a bittersweet longing.

Sarah realized that Liam had given her a gift far more valuable than any tangible possession: the gift of forgiveness. He had shown her the power of letting go of resentment, embracing vulnerability, and allowing love to guide her path. His legacy was a beacon of hope, reminding her that even in the darkest times, there was always the possibility of redemption, renewal, and the enduring power of love.

His influence was evident in how Sarah approached her relationships, work, and life in general. She had learned to prioritize connection, value authenticity, and embrace the imperfections that made life rich and vibrant. Liam's spirit lingered in her heart, a silent guide urging her to live a life filled with love, kindness, and compassion.

The lavender still bloomed, a poignant reminder of the enduring power of love, forgiveness, and the lessons learned from those who have touched our lives in profound ways. Liam's memory was a beacon of hope, a testament to the resilience of the human spirit and the bittersweet beauty of second chances. Sarah, in turn, promised to carry his legacy forward, to live a life that reflected his values, and to share the gift of forgiveness with those who needed it most.

As Sarah looked out at the lavender field, she saw a vibrant purple tapestry, a testament to the enduring beauty of life, even in the face of loss. Liam's memory was a cherished part of that tapestry, woven through the threads of her life, forever reminding her of the importance of living with love, grace, and a heart open to the possibilities ahead. The lavender still bloomed, a gentle reminder of the enduring power of love and the connection that transcended time and space boundaries.

Shattered Reflections

The walls of my office were lined with accolades—plaque after plaque, a testament to years of relentless dedication. I had clawed my way to the top of the legal world, yet every morning, as I settled into my sleek leather chair, I felt more like a fraud than a success. The polished mahogany desk was a fortress, shielding me from the truth buried beneath layers of ambition and desperation.

The distant hum of the city outside was a constant companion, a reminder of the life I had learned to drown out with the clink of glass against glass. It was a ritual, innocently enough at first, a glass of wine to unwind after a long day. But as the months turned into years, that glass transformed into a bottle, and the unwinding became a tightrope walk over the abyss.

My husband, Mark, often commented on my late nights at the office, his brow furrowed with concern. "You work too hard, Rachel," he'd say, his voice laced with admiration and worry. But I brushed him off, returning to my case files, the swirling thoughts of my childhood echoing in the back of my mind. I was a child of chaos, molded by the jagged edges of a broken home, where alcohol had been both a refuge and a curse.

Jake Thompson entered my life like a summer storm—unexpected, electrifying, and entirely captivating. His charisma was magnetic, and he drew people in with stories that danced on the edges of truth and fiction. The first time we met in the conference room, I felt an unexplainable connection, an undeniable chemistry that simmered beneath the surface.

As weeks turned into months, our professional relationship morphed into something more—a secret liaison hidden beneath the guise of late-night meetings and whispered conversations. With Jake, I felt alive, as though I could shed the weight of my responsibilities and embrace the person I had always longed to be. Yet, every stolen moment was tainted by the gnawing guilt that clung to me like a shadow.

One rainy evening, as we shared a bottle of exquisite red wine in his office, I saw the woman I used to be—vibrant, hopeful, and accessible. But that image shattered when I returned home to Mark, who awaited me with eyes full of love and concern. I felt the crushing weight of betrayal each time I looked into his eyes.

It was a Friday morning when the storm finally broke. My phone buzzed incessantly, the screen lighting up with frantic messages. A scandal had erupted, threatening to engulf me and the entire firm. The whispers of my affair with Jake had spilled into the public domain, and suddenly, the fortress I had built around my life began to crumble.

I stood in the bathroom, staring at my reflection, the dark circles under my eyes a testament to sleepless nights spent wrestling with my demons. The woman staring back at me was a stranger, a ghost of the person I once was. Panic gripped me as I realized that I could lose everything—my career, my marriage, and perhaps even my sanity.

Mark confronted me that evening, his voice trembling with a mix of anger and heartbreak. "Rachel, how could you do this? How could you betray me?" His pain was etched into his features, the disillusionment that flickered like a dying candle.

"I didn't want this, Mark," I whispered, tears streaming down my cheeks. "I lost control. I didn't mean to hurt you." But the words felt hollow, inadequate against the weight of the truth.

In the days that followed, I found myself spiraling deeper into despair. I attended meetings at the firm, my eyes glazed over as colleagues shot me pitying glances. I was the pariah, the woman whose choices led to a monumental scandal. I sought solace in alcohol, the very thing that had once been my refuge and was now my prison.

During one of those dark nights, alone in my apartment, I stumbled across an old photograph tucked away in a dusty box. It was of me standing beside my younger self, a girl with dreams painted across her face. I felt a spark of recognition, a flicker of the hope I had lost along the way. At that moment, I knew I had a choice to continue down this destructive path or seek help.

With trembling hands, I reached out to a faith-based recovery program I had heard about through a friend. The prospect of facing my past terrified me, but the thought of losing everything I held dear terrified me more. It was a leap of faith, a step towards a new beginning.

The recovery center was nestled in the serene countryside, a stark contrast to the chaos of my life in the city. The air was fragrant with the scent of pine and earth, a reminder of nature's resilience. I arrived on a crisp autumn morning, the leaves swirling around me like confetti celebrating a new beginning. The program was structured, with a combination of individual therapy, group sessions, and spiritual guidance, all aimed at helping us confront our past and rebuild our lives.

The first few days were excruciating. I confronted the demons of my childhood—my father's rage, my mother's silence. Each session peeled back layers of pain I had buried deep inside. I was surrounded by others who shared their stories, each a thread woven into the tapestry of our shared struggles.

One evening, during a group session, I met Sarah, a woman whose laughter echoed warmly. She had faced her demons head-on and emerged stronger, a beacon of hope. Her story resonated with me, a reminder that I was not alone in this fight. We became inseparable, sharing our fears and dreams, and slowly, I began to rediscover the spark of life.

As the weeks passed, I learned to embrace vulnerability, to confront my past, and to seek forgiveness—not just from those I'd hurt but from myself. It was a process that required me to acknowledge my mistakes, understand the pain I had caused, and make amends. I found solace in prayer, a connection that anchored me amidst the storm. Each day brought new challenges, but I faced them with a renewed sense of purpose.

After months of reflection and healing, I returned to the firm, my heart pounding as I stepped through the familiar doors. The air was thick with tension, and I could feel the weight of judgment in the room. My colleagues, once friends, now looked at me with a mixture of disdain and pity. It was a challenging time, but I was determined to show them that I was not defined by my past mistakes.

But I was different now. The morning of the court hearing, I stood before the mirror, the reflection staring back at me, brimming with resolve. I had a story to tell, one of redemption and strength.

As I walked into the courtroom, a sense of calm washed over me. I stood before the judge, my heart racing, and began to speak. My voice quivered at first, but I found my footing with each word. I spoke of my past, my struggles, and the journey I had undertaken to reclaim my life.

"I am not the woman I was," I declared, my voice growing stronger. "I have made mistakes but also learned the power of forgiveness and redemption. I stand before you as a lawyer and a woman who has faced her demons and emerged stronger."

The courtroom fell silent, the gravity of my confession hanging in the air. For the first time, I felt the shackles of shame begin to loosen. I looked for Mark in the audience, and our eyes met. The love and hurt mingled in his gaze, but I could see a flicker of hope shining through.

In the weeks that followed, I faced the consequences of my actions. The scandal tarnished my career, but I was determined to rebuild. With the support of the recovery program and the newfound friendships I had forged, I began to understand that my worth was not defined by my failures but by my resilience.

Mark and I embarked on a journey of healing together. We attended couples therapy, navigating the rocky terrain of betrayal and trust. Slowly, we began to piece our relationship back together, learning to communicate more openly than ever before.

One evening, as we sat under the stars in our backyard, I turned to him, the weight of my heart spilling over. "I'm so sorry, Mark. For everything. I hurt you deeply and am committed to making this right."

He took my hand, his grip firm yet gentle. "I know, Rachel. It's going to take time, but I believe in us." His words were a balm to my wounded soul, a reminder that love could prevail even in the darkest times.

Months turned into a year, and as spring unfurled its blossoms, I felt a sense of renewal. I had started volunteering at the recovery center, sharing my story with others grappling with their own demons. Each encounter reminded me of how far I had come, and I found purpose in helping others navigate their paths to healing.

One afternoon, as I stood before a group of eager faces, I shared my journey and the struggles that had shaped me into the woman I had become. "You are not defined by your past," I told them, my voice steady. "You have the power to change your narrative. It's never too late to rewrite your story."

Looking at the faces before me, I saw hope reflected in their eyes. At that moment, I realized my journey was not just about me—it was about the connections we forge and the lives we touch.

The sun dipped below the horizon, casting a golden hue over the landscape. I stood on my porch, a warm breeze brushing against my skin, and took a deep breath. Life was imperfect, and I was learning to embrace its messy, beautiful chaos.

I had faced betrayal, addiction, and the ghosts of my past, but I had emerged stronger and more resilient. The journey was ongoing, but I was no longer afraid. With faith as my compass and love as my guide, I was ready to embrace whatever came next.

Life would continue to challenge me, but I learned the most important lesson: it's not about our mistakes but how we rise from them. As I looked out at the horizon, I felt a surge of gratitude for the journey that had brought me here—a journey of rediscovery, love, and an unyielding spirit.

The Ties that Bind

Mark, a respected church leader, encounters Anna, his childhood friend, at a community event. They rekindle their connection, and Mark is drawn to Anna's warmth and understanding, finding solace in her presence. Anna, struggling in her own marriage, also feels a connection with Mark, creating a sense of familiarity and comfort. Mark and Anna's rekindled connection deepened as they found solace in each other's company. Mark, the devoted church leader, felt a strong pull towards Anna's warmth and empathy, a sharp contrast to the judgmental and rigid world he navigated daily. Anna, struggling with her own marital issues, saw Mark as a beacon of familiarity and stability in a sea of uncertainty. Their shared past created an unspoken understanding between them, and their bond intensified.

Mark, torn between his dedication to the church and his growing feelings for Anna, wrestled with his moral conflict. The guilt weighed heavily on him, but the comfort and acceptance he found in Anna's presence made it increasingly difficult to let go. As their relationship progressed, Mark and Anna found themselves entangled in a web of complex emotions. Mark struggled to reconcile his devotion to his faith with his yearning for Anna. He questioned his own teachings, grappling with the idea that his actions might be seen as a betrayal of his values. Anna, equally conflicted, battled her own sense of loyalty and commitment. She knew the consequences of their actions could be far-reaching, yet the connection she shared with Mark felt too powerful to ignore. Their secret world became a refuge from the struggles of their everyday lives. The guilt Mark and

Anna carried became a heavy burden, threatening to expose their affair. They found themselves walking a delicate tightrope, balancing their clandestine meetings with the expectations of their public lives. Every moment spent together was tinged with a mixture of joy and anxiety, as they feared the potential fallout should their secret be uncovered. Yet, despite the risks, they couldn't deny the solace and comfort they found in each other's arms. As their affair intensified, Mark and Anna were forced to confront the difficult choices that lay ahead, knowing that their decisions would forever change the course of their lives.

As Mark and Anna spend more time together, their shared past and growing intimacy lead to a passionate affair. Their secret relationship deepens, fueled by guilt and a desire for forbidden connection. Meanwhile, Emily, Mark's wife, senses a change in her husband, but her insecurities and fear of confronting the truth prevent her from addressing the growing distance between them. As the affair intensified, Mark and Anna found themselves irresistibly drawn to each other, their encounters becoming more frequent and intense. Mark, torn between his devotion to the church and his uncontrollable desire for Anna, struggled with his moral dilemma. He knew his actions were wrong, but the passion and excitement of their secret relationship were overwhelming. Anna, equally conflicted, found solace in their shared past and the understanding that Mark seemed to instinctively have of her. Their bond was unbreakable, and the guilt they felt only served to fuel their desire for each other.

Meanwhile, Emily, sensing the growing distance between her and her husband, Mark, became increasingly insecure. She knew something was amiss, but her fears and doubts clouded her judgment. Unable to confront Mark directly, she retreated further into herself, her insecurities eating away at her. Little did she know that her husband was entangled in a passionate affair with his childhood friend, a relationship that was threatening to destroy the very fabric of their marriage. As the web of lies and deceit tightened around them, Mark and Anna found it harder to extricate themselves from the situation. Their shared past, present, and future were inextricably linked, and the consequences of their actions would change their lives forever. The guilt they carried was a heavy burden, but the forbidden nature of their connection only served to intensify their passion and devotion to each other.

Mark's affair begins to take a toll on him, creating inner turmoil and a growing sense of isolation. His guilt, a heavy burden, begins to manifest in his behavior, eroding his once confident facade. He struggles to maintain his image as a respected church leader, while his fear of being discovered weighs heavily on him. Emily, despite her doubts, chooses to believe in Mark's love for her, but her trust in him is gradually eroded as she witnesses his increasingly erratic behavior. Mark's descent into turmoil was rapid and relentless. The once proud and confident man was now a shadow of his former self, his inner conflict manifesting as a physical erosion of his being. He found himself trapped in a cycle of guilt and fear, his affair with Anna consuming him. The weight of his deception bore down on him, threatening to crush the carefully constructed facade he presented to the community. Mark knew that his position as a respected church leader was at odds with his actions, and the dissonance tore at his soul. Emily, his devoted wife, sensed the shift in Mark. Her insecurities whispered that something was amiss, but her love for him and her trust in his devotion kept her silent. She chose to believe in their marriage, in the vows they had exchanged. Yet, as Mark's behavior became more erratic and unpredictable, her faith in him began to waver. She found herself questioning his every move, searching for signs of the truth she feared. As the days passed, Mark's struggle only intensified. The guilt he felt for betraying Emily's trust was compounded by his fear of losing her. He knew that his actions were causing her pain, and the realization tortured him. Mark found himself trapped in a web of his own making, unable to escape the consequences of his choices.

A tragic event occurs in the community, leaving everyone shaken and questioning their faith. Mark, forced to confront the fragility of life, grapples with the consequences of his actions and the impact they have on those around him. The event serves as a catalyst, prompting Mark to re-evaluate his priorities and his destructive path. The days that followed the tragic event were a blur of grief and soul-searching for Mark. He found himself questioning the very core of his being—his faith, his choices, and the man he had become. The affair with Anna, his childhood friend, now felt like a betrayal of everything he stood for. Mark's position as a church leader, once a source of pride, now weighed heavily on him as he struggled to reconcile his public persona with his private actions. The guilt was overwhelming, and he knew that his actions had not only impacted his own life but also the lives of those around him. As Mark grappled with the consequences of his choices, he realized that the event had served as a stark reminder of the fragility of life and the importance of living with integrity. It was a catalyst for change, prompting him to re-evaluate his priorities and make amends for the destructive path he had taken. Mark's journey was not an easy one. He knew that he had to end things with Anna, but his heart ached at the thought of losing her. Their affair had been a secret haven for him, a place where he could escape the expectations and responsibilities of his public life. Yet, he also recognized that their relationship was built on a foundation of lies and deceit, and it was time to face the truth.

With a heavy heart, Mark confessed his actions to Anna, expecting anger and resentment. But to his surprise, she listened with tears in her eyes, understanding the weight of their actions and the need for repentance. As Mark worked to repair the damage he had caused, he found solace in his faith. He immersed himself in the teachings of the church, seeking guidance and forgiveness. The support of his congregation, who stood by him despite his shortcomings, gave him the strength to persevere. Mark's journey is a testament to the power of grace and the potential for transformation. It was a reminder that even in the darkest of times, there is always the possibility of light and a path towards redemption.

Emily, torn between her love for Mark and the growing evidence of his infidelity, finally confronts him. The truth about his affair is revealed, leaving Emily devastated and heartbroken. Mark, overwhelmed with guilt and remorse, confesses his actions and seeks forgiveness from Emily. The weight of his betrayal hangs heavy in the air, shattering the foundation of their marriage." I can't lie. Would you do this to us, Mark?" Emily said, her voice shaking as she confronted her husband. The evidence of his infidelity lay heavy between them, a weighty silence filling the room. Mark, once a devoted church leader, now stood before her, his eyes filled with guilt and shame. "I never "ended up hurting you, Emily. It just happened, and I couldn't pause," his voice caught in his throat. "I know that I've made a horrible mistake, and I'm so sorry".

Emily realized the depth of his betrayal. She sensed something was amiss, but confronting Mark was difficult because of her insecurities. Now, the truth lay bare before her, and she struggled to process the reality of their shattered marriage. "How could you, Mark? How could you be so selfish and cruel?" she asked, her voice laced with pain. Mark hung his head, unable to meet her gaze. "I know I've let you, and I can't expect you to forgive me. But please believe that I am truly sorry and will do whatever it takes to try and make amends."

Anna, consumed by guilt and the realization of the pain she has caused, seeks solace in her faith. She confronts the consequences of her actions and chooses to find redemption through honesty and self-reflection. The community grapples with the tragedy and the revelation of Mark's affair, a collective reckoning that questions their values and the true nature of love and forgiveness. Anna's faith was her anchor as she navigated the turbulent waters of her guilt and remorse. She found solace in prayer and sought guidance from God, pleading for forgiveness and the strength to make amends. Confronting the harm she had caused, Anna embarked on a journey of self-reflection, determined to rebuild trust and heal the wounds she had inflicted. The path to redemption was arduous, but Anna remained steadfast. Mark, too, was engulfed by guilt and moral conflict. The affair had shaken his foundations, causing him to question his own values and the integrity of his leadership. He struggled to reconcile his actions with his role as a spiritual guide, knowing that his transgression had the potential to shatter the community's inner peace. Mark's guilt was a constant companion, weighing heavily on his heart as he navigated the aftermath of his choices. The community was in a state of flux, grappling with the fallout from the affair. The revelation of Mark and Anna's transition had stirred a collective soul-searching. People questioned their own morals, the nature of love and forgiveness, and the very foundation of their beliefs. It was a time of reckoning, a moment when long-held values were scrutinized, and the true meaning of compassion and redemption was debated.

Emily, shattered by Mark, grapples with the complexities of forgiveness and the possibility of reconciliation. She embarks on a journey of healing, navigating her pain and anger, while seeking guidance from her faith and the support of her community. Mark, deeply remorseful, seeks to rebuild trust and atone for his actions. As Emily grappled with the shards of her broken trust, Mark knelt in his study, head bowed in prayer. He sought forgiveness from God and pleaded for guidance to repair the damage he had wrought. The affair with Anna, his childhood friend, had been a moment of weakness, a lapse in judgment fueled by a midlife crisis and a fleeting desire for the comfort of the past. But now, Mark was determined to right his wrongs and reconcile with his wife. He began attending counseling sessions, delving into the root causes of his actions and working to rebuild the foundations of his marriage.

Meanwhile, Emily, surrounded by the loving support of her church community, found solace in her faith. She poured her heart out to God, seeking strength and clarity. Through prayer and reflection, she began to understand the power of forgiveness and the possibility of redemption. She realized that her journey of healing was intertwined with Mark's forgiveness, which did not mean forgetting or excusing his actions, but rather creating a new path built on honesty and mutual understanding. Mark, filled with remorse and a newfound sense of purpose, reached out to Emily with tentative steps. He wrote her letters, expressing his deepest regrets and the pain he had caused. He offered no excuses, only a sincere desire to make amends and rebuild what they had lost. Emily read these letters with a heavy heart, torn between the pain of betrayal and the hope of reconciliation. With cautious optimism, she recognized Mark's effort and agreed to begin rebuilding their marriage.

Anna heard as she struggled to come to terms with the moral implications of her affair with Mark. She knew she had to choose between continuing down this path of forbidden love and ending it and facing the consequences. But as she reflected on her past and her current journey of self-improvement, she couldn't feel a sense of comfort and understanding with Mark. Despite the guilt and turmoil, their bond grew stronger, drawing them closer. On the other hand, Mark was torn between his loyalty to his wife and his intense feelings for Anna. He had always been a devoted church leader, but his actions with Anna made him question his moral compass. He couldn't describe the connection he shared with Anna, but he couldn't ignore the pain he was causing his wife. As he struggled to find a solution, he found solace in Anna's guidance and unwavering support. Their affair may have caused chaos and turmoil, but it also brought them a sense of healing and understanding. They were both on a journey of self-discovery and in each other, they found the courage to confront their inner demons and seek forgiveness. Despite the challenges and obstacles, their bond grew stronger, and they knew they were meant to find each other and love in the most unexpected places.

Through shared grief, honest conversations, and a commitment to rebuilding their relationship, Emily and Mark find strength in their love for one another. They learn to forgive not only each other but also themselves, finding solace in the power of love and the resilience of the human spirit. The community, having witnessed the fragility of life and the power of forgiveness, emerges more vigorous and united, embracing the lessons learned from tragedy and betrayal. As Mark and Emily navigated their path to healing, Mark found himself drawn to the solace of his faith. He sought guidance from his role as a church leader, leaning on his spiritual teachings to make sense of his actions. The affair with Anna, his childhood friend, had left him conflicted and filled with guilt. Mark questioned his own morals and the example he had set for his community.

In contrast, Emily wrestled with her insecurities, struggling to understand why her marriage had faltered. Through tearful prayers and soul-searching, she found the strength to confront her own role in their marital issues. She recognizes her worth and the value of her bond with Mark and is determined to fight for their love. The community, witnessing the public fallout of Mark and Emily's relationship, found themselves unexpectedly united. The raw display of emotion and subsequent journey toward forgiveness touched the hearts of many. It served as a reminder that even the most respected leaders faced trials and that the power of forgiveness could transcend even the most profound betrayals. The town found strength in their shared humanity, and a newfound sense of empathy emerged. Mark and Emily's journey was challenging, but their commitment to honesty and forgiveness prevailed. They emerged from the shadows of their grief stronger and more resilient. Their love, though tested, became a beacon of hope, inspiring those around them to embrace the beauty of second chances. Through their pain, a deeper understanding of the human condition was born, and the community found solace in the power of redemption.

The Weight of Secrets

Ethan, a charismatic youth pastor, feels a growing weight on his soul. He is admired by his congregation, but his seemingly perfect life hides a devastating secret. He is having an affair with Rachel, a young woman struggling with addiction and a deep sense of self-worthlessness. They seek solace in each other, but their clandestine meetings are laced with guilt and fear. The church, a symbol of hope and community, becomes a stage for their unspoken lies. Ethan feels caught between the moral compass of his calling and the seductive allure of his forbidden love. Ethan stood at the pulpit, his eyes scanning the congregation. He exuded an air of confidence and peace as he delivered a passionate sermon on the power of redemption. Little did they know that he was preaching to himself as much as to them. The weight of his secret affair with Rachel pressed heavily on his heart. He knew his actions were a betrayal of the very principles he preached, but he couldn't deny the intense connection he felt with her. Rachel, sitting in the congregation, felt a mix of emotions as she listened to Ethan's words. She was drawn to his charisma and the sense of acceptance she felt in his presence. It was a sharp contrast to the shame and guilt she carried within her. As their eyes met for a brief moment, an unspoken understanding passed between them. The guilt they both felt was suffocating, yet they couldn't deny the solace they found in each other's arms. Their clandestine meetings were filled with a mixture of passion and despair, each encounter leaving them more entangled in their web of lies. Ethan felt torn between his dedication to the church and his forbidden love for Rachel. The moral compass he so fervently preached from seemed to blur when faced with the complexity of his own humanity. The church, a place of sanctuary for so many, now held a different meaning for Ethan and Rachel. It became a symbol of their hidden truth, a stage where their lies and secrets were carefully crafted and performed. They both knew the consequences of their affair being uncovered would be devastating, yet they couldn't seem to escape the pull of their forbidden connection. As the days turned into weeks, their secret loomed larger, and the weight on Ethan's soul only grew heavier, a constant reminder of his betrayal.

As Ethan and Rachel's relationship deepens, their lies begin to unravel. Whispers of their affair reach the ears of the church elders. The weight of their secret grows heavier with each passing day. They become trapped in a web of deceit, their lives teetering on the brink of exposure. Ethan struggles to reconcile his desires with his commitment to his faith. Rachel, desperately seeking validation, finds herself losing control. Their shared secret is becoming a burden too heavy to bear. The consequences of their actions are looming, threatening to shatter their lives and the trust of those around them. As the whispers of their affair echo through the halls of the church, Ethan and Rachel find themselves ensnared in an intricate web of their own weaving. The weight of their deceit hangs heavy, threatening to crush them under the burden of their hidden desires and fractured faith. Ethan, the handsome and popular youth pastor, struggles to reconcile his passions with his devotion to God. He finds himself torn between his love for Rachel and his commitment to his calling, his inner turmoil intensifying with each clandestine encounter. Rachel, battling her own demons of addiction and self-doubt, seeks solace in Ethan's arms, desperate for validation and a sense of worth. However, as their secret becomes increasingly difficult to bear, she finds her grasp on control slipping away. The whispers are getting louder, and the church elders are beginning to suspect something amiss. Ethan and Rachel know that their fragile world could come crashing down at any moment, exposing their lies and shattering the trust of those around them. Desperation begins to set in as they contemplate their next move. Ethan, torn between his love for Rachel and his duty to his faith, searches for a way to reconcile his conflicting desires. Rachel, fearing the loss of the one thing that makes her feel whole, clings to their secret, hoping against hope that they can somehow escape the consequences of their actions. But with each passing day, the web of lies tightens around them, pulling them deeper into a maze of deceit from which there seems to be no escape.

The cracks in Ethan's facade begin to show. He experiences nightmares, haunted by the consequences of his actions. He tries to push Rachel away, but their bond is too strong. The guilt consumes him, threatening to destroy everything he holds dear. Rachel, fueled by her own inner turmoil, lashes out at Ethan, accusing him of using her. Their connection, once a refuge, becomes a battleground, fueled by their shared desperation and the weight of their secret. The emotional turmoil of the characters is intensified, making their struggles more relatable and evoking empathy from the audience. Ethan's carefully crafted facade was crumbling. The nightmares that plagued him were a stark contrast to his confident, charming exterior. He found himself grappling with the weight of his secret, the affair with Rachel, a vulnerable parishioner. As the guilt gnawed at him, he pushed Rachel away, but their connection was powerful and complex. She, too, was battling her own demons, and the rejection from Ethan only added fuel to her inner turmoil. In a desperate attempt to ease her pain, she lashed out, her words cutting deep as she accused him of using her. Their once safe haven had become a war zone, their shared desperation and secrecy tearing them apart. Ethan felt trapped, his usual composure slipping away as the truth threatened to surface. The dreams were a stark reminder of the potential fallout, and he feared the destruction of his carefully curated life. His position as a youth pastor, admired and respected, seemed at odds with his actions. Yet, he couldn't deny the bond he shared with Rachel, a connection that went beyond their mutual struggles. As their relationship hung in the balance, Ethan questioned his ability to navigate the chaos. As the tension escalated, Ethan and Rachel found themselves at a crossroads. The decision to either confront their secrets or let them destroy them hung heavily in the air. Their once solid foundation was now shaky, and the weight of their choices threatened to crush them. In the midst of their inner turmoil, they clung to each other, unaware that their bond might be their salvation or their downfall.

One fateful Sunday, Ethan's secret is exposed. A disgruntled parishioner, privy to the whispers, confronts him during a service. Initially shocked and confused, the congregation witnesses Ethan's descent into despair. The weight of his lies becomes unbearable, and he collapses under the pressure. Rachel, fearing the consequences, disappears, leaving Ethan to face the fallout alone. Ethan stood at the pulpit, his heart pounding as the disgruntled parishioner, Mr. Adams, revealed the whispered secret. The initial shock on the congregation's faces transformed into a mixture of disbelief and judgment.

Ethan's carefully crafted image as the beloved youth pastor crumbled before his eyes. He felt Rachel's absence keenly; her disappearance left him alone to face the fallout. As the weight of his deception became overwhelming, he struggled to maintain his composure. The once confident and charismatic Ethan now stood broken, his descent into despair playing out in front of the entire church. Fearing the worst, Ethan's mind raced as he tried to process the implications of this exposure. The secrets he kept and the lies he told to maintain his illicit affair with Rachel were now laid bare. The congregation, once a source of support and admiration, had become a jury, passing silent judgment on his actions. He could feel their stares, a thousand accusations, weighing him down. As Ethan's world came crashing down, he realized the true extent of the damage. The trust he had built with his congregation was shattered, and the impact on those who once admired him would be profound. The secrets and lies had taken their toll, and Ethan faced a future filled with uncertainty and shame. Little did he know that this was just the beginning, and the actual test of his character was yet to come.

Stripped of his authority and facing the wrath of his community, Ethan seeks solace in the church he once led. He confronts his own failings, realizing the depth of his betrayal. The walls of his carefully constructed world crumble, revealing a man consumed by his own hypocrisy. He confesses to his congregation in a moment of raw vulnerability, seeking forgiveness and the strength to rebuild his life. Ethan stood in the empty church, the sun streaming through the stained glass windows, casting colorful patterns on the floor. He ran his hand through his hair, his eyes reflecting the turmoil. The once-confident pastor was now a mere shadow of his former self, stripped of the authority that had defined him. He knew his world was crumbling around him, and his secret affair with Rachel, a young woman from the congregation, had come to light. The hypocrisy of his actions weighed heavily on his conscience. With a heavy heart, he approached the pulpit where he had once stood confidently, preaching to his devoted followers. Now, he was alone, facing his own demons and the consequences of his actions. As he sank to his knees, Ethan felt a wave of vulnerability wash over him. He bowed his head, his shoulders shaking with the weight of his confession. "Forgive me, Lord, for I have sinned," he whispered, his voice echoing in the empty sanctuary. "I have betrayed the trust of my congregation and fallen prey to my own desires. I have hurt those I swore to protect and led a double life, hiding my true self from the world." Ethan laid bare his soul in that moment, confronting the depth of his failings. He knew that his carefully crafted image had shattered, revealing a man consumed by hypocrisy. The silence that followed was deafening. Ethan remained kneeling, awaiting judgment, not just from a higher power but from his own conscience. He knew the path to redemption would be long and arduous, but he was willing to face it. Seeking forgiveness and the strength to rebuild, he vowed to confront his demons and emerge a better man.

Initially angered by Ethan's betrayal, the congregation is moved by his heartfelt confession. They offer him forgiveness and support, recognizing the humanity behind the fallen pastor. Ethan's journey to redemption begins, a path paved with humility and a newfound understanding of faith. He begins to rebuild his life, no longer seeking perfection but embracing his imperfections. Ethan stood before the congregation, his heart heavy with the weight of his confession.

The initial shock and anger that had rippled through the crowd now seemed to soften as they witnessed the depth of his remorse. With tears in his eyes, Ethan spoke of his struggle—the internal battle between his faith and human desires. He bared his soul, revealing the secret affair that had threatened to destroy everything he held dear. At that moment, Ethan found the strength to be vulnerable, to lay bare his imperfections, and to ask for forgiveness. And the congregation, seeing the humanity behind the fallen pastor, extended their grace. They recognized that Ethan, despite his position of spiritual leadership, was still a man susceptible to temptation and error. As the weight of their forgiveness lifted some of the burden from Ethan's shoulders, he began his journey toward redemption. It was a path he knew would be long and challenging, requiring him to confront his demons head-on. Ethan embraced humility, no longer striving for the unattainable perfection he had once sought. Instead, he found solace in the understanding that his imperfections were a part of what made him human and that true strength came from acknowledging and learning from one's mistakes. The road ahead would not be easy, but with the support of those around him, Ethan was determined to rebuild his life. He vowed to use his experience as a lesson in compassion and understanding, hoping to help others facing similar struggles.

Ethan embarks on a journey to find Rachel, desperate to reconcile their fractured relationship. He searches for her in the shadows of the city, retracing their paths, seeking to understand the depth of her pain. He finds her in a halfway house, battling her demons, a testament to the destructive power of her own inner turmoil. He confronts the weight of his own actions, realizing the damage he has caused. Ethan's heart pounded as he stood outside the halfway house, his eyes fixed on the weathered door. He took a deep breath, steeling himself for the confrontation. The weight of his past actions bore down on him as he prepared to face Rachel, the woman with whom he had shared a secret and ill-fated affair. He knew that his presence here could be construed as intrusive, but he was desperate to right the wrongs he had done and perhaps, just perhaps, find a path to redemption. As he stepped inside, the memories of their passionate yet tumultuous relationship came flooding back. He recalled the intensity of their encounters, the way Rachel's eyes would light up with a mixture of desire and pain. He knew that her struggles with addiction and self-worth had been a driving force behind their affair, and he carried the burden of having taken advantage of her vulnerability. Now, as he stood in the dimly lit hallway, he sensed the depth of her pain and the extent of the damage he had caused. Ethan found Rachel in one of the standard rooms, her eyes hollow and her once vibrant spirit seemingly extinguished. She looked up, her gaze a mixture of surprise, anger, and a hint of lingering desire. In that moment, Ethan saw their relationship's raw, exposed nerves, the toxic combination of passion and pain that had bound them together. "What are you doing here, Ethan?" she asked, her voice laced with emotions. "I couldn't stay away any longer, Rachel," he replied, his voice thick with remorse. "I know I've caused you pain, and I want to understand the depth of it. I want to face the consequences of my actions and be here for you if you'll let me." The air between them hung heavy with unspoken words and the ghosts of their shared past. Rachel's eyes flickered, silently acknowledging the truth in Ethan's words. Slowly, she nodded, a silent invitation for him to stay. As they sat down together, the weight of their shared history pressed upon them, and they began the arduous journey of untangling their fractured relationship, confronting the demons that had driven them apart, and perhaps, just perhaps, finding a way to heal and rebuild what had been broken.

Ethan, humbled by his experiences, offers Rachel a hand, not in romantic pursuit but in genuine support. He recognizes her strength and resilience, offering forgiveness and a chance to rebuild her life. Rachel, initially resistant, sees the sincerity in Ethan's intentions. They embark on a healing journey, and their shared past reminds them of their mistakes. Ethan and Rachel's journey of healing was not without its challenges. As they navigated their shared past and the pain it brought, they also discovered a newfound strength in their honesty with each other. Once a proud and popular youth pastor, Ethan had his own demons to battle. The secret affair he'd kept with Rachel, a troubled parishioner, weighed heavily on his conscience. He knew his actions had contributed to her struggles and was determined to make amends. Initially guarded and resistant to Ethan's overtures, Rachel began to see his efforts as genuine. His humility and willingness to own up to his mistakes touched her deeply. She found herself opening up to him about her own battles with self-worth and addiction. Together, they embarked on a path of mutual forgiveness and understanding. Their journey was one of slow and steady progress. They leaned on each other for support, offering a listening ear and a shoulder to cry on when needed. Over time, their shared pain became a bond that strengthened their resolve to heal and move forward. It was a testament to their resilience and the power of forgiveness.

Once consumed by guilt and fear, Ethan finds solace in the act of forgiveness. He realizes that true faith is not about perfection but the courage to embrace vulnerability and the power of redemption. Rachel, supported by Ethan and the church community, begins to heal, finding strength in her struggles and forgiveness in her own heart. They find solace in their shared journey, their burdens lifted, their spirits reborn. Ethan stood at the pulpit, his heart heavy with the weight of his secret. The congregation hung on his every word, their eyes fixed on him with admiration and trust. Little did they know that their beloved youth pastor was battling his own demons. The affair with Rachel, a vulnerable parishioner, weighed on his conscience. He knew it was wrong but couldn't deny their shared connection. As he delivered his sermon on the power of forgiveness, his words took on a new depth, born from his own internal struggle. He spoke of the courage to face our flaws and the strength of embracing our vulnerabilities. His message resonated with the congregation, but none more so than Rachel, who sat in the back, her heart yearning for healing. As Ethan concluded his sermon, he stepped down from the pulpit and approached Rachel. She felt a mix of anxiety and hope as he approached. With gentle sincerity, he asked how she was truly doing. Tears welled up in her eyes as she shared her struggles with addiction and self-worth. Ethan listened intently, his guilt and fear melting away in that moment. He saw the raw, unguarded pain in her eyes, and something shifted within him. It was in that instant that he knew he had to end the affair and help Rachel heal. The path to forgiveness was not easy for either of them. Ethan and Rachel faced their own inner demons, wrestling with guilt and shame. However, with the support of the church community and each other, they began to find solace. Their shared journey became a source of strength, and they discovered that true faith was not about perfection but about embracing their vulnerabilities and seeking redemption.

The Faithful Deceiver

Hannah, a seemingly happy wife and mother, discovers a note in Ryan's jacket pocket that reveals his infidelity. The note, a simple "I miss you," throws her world into turmoil, forcing her to confront the betrayal that threatens the foundation of their marriage. Hannah's heart pounded in her ears as she stood in the bedroom, the note crumpled in her hand. She felt a surge of emotions—anger, hurt, and confusion—as she confronted the reality of Ryan's infidelity. The simple words "I miss you" implied a deep connection and a secret world that excluded her. As she grappled with the betrayal, Hannah's mind raced with questions. Who was this note from? How long had Ryan been unfaithful? Had he fallen out of love with her?

The foundation of their ten-year marriage suddenly felt fragile and uncertain. Hannah, summoning all her courage, knew she had to confront Ryan, but it made her sick to her stomach. She loved him profoundly and now questioned whether their relationship could withstand this crisis. With a heavy heart, Hannah steeled herself for the difficult conversation ahead, determined to uncover the truth and face the challenges ahead. As Hannah gathered her thoughts, she noticed a change in Ryan's behavior. He seemed distant and preoccupied, his eyes carrying a weight she hadn't seen before. When they were alone, she confronted him, her voice shaking but resolute. "Who is she, Ryan? Why are you doing this to us?" Ryan's face reflected a battle of emotions—shame, regret, and a hint of defiance. He averted his gaze, unable to meet the hurt in Hannah's eyes. "It's not what you think," he began, his voice hoarse. "It's someone from my past, someone I thought I had let go of. But I made a mistake and am now paying the price."

Hannah's heart broke at his admission, but a part of her also felt a glimmer of hope. They may be able to repair the damage and rebuild their marriage on a firmer foundation. The coming days were filled with painful conversations and tearful nights. Hannah struggled to accept Ryan's betrayal, but she recognized his honesty and willingness to make amends. As they navigated the turmoil together, Hannah discovered a strength she didn't know she possessed. She realized that her happiness wasn't solely dependent on her relationship with Ryan, and she began exploring her passions and interests. Through counseling and heartfelt conversations, Hannah and Ryan slowly rebuilt their marriage, this time on a foundation of trust, honesty, and mutual understanding. The path to healing wasn't easy, but it taught Hannah the importance of self-love and the power of forgiveness.

Hannah learns about Ryan's affair with a woman from his college days, someone he never fully moved on from. The realization brings a wave of pain and anger, leaving Hannah feeling like a ghost in her own life. Hannah felt as though she were living someone else's life. The pain of Ryan's betrayal was a constant, sharp presence, and it left her feeling disconnected and numb. She went through her daily routine, caring for their children and maintaining a facade of normalcy, but inside, she was crumbling. The image of Ryan with another woman was seared into her mind, and the knowledge that it was someone from his past, a flame he had never truly extinguished, cut deep. It made her question the entirety of their marriage—every memory, every moment of happiness, now tinged with doubt and sorrow. As the days turned into weeks, Hannah's anger began to simmer. She refused to be a victim any longer and channeled her pain into a fierce determination to heal and move forward. She sought solace in the company of friends, finding strength in their support and understanding. She slowly began to piece her life back together, focusing on her happiness and the future she wanted for herself and her children. The path to healing was not linear; some days were filled with more heartache than others. But Hannah found comfort in the small moments—her children's laughter, the sun's warmth on her face, and the realization that she was stronger than she knew. She was determined to emerge from this crisis with a renewed sense of self, ready to embrace a future filled with hope and possibility.

Hannah attends support group meetings, seeking solace and understanding among other women who have experienced infidelity. She is surrounded by stories that mirror her own, highlighting the universality of betrayal and the struggle to heal. Hannah found solace in these support group meetings. Here, she didn't have to explain the all-encompassing grief that came with infidelity; they understood the unique pain of feeling lost in your own life. The other women welcomed her with open arms, and their shared experiences created a bond. Each woman carried a story of heartbreak but also of resilience and strength. They became a sisterhood of survivors, empowering each other to piece their lives back together and emerge stronger than before. As Hannah listened to their stories, she realized how infidelity had the power to shatter lives but also the capacity to transform them. These women inspired her, and she began to see a path forward. Their presence provided a sense of community, a reminder that she was not alone in her struggles. They shared coping strategies, rebuilding self-worth, and navigating the complex emotions that came with betrayal. Through their encouragement, Hannah started to heal. She discovered a newfound sense of self-worth and explored her passions and interests. She felt more substantial and confident each day, slowly but surely reclaiming her life. These women became her lifeline, helping her transform her pain into power.

Hannah meets David, a man navigating his own heartbreak, at a support group meeting. They share coffee, and their conversations touch on their hopes, dreams, and struggles. A connection begins to form, bringing solace and a sense of guilt for Hannah. As Hannah and David sat across from each other, the warmth of the coffee shop enveloped them, providing a cozy backdrop to their intimate conversation. Heavy with the weight of her husband's betrayal, Hannah found solace in David's understanding gaze. He, too, had experienced the sharp pain of infidelity, and their shared experience created an unspoken bond between them. Each word they exchanged formed a fragile connection, offering a glimmer of hope in their otherwise tumultuous lives. Hannah felt a sense of peace in David's presence as if she had finally found someone who truly comprehended the depths of her heartache. She shared her dreams for the future, now uncertain and blurry, and David listened intently, his eyes reflecting a mixture of empathy and something else—a spark of interest that caught Hannah off guard. At that moment, she felt a twinge of guilt, as if her budding connection with David betrayed her marriage vows, but the comfort he offered was too alluring to resist. As their meetings became regular, Hannah looked forward to the time spent with David. Their conversations delved into the depths of their souls, exploring the complexities of love, loss, and the fragile beauty of new beginnings. Hannah's heart began to heal, and though the pain of her husband's infidelity would always leave a mark, David's presence brought a sense of solace and the promise of something new. However, with each step towards healing, the weight of her guilt seemed to grow, complicating the already tangled web of her emotions.

Ryan reaches out to Hannah, desperate to talk. She agrees, but the conversation is filled with tension and pain. Ryan apologizes for his actions, confessing his desire to find something he lost, but ultimately losing her. Ryan's voice cracked as he poured out his heart to Hannah. "I know I can't take back what I did, and I don't expect you to forgive me. But I had to try and find what I lost so many years ago. I was a fool, and I lost you in the process." Once filled with warmth and love, Hannah's eyes now held a cold, steely gaze. She had endured countless sleepless nights, grappling with the pain of his betrayal. "You didn't just lose me, Ryan," she said, her voice steady despite the turmoil. "You lost the trust, the love, and the future we built together. Our marriage may never recover from this." Ryan's shoulders slumped in defeat as he realized the full extent of his actions. His regret bore down, and he knew he had inflicted this pain. "I understand if you can't find it in your heart to forgive me," he whispered, his eyes pleading for a glimmer of hope. Hannah's resolve wavered as she saw the man she once loved, broken and remorseful. Yet, once so complete, her heart felt hollow, and she wasn't sure if it could ever be mended.

Hannah and Ryan embark on rebuilding trust, attending counseling, and confronting the demons that drove them apart. Hannah grapples with her feelings for David and learns to forgive Ryan and herself for past mistakes. As Hannah and Ryan began their arduous journey towards reconciliation, they knew it wouldn't be easy. Hannah's heart still bore the scars of Ryan's infidelity, and she found herself constantly questioning whether she could ever truly trust him again. Despite the challenges, she remained committed to their marriage and the life they had built together. After recognizing the depth of Hannah's pain, Ryan embarked on his own self-improvement path. He attended counseling sessions diligently, confronting the demons from his past that had driven him to betray Hannah's trust. He knew regaining her forgiveness would be gradual, so he focused on becoming a better husband and father, striving to be the man Hannah and their children deserved. During this tumultuous time, Hannah found solace in her new friend, David. They had connected instantly at the support group for people navigating infidelity, and David's understanding and empathy provided a much-needed refuge for Hannah. As their friendship deepened, David's feelings for Hannah intensified, complicating the already complex emotions she was navigating. Hannah was grappling with conflicting loyalties, torn between her commitment to her marriage and her burgeoning feelings for David. The path of healing was fraught with obstacles and setbacks. There were moments when Hannah questioned if she had the strength to continue, but her determination to forge a better future for herself and her family kept her going. Witnessing Hannah's struggle, Ryan redoubled his efforts to prove the worthiness of her love and trust. He demonstrated patience, understanding, and a willingness to confront his own flaws, slowly rebuilding the foundation of their marriage.

Hannah confronts her feelings for David, realizing the complexities of love and its potential to comfort and complicate. She chooses to honor her marriage, committing to fighting for it with all her strength. Hannah's heart was heavy as she grappled with the emotions swirling within her. Confronting her feelings for David had brought a new complexity to her tumultuous life. She recognized the solace he offered, the understanding born from shared heartache, and the unspoken connection that had formed between them. Yet, despite the pull she felt towards David, Hannah honored her marriage vows. She knew the path ahead would be arduous, but she was determined to fight for her relationship with every fiber of her being. The thought of her children and the life they had created together gave her the strength to persevere. Hannah resolved to navigate the complexities of love, embracing its comforting warmth and ability to complicate even the most steadfast of hearts. As the days turned into weeks, Hannah threw herself into repairing her relationship. She sought counseling, poured over self-help books, and conversed honestly with her husband. The process was excruciating, forcing her to confront the raw wounds of betrayal and the lingering shadows of doubt. Yet, with each step, Hannah felt a sense of empowerment. She was rebuilding her marriage on a renewed commitment, trust, and understanding foundation. The journey was far from over, but Hannah approached it with hope and resilience, knowing that the fight for love was worth every ounce of effort. David's presence in her life remained a constant reminder of the intricacies of the human heart. Their paths had crossed when both were vulnerable and seeking solace. While Hannah chose to focus on her marriage, she couldn't ignore the impact David had on her. He represented a potential future untaken, a reminder of the 'what-ifs' and alternate paths her life could have taken. As she continued her journey of healing and self-discovery, Hannah knew that navigating the complexities of love meant accepting its capacity to comfort and complicate.

Hannah realizes that steadfast faithfulness lies in honesty with oneself and the people we love. She acknowledges her past deception to herself and Ryan and chooses to embrace her truth. Hannah's realization led her on a path of self-reflection and courage. She recognized that her own deception had been a coping mechanism, an attempt to ignore the truth about Ryan's infidelity. But now, she was ready to confront it head-on. With a newfound sense of resolve, she sought to repair the damage that had been done, not just to their marriage but also to herself. She began to write, pouring her heart onto the journal pages, exploring her emotions and the lessons she had learned about love, betrayal, and forgiveness. As Hannah delved into her own heart, she discovered a strength she never knew she possessed. She confronted Ryan, not in anger, but with a calm determination. She laid bare her soul, expressing the hurt and confusion his actions had caused. Seeing his wife's transformation, Ryan was shaken to his core. He realized the depth of his wife's love and the extent of her pain. In the quiet moments that followed, as their hearts bore witness to the truth, a new understanding emerged. It was a turning point, a chance for them to rebuild what had been broken. Together, they began the journey towards healing, knowing it would be a road of challenges and triumphs, but they would walk side by side.

Hannah and Ryan stand together on Fifth Avenue, both transformed by their experiences. They embrace, acknowledging the weight of their past but hopeful for a new beginning. The city skyline becomes a symbol of their resilience and love. Hannah and Ryan's embrace was a testament to their journey of healing and forgiveness. With its towering skyline, the bustling city of New York served as a backdrop to their renewed love story. As they stood on Fifth Avenue, the city's vibrant energy mirrored the resurgence of their relationship. They had both emerged from a dark chapter, their hearts bruised but not broken. The pain of Ryan's infidelity had cut deep, but Hannah's resilience shone through. She had confronted her fears and insecurities, emerging stronger and more confident. Ryan, too, had faced his past regrets, recognizing the value of the love he had almost lost. Their shared experiences had taught them that true strength lay in vulnerability and that hope could rise from the ashes of heartache. Now, as they held each other, the city's vibrant lights reflected in their eyes, symbolizing their bright future. Their love, tested and tried, had emerged victorious, a beacon of hope in the vast urban landscape. Together, they embarked on a new chapter, leaving the past behind and embracing the promise of a future filled with trust, understanding, and unwavering love.

The Addict's Prayer

Sarah sat in the dimly lit room, the air thick with unspoken fears and shared sorrows. The buzz of murmured introductions floated around her, but she felt worlds away, cocooned in her own turmoil. This was her first recovery group meeting, a leap into the unknown that left her heart racing and her palms clammy. She watched as others shared their stories, their voices trembling yet resolute, while she fought to keep her own bottled up, hidden beneath a carefully crafted mask of indifference. As she wrapped her arms around herself, a familiar ache gnawed at her insides, a reminder of the addiction that had brought her here. Each face in the circle reflected a struggle she understood all too well, yet the thought of revealing her own vulnerabilities felt like standing naked in a storm. Just as despair threatened to swallow her whole, her gaze landed on David. He exuded a quiet strength, his eyes mirroring the same shadows of pain she carried. At that moment, something shifted—an unspoken understanding flickered between them, igniting the fragile beginnings of a bond that could either save or shatter them both.

Sarah was drawn to David's steady presence as the meeting progressed, seeking solace in his silent strength. When the time came for her to speak, Sarah hesitated, her voice catching in her throat. The desire to retreat and hide in the shadows was strong, but David's encouraging nod was a beacon of courage. With a deep breath, she began, her words faltering at first, then gaining strength as she delved into her story of loss and addiction. It was as if a dam had broken, and the torrent of emotions she had kept pent up for so long finally found release. As Sarah spoke, David listened intently, his gaze never wavering, offering her an anchor in the tempest of her own making. When she finally fell silent, the room hung heavy with the weight of her confession, and she dared to look up, searching for judgment or pity in the eyes of her peers. Instead, she found understanding and a glimmer of hope in David's soft smile.

Through conversations and shared experiences, Sarah and David begin to unravel the layers of their past, exploring the roots of their addictions. Sarah reveals her painful childhood trauma while David grapples with the loss of a loved one. They find solace in their shared vulnerability, understanding that they are not alone in their battles.

As Sarah and David continued to bare their souls to each other, they found comfort in their shared struggles. Sarah spoke of the abuse she endured as a child, the pain so deep it had haunted her into adulthood. David listened intently, his heart breaking for her, but he also recognized the courage it took for her to speak these words aloud. In turn, he shared his own story of the loss and grief of a loved one taken too soon, leaving him with a hole in his heart that seemed impossible to fill.

They found solace in the fact that they were not alone in their battles against addiction. Their vulnerabilities intertwined, creating a unique bond between them. In sharing their stories, it was as if they were shedding the weight of their pasts, layer by layer, and beginning to heal. The more they uncovered, the more they realized how their addictions had been a crutch, a way to numb the pain of their traumas.

But now, with each other's support, they were learning to face their demons head-on. It wasn't an easy journey, with setbacks and challenges. Yet, with every hurdle, they grew more robust, their resolve deepening as they navigated the twists and turns of recovery together.

Their shared experiences created an unbreakable trust between them, a safe space where they could be sincere. In that vulnerability, they found strength and a sense of peace they had never known before. It was as if, in unraveling their pasts, they were also weaving a new future—one filled with hope, understanding, and the possibility of a life free from the shackles of addiction.

Sarah faces a personal crisis, tempted to relapse and succumb to the comforting grip of alcohol. She grapples with her desire to escape her pain and the fear of losing her newfound connection with David. David, witnessing her struggle, offers support and encouragement, urging her to fight for her recovery.

Sarah's heart was a tempest, her desires warring within her. The allure of alcohol's embrace beckoned, promising solace from the tempest of her emotions. Yet, the thought of David anchored her, his unwavering support, a beacon of light in her darkness. She knew that succumbing to her temptations would mean risking their newfound bond, a connection that had brought color and hope back into her life. David saw the turmoil in her eyes and sensed her internal struggle. He stood by her side with gentle strength, offering a hand to hold and a shoulder to lean on. His encouragement was her lifeline, urging her to bravely face her demons and fight for the recovery that lay just beyond the horizon. In this moment of decision, Sarah's resolve wavered, but David's steadfast presence gave her the courage to choose life, healing, and a path toward a brighter future together.

As Sarah and David continued on their path of recovery, they found solace and strength in unexpected places. Sarah, once a skeptic, found herself drawn to the quiet chapel in the hospital. She would often sit in the back, head bowed, hands clasped, and pour out her heart in prayer. Here, she discovered a sense of peace and hope that had eluded her for so long. The power of prayer became her anchor, a way to stay grounded and find comfort in her darkest moments. It was through her faith and the support of the group that Sarah found the strength to resist the temptation of relapse and continue her journey toward recovery.

Meanwhile, David threw himself into the support group meetings. He found comfort in his peers' shared stories and struggles. Their vulnerability and courage inspired him to face his own demons head-on. The group became a safe haven where he could let down his guard and be honest about his past without fear of judgment. It was in these meetings that David found the strength to confront his addiction and the courage to support Sarah in her own recovery journey.

As they navigated their recovery, Sarah and David's paths occasionally crossed, and they found great comfort in each other's company. They shared a unique understanding of their challenges and a deep appreciation for the hope slowly blossoming within them. Together, they began to envision a future free from the shadows of their past, a future filled with faith, strength, and the knowledge that they could overcome any obstacle. The road could have been smoother, and there were setbacks and challenges along the way. But with each hurdle, Sarah and David grew stronger, their faith becoming a shield against the storms of their past. They learned to lean on each other and their respective sources of strength, drawing from the wellspring of hope that had sustained them through the darkest times. And as they continued their journey, they inspired others to do the same, paying forward the gift of hope and healing they had received. Little by little, their recovery began to take shape, and a future once shrouded in doubt and

Uncertainty now shone with promise and possibility. Sarah and David had found the courage to face their past and the strength to build a new future. Their shared vulnerability had become a source of power, and their faith in something greater than themselves had given them a sense of purpose and direction. The wreckage of their past was slowly being transformed into a testament to the resilience of the human spirit, and they knew that no matter what life threw their way, they had the tools to survive and thrive.

As the days turned into weeks, Sarah and David's bond strengthened, and they found themselves inseparable. Their shared struggles had created a unique understanding between them, and they instinctively knew how to provide comfort and support to one another. The lines between friendship and romance continued to blur as they navigated this new, uncharted territory. They enjoyed exploring, discovering new feelings, and anticipating what could be. However, the challenges of recovery were ever-present, and some days were more difficult than others. There were moments when old wounds would reopen, and they would have to lean on each other for support, drawing strength from their growing connection. Despite the obstacles, they were determined to face their struggles head-on together. As they continued their journey, Sarah and David discovered a love that healed and empowered them. Their bond, forged in adversity, became a safe haven, a place of solace and comfort. They were no longer just friends or romantic interests; they had become each other's anchors, guiding lights in the storm, and their love was a beacon of hope in the darkness.

Sarah and David's journey towards healing was filled with both challenges and beautiful moments of connection. As they bravely shared their deepest fears and hopes, they found solace and strength in each other's arms. Their growing closeness brought the possibility of a new beginning, a chance to rewrite their stories with love and support. They were keenly aware of the potential pitfalls and how their past traumas could hinder their progress. Yet, with each step, they faced these obstacles together, fostering an environment of honesty and trust. In doing so, they discovered a unique bond, a safe haven where they could be vulnerable and authentic to themselves. As their relationship blossomed, Sarah and David continued to navigate the complexities of their recovery. They embraced the idea that their journey was about healing, personal growth, and transformation. Together, they explored new paths, pushing themselves to try activities that challenged them and encouraged self-discovery. Whether hiking to the top of a mountain, facing their fears, or volunteering at a local shelter, they found purpose and meaning in their shared experiences. Each day, their bond strengthened, and their love became a beacon of hope in their lives. The road to recovery was not always smooth, and there were times when old wounds reopened, or new challenges arose. Yet, Sarah and David remained steadfast in their commitment to each other and themselves.

They learned to navigate life's ups and downs with resilience and grace, remembering the importance of self-care and mutual support.

As they continued their journey, hand in hand, they inspired those around them, showing that vulnerability can lead to strength, and that love can be the greatest healer of all.

Sarah and David's relationship hung in the balance, their future together uncertain. Sarah's heart ached as she grappled with her conflicting desires for love and her need to focus on her recovery. She feared that giving into her heart's desires might jeopardize her hard-won progress.

David, on the other hand, felt a deep sense of worry as he contemplated the possibility of losing Sarah, not just to her addiction but also to the shadows of her past. He wanted to be her rock, her anchor, but the weight of responsibility scared him. The couple found themselves at a crossroads, their paths diverging in a way that threatened their togetherness. They knew their love and commitment would be tested in ways they had never imagined. Sarah and David knew their choices would shape their relationship and individual journeys of self-discovery and healing. As they stood at this precipice, their love for each other was undeniable, but it was a love that needed to be strong enough to face the challenges ahead. Their story, filled with hope and heartache, was one of courage in the face of uncertainty.

Sarah and David's faith journey became a source of strength and comfort. They found solace in their shared belief, a safe haven in the storm of their struggles. Their prayers were honest and raw, laying bare their fears and hopes for the future. This vulnerability brought them closer, forging a deep bond between them. They knew their faith was a powerful tool, a guiding light that could lead them out of the darkness. Together, they sought guidance from a higher power, recognizing the importance of humility and openness to receive divine direction. Their trust in something greater than themselves gave them the courage to face each new day. They believed their challenges were not insurmountable and that they could forge a brighter path forward with prayer, perseverance, and each other. Their story inspired those around them, a testament to the power of faith and the resilience of the human spirit. In their vulnerability, they found strength, and in their shared prayers, they discovered a sense of peace and purpose. This journey was a reminder that hope can flourish even in the most challenging circumstances.

In the quiet sanctuary of their local church, Sarah and David found solace in their shared prayer. Their voices, filled with hope and resilience, echoed off the ancient stone walls, a testament to their unwavering faith. They had both weathered storms, emerging with a love that felt like a gift from above, a blessing they cherished daily. This prayer was a turning point, recognizing their past struggles and a plea for continued guidance. They knew their journey had been challenging, but with each other and their faith, they felt equipped to face whatever lay ahead. The prayer ended, but the silence that followed was comforting and peaceful. In that moment, they felt a profound connection to something greater than themselves, not just to each other. It was as if their prayer had been heard, and a warm sense of calm washed over them. They knew their future may hold challenges, but they also felt unshakeable hope and determination. As they left the church, hand in hand, a gentle breeze seemed to whisper encouragement, a reminder that their prayer had been carried on the wind, and their journey continued with renewed strength and purpose.

The Shadow of Pain

Azim, a renowned psychologist, was intrigued by his new client, Fatima. She had come to him, seeking help to heal from the trauma of domestic violence. Azim was immediately drawn to her resilience and quiet strength. Though haunted by pain, her eyes sparkled with a fierce determination to overcome her past. Azim looked forward to their time together as their sessions progressed. He was captivated by her sharp wit and unwavering spirit. Fatima, unaware of the impact she had on Azim, continued to share her struggles, slowly unraveling the pain inflicted by her abusive partner. Azim's professional ethics battled with his growing attraction towards her. He knew that an affair with a client was unacceptable and could jeopardize his career. Yet, he found himself unable to ignore his intense connection with Fatima. As the weeks turned into months, their relationship evolved. Azim witnessed Fatima's transformation as she healed and rediscovered her self-worth. Their interactions became more intimate, and they shared moments of vulnerability, revealing their deepest fears and desires. Azim's unresolved traumas from his own past added complexity to their connection, creating a bond of shared understanding and empathy. As their relationship deepened, Azim found himself grappling with his own demons. His past traumas, which he had kept buried, resurfaced with intensity. He recognized that his attraction to Fatima was not merely physical but a result of their shared experiences and their profound understanding. Unaware of Azim's internal struggle, Fatima continued to make remarkable progress in her healing journey. She had regained her confidence and was rebuilding her life, free from the shadows of her abusive partner. Yet, she remained oblivious to the power of her own healing on Azim, who found himself drawn to the light she shone on his own darkness. The ethical dilemma weighed heavily on Azim's conscience. He knew that acting on his feelings for Fatima would be a breach of trust and could have devastating consequences for them both. But their connection was undeniable, and as their paths continued to intertwine, the lines between doctor and patient began to blur. In the quiet moments between their conversations, Azim witnessed the strength it took for Fatima to share her story. Her resilience mirrored his own; he found solace in their shared vulnerability. As Fatima's laughter filled the room during one of their sessions, Azim realized that his feelings for her had evolved into something more profound than attraction—a sense of belonging and connection that he had never experienced. The ethical boundaries of his profession loomed over him, but the force of their bond seemed to transcend those constraints. Azim knew that he had to choose—either follow the ethical path, maintain professional distance, or surrender to the connection that was transforming them both. The decision was fraught with consequences, and as he grappled with his inner turmoil, their relationship's impact on their lives became ever more profound.

Azim found himself drawn to Fatima like a moth to a flame, unable to resist the pull of their forbidden connection. He knew it was wrong and unethical, but he couldn't deny the spark between them. As Fatima shared her experiences of domestic violence, Azim saw a vulnerability and strength that moved him deeply. It stirred something within him—a desire to protect her and a recognition of his own unresolved traumas. He knew that his attraction was fueled by a need to save her, to fix something broken within himself. Their affair's danger and secrecy only added to their connection's intensity. They met in secret, stealing moments of passion and intimacy. Azim found himself grappling with his ethics, knowing that their relationship crossed boundaries that could ruin his career. But the pull of their desire was too firm, and they continued their illicit affair, knowing the consequences could be devastating. Fatima, meanwhile, found strength and redemption in Azim's arms. She felt understood and protected, finally free from the abuse she had endured. As their relationship deepened, they knew they were playing with fire, but neither could deny the power of their connection. As their passionate affair intensified, Azim and Fatima were entangled in a web of complex emotions and dangerous secrets. Azim, the successful doctor, knew his involvement with Fatima, his client, breached professional ethics. Yet, he couldn't bring himself to end it. He saw in Fatima a reflection of his own unresolved traumas, and the desire to protect her became all-consuming. With each stolen moment, he felt more alive than ever, the thrill of their forbidden connection fueling his passion. Fatima, once a victim of domestic violence, now felt empowered by Azim's devotion. She found solace in his arms, a safe haven from the abuse she had endured. In Azim, she saw not only a lover but also a savior, someone who understood her pain and offered her the strength to move forward. However, as their relationship deepened, they were unaware of the eyes that watched them, the whispers that followed them, and the ticking clock that counted down to their inevitable discovery. The consequences of their actions loomed over them like a dark cloud, ready to burst at any moment. Azim knew that the ruin of his career would be the least of his worries if their affair came to light. The potential damage to Fatima's fragile state and the repercussions on her recovery were far more concerning.

Despite the warnings ringing in his ears, Azim chose to ignore them, driven by a desperate need to possess Fatima and a desire to keep her safe from the ghosts of her past. Unaware of the potential fallout, Fatima continued to find solace in Azim's arms, oblivious that their secret meetings were being noticed by those around them. As their passion intensified, so did the web of lies and deceit that entangled them, pulling them deeper into a vortex of desire, trauma, and impending doom. The air crackled with anticipation as their secret world teetered on the edge of exposure. Azim and Fatima's hearts raced from the thrill of their forbidden love and the fear of being discovered. Little did they know that their clandestine meetings had already planted the seeds of their downfall, and soon, they would have to face the consequences of their actions. As the truth threatened to surface, they found themselves facing a choice: to confront their demons head-on or to let their forbidden connection slip away into the shadows, leaving them forever changed by the intensity of their secret affair. The decision loomed with the weight of their shared traumas and the ethical boundaries they had crossed.

Fatima's heart raced as she carefully closed the door behind her, ensuring it didn't make a sound. She tiptoed back to her bedroom, where Joseph lay asleep. The moonlight illuminated his face, and momentarily, she remembered the man she had fallen in love with. But that man was a mirage, and the reality was a monster. She knew it, yet she stayed, trapped by her love for him and the chains of her own making. As she slipped under the covers, her mind replayed the forbidden moments she had shared with Azim. Their affair had started innocently enough—a connection formed during therapy sessions, a safe haven from the storm of her marriage. But it had escalated quickly, and now she was caught in a web of deceit and danger. She loved Azim, but she knew their relationship could never be. The guilt weighed heavily on her, but the fear of Joseph discovering their secret was even greater. His temper was unpredictable, and she had borne the brunt of his violence too many times. She lay awake, her eyes fixed on Joseph's peaceful face, and wondered if she would ever find the strength to leave.

The following day, Fatima awoke to the sound of Joseph's voice. He was on the phone, his back to her, and she held her breath, praying he wasn't speaking to someone who might reveal her secret. As he ended the call, she feigned sleep, her heart pounding. "Fatima," Joseph said, shaking her gently. "Wake up. We need to talk." Her eyes fluttered open, and she searched his face for signs of anger or suspicion. "What is it?" she asked, her voice laced with feigned innocence. "I've been thinking," he said, his eyes cold and distant. "I know things haven't been great between us lately. I want to work on this. For us." Fatima's heart sank. She knew this game; he was trying to control her, keep her trapped in their toxic dance. "Of course," she murmured, forcing a smile. "I want that too." As Joseph left the room, she let out a sigh of relief. But her respite was short-lived, as she knew the threat of exposure loomed. Her emotions were in turmoil, torn between her love for Azim and the desperate need to protect herself from Joseph's violence. Fatima's heart hammered in her chest as she lay awake, watching Joseph's chest rise and fall into sleep. The relief she felt upon hearing his proposal to work on their marriage was short-lived. She knew it was a tactic to keep her ensnared, and the fear of their secret being uncovered loomed large. Her mind drifted to the forbidden moments with Azim, the safe haven he had offered during their therapy sessions. She loved him, but the guilt and fear of their affair being discovered were overwhelming. Fatima's emotions were in turmoil, torn between her love for Azim and the urgent need to protect herself from Joseph's unpredictable temper. As the sun rose, Fatima awoke to an empty bed. Joseph was already up, and the house was filled with an eerie silence. Her heart sank as she realized he was giving her space, playing the loving husband, while she knew it was just another tactic to manipulate her. She felt trapped, unable to confide in anyone, and the weight of her secret threatened to crush her. Fatima longed for a way out, the strength to leave Joseph, and the toxic dance they were entangled in. But the fear of his reaction and the chains of her own making held her captive. Azim, unaware of the depths of Fatima's turmoil, struggled with his own unresolved traumas. He knew their relationship was unethical and could ruin them both, yet he could not let go. The connection they shared was intense and unlike anything he had ever experienced. Azim battled his demons, seeking redemption for his part in the affair, but the pull towards Fatima was irresistible. As their forbidden love continued, they were entangled in a web of deceit, each caught in their own personal hell.

The room's initial silence was soon replaced by a cacophony of whispers as the shocked guests began to process the revelation. The air was thick with disbelief and intrigue as the once-admired couple stood there, their faces a mask of shame and defiance. The woman, known for her grace and poise, now struggled to maintain her composure, her eyes darting between the judgmental stares of the crowd. Usually charismatic and confident, the man stood stiffly, his eyes lowered, unable to face the consequences of their exposed affair. As the news spread beyond the confines of the room, the public's admiration for the couple soured. Once synonymous with success and influence, their names were now associated with deceit and scandal. The media pounced on the story, sensationalizing the details and tarnishing their reputations. The couple was engulfed in a firestorm of criticism and shame, their carefully crafted images shattered beyond repair. Amid the chaos, the couple's relationship began to fracture. Once a united front, they turned on each other, each seeking to lay blame and absolve themselves of responsibility. Their luxurious world, built on a foundation of lies, came crumbling down around them, leaving them exposed and vulnerable to the harsh judgment of the public they had once captivated.

The scandal left Azim and Fatima in emotional turmoil, changing their lives forever. Azim, the successful doctor, was drawn into a complex web of emotions, his unresolved traumas resurfacing. He questioned his ethical standing, knowing the affair with his client, Fatima, was a breach of professional boundaries. Yet, he couldn't deny the connection he felt with her. Fatima, a victim of domestic violence, sought solace in Azim's arms. She found comfort and strength in their affair, but the scandal threatened to destroy any sense of stability she had seen. As the truth came to light, they faced the potential ruin of their professional careers. Azim's reputation as a doctor was at stake, and Fatima's redemption story now included a new layer of complexity. The impact of the scandal was far-reaching. Azim's colleagues and patients questioned his judgment, wondering if he had crossed similar lines with other vulnerable patients. His once-respected name was now tainted with scandal, and he found himself defending his actions and motivations.

Fatima, on the other hand, experienced a different kind of fallout. As a survivor of domestic violence, she had already endured judgment and criticism. Now, she faced the additional challenge of being seen as a home-wrecker and a temptress. The public perception of their affair threatened to overshadow her own story of survival and strength. Amid the chaos, Azim and Fatima were more drawn to each other. They recognized the shared trauma and the unique understanding they had of each other's pain. They found a refuge from the judgmental world outside in each other's arms. However, they also knew that their relationship was built on shaky foundations and that their future was uncertain. As they navigated their emotional turmoil, they were faced with a choice: to embrace the potential redemption of their love or to let it go and find healing separately. The choice they faced was a difficult one, and the possible consequences loomed large. Azim and Fatima knew that their decision would shape their lives forever.

On the one hand, they could embrace their love despite the scandal and the breach of professional ethics. Their connection was deep and soulful, offering solace from their respective traumas. Yet, the affair had already caused so much damage to their lives and reputations. The public perception of their relationship was harsh and unforgiving, and the potential for further ruin was ever-present.

On the other hand, they could decide to part ways, heal separately, and attempt to rebuild their lives independently. This option offered a chance for redemption in the eyes of society, but it meant walking away from the comfort and understanding they had found in each other. It would mean facing their traumas alone, without the refuge of their shared connection. Their decision weighed heavily on their shoulders as they contemplated their uncertain future. As they grappled with their choice, Azim and Fatima's paths remained intertwined, their fates linked by their shared secrets. The scandal had already set in motion a series of events that would forever impact their lives. In the eyes of the world, they were now bound together, their names forever linked in a web of gossip and judgment. Despite the potential consequences, they found strength in their shared experience, understanding each other in a way no one else could. Their connection, born out of trauma and pain, offered a sense of solace and redemption that was hard to ignore. Each day, the intensity of their emotions grew, and the choice became even more challenging. The potential for redemption loomed large but so did the possibility of further scandal and heartbreak. Azim and Fatima stood at a crossroads, their hearts torn between love and duty, passion and ethics. The world awaited their decision, ready to judge and scrutinize, but in that moment, they belonged only to each other, their shared trauma forming an unbreakable bond.

Azim found solace in his Islamic faith, turning to it like a beacon of light in his darkest hour. He immersed himself in prayer, seeking comfort and guidance from Allah. The serenity of the mosque offered him a sanctuary where he could reflect on his transgressions and find inner peace. Through supplication, he discovered the strength to confront his unresolved traumas and the courage to embark on a journey of repentance. The power of prayer brought him clarity and a renewed sense of purpose, guiding him toward righteousness. The support of the Islamic community played a pivotal role in Azim's healing process. He found solace in the company of like-minded individuals who shared his values and beliefs. Their empathy and understanding provided him with the safe haven he needed to confront his demons. His community's collective prayers and well-wishes uplifted him, filling him with a sense of belonging and hope. Their non-judgmental support reminded him of the beauty of compassion and forgiveness, inspiring him to extend the same grace to himself. As Azim continued his self-reflection and repentance, he drew strength from his faith and the surrounding community. The Islamic principles of forgiveness, compassion, and redemption became his guiding stars, leading him toward a brighter future. With each prayer and act of support, he felt his burdens lift, allowing him to emerge from the shadows of his past and embrace a life of spiritual fulfillment and tranquility. Azim's journey of self-reflection and healing was deeply intertwined with his Islamic faith. As a successful doctor, he had always prided himself on his ethics and professionalism, but his encounter with Fatima, a client battling domestic violence, had shaken him to his core. The affair that ensued left him conflicted and filled with guilt. However, in the quiet solitude of prayer, Azim found the strength to confront his own demons. He sought guidance from Allah, turning to the Islamic principles of forgiveness and compassion. The mosque became his sanctuary, where he could leave the chaos of his thoughts behind and find inner peace.

The support of the Islamic community was instrumental in Azim's healing. He found comfort in the company of his fellow Muslims, who embraced him with empathy and non-judgment. Their prayers and well-wishes uplifted him, reminding him of the power of compassion and the importance of extending grace to himself. Through their support, Azim began to understand the beauty of redemption and the possibility of a brighter future. As Azim continued on his path of repentance, he drew strength from his faith, allowing it to guide him toward the light. With each prayer, he felt his burdens lift, and the shadows of his past began to fade. The Islamic community's unwavering support was pivotal in his transformation, leading him toward spiritual fulfillment and tranquility.

Azim knew that his decision to end the affair with Fatima was right, but it didn't make it any easier. He had become entangled in an unethical relationship, and now he had to face the consequences of his actions. The affair had been a source of comfort and excitement for Azim, struggling with unresolved traumas. But he realized that his actions were only causing more harm to Fatima, who was already battling domestic violence. He wanted to help her find healing and redemption, and he knew their affair was standing in the way. So, with a heavy heart, he ended things between them. Azim explained to Fatima that their relationship was unhealthy and that they both needed to focus on healing from their respective traumas. He offered her his continued support as her doctor and promised to help her find the strength and courage to move forward. Fatima was heartbroken, but she understood the necessity of their decision. She had come to rely on Azim as a source of comfort and escape from her abusive relationship. Now, she realized that proper redemption lay in facing her demons head-on. With Azim's guidance and support, she began the difficult journey of healing, determined to find the strength to leave her abusive partner and rebuild her life.

Fatima's journey of self-discovery was a treacherous path, riddled with the pain of her past. She had endured domestic violence, a secret affair, and now sought redemption and strength. Her determination to heal was unwavering, and she knew rebuilding her life was entirely in her hands. Fatima's days were spent in quiet reflection, often in the company of nature, where she found solace and a sense of peace. She would wander through the forests, observing the trees' strength, resilience in the face of storms, and ability to bend without breaking. This became her mantra, and she vowed to emulate their strength, knowing that she could weather any storm life threw her way. As time passed, Fatima's wounds began to heal. She found comfort in the small joys of life and learned to appreciate the beauty in simplicity. Her once-heavy heart, burdened by her past, now felt lighter and full of hope for the future. Fatima's journey was one of courage and self-acceptance, and she knew that no matter what life brought, she had the strength to rise above it. As Fatima's journey progressed, she encountered new challenges, but her unwavering determination remained. She sought professional help and found solace in the understanding gaze of Azim, her therapist. Their sessions became a sanctuary, a safe haven where Fatima could unravel the tangled threads of her past without fear of judgment. Azim's gentle guidance helped her navigate the treacherous path of healing, and Fatima's strength grew with each step. Their affair was a secret, bringing comfort and confusion. Azim became her rock, a source of stability in the storm of her life. She confided in him, sharing her deepest fears and shameful secrets. He helped her understand that her past did not define her and that she had the power to forge a new path. Fatima's redemption lay in her ability to forgive herself and let go of the pain that had weighed her down for so long. Fatima's heart grew lighter with each passing day, and the shadows of her past began to fade. She embraced nature's small joys, finding peace in the gentle rustle of leaves and the warm embrace of the sun. The strength of the trees remained her inspiration, a reminder that she, too, could bend without breaking. Fatima's journey was a testament to her courage, and she knew that no matter what life threw her way, she had the resilience to rise again.

Azim and Fatima's paths had collided in a whirlwind of emotion and turmoil. Azim, the successful doctor, found himself drawn to Fatima, his vulnerable client, as she shared her painful experiences of domestic violence. In her, he saw a reflection of his own unresolved traumas, the shadows that haunted his dreams, and the silence that weighed on his heart. Their connection was intense and forbidden, a secret affair that blossomed in the shadows of their pain. But soon, the weight of their actions bore down on them, and they were forced to confront their mistakes. For Azim, it was a battle within. He knew the ethical boundaries he had crossed, and the guilt gnawed at his conscience. He sought forgiveness from himself and those he felt he had let down. In quiet moments of reflection, he grappled with his choices, questioning his own judgment and the impact of his actions on those around him. He found solace in the support of trusted mentors and peers, slowly rebuilding his sense of self and purpose.

On the other hand, Fatima embarked on a journey of self-discovery and empowerment. She recognized the strength within her, a fire that had been dimmed by the abuse she endured. With each passing day, she reclaimed her power, standing tall against the shadows of her past. She sought understanding, not just from those around her but also from herself. Forgiving herself for the choices she made amid her trauma was a pivotal step in her healing process. As Azim navigated his internal turmoil, he found solace in the company of a trusted mentor, Dr. Sharma. With his guidance, Azim began to unravel the complex web of his emotions, confronting the ghosts of his past traumas. It was an arduous journey, fraught with self-doubt and guilt, but with each step, Azim inched closer to reconciliation with himself and those he cared about. He realized that his attraction to Fatima was not just about their shared pain but also a reflection of his own longing for healing and redemption.

Meanwhile, Fatima blossomed like a resilient flower in the wake of her decision to leave her abusive partner. She found refuge in a women's shelter, where she bonded with other survivors, their shared experiences forging unbreakable sisterhood. Fatima channeled her pain into art, her canvases becoming a vivid expression of her emotions, each brushstroke a step towards reclaiming her identity. She discovered a community of supportive friends who embraced her with open arms, providing the family she never had.

Azim fell to his knees, his eyes pleading as he begged for Ashtra's forgiveness. The weight of his betrayal bore down on him, and he knew the path to redemption would be arduous. "I know I've caused you unimaginable pain, Ashtra," he began, his voice thick with remorse. "My actions were inexcusable, and I am truly sorry. I was weak and made a terrible mistake, but I am determined to make amends and rebuild what I have shattered." Ashtra's eyes, once warm and loving, now reflected a cautious wariness. The hurt was still raw, and she struggled to trust that Azim's words were more than empty promises. The challenges were evident. Azim's affair with Fatima, a vulnerable client he had treated, had been a profound breach of trust. Ashtra questioned if their relationship could ever be repaired and if the wounds would genuinely heal. Yet, amidst the wreckage, a glimmer of hope remained. Azim's unwavering dedication to his profession and inherent goodness gave Ashtra pause. She saw his anguish and recognized the trauma he had faced and the unresolved wounds that had contributed to his misstep. The path to redemption would be a delicate dance.

Azim knew he had to earn back Ashtra's trust, demonstrating through actions, not just words, that he was committed to their relationship. He had to prove that his devotion to her was unwavering and that his mistakes were lessons that would strengthen, not destroy their bond. Ashtra, though guarded, recognized the potential for growth and change. She understood the power of forgiveness and the possibility of a new beginning. Azim's voice cracked as he poured out his heart, his eyes never leaving Ashtra's. He knew the depth of his betrayal and the long road ahead to earn her forgiveness. "I understand if you can't offer me absolution, but please, let me show you that my love for you is true and enduring. Let me be the partner you deserve, and together, we can rebuild the life we once had." Ashtra's gaze softened, and she took a tentative step forward. Her heart, once shattered, now beat with a steady rhythm of hope. She saw the sincerity in Azim's eyes and recognized the man she had fallen in love with, whose wounds had led him astray. "I want to believe you, Azim," she said, her voice steady but laced with emotion. "But words are not enough. Your actions must speak for your repentance. Prove that your dedication to our love is stronger than any temptation or trauma." Azim nodded, his eyes filling with determination. He understood the gravity of his wife's words and the task's weight before him. "I will spend every waking moment reminding you of my love and commitment," he vowed. "I will be transparent and accountable and cherish and honor you, as I should have done from the start." The path to healing was paved with challenges, but with each step, Azim and Ashtra found solace in the knowledge that their love, though tested, had the strength to endure.

Fatima stood at the community center entrance, her heart heavy with the weight of her past. The affair with Azim, the domestic violence she endured – it all felt like a dark cloud that had been hanging over her for too long. But today, she was taking the first steps towards a new beginning. As she crossed the threshold, a warm smile greeted her. It was Sister Aisha, a wise and compassionate woman who had offered her support and guidance. Aisha embraced Fatima, and at that moment, Fatima felt a sense of belonging and acceptance that she had never known before. Over the next several weeks, Fatima found solace in the company of other women who had endured similar struggles. She attended support groups, shared her story, and began the arduous task of healing. The community embraced her with open arms, offering a safe haven where she could finally breathe and begin to forgive herself. Fatima's strength returned with each passing day, and a newfound sense of purpose emerged. She volunteered at the center, helping others who were struggling, and found great satisfaction in offering the same support and compassion that had been extended to her. As time went on, Fatima's past began to fade, and a brighter future emerged. She had forgiven herself and those who had wronged her, and in doing so, she found the courage to start anew. With a sense of peace and determination, Fatima took steps towards a life of her own – a life free from violence, shame, and hope and possibility.

Azim and Fatima's journey had been tumultuous, fraught with pain and ethical complexities. But now, as they stood facing each other, a newfound sense of clarity and purpose emerged. Azim, the successful doctor, had come to terms with his unresolved traumas, recognizing their impact on his judgment and actions. He realized that his affair with Fatima, his client, was a result of his own unhealed wounds and a misguided attempt at finding solace. Fatima, once a victim of domestic violence, had transformed into a resilient and empowered woman. She, too, recognized the affair for what it was—a cry for help from two wounded souls. But now, she stood tall, having found redemption and inner strength. The journey had been challenging but also transformative, teaching them invaluable lessons about themselves and the power of healing. With heartfelt sincerity, Azim apologized to Fatima, acknowledging the pain he had caused and taking responsibility for his actions. With equal grace, Fatima forgave him, understanding the complexities that led them down this path. Their reconciliation was a testament to the power of growth and our potential for peace. As they parted ways, it was with a sense of closure and tranquility, knowing that their difficult journey had ultimately led them to a place of self-acceptance and newfound wisdom.

The sun had set, casting a warm glow over the city, as Azim and Fatima found themselves in a quaint café, a world away from the turmoil of their past. The soft jazz playing in the background and the aroma of freshly brewed coffee created a soothing ambiance.

They sat across each other, their eyes meeting with a newfound understanding and peace. The journey to this moment had been arduous, but it had forged a unique connection between them—a bond forged in the fire of adversity. With a gentle smile, Azim expressed his gratitude for Fatima's forgiveness and the opportunity to find closure. He spoke of his lessons and the importance of facing one's demons. "I was lost," he admitted, "but through this journey with you, I've found my way back to myself." Fatima, her eyes shining with a quiet strength, nodded in understanding. "We were both lost," she agreed, "but sometimes it takes getting lost to find your true path." She sipped her coffee, savoring the warmth it brought to her soul. "I'm grateful for the growth that came from our pain," she continued, "and I hope we can both carry this wisdom forward." As they sat in comfortable silence, the weight of their shared history seemed to lift, replaced by a sense of calm and acceptance.

The turmoil of their affair and the ethical complexities had been a crucible, refining their characters and teaching them the importance of healing. Azim and Fatima had emerged from the flames, not unscathed but stronger and wiser. Their story was a testament that even in the darkest times, there is always the potential for growth, redemption, and inner peace. The night bid farewell, and a new day dawned, promising a fresh start. Azim and Fatima went their separate ways, carrying the lessons learned and the strength gained. Their paths may not cross again, but the impact they had on each other will forever be imprinted on their souls. The tumultuous journey had been a necessary chapter in their lives, a catalyst for the healing and self-discovery ahead. Now, they ventured forward as survivors and warriors, ready to face the world with newfound clarity and purpose.

Different Direction

The sun dipped below the horizon, casting a warm glow over the enchanting whitewashed buildings of Oia. Mia and Jeffrey stood side by side, watching as the sky transformed into a mesmerizing canvas of vibrant hues. The air was thick with the scent of the sea, and the gentle breeze carried the soothing sound of waves crashing against the cliffs below. It was in this very spot that they had once dreamed of chasing sunsets together, their futures intertwined. But now, as the light faded, so too did the remnants of their relationship. Mia, with her sun-kissed skin and vibrant spirit, felt the weight of their unspoken words. She had always found solace in the colors that danced across the sky, but now those colors reminded her of what they once had.

As the last rays of sunlight disappeared, Mia turned to Jeffrey, her eyes reflecting her myriad of emotions. "I think it's time for me to go," she said softly, her voice carrying a mixture of sadness and resolve. Jeffrey nodded, understanding the finality of her words. They had come to Oia hoping to rekindle what they once had, but instead, they found closure. Mia took a deep breath, filling her lungs with the salty air as she stepped away from the sunset-bathed cliffs of Oia. She felt a tug on her heart as she left Jeffrey behind, their shared dream of chasing sunsets together now a distant memory. With each step, she moved further away from the vibrant sky, the colors that once inspired her now a painful reminder. Mia's artistic spirit, so attuned to the emotions evoked by color and light, struggled to accept the fading of their relationship. But she knew that sometimes, even the most beautiful things must come to an end. As she wandered through the charming cobblestone streets of Oia, Mia felt the weight of the village's history bearing down on her. The whitewashed buildings, so bright in the daylight, now took on a softer glow in the twilight, as if even the village was preparing for a new day. She imagined the countless lovers who had strolled these streets, their stories of love and loss woven into the very fabric of this picturesque place. Still hanging idle at his side, Jeffrey's camera watched Mia's retreating figure. He knew that their journey to Oia had been a futile attempt to recapture something that was no longer there. The vibrant sunsets, the charming architecture, and the air of this place were all reminders of what they had lost. Jeffrey's pragmatic nature, so often his strength, had failed him regarding his relationship with Mia. He realized now that some moments are too painful to immortalize, too personal to be captured by a lens. Jeffrey turned away from the cliffs as the night sky began to descend, his heart heavy but resolved. As the sun rose over the tranquil village the following day, Mia awoke to find her canvas and brushes calling to her. The night had brought clarity, and she knew that her heart, though bruised, still beat with a passion for life and art. So, she set out to capture the beauty of Oia in a new light, determined to find solace in her art and to embrace the future that lay ahead, uncertain but full of possibility.

Mia and Jeffrey's footsteps echoed on the cobblestone streets of Oia, their voices carrying a mixture of sadness and resignation. The vibrant hues of the village, with its whitewashed buildings and bright blue domes, mirror the emotions swirling within them. Mia, her heart heavy, spoke of her dreams and the need to pursue her art. "I feel like I'm finally finding my voice, and it's leading me down a different path," she said, her eyes reflecting the sunset's golden glow. Jeffrey, his camera always ready, understood her need for freedom. He had his own dreams to chase, his own visions to capture. "I think it's time we accept that our paths are diverging," he said, his voice steady but filled with a hint of pain. They stopped at a lookout point, the Aegean Sea stretching before them in a dazzling display of color as the sun dipped toward the horizon. It felt like a metaphor for their relationship, the end of a beautiful day marked by the setting sun. Mia and Jeffrey stood in silence, watching as the sun's final rays painted the sea in hues of orange and pink. The moment's beauty seemed to comfort and pain them as if the sunset understood their conflicting emotions. "I'll always cherish our time together," Mia said, her voice soft and filled with warmth and sorrow. "How we explored this island, discovering hidden gems and capturing their beauty—it's been magical." Jeffrey nodded, his eyes never leaving the horizon. "This place has a way of making you see things differently," he replied, his voice quiet, as if speaking to himself. "It's like the island is alive, breathing life into our dreams and urging us to chase them." As the sun slipped below the horizon, casting a final glow across the sea, Mia and Jeffrey turned away, their footsteps carrying them in opposite directions. With its vibrant hues and charming cobblestone streets, the village of Oia bore witness to their silent farewell, marking the end of one chapter and the beginning of another.

As the vibrant hues of the sunset painted the sky, Mia and Jeffrey stood in silence, their hearts heavy with the weight of their impending parting. Mia, her eyes reflecting the melting pot of colors above, spoke first, her voice soft and laced with sadness. "I'll miss the sunsets with you, Jeffrey. The way we'd chase the light, trying to capture its fleeting beauty. But I know we both need to follow our own paths now." Jeffrey, his camera usually eager to capture the world, hung idly by his side. He nodded, his expression pained. "I know, Mia. It's just—it's hard to let go of what we had. The adventures we went on, the art we created... it meant something." Mia reached for his hand, her heart aching for the pain she saw in his eyes. "It meant everything, Jeffrey. And it will always be a part of us, even as we grow and change. We'll carry those memories with us, and they'll shape the people we become." Jeffrey smiled, his thumb gently brushing against Mia's hand. "I guess this is where our paths diverge," he said, his voice steady despite the turmoil. Now a fading memory, the sunset began a new chapter for Mia and Jeffrey. As they turned away from each other, their hearts, though heavy, were filled with a sense of purpose. The road ahead would be challenging but also bring new adventures, creations, and a deeper understanding of themselves and the world around them.

Mia and Jeffrey's steps echoed on the cobblestones as they walked away from each other, the sunset's afterglow painting their surroundings in a soft, dreamy light. Mia's heart felt raw and exposed as she thought about their countless adventures—how they had explored hidden corners of the world, always seeking to capture its beauty through their unique lenses. She knew that their creative passions had brought them together, but the depth of their emotional connection had kept them intertwined for so long. As Mia returned to her art studio, she passed by vibrant markets and bustling city streets, but her mind remained in the realm of memories. She thought about the late nights spent painting on the rooftop, Jeffrey by her side, their laughter ringing out into the darkness as they shared stories of their dreams and fears. The thought of never experiencing those moments again brought a lump to her throat, but she reminded herself of the truth in their decision to part ways. The following days were a blur of paint, canvas, and emotional turmoil for Mia. She threw herself into her art, seeking solace in the familiar ritual of mixing colors and translating her emotions onto the blank canvas. During these solitary moments, Mia truly understood the impact of her time with Jeffrey. He had not only been her lover and friend but also a mentor who had pushed her to see the world through a different lens, to appreciate the beauty in the ordinary, and to seek out the extraordinary.

The sun began its slow descent over the Aegean Sea, casting a warm glow over the whitewashed buildings of Oia. Mia stood amidst the bustling crowd, her heart fluttering as she took in the vibrant scene before her. The annual Oia Sunset Festival was in full swing, and her mural, a stunning depiction of the intertwined trees, stood proudly on display. It was a testament to her artistic journey and the emotions she had endured. As she scanned the crowd, her eyes landed on Jeffrey, his tall frame leaning against the stone wall, his camera hanging idly by his side. Their eyes met, and an unspoken tension hung heavily between them. Mia's heart ached as she recalled their passionate yet complicated relationship. Jeffrey had been her confidant, her lover, and her muse. But now, as their paths diverged, their silence spoke volumes. She approached him, her steps measured, and her voice caught in her throat. The sunset bathed them in a golden light, starkly contrasting the turmoil within.

The festival buzzed around them, yet they were the only two people in existence at that moment. As Mia and Jeffrey stood amidst the breathtaking sunset, the unspoken words and emotions threatened to overwhelm them. Mia's artistic passion and Jeffrey's pragmatic eye had once complemented each other perfectly, but now, they needed help finding common ground. The festival's celebration of beauty and change mirrored their own internal journeys. Mia's mural, symbolizing their intertwined past, was a poignant backdrop to their encounter. It was a moment frozen in time, where the beauty of the sunset and the charm of Oia couldn't mask the heartache and uncertainty ahead. The sun sank lower, the golden hour illuminating the festival and casting an even warmer glow on the vibrant scene. Mia felt a sense of wonder as she took in the sights and sounds around her—the lively music, the laughter, and the crowd's murmur, all set against the backdrop of the stunning Aegean Sea. It was as if the world had conspired to create this perfect moment that both celebrated and mirrored the beauty and complexity of her own life. She felt a tug on her heart as she thought about the man who now stood before her. With his quiet strength and unwavering gaze, Jeffrey had been her anchor through the storms of her artistic journey. Their relationship, once a source of comfort and inspiration, now hung in the balance, a victim of their diverging paths and unspoken words. Amid this enchanting festival, with her mural as a testament to their intertwined past, Mia was at a crossroads, grappling with the essence of love, loss, and the beauty that lay in between. As the sunset painted the sky with hues of pink and orange, Mia and Jeffrey remained still; their silence speaks volumes. The festival buzzed around them, a blur of colors and sounds, yet they were lost in their own world, their hearts caught between the beauty of the present and the uncertainty of the future. Mia's eyes flickered to her mural, the intertwined trees reflecting the connection they once shared. She wondered if Jeffrey saw what she saw—the symbolism of their journey, the pain of their separation, and the hope that perhaps, just perhaps, they could find their way back to each other. At that moment, as the sun dipped below the horizon, casting its final rays over the Aegean Sea, Mia and Jeffrey stood, bathed in the golden light of possibility, their story still waiting to be written. The night of the festival unfolded a tapestry of music, art, and conversation. Mia and Jeffrey were drawn into the whirlwind, their silent standoff momentarily forgotten. As they wandered through the cobblestone streets of Oia, the glow of the setting sun giving way to the warm glow of lanterns, they felt the pulse of the village surrounding them. It was as if the very essence of Oia, with its charm and beauty, was urging them to embrace the moment. They shared a smile, a silent understanding passing between them, as they allowed the energy of the festival to guide them. It was a night of discovery, not just of the vibrant culture surrounding them but of themselves and the path that had led them here. As the moon rose over the Aegean Sea, casting a silvery light, Mia and Jeffrey stood on the cliffs, taking in the breathtaking view. It was then that they knew that regardless of the future, this moment, this festival, and this sunset would forever be etched in their memories.

Mia and Jeffrey sat across from each other in the quaint café, their eyes reflecting myriad emotions. The afternoon sunlight streamed through the window, casting a warm glow on their faces. Mia's heart felt heavy as she traced the patterns on the table with her finger. She took a deep breath and spoke softly, her words carrying their own weight. "I know we've been through a lot together, and I cherish every moment we shared. But it's time we accept that our paths lead us in different directions." Jeffrey's gaze remained fixed on the table, his hands clasped tightly together. He nodded slowly, his silence speaking volumes. Mia continued, her voice steady despite the turmoil within. "I want you to know that I understand your dreams and ambitions. I've always admired your pragmatic approach to life, and I know you'll achieve great things. We may not be together like we once were, but I'll always be here to support you." Jeffrey lifted his head as Mia spoke, his eyes meeting hers with a mixture of sadness and gratitude. The air between them softened as they shared a moment of unspoken understanding. In that instant, they forgave each other for the heartaches and missteps of their relationship. They acknowledged the love that remained, even as their paths diverged. With a gentle smile, Mia extended her hand across the table. Jeffrey took it, their fingers intertwining one last time. It was a silent promise that, despite the heartbreak, their connection would endure.

Mia watched Jeffrey walk away, his figure blending into the bustling cityscape. She felt a pang in her heart as she realized this might be the last time she saw him. Turning on her heel, she returned to her apartment, the weight of their conversation lingering. The sun had set, casting a soft orange hue over the city, and Mia felt a pull to capture this moment on canvas. She quickened her pace, eager to translate her emotions into art. As she painted, the vibrant hues of the sunset reflected the turmoil of her heart—the orange a fiery passion, the purple a melancholy sadness. Brushstroke by brushstroke, she poured her soul onto the canvas, creating a vivid testament to the beauty and pain of their relationship. The days turned into weeks, and Mia found solace in her art. Each painting was a journey through her emotions, a way to make sense of the heartbreak. She explored new techniques, incorporating the vibrant colors of her Filipino heritage, a reminder of the warmth and strength that ran through her veins. As time passed, her heart began to heal, and she thought of Jeffrey less and less. Yet, her heart always had a soft spot for him, a tender memory of their shared connection. One sunny afternoon, as Mia strolled through the city, she found herself outside the quaint café where they had parted ways. A wave of nostalgia washed over her, and she stepped inside, sitting by the window. The sunlight bathed her in its warm embrace, and she felt a sense of peace. Mia knew that despite the heartache, she had made the right decision. Their paths had diverged, but their connection remained immortalized in the art they created and shared memories.

Mia's journey of self-discovery unfolds through her art. Each brushstroke becomes a testament to her healing, a vibrant expression of her emotions. She finds solace in the canvas, a safe haven where she can explore the depths of her heart and the complexities of her cultural identity. Mia discovers a newfound sense of purpose and resilience as she pours her soul into her artwork. Her growth becomes her muse, inspiring her to create pieces that reflect the beauty of transformation and the power of the human spirit.

On the other hand, Jeffrey sees the world through a different lens. His photography captures the raw, unfiltered beauty he discovers in his travels. As he navigates the aftermath of his relationship with Mia, he finds freedom in exploring new places and connecting with nature. Each click of his camera becomes a step towards self-discovery, a way to freeze moments of tranquility and serenity in time. Jeffrey's pragmatic nature slowly gives way to a more adventurous spirit as he embraces the unknown and life's unexpected twists and turns. As Mia and Jeffrey continue on their separate paths, they unknowingly mirror each other's journey of healing and self-exploration. Their shared passion for art becomes their anchor, a constant reminder of the beauty within the chaos of life. Though their relationship has ended, they find solace in the knowledge that they are both thriving in their own unique ways, embracing new beginnings and discovering the resilience within them. As Mia delved deeper into her art, her brushstrokes reflected her Filipino heritage. The vibrant colors of her palette danced across the canvas, mirroring the vibrant traditions and culture that ran through her veins. Each painting became a window into her soul, a way to explore the intricacies of her identity and the emotions that came with it. She found comfort in expressing her heart's deepest longings and fears, using art as a language to communicate what words could not. In her studio, surrounded by the scent of fresh paint and the soft classical music playing in the background, Mia uncovered a strength she didn't know she possessed.

Meanwhile, Jeffrey's journey of self-discovery took him to remote landscapes and untouched natural wonders. His photography evolved, capturing not just the beauty of nature but the essence of its tranquility. As he hiked through forests and stood atop mountains, he felt a sense of liberation from the constraints of his past relationship. Each shutter click became a way to immortalize the peace he found in these solitary adventures. The pragmatic man who once carefully calculated each step now embraced the unknown, allowing life to surprise him with its twists and turns. Unbeknownst to them, Mia and Jeffrey's paths were mirroring each other in unexpected ways. Their art, a common thread that still connected them, became a testament to their shared ability to find beauty in chaos. As they continued their journeys, they unknowingly inspired each other from a distance, their creative spirits intertwining across space and time.

Mia's heart swelled as the sun dipped below the horizon, painting the sky in hues of crimson and gold. Standing on the cliffs of Oia, she felt a sense of peace wash over her. The charming village, with its whitewashed buildings and cobblestone paths, had become her sanctuary these past few months. Here, she had learned to heal and embrace the twists and turns of her journey. As an artist, Mia had always found solace in the vibrant colors of Santorini. The island's beauty inspired her to capture its essence on canvas, expressing her emotions through bold strokes and vivid palettes. And now, as she stood witness to yet another breathtaking sunset, she felt a profound sense of gratitude for the life she had been given. Though Mia's heart still carried the scars of past heartbreak, she knew that love could evolve and transform. It was a message imprinted on her soul during her time in Oia. With each sunset, she was reminded that every ending marked a new beginning and that the passage of time brought the promise of hope and acceptance. The gentle breeze carried a hint of the sea's salty embrace as Mia turned away from the sunset, her heart full and her mind at ease. She strolled along the familiar cobblestone paths of Oia, the charming village that had become her sanctuary. The whitewashed buildings, bathed in the fading glow of dusk, created a serene ambiance that mirrored the peace within her. In the distance, the gentle rumble of the ocean provided a soothing backdrop to her thoughts. Mia reflected on the twists and turns that had led her to this moment of tranquility. The heartbreak that had once threatened to consume her now felt like a distant memory, its scars a reminder of her strength and resilience. As an artist, she had learned to channel her emotions into her craft, and the vibrant colors of Santorini had become her palette, a means to express the beauty she found in the world around her. The following day, Mia woke up to the soft glow of morning light filtering through her window. She rose, eager to begin a new day, her spirit feeling lighter than it had in a long time. After a leisurely breakfast, she gathered her art supplies and set up her easel on a secluded cliffside spot she had discovered during her stay in Oia. The canvas in front of her was a blank slate, waiting to be filled with the colors of her imagination. As she began to paint, the vibrant hues of the village and the dazzling Aegean Sea came to life under her brushstrokes. It was as if she were casting a spell, weaving the magic of Oia into her artwork. As the days turned into weeks, Mia found herself fully immersed in the rhythm of life in Oia. She would rise with the sun each morning, eager to explore the village and its surrounding landscapes. Some days, she would hike along the cliffs, discovering hidden coves and breathtaking vistas. Other times, she would wander through the cobblestone streets, chatting with local shop owners and soaking in the vibrant culture. But every evening, as the sun prepared to dip below the horizon again, Mia would return to her beloved cliffside spot, watching the sky transform into a canvas of crimson and gold.

During these moments of serene beauty, Mia truly felt alive, her heart open to the possibilities ahead.

www.ingramcontent.com/pod-product-compliance
Lightning Source LLC
LaVergne TN
LVHW100506110826
845146LV00002B/530
9798888705223